HOLLOW CITY

SONG OF KARMA, BOOK ONE

KAI WAI CHEAH

SILVER EMPIRE

1

DO UNTO OTHERS

How do you take down someone who always hits what he shoots at?

Take him before he gets his hands on a weapon.

And if he does grab a gun, do unto him before he does unto you.

I felt those thoughts percolating in the team's heads. They were all quiet, coiled tight as springs, bunched up against each other on the narrow benches, carefully checking and re-checking their gear. No one said a word. The only sound was the humming of the engine and the occasional radio call emanating from the cab.

They were getting their heads in the game.

I ran my hands down my head and chest, confirming that everything was where it needed to be. Helmet with rifle-grade ballistic applique. Soft armor inserts and joint pads integrated into my tactical uniform. Tactical vest, laden with trauma plates and pouches filled with ammo and gear.

Sergeant Jose Oliveira had insisted that everyone run heavy today. No one objected. When facing a rogue gifted with supernatural accuracy, there was no such thing as running light.

Carbine pointed at the floor, finger safely off the trigger, I rotated the selector lever through safe, semi, auto, and back again. The weapon was a SIG MCX Virtus, one of the many incarnations and evolutions of Eugene Stoner's timeless AR-15 design.

The Virtus was an old friend. I'd used one just like it in another life, on similar missions. This Virtus was configured as an SBR, a short-barreled rifle, with an eleven and a half inch barrel mated to a compact suppressor. An EOTech holosight rode atop the upper receiver, and the handguard sported a flashlight at the 3 o'clock rail, a laser right in front of the holosight, and a hand stop at 6 o'clock.

"Amp, you playing with your gun?" Oliveira asked.

"Just a function check," I replied.

"Don't put a hole in the floor, ya hear?"

"Finger off the trigger, Sarge."

"If you put a hole in the BearCat, it's coming out of your salary."

"Aye, aye, Sergeant."

Not that that would happen. The BearCat's armor would stop .50 BMG rounds and resist explosions. Not too long ago it would have been overkill for a simple search warrant. Today, in an age of super-heroes and supervillains, it was merely the minimum level of protection necessary to serve a warrant on a Prime.

The team smiled grimly around me and continued inspecting their kit. There's no margin for error for this op, but too much tension would slow them down. Oliveira was just lightening the mood, keeping everyone from worrying too much about the reaper lurking around the block.

Today's customer was Emmanuel Ruiz. An El Trece heavy hitter, he had his fingers in many pies: smuggling, robbery, home invasion, but his true calling was murder for hire.

Most homeboys couldn't aim worth a damn, but Ruiz always hit what he shot. With at least a dozen bodies to his name, his gift allowed him to command premium prices within the criminal underworld. His father, Ricardo Ruiz, a shot-caller in his own right, brokered hits within the gang and Emmanuel faithfully executed them.

According to the Special Investigation Section, Emmanuel was one of the rarest of American criminals, a gunfighter gangster, a dark-sider who walked the way of the gun. His favorite weapon was an AK-47 rifle, with .45 pistols in second place. In his clique, he was the leader and the trigger-puller, with the rest of his crew running backup and support.

Unknown to young Emmanuel, SIS had tapped his phone. They knew he and his clique were throwing a party tonight at his house. But the gangsters didn't know we were coming for them.

Too bad.

There was a time when if the police wanted to take down a Prime, they commissioned another Prime to hunt him down. The Halo City Police Department didn't do that anymore, and they won't make exceptions for Emmanuel Ruiz.

The last time a Prime tried to arrest Ruiz, the alleged hero made the rookie mistake of announcing on the Internet that he had spotted a rogue and live-streamed his approach. Ruiz's buddy tipped him off, and Ruiz suckered the Prime into an ambush and put three rounds in his face.

Most so-called heroes were amateurs and glory hounds. Nine in ten heroes were so focused on chasing sponsorships and crowdfunding, if they ran up against a hardcore killer, they would be chewed up and spat out. There was no room for amateurs today. Today, the professionals came out to play.

There were eight other officers in the BearCat, plus one more up front in the driver's seat. Standard size for an HCPD Special Tactics and Rescue team. But I was the only Prime among us, and we were expecting six subjects today. Ruiz, his five *carnales*, and his girlfriend, Sophia Vega. Ruiz and his buddies were in the Life, SIS had confirmed that, but Vega was an unknown.

We would have been much more comfortable if there was a second team with us. Never engage an entrenched enemy with anything less than a three-to-one numerical advantage. But all the other STAR teams were out serving other warrants and responding to supervillain incidents. With so few officers, if the subjects tried something...

Do unto others before they do unto you.

The BearCat rolled to a halt. Oliveira threw the doors open. "Every day is a holiday and every meal a feast!" he shouted. "Let's go!"

We jumped out of the BearCat in pairs, gear held close to hand. Stepping up on the running board, I grabbed the roof-mounted grab handle with my left hand, hoisted myself up and turned on my helmet-mounted camera.

In front of me, Shane O'Neil took her place. The designated shield officer, today she was running the Reaper, an exoskeleton with a swinging arm that mounted a ballistic shield. The heavy shield would stop even armor-piercing rifle rounds, but it was so large it threatened to dwarf the petite redhead.

Shane and I were the bunker team. She went in first to soak up fire, I took down whoever dared to resist us. I'd only been on the team for a little over a year, but we'd grown tight. I could read the tension in her muscles, the tightness of her jaws, the stiffness in her neck.

"Hey, Shane, relax," I said. "We'll be fine."

She sighed and nodded, still looking dead ahead. "Easy day, huh?"

"Easy day."

A heavy hand slapped my shoulder. I patted Shane's.

"Port side ready!" Oliveira yelled.

"Starboard ready!" Shane reported.

"Let's go!"

The BearCat rumbled down the road and turned a sharp bend. Scanning, I saw the two other cars in the convoy. Behind us was an unmarked car from Gangs and Narcotics, carrying the detectives who would handle the post-search investigation. The tail-end Charlie was a K-9 team in a black-and-white. STAR would make entry first, the ones behind us would come in after the scene was secure.

Hand on my Virtus, I sized up the street. A long row of brown two-story houses stared back at me, all of them in varying states of disrepair. More than a few had bullet holes in the walls. All of them had security gates and window grilles.

The last rays of the sun streaked across the sky, but the streetlights were dark. They had all been shot out long ago. It was much cheaper, not to mention safer, to blast streetlights with BB guns than to replace them. Eventually the utilities department gave up.

Youths sauntered down the street. They were all young Hispanic men, many of them with crude tattoos and empty eyes, flying the green bandannas that marked them as El Trece *carnales*. As we drove past, most of them stuffed their gang flags into their pockets and studiously looked away. A few stared defiantly at us, as though daring us to take them down.

Today was their lucky day.

But one of them locked eyes on us, on *me*, nodded ever so slightly to himself, and raised his phone to his ear.

Spotter.

Syria, Mindanao, Mexico, in hellholes the world over, spotters were everywhere. Whenever bad guys were prepping an ambush, doing business, or just meeting up, there would always be someone ready to sound the alarm or call the trigger. This close, even from a moving vehicle, it was so easy to take a shot, and my arm—

No.

This was Halo City. This was America. The rules were different.

Instead, I yelled, "Halcón! Three o'clock!"

"Copy!" Oliveira replied. "Speed it up!"

We barreled down the street, eating up the last few yards to the target. As we approached, a chill washed down my spine, and a void invaded my mind.

Danger.

I looked around. No signs of threats. Yet. I gripped my weapon and steadied myself.

The BearCat screeched to a halt right outside the target block. I jumped off the running board, taking the carbine in both hands. Shane sprinted for the front door, orienting her shield to the door. The inhabitants had drawn curtains across the glass, but I could hear faint music. Sugary high-energy electronic trash melded to a female voice.

And just over the music, I heard a faint pattering sound.

A dark brown blur blasted out from around the corner of the house. A Doberman. Barking and growling, it charged at us. At Shane.

She hit the shield's light switch. Six hundred lumens glared into the dog's eyes. Undeterred, it leapt at her. She swung the shield just so, and it bounced off the heavy ceramic. Growling, it shook its head, moved to circle around her—

And a noose dropped over its head.

"Here boy!" Ray Monteiro called.

Ray was running the animal capture pole. The dog barked and scratched and yelped, to no avail. He tightened the noose and dragged it away to a waiting cage.

Carl Duncan and Tom Rodriguez sprinted around the corner where the dog came from. As Shane and I stacked on the door, Miguel Herrera stepped up on the other side, hefting his sledgehammer. Eric Williams dashed to the door, assault hook in hand, and fastened the hook to the heavy-duty security gate. A bright yellow sling connected the hook to the BearCat's front bumper.

All of us took a step back.

"Pull!" Oliveira commanded.

The BearCat reversed explosively. Metal shrieked for a single, terrible, instant, and the gate went flying.

Miguel wound up his sledge. I grabbed a flash-bang from my pouch and pulled the pin. With a mighty swing, Miguel smashed the door in. I tossed the stun grenade into the room beyond.

The banger erupted in thick smoke and blinding light and thunderous sound. My ear protection kicked in, muting the noise. A split second later, another flash-bang detonated around the back of the house. Shane charged through the smoke, through the open door, and headed right. I was right behind her.

"POLICE! SEARCH WARRANT!" I shouted.

We were in the living room. Five subjects, scattered across sofas and couches. Three huge pizzas and cans of soda covered the table. A barely-clad woman gyrated on the enormous TV screen. They were all reeling, covering their ears and screaming, disoriented from the shock of entry.

At the far right corner, halfway up the stairs, there was a sixth subject. Emmanuel Ruiz.

"POLICE! FREEZE!" Shane yelled.

Ruiz's face contorted in fury. He held a small dark object in his right hand. A phone.

Twisting around, Ruiz brought the phone up to his ear. His eyes narrowed, his muscles contracted, and as he wound up, I saw the trajectory of his throw. I ducked and slipped right, and instead of slamming into my throat the phone merely bounced off my helmet.

Ruiz turned and ran upstairs.

"Suspect headed to level two!" Shane called. "Amp! On me!"

I followed her, flowing around the room and following the walls. The rest of the team surged in, converging on the subjects.

Shane halted at the foot of the stairs, aiming her carbine up the stairs. I patted her shoulder.

"On you!" I called.

We headed upstairs. Heavy footsteps pounded the floor, Ruiz cursing as he ran. A woman yelled something in Spanish. Staying behind the shield, we sliced the pie as we ascended, leaning out and sidestepping to minimize our exposure.

No sign of Ruiz on the upper floor. There were four doors, all open. Bedroom to my right and front, bathroom next to the room before me, another bedroom to my left.

"Where'd he go?" Shane whispered.

"Emmanuel Ruiz!" I yelled. "Come out with your hands up!"

No response.

I Amped.

Electric fire surged through my ears, supercharging my hearing. Men yelled and complained on the lower floor, every word and obscenity amplified and articulate. Heavy boots pounded up the steps, the rest of the team following us. Fabric rustled, metal clanked, men inhaled and exhaled deeply.

I shut them all out and focused on the sounds on this floor.

To my right, I heard hands scrabbling against wood, plastic crackling, metal clashing on metal.

And breathing.

"Go right," I whispered, stepping down my power. "Two subjects."

"Copy," she said.

She swung the shield to cover her right, shifted her carbine to her left shoulder, and pushed on the door. I was right behind her, peeking over her right arm, studying the room beyond—

My spine tingled again.

DANGER DANGER DANGER

Lowering my left hand to my other grenade pouch, I whispered, "Wait."

Shane stepped through the door.

I Amped again.

Power roared through my belly, filling my hands and feet and head. I concentrated the energies, focusing them on my nerves.

The world slowed and sharpened into crystal clarity. I saw every strand of auburn hair peeking out from under Shane's helmet, every crease on her uniform, every scuff mark on the edges and back of the shield. She rested her carbine on the shield's left-hand cut-out and took one step. A second step. A third. And went right.

I blew past her, following the wall to the far corner of the room, pivoting as I went, carbine rising to dominate the room.

Next to the door, Ruiz and Sophia Vega rummaged through a massive closet. The bed stood in between them and me. The closet doors were flung wide open, right in Shane's face. She wouldn't be able to see them.

But they saw me.

And Ruiz had an AK-47 in his hands.

He turned, slowly, slowly, trying to track me. I mashed the laser pressure switch, training the bright green dot on his chest. I didn't need it, but it was his final warning that he was one trigger pull away from the point of no return.

"POLICE!" I roared. "FREEZE!"

He kept turning, turning, his left foot stepping back, his torso blading towards me, arms swinging up the AK to greet me.

I snapped my carbine to the shoulder, cheek welding itself to the unyielding buttstock, found the blazing green dot-in-circle of the holosight centered on his chest and the smaller green laser dot just beside it, rotated the selector lever down with my thumb.

Fired.

Once, twice, the classic controlled pair. He shuddered, his lips drawing back in an involuntary grimace. I lifted the carbine a touch, found his face framed in the holosight window, stroked the trigger twice more.

He dropped.

Lowering the Virtus to the compressed ready, I saw Ruiz crashing to the floor in slow motion. His hands sprang open and the AK clattered under the bed.

"NOOOOOOOOO!" Vega screamed.

Shane bashed the door out of her way.

"POLICE! HANDS UP!" she yelled.

Vega ignored her, diving to the body on the floor, to the AK under the bed. The alarm in my head screamed again.

I aimed at her.

"HANDS IN THE AIR! BACK UP NOW!" I yelled.

Vega looked up at me, face twisted in hate. She rose from the floor, her arms shifting with her, her hands still out of sight. My eyes trained on her collarbone, with my peripheral vision I hunted for her hands, where are her hands—

Wood.

Metal.

I fired.

One round to the upper chest, second to the throat, third to the mouth and forth between the eyes and down she went, arms splaying out, head haloed in blood.

Her hands were empty.

I stepped my power down. The world accelerated, snapping back to regular time.

"Shots fired! Shots fired!" Shane called.

"Roger on the shots fired," Oliveira radioed. "Who fired? Everyone okay?"

There was still one more room to clear. The attached bathroom. Shane moved to the corpses. I burst into the bathroom, peeled back the shower curtains, peeked into the tub.

"Amp fired the shots," Shane replied. "Wait one."

"Bathroom clear!" I yelled.

"Room clear!" she called back.

"Coming out!"

"Come out!"

Stepping out, I saw Shane kneeling over Ruiz, her fingers pressed to his neck. I took a deep, stabilizing breath and hit my push-to-talk switch.

"This is Amp. I fired the shots. Two suspects down in main bedroom, GSWs to the chest and head. Room is clear."

Shane scooted over to Vega and felt for signs of life.

"Copy that. Is everyone okay?"

I patted myself down. "Shane? Are you okay?"

"I'm fine!" she replied.

"Shane and I are okay," I reported. "No injuries."

"Copy that," Oliveira replied. "Entry team, secure the house and lock it down. Shane, Amp, check in on the suspects. EMTs inbound."

Shane looked up at me, a mask of dread on her face.

"They're dead," she said.

"I know," I replied.

2

THE TWO SAMS

Night had fallen by the time Shane and I stepped out of the house. Green chemlights marked the perimeter of the building, supplementing the weak light spilling out the windows. Everyone around the house must have heard the shots. No one asked about them.

The five surviving suspects were proned out on the dead grass, their hands zip-tied behind their backs. As Miguel and Ray patted them down, the others stood watch around the perimeter. A couple of nosy neighbors poked their faces over chain-link faces, but no one asked too many questions. Ruiz's Doberman, still caged, pawed at the bars, barking furiously.

Standing by the BearCat, Oliveira waved me over.

"Over here."

I sidled up next to him, keeping an eye on the detainees.

"How are you doing?" he asked.

"I'm okay," I said.

As okay as anyone would be after a shoot.

He nodded. "Shane, what about you?"

"Just fine," she said.

"Good, good. I know this can be a difficult time for you, but right now we're deep inside El Barrio. I need the both of you to stay put until backup arrives."

"Got it," I said.

"Roger," she replied.

"Good. Amp, I want you on perimeter security. Shane, watch the BearCat, make sure no random *carnal* tries to do something funny."

Shane and I moved off. With the scene secure, the other cops went to work. The K-9 handler released his hound. The dog bounded into the house, nose pressed to the floor, sniffing and panting away. The two gang detectives, in balaclavas and plainclothes, brought out their biometrics collections devices. Each device was a combination of a computer, fingerprint reader, digital camera and iris scanner, enabling the detectives to quickly identify the subjects and run them against the police database.

As I watched, Miguel stepped away from a handcuffed suspect, holding up a pistol.

"Hey *ese*, I thought you said you weren't packing?" Miguel asked.

The gangbanger looked away.

"Are you hiding anything else I should know about?" Miguel pressed.

"Nothing to say to you, five-o," the banger mumbled.

Miguel paid him extra special attention, carefully patting down every inch of his body.

Safely away from the subjects, the team laid out the confiscated hardware. Four pistols, a revolver, eight knives. But no spare ammo. As I stood guard, they unloaded the weapons and bagged them up as evidence.

The police dog woofed excitedly. It must have found something. The detectives packed up, headed inside, and turned on the lights. Soon after, the K-9 officer returned in triumph, hefting bags of snow-white powder. The gang detectives followed, one of them with an AK-47.

"Where'd you get the AK from?" I asked.

"In the kitchen," the detective carrying the gun replied.

"There's another one up in the master bedroom. You should document it before IA takes it away."

"Gotcha. Thanks."

As the detectives and K-9 continued searching the house, a van from Animal Services arrived. I picked up the caged Doberman, carefully keeping my fingers away from the bars, and handed it off to the two AS officers. The dog was still hostile, barking and biting and growling, but its teeth couldn't reach our gloved hands. I signed the paperwork, the ASOs loaded it up and drove off.

I didn't blame the dog for attacking us. It just didn't know better. All it knew was that a bunch of strangers had invaded its home and attacked its owner. Maybe this time, a second family will take care of it, one that deserved its loyalty and love.

A group of patrol cars rolled up to take the arrestees away. As we handed them over, two more vans arrived. One came from the coroner's office, the other from the HCPD's Forensic Science Division. Hauling cases filled with equipment, the coroner team, and the crime scene unit entered the death house.

Last of all came the Inquisition.

Two unmarked cars parked across the dark street. Two figures crossed the road. It was so dark I could barely make out their silhouettes. I aimed my flashlight at their feet and lit them up.

The one on the left was a bald, heavyset man in a cheap gray suit and cheaper shoes. My light reflected off his frameless spectacles. His belt strained against his belly, and his suit jacket parted to reveal a hint of a holstered Glock on his right hip. A badge in a case swung from a lanyard around his neck.

The woman on the right might have been pretty once. The years had etched stress lines on her face and frozen her lips in a semi-permanent frown, and she had done up her raven hair in a severe bun. Nonetheless, her sharp black-and-white pantsuit flattered her figure and did a much better job at concealing her pistol. Like her partner, she wore her badge case on her lanyard, opened to reveal her gold shield.

Sam Byrd and Samantha Cho. The Two Sams of Internal Affairs.

The rank and file didn't like them—nobody liked IA—but they had a reputation for being fair, and that was more than I could say for most people.

"Get that light out of my eyes," Byrd grumbled, covering his face with his hand.

I put my light away. Oliveira waved them over.

"Sam and Sam," Oliveira said. "Caught this shooting?"

"Yup," Byrd replied. "What've we got?"

"Two deaders, master bedroom on level two," Oliveira said. "The action was contained inside the room. Officer Shane O'Neil witnessed the shoot. Officer Amp discharged his weapon."

"Jesus," Cho muttered. "Amp? Again?"

I sauntered over. "Hey, guys."

"Amp," Byrd said, his voice a dead monotone. "We keep meeting each other."

I shrugged. "Not my fault."

"Of course," Cho said dryly. "I'm sure you know the drill by now."

"Unfortunately."

I unslung my carbine and checked that the safety was on. Ejected the magazine and handed it to Byrd. Aimed the weapon at the grass, Amped just a tiny bit, and worked the charging handle. The chambered round jumped out of the ejection port, describing a slow arc through empty space. I caught the bullet in mid-air and powered down.

"Cute trick," Cho remarked.

"Thanks," I said, and handed my weapon and spare magazines to her.

As Cho prepped her firearms testing kit, I turned off my helmet cam, freed it from its mount, and gave it to Byrd.

"We need your other weapons too," Byrd said.

"I only fired my carbine."

"We need to verify that. It's policy."

I sighed.

First to go was my sidearm, a Glock 19 in a hip holster. Then my secondary, another Glock 19 in a chest holster, and my tertiary, a

Glock 26 worn at my ankle. Last of all was a Taser on a cross-draw holster on my left hip.

"Why do you carry so many guns?" Cho marveled.

"We're STAR. Outgunning the bad guys is our job."

Her eyebrows disappeared into her hairline. Off to the side, Oliveira chuckled into his palm. Byrd gestured at my pockets.

"Your blades, too."

"Come on," Oliveira interjected. "It's a shooting, not a stabbing."

"It's policy," Cho said.

"Are you serious?" I said. "Look, if you find any knife wounds on the bodies, which you won't, you can come back for my blades."

"We're just covering the bases," Byrd said.

Oliveira shook his head. "He keeps his blades, until or unless you find knife wounds."

Byrd raised his hands in mock-surrender. "Fine."

The IA detectives went to work, examining the weapons, checking their chambers and magazines, swabbing the muzzles for powder. Byrd glanced at the Taser and saw it was unfired.

As they worked, a second pair of visitors arrived. The leader was a young woman in a dark jacket with matching pencil skirt. Her posture upright, her handbag hanging from her shoulder, she walked with purpose and confidence. Behind her was a stout middle-aged man with a neat graying beard and sad eyes. Everything about him, the way he surveyed the scene, the faded but serviceable white shirt and gray pants just a little too big for him, the tension in his hands and jaws, screamed *cop*. Both wore identification cards on lanyards.

"Can I help you?" Oliveira asked.

"Deputy District Attorney Keira Conway," the woman said briskly. "This is my investigator, Herbert Franks. We're responding to the OIS."

Following an officer-involved shooting, Internal Affairs and the District Attorney's Office would conduct parallel and independent investigations. The procedure was designed to uphold the integrity of the justice system, and coincidentally doubled an officer's chances of being charged for a crime.

"Just in time. We've just collected the officer's weapons," Byrd said.

Conway glanced at me. "You're the shooter?"

"Yes," I replied.

"Amp?"

"Yes."

She held my gaze for a fraction of a second, as though trying to see past my balaclava.

"It's my first time seeing a Prime in person," she said, finally.

"Don't worry. The power isn't contagious," I said.

She blinked, her face caught between confusion and amusement.

Oliveira cleared his throat. "We're ready for initial statements and the scene walk-through."

"Let's do it," she replied.

"Wait up," I said.

"What is it?"

I held out my hand towards the IA detectives.

"May I have my pistols back?"

Byrd returned my Glocks while Cho bagged up the carbine and locked it in her car. Now re-armed, I led the inquisitors into the house, retracing my footsteps and recalling my actions. On the second floor, the coroner team and the crime scene unit were taking photos of the death room and laying out their kit. They paused long enough for me to walk in and point out the bodies and the angle of the shots.

When she saw the corpses, Conway's face paled and her hand crept to her chest. Franks' lips pressed together into a tight line. The Two Sams remained stoic.

When I was done talking, the quartet whipped out their cameras and took their own photos and videos of the scene. After they were satisfied, they gave the go-ahead to the specialists to do what they had to do.

"Amp, you seem unusually composed," Conway said.

"Thanks," I replied.

"This ain't his first ride at the rodeo," Cho added.

"How many shootings have you had under your belt?" Conway asked.

"Including this one, five," I admitted.

She goggled. "Five? In how many years?"

"Six."

Her jaws dropped. "Are they... Were they all fatal?"

"Yes. For the bad guys, that is."

"My God..."

"Amp's a real cowboy," Byrd quipped.

"Detective Byrd, I'd advise you against making any comments that might prejudice the investigation," Franks said balefully.

"Sorry," Byrd said, his voice completely insincere.

Back outside, the investigators gathered statements from the rest of the team while the DDA dictated her initial findings into her smartphone. I hung back and kept eyes on the street. This deep in El Barrio, there was no telling if or when an El Trece wannabe would decide to make his bones by jumping a cop.

As I stood guard, I spotted Shane occasionally sneaking glances my way. Finally, I gave her a thumbs-up, and she nodded once at me before turning her attention outwards.

When they were finally done, the Inquisition gathered around me. Oliveira butted in and stood by my side.

"Amp, you're done here for now," Byrd said. "But we'll need to make arrangements for a full statement within the next seventy-two hours."

"Not tomorrow," Oliveira said. "Per policy, Amp gets the next twenty-four hours off."

"Of course," Byrd agreed.

HCPD policy required two post-shooting statements. The initial statement was just a simple walk-through of the scene, where practical. The second statement was an in-depth examination of events prior, during and after the shoot. The day off was mandatory, to allow officers to gather their thoughts and prepare for the interview.

"I can speak to you at your office the day after tomorrow," I replied. "Oh nine hundred."

"Works for me," Cho said.

"Same here. Ms. Conway?" Byrd asked.

Conway looked at Franks. Franks nodded.

"We'll be there," Conway replied.

"Nine o'clock it is," Byrd said. "You should know this by now, but you are entitled to have legal counsel present during the interview."

I nodded. "Got it."

"Excellent. Amp, be advised that from this moment on you are formally sequestered to preserve the integrity of statements. Barring an emergency, you may not contact anyone on your team until we give the go-ahead. Furthermore, within the next seventy-two hours, we will require a full written report detailing your responsibilities and actions during the raid."

Byrd spoke formally and lifelessly, like a mechanical man reciting from a script.

"Understood," I said.

"You can go home now," Conway said. "We'll see you in two days."

I nodded. "I'll need a lift back to headquarters."

"I can drive you," Cho offered.

"An excellent opportunity to interview Amp in private," Oliveira observed.

She scowled. "There won't be anything like that. I'm going back anyway; I need to turn in the weapons and file our preliminary report."

"Thanks for the offer," I said. "Let's go."

"You sure you'll be okay?" Oliveira asked.

Meaning: don't say or do anything stupid in front of IA.

"I'll be fine," I said.

"All right. Take care now."

"See you on the other side."

Sequestered I may be, but at least IA allowed that one interaction.

3

DUKKHA

My dead came for me.

A procession of ghosts lurched towards me, their wounds on full display. The hopped-up Chechen I'd shot eight times before he decided to die. The kid who thought it was a great idea to pull a knife on a cop. The Prime who bet his ice-manipulating powers against my shotgun and lost. And more.

More and more and more of them, the ones I'd slain by my own hand, the ones I'd helped others to kill, so many of them destroyed with grenades and rockets and shells and bombs. They marched on me, a phalanx of the dead, and spoke with one voice.

"Why did you kill me?"

And my answer was always the same.

"Because I had to."

I forced my eyes open and sat up. The first rays of the morning sun burned away the final images of the nightmare. Yet deep within, I felt toxic shards clinging to my soul, so deeply embedded no amount of psychic surgery would remove them.

It was just a burden I had to carry. I couldn't sit here forever; life was waiting.

I slipped out of my futon and checked the clock. A quarter to six.

Later than I was used to waking, but in fairness, I'd come home late too.

During the long drive to HCPD HQ, Cho had gently probed me to call my parents. After all, and unfortunately, it was HCPD policy. I braced myself, called them on my police-issue phone, and told them I was involved in an OIS but I'm well, and everything is fine.

"You what? You killed someone *again?*" Father said.

"Adam! How? Why?" Mother added, her voice filled with sorrow and pain and disbelief.

"Why like that?" Father nagged. "How come you keep killing people so often? Do you like—"

"I don't have time for this," I interrupted. "I'm just letting you know I'm safe."

"It's so dangerous, you know? You must—"

"Look," I interrupted, "I'm in the middle of the post-shooting investigation. I'm telling you this now so you won't be caught off-guard, okay? And I have to go now."

"Adam... be careful," Mother said.

I hung up before Father could chip in.

Cho must have noticed, but she didn't comment.

Back at HCPD HQ, I changed out of my uniform and gloves and handed them to Cho as evidence. I was still hopped up, so I headed to the gym and worked the heavy bag. I smashed it around for a half hour, giving it everything I had, burning out every last drop of adrenaline.

Fortunately, I didn't destroy the bag this time.

After a long cold shower and a quick dinner of vending machine sandwiches, I drove home. I didn't bother checking the time when I finally entered my one-room apartment; I simply brushed my teeth and changed into my sleepwear and crashed.

Here was the morning after. The world was still here, the world has moved on, it was time for me to move on too.

I washed up in the attached bathroom and changed into a faded sweatshirt and running shorts. Summer had come, and the news advised joggers to dress appropriately. It always made me smile. I'd spent half my childhood in Singapore, where the only seasons were summer and monsoon, either blistering wet heat or chilly rains. Barring heatwaves, Halo City was cooler and drier than Singapore. But when in Halo City, dress as the Halos do.

And when you're a cop, dress as a cop would.

I opened the pistol safe in my closet. There were two shelves inside, each carrying a loaded Glock 19 and two spare magazines.

Both Glocks were my duty pistols, one issued after graduating from the Academy, one purchased after I'd joined STAR. I didn't favor the ugly, blocky weapons, and I was authorized to carry a half-dozen other pistols, but Glock was the brand of choice for most of the HCPD, and with the life I lead now, standing out was suicide.

My runner's rig was propped up against the safe. It was a low-profile two-compartment pouch fastened to a chest harness. I donned the harness, securing the pouch high and tight against my chest, and slipped the magazines into the front compartment. The main section in the rear was just about large enough for a Glock 19. Tied to a Velcro loop on the floor of the main compartment was a VanGuard holster from Raven Concealment Systems, really just a tiny strip of molded plastic, large enough to cover the trigger guard of a pistol but no more.

I carefully slipped one of the G19s into the holster, fitted the pistol into the rig, and zipped up and secured the rig to my chest.

I filled the secondary compartment with other tools. A Spyderco Delica folding knife, the model with the Wharncliffe edge, to make the most of its street-legal 2.875-inch blade. A Shinobi koppo, a pocket stick that doubled as my keychain. Most importantly, my phone. Last of all, I clipped on a Platypus SoftBottle to an external fabric loop and headed out.

My studio apartment was on the top floor of a six-story apartment building. Between the street-facing balcony and easy access to the rooftop courtyard, it commanded the highest rent in the building. But that was fine. In Chinese culture, six was a lucky number.

I walked briskly down the stairs, using the opportunity to stretch and swing my arms. There was a small gym with storage lockers on the ground floor, which I'd never used. For one thing, HCPD HQ's gym was larger and more lavishly equipped. For another, where I was going, I wouldn't need it.

There were three parks within easy access of my apartment. I picked the furthest, Bishop Park. I power-walked there at a smooth, easy pace, just fast enough to get the blood going.

Chinatown awoke around me. Storekeepers set out signs, raised shutters and swept the floors. A few of them greeted me in Mandarin and Cantonese, and I returned the favor. The scent of fresh bread wafted from Aunt Wong's bakery, the oldest and cheapest bakery in the neighborhood, and already there were customers lining up outside. Cars flowed through the narrow streets, racing to beat the morning rush, in doing so inevitably building it up. Joggers and dog walkers took to the pavement, many of them familiar faces, too many wearing earphones or headsets blaring loud music, trusting their lives to the kindness of strangers.

Just another morning in Chinatown.

It's been a year and a half since the second Hadron collider event at Serenity City. A year and a half since I became a Prime. I couldn't speak for other Primes, but my empowerment was fairly mundane. I simply came home at the end of a long watch, fell asleep, and awoke the following morning to a living hell.

I could hear *everything*. The growling of car engines and the softer crackling of rubber tires sweeping aside gravel on the road. The unbearable tap-tap-tap of high heels on hard floors. The unmistakable high-pitched screams of babies demanding attention. The rapid thump-thump-thump of my heart. A thousand other sounds, strange and overwhelming, flooded my brain, and I had to shut the windows and don my earplugs.

The rest of my senses were equally supercharged. I felt every single fiber of my clothing, my blanket and my mattress against my naked skin. Vibrations in the wall betrayed pipes and movement in the other apartments. Looking out the window the world suddenly became bright and sharp and clear, and I could pick out tiny details —individual strands of hair on the head of a passer-by, scuff marks on a wheel well, tiny blemishes on the facade of the coffee shop across the road.

When I tried to wash up I broke off the handle of my tap. I damn near put holes in the floor just by walking and almost destroyed my phone while calling the nurse hotline of Halo City General Hospital —and other hospitals. The lines were all jammed, and it took hours before I could reach someone who could tell me what was going on.

It was Rebirth Day. The day new-generation Primes were born.

It took a week of extensive testing and re-training at Halo City General's Special Wing before I learned how to control my power. How to dial it down all the way to near-human levels, then how to amp it up to become a demigod. For a while, the hospital thought I was the next Wraith or Death Shroud, until I showed them what else I could do. Even with my power at the lowest setting, I tested in the top one percent of males my age in all fitness categories—and in the top ten percent of all people in sensory sensitivity tests.

When I returned to work, the brass quietly 'suggested' I join STAR. I didn't mind; I had my sights set on STAR from the moment I entered the Academy. I graduated from selection and training at the top of my class. Immediately after that, some quiet men in sharp suits from the alphabet agencies sat me down and explained the facts of life.

As a Prime *and* a cop, I was a target. A quick way for name makers —low-level gangsters and wannabe supervillains—to climb the underworld career ladder was to cap a Prime, especially a Prime police officer. Terrorists targeted Primes in public service to gain publicity and undermine authority. And, inevitably, there would be the rogues I would be called upon to handle.

My old life was over. My best defense was anonymity. When on the job, I had to go masked. When I spoke to the media as Amp the supercop I used a voice synthesizer. My police records were sanitized, and no one outside STAR and the brass could know of my identity as Amp.

More than that, I had to disappear. And in Halo City, with my skin color and facial features, that meant living in Chinatown.

It wasn't that bad. I always preferred anonymity to fame. Celebrity superheroes might win patrons, wealth and hearts, but the hardest hitters were the ones you didn't see coming.

The largest park in Chinatown, Bishop Park attracted visitors from neighboring districts. The morning crowd was mostly retirees, with a scattering of working adults and dog walkers. Now warmed up, I headed to the fitness corner.

I never use my power when I train. It was a boost, not a crutch. It couldn't compensate for weakness—but it would make a strong man even stronger.

For the next half hour, I cycled through the stations. Pull-ups, parallel bar walks, dips, L-sits, planches. I sucked down some water, paused long enough to catch my breath, then hit the track.

I remembered a time when I could run a mile in four minutes. To max the US military fitness test, you need to run three miles in eighteen. But the workout had worn me down, and my age was catching up to me, so I settled for a pace of seven minutes a mile.

As I ran, I kept an eye on the people around me. In a grassy plain, an all-female yoga class flowed through a series of poses. A man jogged alongside his dog, interrupting his exercise whenever it wandered off to sniff a tree or streetlight. By the lake, Leong *Sifu* conducted his daily morning Taiji class for senior citizens.

I was the only killer among them.

The mark of Cain is in the eyes. It's an ever-vigilant gaze, constantly assessing everybody as friend or foe or neutrals, always studying the environment for escape routes and signs of ambush. And behind that gaze is a primordial emptiness where your innocence once lived.

No one else around me had that look. Maybe it was a good thing.

Five miles later, I was done. I power-walked back home, took a long cold shower, and prepared breakfast. Four soft-boiled eggs, the breakfast of champions.

I checked my mail as the eggs cooked. Confirmation of tomorrow's interview, coupled with a reminder to get union and legal representation. Messages from the rest of the team expressing their support. A mail from the Public Relations Office informing me not to speak to the media unless otherwise instructed. Bills. And spam.

Over breakfast, I rehearsed what I had to say. The moment I loaded the utensils into the dishwasher, I called the Halo City Police League.

"This is Detective Adam Song," I said. "I have been involved in an officer-involved shooting, and I require representation."

It had been a while since I used my formal rank. Before joining STAR, I was in the Asian Gang Unit. After the move, I retained my rank, and the pay that came with it, at the price of helping the actual detectives whenever they needed tactical support. I didn't mind it; it was just part of the job.

"Understood," the receptionist replied. "Please state your badge number."

"One-eight-three-two."

"Thank you, Officer. Putting you through to Legal Services."

When the call came through, I spent a few minutes describing the basic facts of the OIS and the coming interview. The administrator promised that she would mail me the details of my union rep by the end of the day.

With that out of the way, I called my *other* union: the Halo City Prime Association. The HCPL rep may be well-versed in police procedures and internal investigations, but as a Prime, I was held to other laws, laws that only a lawyer who specialized in Primes could use in my favor.

Once again, I described my situation to HCPA's legal department. This time, instead of assigning me a lawyer, the administrator had a question for me.

"Do you wish to engage an attorney of your choosing, or should we assign one for you?"

"I'd like to choose, please."

"Very good. Whom should I contact?"

"Will Dawson."

He was one of the most prominent lawyers in Halo City, a nonspecialist specializing in everything related to Primes. If a Prime wanted to file a class action lawsuit, if a company needed to draft an employ-ment contract specific to a Prime, if a Prime needed representation in court, Dawson was the one lawyer everybody needed on their side. Ordinarily, cops couldn't hope to begin to afford his fees, but he and I had a special arrangement.

"Understood. Should I also contact Thomas Plutarch?"

Better known as the Historian, Plutarch was gifted with the power of perfect recall and worked as a chronicler for Prime communities. I'd met him once when he was shooting a documentary of high-profile Primes.

Shame the documentary ended the way it did.

"No need for that, thanks," I replied.

The moment I hung up, I sent a mail to Will, explaining the situa-tion. While I had to formally engage him through the HCPA to ensure the Association would step up to the plate for me if necessary, he appreciated personal touches like that. For a case like this, it didn't hurt to start out on his good side.

One last phone call, this time to the police psychologist. Before I could be returned to duty, she needed to conduct a formal assess-ment and verify that I was fit for duty.

After scheduling my appointment, I spent the rest of the morning doing paperwork, dictating my report on my police-issue smart-phone. As I talked, I paced around the room, recalling the drive, the raid, the shoot.

With every word I relived every sensation from last night. The wind in my ears, the unyielding polymer grip of the carbine, shouts of "POLICE!" and "SEARCH WARRANT!", Ruiz running up the stairs, the rustling from the closet, Shane charging in when she should have stopped, green dot over olive skin, finger on the trigger, the muzzle blasts that ended two lives.

I breathed. I spoke. I carried on.

I finished my first draft at eleven. I checked my clock, ran a few mental calculations, and dressed up again. This time in a white shirt, gray pants and black leather shoes.

I didn't expect any trouble today, but I would be in close proximity to civilians. Low-pro was the way to go.

Glock 19 at my hip, two spare magazines and flashlight and Delica spread across my waistband. Minimalist as kit went, but where I was going, minimalism was a virtue.

Bright Moon Temple was the largest Chinese Buddhist temple in Halo City. Tracing its lineage to the world-famous Northern Shaolin Temple, it ministered to the Buddhists of Chinatown and neighboring Koreatown, and anyone else in the city drawn to Chan teachings.

When I was a kid I wanted to be a Shaolin monk. Blame it on the dramas and movies Mother liked to watch. In the monks, I saw the perfect synthesis of faith and war, holy men who upheld both secular and divine law while taking care to avoid spilling blood. I might have outgrown my childhood dreams, but the sutras still echoed in my head.

The walk to the temple took forty-five minutes. I used the opportunity to practice mindfulness, paying attention to the tension in my muscles, the subtle weight shifts in every step, the breath flowing in and out of my lungs, the clothing and behaviors of the people around me, the cars passing by on the street, the buildings around me.

Situated in the middle of modernity, Bright Moon Temple was a throwback to another time and place. With sweeping roofs of bright yellow tiles and red-painted walls, it was an island of color in a world of gray. The triple gate, a large main entrance flanked by two smaller ones, loomed over me. In bold gold, the characters *Guangyue Si* shouted from the main signboard, the English translation right below it. A stone path led from the gate to the main hall.

It was almost noon, and a small crowd was building up. Young adults, almost all of them Caucasians; middle-aged women and elderly men, all of them Chinese; a few tourists I identified by their pink sunburnt skin and their expensive cameras.

Passing through the main gate, I entered the main courtyard. The scent of burning incense tickled my nose. Trees and bushes lined the inner perimeter, subtly drawing the eye to the pagoda-shaped stele in the center of the courtyard and the worship hall beyond.

Through the open doors of the worship hall, I saw a trinity of statues gilded in gold leaf. On the left was Bhaisajyaguru Buddha, the Medicine Buddha, and the Buddha in charge of the past. On the right was Amitabha, the Buddha of Immeasurable Light and Life, he who controls the future. In between them, seated on a lotus, his right palm raised in benediction, was Shakyamuni Buddha, the Buddha of the present, and the principal Buddha of the faith.

An elongated trough stood before the hall, filled with burning incense sticks sprouting from a bed of soft gray ash, and flanked by a pair of oil lamps.

There were two smaller halls, one on either side of the courtyard. I followed a small group of people heading to the right-hand hall. Past an antechamber, down a short passage, we entered the meditation room.

The room was deliberately sparse. Ottomans and neatly-folded blankets lined the walls. The tinted windows allowed in light and trapped the cool air from the air conditioner. A statue of the Buddha sat on an altar. Before the altar sat a bald, smiling man in saffron robes. Shi Jin Kong.

Like me, Shi Sifu was a Prime. Born in a hardscrabble farming town, as a child his parents discovered he could work and play all day and night without rest. As a Prime, he could have secured a powerful position in the police or military, enjoyed the respect of the government and society, and brought great honor to his family and village.

Instead, he renounced the material world to follow the teachings of the Buddha.

In the Shaolin Temple, he studied martial arts and the sutras, mastering his mind, body, and gift. State security kept a watchful eye on him, monitoring his every move and forbidding him from casually contacting foreigners or traveling overseas.

Two decades ago, Beijing organized a cultural exchange performance in Halo City. Shi Shifu jumped at the chance and pulled every string he could to join the performers. On the last day of the exhibition, he sneaked away from his group and defected to the United States.

After the controversy died down, he opened a Chan temple in Chinatown. Since then, he kept the core regimen of his teachers, with meditation classes in the morning and lunchtime, and *qigong* and *gongfu* training in the evening.

"Thank you for coming," Shi Shifu said, in accented English. "Please, find a seat."

I took my place at the far corner, where I could see the room and the door. When the others were ready, Shi Shifu pressed his palms together at his chest and bowed. We echoed the motions. He sat on his cushion, and we did the same.

I eased into a cross-legged position on my smooth faux-leather ottoman. My hardware dug into my flesh. Around me, more advanced practitioners gracefully sank into half- or full lotus postures. Others resorted to sitting with their feet firmly pressed against the floor.

In gentle, soothing tones, Shi Shifu instructed us in proper meditation form. Hold the spine and head erect. Keep the eyes half-closed and cast downward, or in a state of soft focus. Place your hands in the cosmic mudra by touching the thumbs together in front of your belly and placing the fingers of one hand above the other to form a shape of the bowl. Breathe deep, breathe naturally, and be.

When he was sure we had settled in, Shi Shifu walked to the altar, lit an incense stick, bowed to the Buddha, and planted the incense in a small brass bowl. When the stick burned down, the session would end.

Shi took up a large stick by his cushion and walked the floor, ready to awaken dreamers and sleepers with a sharp rap. I tuned him out and breathed.

Breathe in for four counts. Exhale for four. Breathe in. Out. In. Out.

In again and—

Ruiz's face swam before my mind's eye. Blood poured down his chest and shattered skull. He pointed his AK-47 at me, screaming curses and demands. Vega materialized next to him, her wounds on full display, shouting in my face.

I continued breathing.

One by one, my ghosts returned. Spectral faces arose in my mind's eye, reaching for me with bony fingers. Half-formed words reverberated in my ears, orders and demands and accusations. Immaterial blood seeped from my clothes and spilled out on my hands.

I breathed and let the sensations pass through me. Still they come in relentless waves, demanding attention. I continued to breathe, to acknowledge these sensations, and let them pass.

The dead were dead. These sensations were not real, merely phenomena arising from an unquiet mind, a mind disturbed by the weight of unwholesome deeds.

You can't outrun what you've done. The fruit of your actions will come back to haunt you, and actions that cause suffering to others inevitably cause you suffering also. Year after year, lifetime after lifetime, karma bites at your heels, piling sorrow upon sorrow. To escape the eternal recurrence of sin and suffering, you must awaken.

I couldn't. Not today. Maybe not in this life.

But as I breathed, the phantoms vanished.

Shi Shifu rang a brass bell, signaling the end of the session. I swayed my body from side to side, limbering ligaments and muscles, and slowly stretched and unfolded my legs. I gingerly got up to my feet, feeling blood rush into my muscles. Around me, the rest of the class did the same, some more fluidly than others.

Shi Shifu pressed his palms together and bowed. "Thank you for coming today."

We bowed back. "Thank you for teaching us."

As we filed out the door, Shi Shifu walked next to me.

"*Ni de fudan hen zhong ba,*" he said.

You're carrying a heavy burden.

Heavy. As appropriate a word as any other.

I'd joined the Marine Corps right out of high school, and spent a decade exploring the world. After I was discharged, I came home to find myself. One evening, I wandered into one of Shi's weekly lectures. He spoke of *dukkha*, of suffering, of how all life was suffering and how suffering could be overcome through a proper understanding of existence.

During the lecture, he fixed me with a piercing stare, one that seemed to penetrate the depths of my soul. He knew who I was. What I was.

When the lecture ended, I explored the temple grounds. I bumped into him again at the entrance, and he had said the same thing to me. *Ni de fudan hen zhong ba.*

"*Ze ji tian zhen daomei,*" I replied.

These been a rough few days. The same words I'd said to him so many years ago.

"Do you wish to talk about it?" he asked, continuing in Mandarin.

"I'm not sure if I should."

Shi Shifu usually spoke to me in Mandarin. I obliged whenever possible. This far from his native land, few people spoke his mother tongue. He needed the connection as much as I needed the practice.

"During meditation just now, I felt you were struggling with something. Was it your dead?"

"Yes."

"There are more of them today."

"Yes."

He sighed. "I see."

He knew I was once a Marine, now a cop, forever a killer. I never told him anything more than the broad strokes of my work—killing least of all—but he had this uncanny sense of *knowing*, and more importantly, understanding.

Stepping out into the sunlight courtyard, Shi Shifu fixed me with his eyes, at once gentle and brilliant and piercing.

"Death is inevitable. Yet violence is always regrettable," he said.

"It comes with the job," I replied. "When persuasion fails, when villains no longer respect authority and persist in visiting violence upon others, to uphold the norms and customs of civilization the only option we have left is naked force."

"A pity. Yet so long as you continue this path, I fear you will be forced into making more of such decisions."

"Fortunately, I'm not a monk."

Shi laughed. "Fortunate indeed."

I smiled. "I did what I had to do. I'll continue doing it."

"Yes, but who are you justifying yourself to? And why?"

I blinked. He was a monk and had long ago renounced the material world. Why did I have to justify myself to him?

What else was hiding behind my words?

"I'll have to think about that," I said.

"Please do. Do you need help?"

"Not today."

"If you need help, our doors are always open." Shi's smile grew sad. "I'll pray for you. And for the unquiet ghosts."

"Thank you."

I hoped they could find peace. I'm still searching for it.

Near the entrance, an elderly volunteer sold incense and other ceremonial items at a small kiosk. I bought a packet of joss sticks and lit them at an oil lamp. When the tips caught fire, I fanned the sticks, watching the brown incense coating and sandalwood core transmute to smoke and dissipate to nothingness.

I stood before the Buddhas, joss sticks held at chest height, and waved the sticks back and forth, just enough to spread the cloud of incense. Other devotees around me made exaggerated bowing motions, some lifting their sticks to their heads and bringing them back down to their hearts. A few insisted on facing the gate and praying to the sky before turning their attention to the Buddha.

They had their ways of worship. I had mine.

I planted the joss sticks in the ash-filled vessel, bowed to the Buddha, and left. The secular world was calling, and it wouldn't wait.

4

THE FIFTH ESTATE

Lunch was bibimbap at a Korean eatery around the corner. Back home, I hung my futon out to air on the balcony and returned to work.

Editing and saving my report consumed another half-hour. When I was done, I opened a new page on my processor and touched my fingers to the keys.

Something bubbled in the depths of my mind. Something that sought expression. I set my ego aside and let it rise from my deepest self and out into my hands. Of their own accord, my fingers moved.

Six and a half pounds of pressure flings
A metal bus with exposed needlepoint heart
To ignite a rocket of brass and powder
Blasting 62 grains of copper alloy and plastic tip
At 2600 fps down an 11.5-inch barrel
Yearning
To fulfill its purpose.

. . .

I DON'T CONSIDER myself much of a poet. Maybe someday, but not today. I saved the file anyway.

With my work out of the way, I could relax. I opened my web browser and headed to the website of the *Halo City Herald*. Right at eye level, a headline screamed, *Amp kills two in deadly police shooting.*

I sighed. Trust the *Herald* to concoct headlines like that. I steeled myself and clicked on the article.

A PRIME POLICE *officer codenamed Amp shot and killed two suspects Wednesday evening in Franklin Boulevard, according to police.*

Amp, who serves on the Halo City Police Department's Special Tactics and Rescue team, was serving a high-risk search warrant when he encountered two suspects. The suspects reached for an AK-47 assault-style rifle, forcing Amp to open fire, the HCPD said.

Amp reportedly shot both suspects multiple times in the chest and head. The suspects were declared dead at the scene.

SENSATIONALIST HEADLINE and inaccurate firearm terminology aside, it was a fair take. But I didn't need the reminder.

It was a bright, warm day outside. Too pleasant to stay indoors. I grabbed my Glock and Kindle and headed to the rooftop garden.

As I stepped out the door, greenery welcomed me. Vine-adorned fences flowed along the edges of the parapet. I followed the gravel path curving sinuously through the carefully-cut turf, studying the potted shrubs and flowers by my sides. A blue-painted gazebo stood at the corner of the roof, and under its roof there were wooden benches and tables and sofas. Small bridges connected this apartment to neighboring buildings, forming a four-block square of green.

The realtor had boasted that the garden was the social hub of the neighborhood. In all my months here I'd never known the inhabitants to mingle much with each other. At the block diagonally across mine, Mrs. Jones coached her children through their homework under a gazebo. An elderly couple, Mr. and Mrs. Wood, walked their cat around the four gardens, stopping to stroke it every now and then.

I exchanged greetings with them as I passed by, then settled into a bench under a nearby gazebo and opened my Kindle. Today's reading material was the latest translation of the *Shoninki*, an instruction manual written for 17th-century shinobi.

This was my third read-through, and every time I gleaned more information from the ancient text. On the surface, much of the teachings were outdated, but they illustrated timeless principles still relevant today. Mindset, camouflage, deception, social engineering; the modern operator could find much to learn from here.

As I read, I took notes on my phone, occasionally pausing to ponder the implications of a sentence and attempting to frame it in a modern context. My neighbors left me alone, and I returned the favor.

Near the end of the book, my phone rang. The caller ID said 'Thomas Crane.'

Like me, he was a new-gen Prime. Some years ago, Tom left the Army to start a private security company. When he gained his gift, he rebranded himself with his power as his touchpoint, and Aegis Security Group quickly became one of the premier PSCs in the state.

He was private security, I was a public servant, but we walked in similar circles. Our paths had crossed enough times that we were on friendly terms.

I picked up immediately.

"You're on the news again," Tom said. "You heard what they said about you?"

"Nothing good, I trust."

He barked a laugh. "They say you shot two people."

"Guilty."

"They needed killing?"

"Absolutely."

"Good." His jovial tone took a darker tone. "Listen, you doing okay?"

"Yeah. What's wrong?"

"El Trece thinks it can become the Cartel Del Norte. They've been emulating the tactics of the cartels down south. Expect reprisals soon."

"I appreciate the heads-up. I've been taking precautions."

"Good, good. I've run into them recently myself."

"What happened?"

"A journo went down south to investigate the links between El Trece and the narco cartels and hired us to protect her. I had a bad feeling about this job, so I personally led her personal security detail. She must have asked the wrong people the wrong questions. After she returned to our side of the border, some *sicarios* tried doing a drive-by on her. With an AK-47."

"Damn. What happened next?"

"We saw them coming. Me and my boys did our thing, and now there are three less *sicarios* in the world."

I heard the grin in his voice. He had never outright told me what he had done in the Army, but he had The Look, and his website said he had spent time in the Special Forces. We could talk guns and ammo and tactics all day long, and his preferences screamed high-speed low drag. He didn't care about three-gun competitions or sports or mere 'self-defense'; he was obsessed with slinging lead downrange and putting bad guys in the ground in the shortest possible time. In that sense, he was like me.

And, well, I never did tell him what I used to do in the Marines either.

"Bravo Zulu," I said.

"Thanks. But anyway, El Trece are animals. If you kill one of them, they are honor-bound to kill you. Doesn't matter if you're a cop or a Prime, if they see you they *will* come gunning for you. And if they can't get you, they'll go after your family."

"No doubt about that."

"If you need help, any kind of help, just call me. Me and my boys will take care of you."

"Thanks."

"No problem, bro. You take care now."

Lots of people called me 'bro.' He meant what he said. We'd seen each other around HCPA functions now and then, but our paths had collided in blood and fire six months ago at the Morgan Arts Center, and there is no greater bond between men than those forged in battle.

I finished my read-through at half-past five. Returning to my apartment, I grabbed my training bag. It was chock-full with rattan sticks, training blades, foam batons, and safety gear, with a pouch holding a dedicated first aid kit. I stuffed my towel and a change of clothes into the bag and went out.

Two blocks down the road, I stopped in at a dim sum place for a light dinner. Two *dai bau*, large buns stuffed with pork and mushrooms and sausage and hardboiled eggs, just enough to keep me going without slowing me down. Then, I donned my earplugs and entered the metro.

When I was a child, the metro was fast and smooth and pleasant. As a Prime, it was an ordeal of unrelenting noise. Shoes shuffled and high heels clicked. Ticket and gantry machines beeped in a constant cacophonous din. Businessmen gabbed into phones, children screamed for attention, a crew of street dancers blared hip-hop from a boombox as they hopped and skipped and gyrated and twitched next to the stairs, people clapping and cheering in appreciation. The sonic tide assaulted my ears from every direction, and without my earplugs I'd have a splitting headache by now.

When the next train pulled in, I saw it was mostly empty. Not good. Passengers absorbed and dampened noise. Without them, the thunderous announcements from overhead speakers, the humming of the electric motors, the blaring of door closing alarms, the deafening screech of the brakes, every sound, sharp and subtle, flooded my ears.

I endured.

I had to. Rush hour was setting in, and where I was going, the train would be faster than a car. And in this line of work, you couldn't afford to shun loud sounds. If nothing else, this was training, what autistics called desensitization.

The train conveyed me to the Harbor district. I leapt out the
second the doors opened and took to the streets. Ducking down
winding roads and cobblestone streets, staying clear of the clogged
thoroughfares and the jammed-up avenues, I strolled through one of
the oldest neighborhoods in the city, so old it traced its history to the
early 19th century, to the days when Halo City was just a collection of
scattered farms, fishing villages and mining towns. There were few of
the dazzling modern glass and steel and concrete edifices that domi-
nated the Halo City landscape here, and everywhere I turned there
were brick-and-mortar buildings drenched in faded reds and blues
and greens and grays. As I walked down the streets, the scent of
asphalt and rubber mingled with mouth-watering aromas wafting
from hot dog stands and taco wagons.

My route ended at the Wilshire Community Center. Men in rough
clothes and women in tight spandex made their way to the ground
floor gym. On the second floor, I saw youths gathering near the
library and mothers picking up their children from the daycare
center. The third floor was given over to conference rooms and events
halls. Mostly empty, save for one room.

The Southeast Asian Martial Academy.

I changed into my training clothes and entered the hall. There
was still five minutes to go before class began proper, but already
there were a handful of students warming up and laying out their
gear. Near the front of the room, unloading a massive duffel bag of
equipment, was the owner and founder of the academy, Jim Wilson.

Built like a fireplug, Jim was a human weapon. With over thirty-
five years of martial arts training under his belt, he held instructorship certificates in kali, silat, kuntao and Jeet Kune Do; he had
studied kickboxing, judo, wrestling; and was even now working on a
black belt in jujitsu. His green eyes sparkled as I approached.

"Yo, Adam. I was hoping you'd show up today."

"Let me guess," I said. "You need a guinea pig for later."

He laughed. "I was at a seminar last week, and I learned some
really cool techniques. You should've been there."

His voice held a hidden edge. I was an assistant instructor in his school, and part of my unspoken duties was to keep up with training as best as I could. But last week, STAR ran a series of drug busts, taking down one crack house after another, working our way up the chain to snatch the suppliers. There was so much to do, there was barely time to breathe.

I shrugged. "Work. You know how it is."

"It's all good. We'll try some of those concepts later."

"I can hardly wait."

I slipped my earplugs in place. In such close quarters, the cracking of stick on stick was as deafening as gunfire. The first time I attended training after my empowerment, I lasted fifteen seconds under the sonic barrage before my ears, and head hurt too much to continue.

Also, I'd shattered my sticks. All six of them.

Jim graciously asked no questions. I simply fashioned earplugs from wads of wet tissue paper and carried on. He transitioned to knives and empty hands for the rest of the session.

For the next class, I'd equipped myself with earplugs—high-end ones, made of transparent medical-grade silicon—and fresh rattan sticks, the upper ends taped down for additional reinforcement and sound insulation. This time, my ears survived the class. My sticks, too.

Jim never asked about the earplugs or the sticks. I never told him.

At nineteen hundred on the dot, class began. There were twelve students today, all of them regulars, an even mix of seniors and juniors. We opened with footwork and coordination drills, training the movement patterns, platforms and concepts we would be working with tonight.

Pairing off, we took turns feeding attacks and responding to them, rotating out every few minutes. With the newcomers I went slow and precise, helping them sharpen their movements and passing on the principles of positioning and angles and body mechanics. I pushed the veterans to the limit of their abilities, going as fast as they could keep up, and sustained the pace.

I didn't use my power, of course. For one thing, overwhelming the students in training wouldn't teach them anything; for another, hurting training partners was bad form.

True to his word, as training progressed, Jim demonstrated different concepts on me. How to destroy a weapon-bearing limb and follow through with strikes and locks and takedowns. How to turn an opponent's weapon against him. How to maneuver around multiple armed opponents. Jim held back just enough to prevent injury; I gritted my teeth and soaked up the pain. I'd experienced far worse than this.

Class always ended with full-contact work, either sparring with training weapons or scenario work. Jim elected for the former today. I donned protective eyewear, grabbed a rubber knife and a foam baton, and went to work.

The junior students posed no threat. I simply kept my distance and sniped at their hands. The experienced ones were more difficult to handle, and they got in a few hits. One of them gave as good as he got, and he might just be ready to take on an instructorship position. When it was my time to go toe-to-toe with Jim, I pulled out all the stops, and even then, for every hit I got in, he landed four or five.

If I'd Amped up, I could have wiped the floor with all of them. But that wasn't the point of today's training. The chief weakness of almost all Primes was over-dependency on their powers. Once their power failed, or when someone found a way to work around their gift, they were helpless.

I preferred to develop the skills I needed to hold my own. My power was simply the icing on the cake. Being a well-rounded operator was always better than being a one-trick pony.

Training ended at 2100. My muscles were sore, sweat soaked through my clothes, and my brain felt like it was stuffed to the brim. Good training.

As the students packed up, Jim sidled up to me.

"Good work today," he said. "You really should come by more often. I need people who can help with class."

SEAMA was expanding. That wasn't a bad thing, except that Jim could only be in so many places at once, and the only other full-fledged assistant instructor couldn't attend weekday sessions. Jim couldn't pay me for my time either, but at least I didn't have to pay for classes anymore.

"The badge is a harsh mistress," I replied. "But I'll show up whenever I can."

"Good, good. I didn't think you were coming today."

"I had some unexpected time off."

"Glad you came here to spend some of that time with us."

"Me too."

I'd dabbled with martial arts here and there in my youth, but none stuck with me. After joining the Marine Corps, I'd stopped training altogether. Then came the fateful day when I was deployed to the Philippines to train with their renowned Force Recon Battalion. The Filipinos introduced me to Pekiti Tirsia Kali, and its emphasis on weaponry resonated with me in a way no other art did. Since then, I'd sought training in Filipino martial arts whenever I could.

After separating from the Marines, I wanted to get into training FMA in a big way. Soon after, I saw Jim Wilson on a local news station discussing self-defense and promoting his school.

I joined up on the spot.

Three years later, I picked up my instructor certificate. Since then I helped Jim with classes, sometimes taking over for him when he was busy. In a life filled with constant change, martial arts was my one constant, an anchor to my deepest self.

During the journey home I stopped at a convenience store and fueled up on a pair of tuna sandwiches. The moment I returned home, I took a cold shower and checked my mail.

Will Dawson had replied to my email, thanking me for the heads-up and listing a long set of instructions and questions. My union rep, James Moss, had mailed me as well, and offered a similar set.

I answered their questions, cc'ing them in the same thread. Then I spent the rest of the evening preparing for tomorrow, rehearsing answers to likely questions, reading and meditating.

As I voided my conscious mind, my dead rushed in to fill the space. But this time, only Ruiz and Vega showed their faces. The rest were indistinct shadows, lurking at the edge of my subconscious. I breathed and held space, and watch them fade out.

I woke up early the following morning, headed to Bishop Park and exercised for an hour. On the way home, I bought a pair of *dai bau* and ate them on the move. After a quick shower, I dressed myself in my best suit and headed out.

My car was a silver second-hand Honda, bought cheap and meticulously maintained. With so many Hondas on the road it was virtually invisible. Just the way I liked it. I melted into traffic and followed it downtown.

HCPD Headquarters was a soulless monolith, a great glass box ten stories tall encased in a concrete frame. Its sole concession to aesthetics was the driveway, supported by a blocky colonnade. In front of the building was a wide plaza, dotted with carefully-pruned trees and unobtrusive bicycle parking spots.

A plaza presently filled with protesters.

I slowed down, eyeballing the crowd. There were about a hundred demonstrators, mostly Hispanics with a scattering of whites. A thin blue line of barricades held them off from the entrance of HCPD HQ, reinforced by a platoon of Rapid Enforcement and Counter-Terrorism Team cops in riot armor and clear shields. More uniformed cops surrounded the protesters, hemming them in. In the no man's land between the police and the civilians, cameramen and journalists stalked for quotes and optics.

The crowd hammed it up for the media, chanting and waving signs in English and Spanish. Through the window glass, I only heard indistinct murmurs. But their signs were plain to see.

NO POLICE VIOLENCE! NO KILLER CAPES!

JUSTICIA POR SOFIA Y EMMANUEL!

JAIL AMP NOW!

"What the fuck?" I said.

THE INQUISITION

I aborted my approach, blended into nearby traffic, and sneaked into a public parking garage. The protesters were content to stand and shout in the plaza for now, but there was no guarantee things would stay that way.

I slipped on a cap and jacket and made my way to the station on foot. Across the street, I heard the protesters chanting.

"NO JUSTICE, NO PEACE!"

"NO KILLER COPS! NO KILLER CAPES!"

"HEY HEY! HO HO! KILLER AMP HAS GOT TO GO!"

They punctuated their chants with air horns and shrill whistles, foot stomps and synchronized claps. The REACT platoon stood impassively in the face of the sonic assault, while their uniformed backup covered their flanks.

Ripples passed through the crowd. The demonstrators were reorganizing themselves, packing as many people in front of as many cameras as they could. As a squad of broadcast reporters addressed video cameras, a legion of journalists waded into the crowd, digital cameras and recorders and press passes held high.

I donned my earplugs and slipped into the main entrance. Inside, the thick bullet-resistant glass blunted the shouting. A half-dozen

REACT cops stood by the doors, armed not with riot gear but with carbines and body armor, forming the last line of defense against a sudden infiltration or a terrorist attack.

REACT responded to all high-profile, large-scale events in Halo City. Parades and diplomatic talks, civic unrest and terrorist attacks, anytime the PD needed to flood an area with cops and guns, they got the call. And if STAR needed backup, REACT would be there too.

The security measures had spooked the locals. The cops manning the front desk were on edge. Uniforms reporting to duty kept their hands on their guns, and plainclothes detectives fidgeted with their gear. Civilian administrators hustled through the security checkpoint. At the far end of the lobby, the in-house cafe, Angel's Beat, was mostly empty, the only customers a short queue of cops ordering coffee to go.

And Will Dawson.

Seated at a small table, he was clearly out of place. Every inch of him screamed wealth and status. His bespoke blue suit, red silk tie, and polished leather shoes were understated and elegant, flying under the radar of the proletariat, yet screaming his true colors to people with the eyes to appreciate them. His chunky gold watch gleamed on his wrist, his one obvious sign of opulence. His sliver-thin Apple laptop lay open on the table, focused utility and functional beauty in a 12-inch package.

"Morning," I said.

"Morning Adam," Will Dawson boomed, standing and extending his hand. "How are you doing?"

I shook his hand. He had a firm, powerful grip, and I matched him ounce for ounce. But no more—if I didn't modulate myself I could accidentally crush every bone in his hand.

"As well as can be, given the circumstances. And you? How's the family?"

Shadows fell over his eyes. His crow's feet deepened.

"They're good. We're good."

"Glad to hear it," I said.

The Dawsons were among Halo City's most famous supercouples.

Will was a mundane lawyer who was among the first in his profession to handle Prime-related cases, and over thirty years built his empire on a reputation of success. His wife, Dr. Angela Marie Dawson, was a Prime with that most treasured of gifts: the power of healing.

A mere mortal like me couldn't hope to break into their social circles, until the day of the Morgan Arts Center Massacre.

Six months ago, Angela had organized a charity gala at the Morgan Arts Center to raise funds for research into childhood diseases. The Dawsons had invited the glitterati of both coasts, among them some of the most famous Primes in the nation.

It should have been the safest place in America, until the moment the One World Coalition struck.

OWC was one of the many anti-Prime terrorist groups that had sprung up over the past decade. Unfortunately, they were also among the more competent ones.

Posing as MAC employees, OWC operatives smuggled ceramic blades into the building before the event. When the gala began, the operatives took their places, mingling with the Primes and security.

An hour after kick-off, the insiders struck. Two operatives stabbed the cops guarding the front door and allowed a squad of gunmen to charge in. As the shooters entered the event hall, the other insiders cut the throats of nearby Primes. The shooters went to work, first firing on Primes, then seizing other visitors as hostages.

Unfortunately for them, the Dawsons had engaged Aegis.

Aegis and his men were working the crowd incognito, posing as guests and waiters and event staff. Shortly after the massacre began, they broke cover and sallied forth to meet the terrorists. Armed only with knives and flashlights and their powers, the protectors hustled the survivors to safety. Aegis deployed his electromagnetic shields, holding off the terrorists long enough for STAR and REACT to respond.

My team had caught the call.

I did what I had to do.

And at that time, Thomas Plutarch was doing a ride-along with a film crew.

That incident propelled my team, and me, into the national spotlight. In the week that followed, the media insisted on interviewing me, and the brass insisted I deliver the script they gave me. When the fifth estate finally moved on to other news, the Dawsons insisted on meeting everyone who had helped them. Since then, the Dawsons had treated Aegis and me as personal family friends. In public, Angela and Will seemed to have bounced back, but his face hinted at another story.

But it wasn't a story I could investigate today.

"Did the protesters give you any trouble?" Will asked.

"No. They're behaving themselves."

"Damned thugs," he said, shaking his head. The sweet floral fragrance of his cologne invaded my nostrils. "I'll bet a million dollars there's El Trece mixed up in the crowd."

"No bets," I replied. "El Trece's been dabbling in politics lately. I wouldn't be surprised if they had a hand in organizing the protest."

"I remember a time when they were just street punks."

"I remember a time when nobody knew them."

He laughed bitterly. "Ain't that the truth."

We had an hour before the interview. Will and I discussed our interview strategy, rehearsing and refining answers to potential questions, identifying topics which he should handle in my place.

A few minutes later, a slim Caucasian man in a gray suit approached us. Briefcase in one hand, he carried himself with a confident air. Lawyer, no doubt, but he was a moon to Will's sun.

"Mr. Song? Mr. Dawson?" he asked.

I stood. "Yes. You must be Mr. Moss."

"Indeed," he confirmed.

After a round of handshakes and an exchange of business cards, we got down to business. The lawyers discussed their division of labor, with Moss monitoring all questions related to police procedure, and Will handling everything to do with my powers. We continued our preparations until ten minutes to the hour.

The civilians exchanged their ID for visitor passes and followed me upstairs. Internal Affairs was sited on the ninth floor, just one floor removed from the chief's office. I was intimately and unfortunately familiar with the way to IA; by now I could walk there with my eyes closed.

Inside the office, past the glass double doors, the Inquisition was waiting for me. The Two Sams on my left, DDA Conway and Investigator Franks to my right.

"Detective Song," Sam Byrd said. "Just in time. Are these your attorneys?"

"Yes," I replied. "Will Dawson and James Moss. Mr. Dawson is my defense counsel, and Mr. Moss is from the union."

"It's a pleasure to meet you, Counselors," Conway said. "I'm Deputy District Attorney Keira Conway, and this is Investigator Herbert Franks."

"Same here," Moss replied.

"Charmed," Will said congenially.

Conway's eyes narrowed. "I've never seen two lawyers present during an OIS interview before."

"First time for everything," Will said, a bright smile on his face.

"We've got the interview room set up," Byrd said. "Are you ready?"

"Let's get it over with," I replied.

THE SEVEN OF us barely fit into the interview room. The table had just enough room for Byrd's laptop and the Inquisition's and lawyers' recording devices. We brought in chairs and squashed ourselves around the table as best as we could. After everyone turned on their recorders, Byrd stated the subject of the meeting, the names of the participants, and the date.

"Detective Song," Byrd said formally, "let's start from the beginning. Please state the purpose of the STAR call-out two nights ago."

"We were serving a high-risk warrant targeted at Emmanuel Ruiz and his clique," I replied.

"Mr. Ruiz was one of the subjects you shot, correct?"

"Yes."

"Was there a warrant on the other decedent, Ms. Sofia Vega?" Cho asked.

"Not to my knowledge."

"What do you think she was doing there?" she asked.

"I don't know. I only know that they lived together in the same house," I said.

The opening questions were designed to establish the circumstances of the day, before moving on to the main event. As the DDA and the investigator observed, the IA detectives probed me about the shooting, the steps that led up to it, the moment after.

No detail was left unchecked. The number of steps I took. How everyone else moved and acted. The tactics we employed. The number of shots fired. Why I fired. What I sensed before, during and after the shoot. The Two Sams employed memory-jogging questions, framing every action in time and place, building a timeline of events.

When the first round of questioning was over, Byrd spoke.

"We have recovered footage from your helmet camera. Now we're going to watch the footage and compare it to what you said earlier."

"Go ahead," I said.

As Byrd started up the computer, Conway asked, "Detective Byrd, did you say helmet camera? I thought all officers wore body-mounted cameras."

This time, Moss answered.

"STAR routinely wears helmet-mounted cameras. It is accepted practice."

"Why?" she asked, her tone genuinely curious.

"We carry lots of specialized gear on our vests," I replied. "Body-cams can interfere with access."

More importantly, when aiming a weapon, an officer's arms might obstruct the lens.

"Department policy holds that so long as citizen interactions are clearly recorded, the actual positioning of the camera doesn't matter," Moss added.

Byrd spun the laptop screen around. A full-screen window

showed a still image. The moment I had turned on the camera. As we craned forward, Byrd hit the play button.

The camera saw everything I saw. The drive up, the door breach, the sweep of the living room, the initial encounter with Ruiz.

Pausing the video, Cho asked, "Detective Song, is it STAR policy to chase fleeing suspects like that?"

"I thought this interview was about a shooting, not about tactics," Dawson said.

"Let me clarify," Cho said. "Detective Song, you said earlier that you and Officer O'Neil pursued the suspect upstairs. Correct?"

"Yes," I agreed.

"Just the two of you?"

"To my knowledge, yes. But I had to cover my area of responsibility. I couldn't look back to see if the rest of the team was behind us."

"Is it STAR policy to send just two officers to chase a suspect, known to be armed and dangerous, and gifted with a power, into an uncleared space?" Byrd pressed.

I sensed a trap here. But I couldn't feel its shape just yet.

"Our tactics are driven by the situation on the ground," I said carefully. "If we have just two officers to resolve a situation, we make do with what we have."

"Detective Byrd," Moss said, "I should point out that the rest of the team was at that time taking the other suspects in the living room under control."

"Did you feel the decision to follow the suspect was dangerous?" Conway asked.

"Everything STAR does carries an element of danger," I said. "But Shane had the Reaper. I felt it was a manageable risk."

"Reaper?"

"The ballistic shield. More properly, the exoframe we used to carry the shield."

Conway blinked. "That's a scary name."

Conway was a civilian. Not a cop. I had to remember that.

"We can't do anything about how a company names its products," I said.

"Tell us more about the shield," Franks probed. "What about it made you feel the risk was manageable?"

"It was rated to stop armor-piercing rifle rounds. I was reasonably confident that even if Ruiz grabbed one of his AK-47s, he wouldn't be able to hurt us."

"But shields leave your legs exposed," he said.

Many DA investigators tended to be former or retired cops, and they took their knowledge of tactics, weapons, and equipment with them.

"Legs are small, fast-moving targets," I said. "We—STAR, that is—decided that it was an acceptable risk."

Byrd played through the next half-minute and paused again.

"Why did you call out to Ruiz?" Byrd asked.

"If we could convince him to come out and surrender, it would minimize the risk to everyone," I said.

"Is that STAR policy?" Conway asked.

"Yes."

"Under what circumstances do you do it?"

"When the suspect has broken contact with us, but does not presently pose a threat, and when we suspect he is somewhere in the immediate area."

"Does it work?"

"Sometimes."

Usually with assistance from chemical agents or flash-bangs.

"Why did you say, 'go right'?" Franks asked.

"I heard movement in that direction."

"The helmet cam didn't," Cho said accusingly.

"My power, among other things, grants me enhanced hearing. I heard rustling from the master bedroom, and I inferred that Ruiz was in there."

"Did you activate your power?" Conway said.

"Not consciously. Not at that point. The enhanced hearing is a passive effect of my power."

"So you and Officer O'Neil chose to clear the bedroom at that point," Franks stated.

"Correct."

"You didn't wait for backup?"

"We couldn't. He could have been destroying evidence or accessing a weapon. Besides, the room was so small, there was only enough room for two officers anyway."

"In this case, Mr. Ruiz *did* grab a gun," Moss added. "The officers had no choice *but* to act."

The IA detectives played the video for a few seconds longer. Up until the moment Shane stepped through the door.

"Hold up," Cho said. "Detective Song, you didn't tell us you told Officer O'Neil to wait."

The eight eyes of the Inquisition fell on me.

"Sorry," I said. "It slipped my mind."

It truly had. I was so caught up recounting the shoot that I'd missed that word. And no one had asked me what I had done prior to entering the room.

"Why did you tell her to wait?" Cho asked.

I took a moment to recall what, exactly, I had been doing then.

"I wanted to deploy a noise flash diversionary device prior to making entry."

This interview was going on the record; by using the official police nomenclature it made my life just a bit easier.

"But you did not."

"Shane moved in before I could."

"Why did you want to deploy the NFDD?" Byrd asked.

My instincts told me to. But it was the ace up my sleeve. No one knew about that, not even STAR.

"I wanted to surprise and disorient the suspect, making it easier for us to gain compliance."

"At that time, did you suspect Ms. Vega was inside the room?"

"No. All I heard was rustling. I couldn't tell how many people were inside the room."

"Did you feel deploying the NFDD was necessary?"

"Yes."

"But Officer O'Neil did not."

Now I saw the trap, a gleaming tripwire an inch from my foot.

"I can't say for sure what she was thinking at that time," I said.

"You didn't communicate your plan to use an NFDD," he accused.

"Detective, what exactly are you implying about my client?" Moss said.

"Would Officer O'Neil have gone along with your plan had you told her exactly what you intended?"

"She would have, but I didn't have time to do so."

"Why not?"

"In close quarters battle, there is no time for hesitation. You must maintain your momentum, or the subject will have room to act. If I'd said, "Wait. I want to deploy a flash-bang", it would take too long. Moreover, this close to the subject, he could have overheard me and prepared himself. Without the element of surprise, an NFDD wouldn't be nearly as effective."

"Why didn't Officer O'Neil wait for you?" Cho asked.

I shrugged. "I can't tell you why. You'll have to ask her yourself."

"But what do you think?"

"Detective, this interview is about my client, not Officer O'Neil," Dawson interjected, his foot brushing up against mine.

"I don't know," I said. "You'll need to speak to her."

"I think I will," Byrd said.

Sorry, Shane.

"Why didn't you stop her?" Franks asked.

"We take our cues from the shield officer," I replied. "Once we make entry, the shield officer controls the team and tactics. As Shane decided to make entry, I moved in to support. If I had stopped her as she entered, it would have left her vulnerable. Once committed, we had to act."

I could see IA's case now. A pair of aggressive cops charged into the room and shot up the suspects without taking measures to degrade their will to resist. I had to stop them from reaching that conclusion.

"Was it, in your opinion, a tactical error?" Cho asked.

"No," I said.

"Why not?"

"What she did was in line with our training. She simply didn't wait for me, for reasons unknown to me, so I adapted to the situation. And to be clear, it's not a STAR tactical requirement to deploy an NFDD against an aggressive suspect after we make entry. It's left to the officers' discretion."

"What about powers?" Conway asked. "I recall that you saying that you activated your power right before you entered the room."

"HCPD policy is that on-duty Primes must seek approval from their supervisors prior to activating their powers," Cho said, a steely glint in her eye. "Could you explain why you did not?"

This was one of the many questions Moss and I had rehearsed earlier.

"Powers differ from Prime to Prime," Moss said. "The purpose of seeking supervisory approval is to prepare nearby officers for the power and to mitigate the risk of collateral damage. My client's use of his power at that moment did not pose any risk of collateral damage."

"Even so, failure to notify a supervisor is still a breach of policy," Byrd said.

"Due to the unique nature of my powers," I said, "my team leader, Sergeant John Oliveira, agreed that I could activate my power at will when I needed to boost my senses and reaction time."

"Could you explain why?" Byrd asked.

"Close quarters battle is like a complex dance. To succeed, everyone needs to know what everyone else is doing, and predict what they are going to do next. If I had to amp my speed or strength, the team needs to know so they can adapt their actions to mine. Amping reaction time doesn't alter the tactical equation. It doesn't change the dance steps, if you will. It simply makes it easier for me to react to changing situations, and it poses no potential harm to anyone."

"In summary, you obtained prior approval from Sergeant Oliveira to amp your reaction time at will?" Franks asked.

"Yes. Captain Steve Irving also signed off on it. I believe he kept a record."

"Understood," Franks said.

Byrd's eyes hardened behind his frameless glasses. He hadn't gotten the policy breach he was looking for. Instead, he continued playing the video. I braced myself with a breath and watched myself enter the room.

"POLICE FREEZE!" I yelled.

"FUCK YOU!" Ruiz replied.

I was sure I'd spoken slowly and clearly, while Ruiz had dragged out his words. But that was one of the side effects of enhanced reflexes.

Ruiz swung up his AK-47. Four metallic coughs erupted from my suppressed Virtus in double-quick time. Blood and brains burst over the cabinet interior.

Byrd stiffened. Cho pressed her lips together. Franks' eyes narrowed. Conway went pale and paused the video.

"Was that automatic fire?" Conway asked.

"No," I said. "Semi-automatic."

"It sounded like full-auto to me," she insisted.

"Passive effect of my power," I said. "It enhances my motor skills and coordination."

"STAR has access to select fire weapons, doesn't it?" Cho asked.

"Yes. Our carbines are capable of automatic fire, but we don't use full-auto except under very specific circumstances," I replied. "This wasn't one of them."

"That was too fast to be semi-auto," Conway said accusingly.

"I can show you," I said. "You take videos if you like."

"Please," Cho said.

The four inquisitors whipped out their phones and aimed their cameras at me. I held up my index finger.

Amped.

Curled four times.

"Done," I said.

"Isn't that enhanced speed?" Byrd said accusingly.

Translated: didn't you break policy?

"No," I replied. "Enhanced reflexes allows me to sense the

moment the trigger breaks and the gun fires. This lets me reset the trigger quicker, which leads to a faster rate of fire. The power doesn't make my finger any faster. It's just that reflexes, technique, and genetics combine to make my shots sound like full auto."

But only to civilians. I've heard actual full auto fire too many times.

"It's hard to believe that," Conway said.

"My shot timings with semi-auto weapons are on par with Jerry Miculek," I said. "The records are on file with the HCPA and the National Rifle Association."

"Who's that?"

"The world's fastest shooter. He can fire a revolver so fast it almost sounds like a machine gun."

"I see," Conway said. "Why did you have to shoot Ruiz so many times?"

I'd lost count of the number of times I'd heard that question.

"HCPD policy is to shoot until a threat stops," I said. "Ruiz did not stop until after the last shot."

"You shot him in the heart with the first two rounds," she said accusingly.

"Have you personally seen the autopsy report?" Moss asked.

"Well... no."

Moss smiled. "Then we can't say that for sure, can we? Besides, even if my client had completely destroyed Ruiz's heart, there would still be enough oxygen in Ruiz's blood to facilitate brain function for up to two minutes. In that time Ruiz could easily have killed my client."

"Detective Song, you had amped reflexes at that time, yes?" Conway asked.

"Yes," I said.

"Your file says you experience amped reflexes as a slowing down of time, yes?"

There was another trap coming. I could taste it.

"Yes," I said.

"Did you take the time to observe Ruiz after you'd shot him in the chest, to see if he still posed a threat?"

"I didn't have time."

"Why not?"

Will cut in. "Ms. Conway, are we in agreement that Mr. Ruiz was armed and posing a threat when he was shot?"

"We ask the questions here," she said. "That's how it works, Counselor."

"But he was armed, yes?"

"Yes. What about it?"

"Was he still armed when he was shot in the head?"

"Yes..." Conway said, now unsure.

Will spread his arms. "Does this satisfy the HCPD's use of force policy?"

"I believe so," Moss agreed. "Mr. Ruiz was still capable of posing a threat even after being shot in the chest."

"Well, then," Will said. "I fail to see the issue here."

"The issue is whether Amp knew Mr. Ruiz was still armed at the moment of the brain shot." Conway looked at me. "Were you?"

In the Marines, and later in STAR, we trained the failure drill obsessively. Two to the chest, two to the face. If the first two doesn't neutralize the threat, the last would finish the job. If the threat were still active, there would be no time to lower the gun, see if he were still armed, then go for the headshot. Instead, after the first controlled pair, we simply raised our sights to head height and, if we saw a face, we fired.

"Yes," I said.

"How did you know?"

"He was still standing. He was still capable of aiming his weapon, still capable of posing a threat. Ruiz has the power of hitting everything he shoots at, and I could not give him a chance to fire."

Conway eased off, and we continued the video. Ruiz fell. His AK disappeared under the bed. Shane ordered Vega to show her hands. Vega dove to the corpse.

Someone shouted gibberish.

"What was that?" Conway asked.

Byrd replayed the scene at quarter speed.

"HANDS IN THE AIR! BACK UP NOW!"

"Detective Song, was that you?" Franks asked.

"Yes," I admitted.

"I don't think anyone here understood what you said."

Crap. In the stress of the moment, I didn't realize I was speaking too fast.

"Does it matter?" Will asked. "Officer O'Neil was clearly audible. It stands to reason that Ms. Vega would have heard her."

"Not necessarily," Franks said. "Adrenaline alters sensory perception. She may not have heard Officer O'Neil or understood what she said."

"Ms. Vega went for the weapon, didn't she?" Moss said. "Police officers are not obliged to issue a final warning to a suspect if they believe the suspect poses a significant threat of death or serious injury."

"We'll see," Cho said, and continued playing the video.

Still in slow motion, Vega looked up at me. Her eyes widened, her teeth bared. She rose, taking Ruiz with her.

What the hell? I hadn't seen her carrying the corpse with her. Where the hell had it come from?

No. I was too fixated on Vega, on whether she posed a threat. Everything else in the world ceased to exist in my eyes. Everything but the AK.

The AK in Ruiz's hands.

Wait. What?

Suppressed gunshots rang out, slow as molasses. Blood bloomed over her chest and throat and face. As she fell, she flung her arms open.

There was no sign of the AK.

My blood ran cold.

"Could you rewind that please?" Franks asked.

Byrd obliged. We watched the video a couple more times. I saw nothing new.

"Detective Song," Byrd said, "did you believe that Ms. Vega posed a threat at that time?"

"Yes," I said quietly.

"But she was dragging the body of Mr. Ruiz," Conway said. "She wasn't armed."

Moss pointed at the screen. "Are you sure? As you can see, the bed obstructed the camera's view. It obstructed my client's view too. Correct?"

"Yes," I said.

"We can't see her hands, only her arms. But we *can* see the rear end of the AK-47."

"Which was in Mr. Ruiz's hands," Conway said.

"Really? Let's look closer."

I did. The stock of the AK and part of its upper receiver was visible. The weapon was pointed down at the floor, and the bed prevented us from seeing the location of Vega's and Ruiz's left hands. But the stock of the AK was resting against Vega's right forearm, which was angled towards the weapon's pistol grip.

Vega's arm was *above* the stock.

"Look at her arm," I said, pointing at the screen. "It looks to me like she was reaching for the AK's grip."

"Were you aware of that at the moment of the shooting?" Franks asked.

"Subconsciously."

"Subconsciously?"

"I was... At that time, I was taking in a huge amount of detail at once. The positioning of the bodies. Shane's location. The way Vega was reaching for the weapon. Her face."

"What about her face?"

"I saw her face. The way the muscles of her face bunched up in anger. Let's go back and see it."

Cho dutifully backed up to the moment she bared her teeth at me.

"That's a sign of aggression," I said. "At that moment, I realized she was a threat."

Byrd pounced in. "She was not armed at that time. She was not a threat, was she?"

Damn. That was a mistake.

"I think my client means that at that time, he felt that Ms. Vega was about to do something dangerous," Moss said.

"Yeah, that's what I meant," I said.

"I see," Byrd said, unconvinced. "So her facial expression, coupled with her body language, led you to think she was armed and about to kill you."

"Yes."

"But you can't say for certain she was actually armed."

"No one can, not with this video," Will protested.

"But when did you make the decision to shoot?" Byrd asked.

"When I saw the AK."

"You noticed her facial expression, the positioning of her arms, the AK-47, and you decided to shoot. Is that right?"

"Yes."

"You did not actually see her hand on the rifle. Is that right?"

"Yes," I admitted. "But I inferred from the positioning of her arm that she was either holding the weapon or was about to grab it."

Byrd let the video play to the end. But the detectives had no more questions for me.

"I think that's everything from us," Byrd said. "Ms. Conway, Investigator Franks, what about you?"

"Detective Song, do you presently suffer from post-traumatic stress disorder?" Franks asked.

"No."

"Even after experiencing five shootings."

"Correct."

He frowned, rubbing his chin. "Before you joined the HCPD, you served ten years in the Marine Corps."

"Yes. What about it?"

"I requested for your service record yesterday." He looked at me square in the eyes. "Most of the details are sealed."

"Wait a second!" Moss interjected.

"Hold on," Will said at the same time.

The attorneys looked at each other. Moss nodded.

"What does my client's military service have to do with this investigation?" Will asked.

"I second the question," Moss said. "I don't see any relevance whatsoever."

"I'm merely interested in seeing if he has any psychological illnesses, or if he has any special expertise in reading body language in combat. As I understand it, Detective Song enlisted as a Recon Marine before joining the Marine Raider Regiment. The Raiders are the Marines' Special Operations unit, yes?"

"Yes," I said.

"Did you have any special training or experience in assessing whether someone posed a threat?"

"Training or experience?" I asked.

"Both."

"Is combat experience included?"

"Yes."

"Detective Song, you don't have to answer any questions if the answer is classified," Moss said.

"I can't answer your question," I said.

"What about training?" Franks asked.

"I can't go into specifics. All I can say is that we had plenty of CQB training."

"Investigator, where exactly are you going with this?" Will asked.

"Let me clarify," Franks said. "Detective Song, based on your training and experience, both in the Marine Corps and in the police, did you assess that Ms. Vega was a threat at the moment when you shot her?"

"Yes," I said.

"Thank you. No further questions."

With the interview formally over, I escorted the attorneys down to the lobby.

"It wasn't too bad, all things considering," Moss said.

"How so?" I asked.

"You didn't do anything outright illegal. The evidence points towards a good shoot. But... there might be a problem."

"What is it?"

"Necessary force rule."

Recently signed into state law, the necessary force rule imposed a higher standard of conduct on law enforcement officers. It wasn't enough for LEOs to be in reasonable fear for their life or the lives of those around them to use lethal force; they had to exhaust all possible options before shooting. If a cop didn't use a lower force option, if by action or omission he created a situation that made lethal force necessary, he was liable for criminal prosecution.

"Do you think not throwing the flash-bang is a necessary force violation?" I asked.

"I'll be honest: I don't know," Moss admitted. "As you said, it's not policy to throw flash-bangs before making entry, but an aggressive prosecutor might pin it on you and claim that you created a lethal force incident through negligence."

"It's going to be a bear to fight off," Will said.

"What can we do?" I asked.

"We've done everything we could," Moss replied. "If they thought they could charge you with something, you'd be in handcuffs by now. Since you're walking, though, there's a chance you'll be cleared of any wrongdoing."

Will shook his head. "Or they might simply be gathering more ammo to use against you. I'd place the chances at fifty-fifty."

"Agreed," Moss said. "If they come back for you, give us a call."

"Thanks," I said.

I hoped this was the end of it. Will might handle my cases pro bono, but I couldn't afford Moss' fees for a second consult.

Outside the station, the protest had quadrupled in size. A sea of people, many of them dressed in green or black, stretched from one end of the plaza to the other, carrying a forest of signs and banners. Some blew whistles and air horns, others banged pots and pans over their heads. Even through the glass and concrete of HCPD HQ, there was so much noise that I had to don my earplugs.

REACT had turned out in force. There was a full company of them now, over a hundred cops in all, turned out in body armor and shields and batons. Surrounding the protesters, they kettled them into a narrow strip on a grassy patch, keeping them away from the roads and the main entrance. No one was going anywhere, not the police, not the media, most certainly not the protesters.

"Don't these people have to work?" Will grumbled.

"This *is* their work," Moss offered. "They're just not being paid for it. Most of them, anyway."

We shared a brief chuckle. I saw the lawyers out, made my excuses, and headed back inside. I still had work to do.

The office of the Special Operations Bureau was located on the ground floor on the west wing, within easy reach of the underground parking lots dedicated to STAR. STAR didn't use the office much—we spent most of our days training, serving warrants or out on the street—but we still needed a place to do our paperwork.

The team room was empty. The guys were out, and the schedule on the noticeboard said they were out at the range for the morning. Just as well. I settled down at my ancient computer, so old that islands of dead pixels dotted the faded LCD monitor, and tapped my foot until the machine deigned to boot.

It only took a minute this time. It might yet be saved. But no matter how many service requests I'd filed to IT, they still didn't bother replacing the team's computers.

I navigated to the report-filing program. The draft I'd composed back home, through the wonders of cloud computing, was accessible on this computer. I read through the report one last time, filled in a few more details, then sent it on.

With that out of the way, I checked my inbox. Six new emails. Three of them were routine administrative matters. One discussed next week's training plan, the second was an update from the Intelligence Bureau discussing trends in criminal activity in high-crime areas. The last was from Captain Irving, addressed to me.

It was a pro forma post-shooting email, the same mail he always sent STAR officers after a shooting. This was my second time receiving it. He began by asking after my health and wishing me well, then confirming that I was placed on five days' administrative leave, beginning yesterday. Today was Friday; come Tuesday I should report to work.

Administrative leave came with caveats, of course. I couldn't leave the city. I had to remain contactable. I had to be ready to report to duty to assist with investigations.

The email concluded with a formal reminder to schedule an appointment with the psychologist before returning to work. Fortunately, I'd already beaten him to it.

I sent him an email to acknowledge receipt and stuck around reading emails and intel reports for a few more minutes. As I made to go, the rest of the team came in, dressed up in tac gear.

"Yo, Amp!" Miguel called out. "Came back to run with the big dogs, eh?"

"Good to see you guys too," I said.

"Have you spoken to IA and the DDA yet?" Oliveira asked.

"Yeah," I replied. "And you?"

"Yup. Yesterday. They spent the whole frigging day talking and talking and talking. Barely got any work done."

"Nature of the job," I said.

"Are you still sequestered?" Shane asked.

"They didn't tell me I wasn't. They must still be going over my statement."

"You didn't say anything that makes us look bad, right?" Miguel asked.

"Nah. Only you," I said.

The team broke out into good-natured laughter.

"Whatcha doing back here anyway?" Ray asked.

"Paperwork." I shrugged. "You know how it goes."

"You done with it?"

"Yup. What about you guys? Today was a range day, right?"

"Right," Oliveira said. "Good shooting today. Pistol, carbine, shotgun, precision rifle. You shoulda been there."

You shoulda been there. I keep hearing that phrase.

"Next time," I promised.

"We've got DT scheduled for the afternoon. You can join in if you want. No one's going to tell IA, and I know you're into martial arts big-time."

DT meant Defensive Tactics, a catalog of techniques designed to quickly and safely take down and arrest a non-compliant suspect. They weren't bad, they were just almost adequate.

"Thanks, but I've got an appointment with Dr. Murphy."

"Ah, well, another time then."

As the team dispersed, I tapped Shane on the shoulder. "Could I speak with you outside for a second?"

"Sure," she said. "What's it about?"

"Not here."

The hallway outside the office was empty. Leaning into her, I said, "IA may be coming after you."

Her emerald eyes widened. "What do you mean?"

I told her about my interview with Internal Affairs, about the moment they focused on her actions prior to entering the bedroom.

"They might dig up dirt on you and push for a necessary force violation," I finished.

Her tanned skin turned pale.

"I'm... I'm sorry," she said. "I honestly didn't hear you say anything. I was so focused on getting through the door and stopping them from getting a gun. I..."

"Hey, relax. I'm fine, you're fine. That's the important part. I just wanted you to be ready in case the Two Sams try something."

She pressed her lips into a tight smile. Nodded.

"Thanks."

"No problem."

NO PROMISES

"All things considered, you're doing well," Dr. Rachel Murphy said.

"Lucky me," I said.

Shaking her head, Murphy leaned back into her sofa and sipped at her white ceramic coffee mug. A slight smile played over her features. She had aged well, but her pale auburn hair, tied into a neat bun and secured with a hair net, was turning white. The warm amber light accented her cream dress and matching jacket but failed to hide the lines radiating from her eyes and nose and cheeks. I guessed she was in her late fifties, maybe early sixties.

"What are you thinking?" I asked.

The smile turned into a grin. "I'm thinking that you're thinking that I'm thinking that you think you're a tough guy."

"Real funny, Doc."

"To be fair, I've never seen anyone as stable as you after a shooting."

"Never?" I asked.

"Never," she confirmed.

We'd spent the first forty-five minutes of the session walking through the shooting. I told her about what I did, what I saw and heard and felt, what happened after the bodies settled.

"It's not like I don't feel anything," I admitted.

"What's wrong?"

"It's... it's been hard to sleep."

"Nightmares?"

"Yeah."

"Describe them."

I exhaled sharply. "I see my dead. Everyone I've killed. They come up to me, showing me their wounds, and demand answers. Why did I kill them? Did I have to do what I did to them? Was killing them necessary?"

"*Was* it?" she asked.

"Always."

"But your dead still haunt you."

"Yeah."

"Nightmares following a shooting are a common reaction," she said. "It seems like you're carrying around pent-up guilt."

"It's not affecting my performance."

"But it's affecting your sleep."

I shrugged. "Not as much as it used to."

"Are you still able to get a full night's sleep?"

"I don't think I've had one since... I don't know when."

She spread her arms out, as if to say, *See?*

"You may not feel it's affecting you, but your nightmares suggest you have lingering guilt. I'm sure you think you're tough, but you're not immune to emotional stress."

I inhaled deeply. Exhaled sharply.

"I do my best to cope with it. Meditation, martial arts, exercise."

She smiled again. "Where most people turn to the bottle, you turn to the stick, eh? I wish my other clients were more like you."

"Thanks."

"You told me before you visit a temple often. Do you still do that?"

"Yes."

"Does it help?"

"Yes."

"How so?"

"I think I answered that the last time."

"Humor me."

I chuckled and took a moment to ponder my answer.

"The environment is calming. Shi Shifu's meditations and lectures help put things into perspective."

"I heard Buddhism is a religion of non-violence. How exactly do you square the teachings with what you've done?"

"I'm not a monk. I'm not required to abstain from killing, though it's strongly encouraged. Besides, the prohibition against violence isn't set in stone. Not the way the Ten Commandments are."

"Oh? What do you mean?"

"In the Buddhist ethical framework, every action carries eternal consequences, be they bitter or glorious. The ideal is to undertake every action in full recognition and acceptance of the fruit of your deeds. Thus, if you must take a life, it must be for the right reasons. Usually to save a life, either yours or someone else's. Killing must never be done lightly, or with pleasure."

"I guess this explains why you don't register any positive emotions after a shooting," she said.

"Killing isn't meant to be pleasant," I said. "But sometimes it's the only option left."

"I see. I noticed you don't talk much about support from the rest of the lay community."

"I don't socialize much with them. Not the ones who visit the temple."

"Why not?"

"Honestly? Many of them are hippies."

She laughed. "Seriously?"

"Seriously. They... they're the kind of people looking for peace and love and light and all that good stuff. They're not bad people, but they wouldn't begin to understand what it's like doing what I do."

"How do you know that?"

"I tried socializing with them. After I told them I was a cop they just... tuned out."

"I see. But you said 'most' of them. What about the rest?"

"They're Chinese. Well, Chinese and Koreans, but mostly Chinese. Their attitudes towards police are... complicated."

"Complicated? How so?"

"It's a cultural thing. When you grow up in a Chinese family, you're told to go to school, study hard, get good grades, get a good job. A stable job, with a high income and social prestige. Jobs like doctor, lawyer, engineer... you know the stereotype."

She nodded. "I take it being a cop doesn't count."

"It doesn't. Don't get me wrong, many people view police officers as necessary. It's just that they'd rather someone *else* do the policing. It's a stable job, sure, but it's also dangerous, especially in America, and Chinese are risk-averse."

"'Especially in America'? What do you mean?"

"I was born in Hong Kong and moved to Singapore when I was six years old. My parents brought me to Halo City when I was thirteen. Compared to Hong Kong and Singapore, the crime rate here is unbelievable."

"Ah. 'Unbelievable,' you say? And yet you became a cop."

"Someone had to do something. Might as well be me."

"That's an admirable attitude," she said. "It seems to me you value duty, tradition, moral values and religion. Is that right?"

"You can say that."

"But you don't have much in the way of community support."

"Yeah."

"And your family?"

I sighed. "Same."

"Same reasons?"

"Yup."

"It must be difficult."

"I get by."

"You sound distant from them."

"They live their lives. I live mine."

"I see. Do you experience any conflict between your religion and killing?"

"I'm not a Buddhist."

"You're not?"

I shrugged. "Visiting a temple doesn't make you a Buddhist, and I haven't formally taken refuge in the Triple Gem. But, to answer your question, I don't."

"That could explain why you don't experience crippling guilt. You don't feel severe inner conflict or emotional turmoil. Not to the point where it causes you lingering discomfort or suffering."

"I don't."

"As I said, you're unusually stable."

"What's done is done. I just have to live with it and keep on keeping on."

"An excellent attitude. But you're still having problems with nightmares, yes?"

I sighed. "A bit."

"Come on, you don't have to pull that macho act here."

I sighed even louder. "Fine."

"Do you need sleeping pills?"

"No."

She nodded. "Thought so. In your case, your training regimen would do wonders for your sleep. Don't worry too much about the nightmares; usually, they fade without requiring intervention. Just keep telling yourself that things will get better."

"They always do."

"That's the spirit!"

As the session ended, Dr. Murphy finished her coffee and looked me square in the eyes.

"I take it you don't have any lingering issues or concerns?" she asked.

"I don't," I confirmed.

"Excellent. My take is that you're feeling well and are ready to return to work. Is that correct?"

"Yes."

"Great. I'll recommend that you'll be returned to duty. But if you need any help, feel free to come back. My doors are always open."

"Thank you."

"Oh, and one more thing."

"Yeah?"

She smiled tightly. "Please try to stay out of trouble next time."

"No promises, Doc."

FIFTEEN MINUTES after I returned home, my smartphone screamed in my pocket. The caller ID said 'Daniel Gonzalez.' I took the call.

"*Que onda?*" Danny asked. *How's it going?* "It's been a while, hasn't it?"

"It feels like the whole world's been calling me lately," I replied.

He laughed. "You're a bona fide celebrity, Amp. Embrace it while it lasts."

Danny Gonzalez was one of the few cops outside STAR and the brass who knew what I was because he was the longest-serving Prime in the HCPD. And one of the few Primes in the HCPD, for that matter.

His official handle was 'Phantom,' but everyone called him 'Speedy.' I don't know why, but I heard it had something to do with an old-time cartoon. He was the last of the second-generation Primes, or maybe the first of the third-gens. He could transform himself and everything on his person into a gray cloud and zip right through anything at warp speed. Walls, cars, people, he could pass through them like a ghost. I heard that once he ran from one end of Halo City to the other in just fifteen minutes—only because he had to maneuver around the city's many canals and tributaries.

"You saw the protests outside HCPD HQ, didn't you?" I said. "I wouldn't call that being a celebrity."

"You're in the spotlight. That's all that matters."

"I don't suppose you're calling me for a book deal, then."

"Nope. I got a call from the brass assigning me as your peer support officer. They said you were involved in a shooting a couple days back." His voice grew sober. "You alright, *hermano?*"

"I'm good. Just got back from Doc Murphy, actually. She said I'm stable and ready to return to duty."

"*Que padre.*" Awesome. "Wanna have dinner together?"

"I've got evening class tonight."

"Oh? How about supper then?"

"Well..."

"I could pick you up. What d'you say?"

"You sound eager to meet."

"It's been a while since we last got together, 'mano. Besides, the brass wants me to make sure you're doing alright, write up a long report for 'em. You know how they want to check all the boxes. Or would you rather do it another day?"

I wasn't much of a socializer. But I might as well get all my engagements out of the way today.

"I'm good for supper."

"A'ight man. When do I pick you up?"

"Nine thirty."

"Ten-four, Amp. See you soon."

The news said the protests were still going strong. That didn't sit right with me. There was always some degree of blowback after police violence, but it usually took the form of angry letters, spiteful phone calls and online trolling. Not a hundreds-strong protest. That took organization, resources, and most importantly, motivation. Who did it?

The website of the *Halo City Herald* held the answers I was looking for.

PROTEST DECRIES *Prime police shooting*

FIVE HUNDRED PEOPLE *have gathered outside the Halo City Departmentment to protest the slaying of two people by Prime police officer Amp.*

On Wednesday evening, Amp shot and killed two suspects, Emmanuel Ruiz, 25, and Sofia Vega, 23, while serving a search warrant. Police claim the suspects were armed, but activists argue otherwise.

Emmanuel Ruiz's father, Ricardo Ruiz, said, "My son didn't do anything wrong. He hung out with a tough crowd, but he supported his family, his friends, his girlfriend. They were planning to get married and start a family together."

Mr. Ruiz, a local businessman, and community organizer, organized the protest in solidarity with victims of police brutality.

I GOT UP, walked away from the screen, looked out the balcony, and breathed.

'Local businessman and community organizer'. Was that what they called being a shot-caller these days? There was no way in hell the *Herald* had checked in with the HCPD. Or, if they did, they hadn't bothered telling the HCPD's side of the story.

On the other hand...

As Tom had said, El Trece wasn't just a street gang anymore. They've been studying the strategies of the cartels down south and applying them here. Business, criminal and political strategy.

They presented themselves as businessmen, selling drugs, guns, counterfeit goods, sex, every temptation of the flesh and then some, just good honest *carnales* providing what the people wanted. They protected El Barrio, chased out or crushed anyone who tried to move in on their turf, and delivered some street justice on the side. These days, some of their higher-profile members ran soup kitchens and charity programs to rebrand the gang's image.

Businessman and community organizer. Christ. In El Barrio, there was no difference between a gangster, a businessman and a politician.

I returned to the article and kept reading.

Cape Watch, an activist group that advocates Prime regulation measures, agreed to support Mr. Ruiz's protest.

"For too long, Primes have hidden behind badges and uniforms to oppress ordinary citizens," Cape Watch spokeswoman Joanna Goh said. "We stand behind Mr. Ruiz to bring justice to tyrannical Primes who abuse their powers."

Ms. Goh claims that Cape Watch has mobilized over 200 supporters, volunteers and activists for the protest, and expects more people to join in.

Amp, whose identity remains secret under the Prime Privacy Protection Act, was not available for comment.

CAPE WATCH. Should have known. Ever since Achilles and Blackout had destroyed half of Serenity City two decades ago, pro-regulation groups have proliferated all over the world. In North America, Cape Watch was the largest of them all, an umbrella group that welcomed anyone and everyone who championed the cause of Prime control.

The mildest among their ranks advocated 'reasonable power control laws' to prevent Primes from abusing their power. The extremists demanded mandatory identification, government registration and education, and harsh punishments for Primes who failed to toe the line.

Day by day, it seemed that the extremists were winning.

I could count on the HCPD's Public Relations Office to speak to the press on my behalf. All I had to do was keep my head down, stay far away from the reporters, and this would blow over soon enough. But it didn't hurt to keep an eye on on-goings.

With that said, there were no public records of my face. Of Amp's face. The few times I spoke to the press, I was masked and used a voice synthesizer. I don't think the journalists even knew I was Chinese. Likewise, I kept my social media presence minimal, with no photos of my face. There was little risk in going out with my real face.

All the same, I prepared a light disguise kit. Just in case.

Nobody accosted me on the way to training. In class, Jim ran through two hours of stick and knife work, with occasional segues into empty hands to demonstrate principles of motion. I allowed myself to stop being Amp and step into my role as an assistant instructor.

After class, I took a mixed hot and cold shower and waited for Danny outside the community center. At exactly half past nine, he drove up in his personally owned vehicle, a blue Honda Legend. The second I climbed into the shotgun seat, he shot off.

"Looking good, *hermano*," he said.

"Thanks. You're not too bad yourself," I replied.

Danny was around my age, but he wore the lined face of an older man and silver strands ran through his dark hair. He hid his frame under a gray jacket, loose white shirt, and blue jeans, but even in the low light I could see his muscular neck, the cords running through his hands, the lean and tight muscles of his legs. On his left ring finger, he wore an engraved titanium band.

The power had come for Danny late in life. Most second- and third-gen Primes expressed their powers after birth or during puberty. Danny's had manifested during the track and field meet of his senior year in high school. When the starting pistol went off, he faded into a blur and reappeared at the finishing line scant moments later.

He was immediately disqualified.

From that moment, his life changed dramatically. Overnight, he became the world's fastest man. He smashed every record on the history books, even a few set by other Primes. But the International Olympics Committee had long ago ruled that Primes were not eligible to participate in the regular Olympics, as their powers gave them an unfair advantage over regular humans. And as there were no Primes out there with the exact same power as Phantom, he could not compete with the Prime Olympics either, not in the track events he had spent years training for.

With his dreams simultaneously fulfilled and shattered, Danny decided to do something else. Something that allowed him to use his talents and his powers. Fortunately, the HCPD was hiring—and offering bonuses to Primes.

A decade and a half later, here he was, still going strong.

"Do you have any place in mind for supper?" I asked.

"Long Moon."

"Loong Moon," I corrected, pronouncing it as '*lung mun*.'

"You know what I mean. Your family's restaurant. It's been a long time since I've been there."

"I had dim sum this afternoon."

"Yeah, but when was the last time you saw your family?"

I didn't say anything.

"Thought so," he said.

I sighed. "It's complicated."

"'*mano,* do they even know you shot someone?"

"Yeah. I called them."

"That's it? You didn't see them?"

I sighed again. "We're not exactly... close."

"They're *your* blood. You've only got one family in this world, man. Calling them isn't enough. They have to see for themselves that you're alright. Or would you rather Cape Watch tell them how to feel?"

I sighed once more. Danny had walked me right into a trap.

"Is there any compelling reason why we shouldn't do this?" he pressed.

"Let's get it over and done with," I said.

He grinned. "Be nice to them, okay?"

"No promises."

7

GOOD IRON AND GOOD SONS

L oong Moon Dim Sum Restaurant was nestled deep in the
heart of Chinatown, in the historic district that predated the
architectural codes and aesthetics of the modern era. Everywhere I turned I saw sweeping roofs and towering pagodas, paper
lanterns and flying streamers. Every building sported wildly different
paint schemes, creating a garish riot of colors that both repelled and
attracted the eye.

Sandwiched between a gift store and a Vietnamese restaurant,
Loong Moon was a two-story shophouse built in the traditional fashion. The first floor was given over to customers, while the inhabitants
lived and worked on the second floor. Above the door, a huge red
signboard proclaimed the restaurant's name in gold Chinese characters; squashed under the ideograms, five font sizes smaller, was the
English translation.

At the front door, a scrawny Chinese man bowed at us apolo-
getically.

"Sorry. It is after last orders. We can't take any more customers."

"Aw, man," Danny said, crestfallen.

Here was all the excuse I needed to walk away, to leave my family
to their affairs. But I'd already come all this way, and Marines don't

quit. I remained present in the moment, breathed through it, and spoke.

"Tell Aaron it's Adam," I said. "We're here to visit."

He looked at me in puzzlement. "Adam who?"

"Just Adam. He'll know."

"One moment."

He stepped inside. As I waited, I peered through the window glass.

The restaurant was doing a roaring trade. Young adults, couples or small groups, filled the tables near the front. Larger groups and families sat near the rear. Almost all of them were Chinese, reflecting my father's preferred target market, but the younger set came from outside Chinatown.

On the left-hand door, a large sign proclaimed the shop's business hours. Ten to two, five to ten, every day of the week. On the right door was a slightly smaller sign showing a large black revolver in a slashed-through circle.

Danny shook his head. "Still a gun free zone?"

"One of the reasons I don't visit. Or most of the PD, for that matter."

"I thought you'd have educated them by now."

"They're stubborn."

He smiled and shook his head. "The apple sure fell far from the tree, huh."

More like it bounced off barren earth and kept on rolling.

"There's still time to walk away," I said.

He waved his hand dismissively. "I'm not scared of a little sign like that."

"No one is."

A minute later, the maître d' returned, all smiles.

"Thank you for waiting. Please, come in."

Danny and I followed the maître d' inside. The sticker failed to stop us or do anything about our concealed hardware. The man led us to a large table near the back of the restaurant, handed us a menu and bowed.

"Please order whatever you like. Aaron says it's on the house."

"Sweet," Danny said. "Much obliged."

The menu listed all manner of traditional Chinese delicacies. Dumplings, rolls, buns, cakes, three kinds of sticky rice, a selection of meat and vegetables, a half-dozen types of tea. A nook under the table held a clipboard with order sheets and a pencil on a lanyard.

As Danny perused the menu, a Chinese man approached the table. In his white shirt and gray pants, he was almost indistinguishable from the customers. His silver spectacles lent him a scholarly air. But his soft round face was almost like mine.

"Adam!" my brother said, breaking into a grin. "It's been ages!"

"I thought I'd come by, see how the family's doing," I said.

"Good, good." He nodded at Danny. "Officer Gonzalez, how are you doing?"

"Peachy," Danny said. "But I'm off-duty. Just call me Danny."

"Of course, Danny." Turning back to me, he continued, "What brings you here?"

I cocked my head at Danny. "His fault."

Danny laughed. "I wanted him to come here. He needs to learn what's important in life."

Aaron smiled. "Thanks for bringing him." Leaning in, he added, "Does this have to do with the shooting?"

"Yes," I said.

"I... see. I'm, well, I'm happy you're fine."

"Thanks."

"If you'd like to meet the family, I could bring them down at ten fifteen, ten thirty or so."

"Sure."

"Okay. If you can wait, just make your order, and we'll serve them when everyone's ready."

"I can wait," Danny confirmed.

"Great! I've got to get back to work. I'll see you later."

"Bye," I said.

As Aaron left, Danny turned to me.

"That wasn't too bad now, was it?"

"For now," I said.

"One step at a time, *hermano*. Take things one step at a time."

Danny leisurely scrolled through the menu, occasionally consulting with me, and picked out enough dishes for a full meal. I contented myself with a plate of *liu sha bao*, another of pork rice noodle rolls, and a cup of warm water. We filled up the order sheet and handed it to a passing waiter.

As we waited, Danny and I made small talk. We kept things light, talking about the upcoming administrative paperwork, the stupid and the insane things we've seen, the latest books and movies. Mundane things.

I wondered how Danny kept his sanity. Right after leaving the Academy, Danny walked the street unmasked. The brass reasoned that a police Prime who engaged the public using his real name and face would forge better relations with his community. Danny agreed, and it paid off.

Danny quickly became the highest-profile Prime in the HCPD. When a supervillain showed up, he would fly to the scene to support STAR. Whenever an officer needed help, there he went, materializing out of thin air with long gun in hand. Often he single-handedly resolved situations before his partner could catch up. Patrol sometimes loaned him out to the Youth and Family Services Bureau, where he toured schools and libraries and community centers, giving talks on law enforcement, crime control measures, and being a Prime in Halo City. By the time the Prime Privacy Protection Act was signed into law, everyone in the city knew who he was. The brass gave him special dispensation to continue working unmasked.

But fame always came at a cost.

He had six shootings in his career. The highest number of shootings among active-duty officers in the department. Half of those were retaliatory attacks. Word on the grapevine was that he was married, even expecting twins, until the day gangbangers kicked down his door and killed his wife.

He still wore his wedding ring, but he never spoke of her to me.

These days, Danny worked solo. He was senior enough for the

privilege, and no one else could keep up with him anyway. The brass had long pressured him to join STAR, but he'd demurred, saying that his powers were not suitable for close quarters battle in a team-based environment. He had, however, signed up with REACT, and these days he ran a one-man crime suppression detail on a citywide beat. A special dispensation for a special cop.

"You heard about the protests outside HCPD HQ?" I asked.

"Heard about them, yeah, walked past them too. But I haven't seen them up close," he replied.

"They didn't call you out for that?"

"Nah. I'm not on public order detail. But if this keeps up they might just redeploy me."

"How so?"

"The protests are still ongoing. Captain Scott says if it grows legs, if they start blatantly breaking the law, he'll put me on a snatch squad."

A snatch squad penetrated unruly demonstrations to arrest and extract troublemakers and violent individuals.

"The protesters are blowing horns and whistles, and banging pots and pans. Isn't that a violation of noise ordinances?"

"It is. But the captain doesn't want to escalate. Not for something like this."

"I guess we can let that slide. I mean, the only ones complaining about them are cops."

Danny chuckled. "Yeah, and who cares what cops have to say, right?"

One by one, the patrons left. Eventually, Danny and I held the only occupied table in the restaurant. The staff hustled around us, cleaning the tables and chairs, wiping down the counter and the windows, mopping the floor and checking the cashier.

Aaron took a chair at the table. "The parents will be coming soon."

I nodded. "How's Julie?"

"She's fine. She's taking care of the kids upstairs."

"She's not coming?" Danny asked.

Aaron shook his head. "We can't leave the kids alone."

Over Aaron's shoulder, I saw an aging couple approach. The patriarch wore an all-white uniform, crowned with a tall hat. He held a stern expression, augmented by his huge black-rimmed glasses. Next to him was his wife. Her shoulder-length hair was dyed a deep brown, but there was no hiding the years etched on her face. Dressed in a red jacket and dark dress, she walked with her arms held tight and stiff by her sides.

"*Ma, Ba,*" I said, nodding at my parents. "*Nei ho ma?*"

Mother, father, how are you?

My mother smiled. My father's expression grew sterner.

"Adam ah, *hou loi mou gin la,*" she said. *Adam, long time no see.*

My father grunted. "You came."

I nodded. "Yes."

Danny stood, extending his arm.

"Mr. Song, Mrs. Song, good to see you again," he said in English.

They shook hands. Mother smiled. Father's expression merely lightened a fraction.

"I'm sorry to impose on you so late today," Danny continued. "But it's been so long since I had the best dim sum in Halo City."

Mother smiled. "You really know how to talk."

"No problem," Father said. "We were going to have supper anyway. Come, sit. I've prepared the dishes myself."

The waiters arrived, laying out a spread of dishes in rapid succession. Half of them were Danny's.

Aaron smiled. "Danny, you really can eat, can't you?"

"This is dinner for me," Danny said.

"It's not healthy to eat dinner so late," Mother said.

"I had a long watch." Danny shrugged. "It can't be helped."

Father gestured at the food. "Come, eat."

We dug in with spoons and chopsticks. Danny had long ago abandoned the idea of learning how to use chopsticks, so he simply forked everything on his plate.

"What brings you here tonight?" Aaron asked.

"Just wanted to see you," I said.

Aaron nodded slowly. "I read about the shooting in the news. I'm glad you're safe."

"Thanks."

"You only visit after you kill someone," Father said.

"Aiyah, *Ah Die ah*," Mother scolded. "Better he come visit now than not at all."

"I came for the reunion dinner," I said.

"That counts, right?" Danny added.

Father shrugged. "It's expected."

Expected. The word that hung over my family like a pallor for decades on end.

My parents met in Hong Kong. My father was a Singaporean, working as a chef in a popular dim sum restaurant chain. My mother was a Hong Konger, born and bred. Six years after they had me, my father returned to Singapore as head chef of a local franchise. Six years after that, they moved on to Halo City and opened their own dim sum restaurant.

As the elder son, my parents expected me to take over the family business. I hadn't displayed any talent for cooking, so the second-best option was to get a good job. Instead, I was drawn to the Marine Corps.

The guns, the uniforms, and the machinery appealed to my 13-year-old self. But more than that, I sensed in the Corps an iron discipline, an unbreakable spirit, an espirit de corps that transcended the origins of every Marine.

Aaron and I were outsiders. Always had been, always were. In Singapore, primary schoolers made fun of our funny accents and weird speech patterns. In Halo City high schoolers did the same. Everywhere we went, the old rules no longer applied. We had to learn quickly, adapt even faster.

Aaron kept his head down, submerged himself into the local Chinese community, and followed in Father's footsteps. I almost did the same, until I saw my first USMC recruiting advertisement. In the Marines I saw a way to become a man. I wanted to prove I was an American, more American than everyone else around me.

The first time I told my parents I wanted to be a Marine, they laughed at me. I kept pushing the issue, and the laughter turned to anger.

"Good iron doesn't make good nails, and good sons don't make good soldiers," Father said.

Sons were expected to carry on the family name and make a living. Four millennia of war and unrest firmly cemented the soldier's place in Chinese history as murderers, robbers, and rapists.

But China was not America.

After four years of non-stop arguments and a couple of visits from the local Marine recruiter, my parents finally signed the waiver allowing me to enlist right out of high school.

Since they couldn't talk me out of enlistment, my parents tried to convince me take a 'safe' job. Drone operator, information systems specialist, even water support technician. Anything but a frontline position. When that failed, they tried to talk me into going into college, hoping I'd reconsider my career, while leaving open the option of becoming an officer.

They never did understand why I wanted to join the Marines.

I ignored them and took the UZ contract, the toughest enlistment option I could find, and spent the rest of my high school years preparing for basic training.

Boot camp, followed by Selection and Indoctrination, was the third-hardest thing I'd ever done. I barely scraped through. But at the end of it, I was a full-fledged Recon Marine.

The Corps didn't care about where I came from, only what I did, and I took to that environment like a fish to water. If anything, it valued my ability to speak multiple languages, which contributed to early promotions and a shot at the holy of holies, the Marine Raider Regiment.

Assessment & Selection was the second-hardest thing I'd ever done. The Individual Training Course was the hardest. But I'd made it.

After completing my tour with the Raiders, I took my discharge papers and returned to Halo City. I had thought it was a homecoming. Instead, I found a city hollowed out by El Trece in one corner, the triads in the other, and power-hungry politicians in the middle.

My parents thought I'd had my fill of excitement and adventure. They pushed me to go to college, get a job, do something with my life. But I couldn't walk away from the gang-infested barrios, the desperate poverty spilling out into the streets, the sight of triad members openly collecting 'protection money' from hapless store-keepers.

I joined the HCPD.

And walked away from my family.

Mealtimes with my family was always quiet. No one spoke during dinner unless absolutely necessary. Danny's presence shook things up. He regaled them with tales from the street, the most absurd and hilarious tales he could summon from his many years of experience.

"Last month, I stopped this guy for speeding. He was running twenty over the limit. When I approached the vehicle, he lowered the window and looked at me all remorseful-like. Right there I knew something was up.

"I shone my light on him. His face and armpits were covered in sweat, his pupils were dilated, and he was scratching furiously at his hands.

"I asked, 'Do you have a medical condition?'. He said, 'No officer, just a mild rash, that's all.

"I didn't buy it. Not one bit. I asked him if he knew why I stopped him, and he said he was speeding. I asked him for his license and registration. He said it's in his glove compartment. I asked him to open it. He complied, and right there, in plain sight, were three packets of white powder.

"I said, 'Sir, is that cocaine?' He said, 'Yeah, it is'. I said, 'Sir, I need you to step out of the vehicle. He said, 'Are you going to bust me?' I said, 'I'm afraid so.' And you know what he said next?"

"What did he say?" Aaron asked.

"He said, 'Can you let me snort it first?'"

Everyone laughed. Even Father smiled.

"Being a cop is dangerous, isn't it?" Father asked.

"It has its moments," Danny said. "But ninety percent of the time, it's pretty boring."

"What about the other ten percent?" Mother asked.

"You get idiots like the guy I just told you about."

They laughed again.

Father nodded at me. "What about STAR? Is it dangerous?"

"If we do our jobs right, if the subjects don't do anything stupid, it's pretty safe," I said.

"The media said you used excess force," he said, an accusing tone creeping into his voice.

"The helmet cam clearly shows the subjects reaching for a gun," I said. "Once the video is released, it'll all blow over."

"You have powers, what. Did you have to kill them?"

Mother clicked her tongue. Aaron pursed his lips. Danny looked at me.

Heat rushed to my face. My hands and jaws clenched. There was a time when I would have lashed out at them. When I had. But... even now, I could always choose to be better than I was.

I stayed in the moment. Breathed. Spoke.

"My power doesn't make me bulletproof. It was either them or me."

Father chewed on a chicken claw and mulled his answer.

"It must be difficult," he said, finally.

I sighed. "It always is."

"If you need help, you can always come back to us," Mother said.

Heat crawled in my chest and ears. Tension gathered in my throat. My eyes itched. It was the first time my parents had said anything like that to me.

"Thanks," I said.

I picked up a *liu sha bao* with my chopsticks and peeled off the paper backing. Brought it to my mouth and bit deep.

Hot sweet and salty egg yolk custard spurted into my mouth. It was a delicate mix of buttery richness and grainy consistency, perfectly complimenting the feather-soft bun.

It was the taste of my childhood.

Danny took his time eating, spending long periods talking and drinking tea and complimenting Father's cooking. When we were finally done, it was a little past eleven, and the other employees were ready to leave. We made our goodbyes and walked to the car.

"Your parents still care about you," Danny said. "You can see it in their faces."

"Yeah," I replied.

"Times like this, you gotta stick close to *la familia*. Blood is thicker than water and all that."

"Yeah."

"Don't give up on them. Okay?"

I sighed. "Yeah."

8

SICARIO

The following morning, Shane called just after breakfast.

"Hey," she said. "Got a minute?"

"Yeah," I replied. "Aren't we supposed to be sequestered?"

She giggled. "I won't tell IA if you won't."

"Me too. What's up?"

"IA and the DAO called me up for a follow-up interview. They wanted to know if I heard you telling me to stop if I'd thought about prepping the entry with a banger, that sort of thing."

"How did it turn out?"

"My defense rep and I were ready for them. I'm off the hook. I think."

"You think?"

"Nobody's complaining. No indications that they're planning to bust us. It's a good shoot."

She tried to sound optimistic, but I heard the desperate note in her voice.

"I'm glad you made it through."

"Hey, couldn't have done it without the heads-up."

"No problem."

"Say, um... when this is over... when will you be back?"

"Tuesday."

"Would the sequestration period be over?"

"It's over when IA says it's over."

"I see. Uh... well, see you when I see you then."

"Same here."

The rest of weekend passed without incident. Life continued to move on, the world rotated on its axis, the streets of the city pulsed and flowed to their secret rhythms. It might have been just another weekend, but the protests outside HCPD HQ were still going strong. I didn't know why the brass hadn't ordered them dispersed, or how the protesters sustained themselves. But they would leave.

Protests always ended someday.

Cheered with that thought, I kitted up with my duty Glock 19 and two spare magazines, running shoes and runner's rig, and stepped out. Mondays in Chinatown always carried that extra edge. It was the start of the working week, and it was time to make money, go to school, to do *something* that justified your continued existence.

I saw it in the way the shopkeepers paid just that extra bit of attention cleaning up before opening the stores; the sharp decrease in early-morning joggers, those who had real jobs; the cars rushing through the streets; those school children who didn't have parents willing and able to drive them to school, shuffling along with rounded shoulders and sleepy eyes to the bus stops and train stations.

I didn't go to Bishop Park today. It didn't pay to be predictable. Today I headed south, out of Chinatown, following the thoroughfares to Grand Park.

Despite the name it was a tenth of the size of Bishop Park. It made up for that by being situated near City Hall, the Hall of Justice, and the Hall of Records. Sited near the Civic Center, the major government and administrative buildings of Halo City radiated outwards from Grand Park in a three-block radius.

Grand Park didn't have a fitness corner. At least, a serviceable fitness corner. The metal parallel bars were rusted, the wooden steps and benches and logs were splintered and vandalized, and large chunks of the rubberized floor had been ripped out. The children's playground wasn't much different, with the bonus of dirty needles and used condoms strewn across the ground.

This city was going to the dogs. I'd clean up the trash myself, but handling biowaste with bare hands was suicide. Instead, I called the Department of Sanitation and left them to it. Their office was right across the street in City Hall, but it was faster this way.

With any luck, they might respond quickly.

I found a clean patch of grass and flowed through bodyweight exercises. I began with a series of yoga and pilates poses, stretching and loosening my muscles and tendons and joints. Then I did push-ups, bridges, pistol squats, and tuck jumps. For the finale, I ran around the park, pushing myself to the limit with 60-60 interval runs.

Grand Park appealed to a different crowd. No morning taiji classes here, but many more runners in athletic sportswear. A film crew shot a scene by the pond, and I swerved well clear. In a corner, there was a fenced-off patch of bare land with a few ancient benches and a lonely tree that pretended to be a dog run. There were only three people in the dog run at this time of the morning, seated at the benches and playing with their phones while their half-dozen dogs played with each other.

When I completed my sprints, I walked back home. The morning rush had begun, and the roads were clogged up with never-ending streams of cars. Most of the stores along the street were still shuttered and darkened, but a rare few were already open for business. A bakery, a coffee shop, a sports apparel store that stocked nothing but Prime-endorsed gear. It seemed like every few months a store closed forever, to be immediately replaced by another interchangeable contender.

Approaching my apartment, I saw a beat-up green Chevrolet parked right outside my front door. Only residents could park there, and I didn't recognize the license plate.

A cold shiver ran down my spine.

DANGER DANGER DANGER SCAN NOW

Two Hispanic males stood next to the front door. The closer one was young, young enough to still be in high school. The other wasn't much older, just barely in his twenties. Both men wore cheap dark jerseys, bargain-basement baggy pants, and expensive Nike sneakers. Their hands drifted near the waistbands, and the older guy patted his belly.

Weapon.

I kept scanning. A green Ford with tinted windows lingered in front of the entrance of the apartment, its engine grumbling. More cars were parked across the street, all of them empty. A gaggle of schoolchildren laughed and skipped as they made their way to the nearby bus stop. A man climbed into his car. A grandmother pushed a shopping cart.

All of them were Chinese. The Hispanics stood out like the proverbial sore thumb. That might simply mean that the Hispanics were a distraction, that there was someone else posing as an innocent bystander nearby. I stopped to retie my shoelaces, using the opportunity to scan all around me, but I didn't pick up any dangerous vibes from passers-by. They were all focused on their affairs, not on me, not on the Hispanics.

I refocused my attention on the strangers. Most people in the First World couldn't stand still and look about for five minutes. They would whip out phones and tablets and stare at screens. These men weren't distracted. They were scanning the street, one guy looking left, the other looking right. They had no cigarettes in their hands, they weren't talking to each other. They had no reason to be here.

They were hunting.

As I framed that thought, the younger guy looked at me.

He had The Look. The soulless look of a hardened killer, a man who had killed before and was perfectly willing to kill again. His eyes narrowed for a fraction of a second.

Then he turned away and whispered something into his friend's ear.

The two continued chatting. Young Gun had turned his face from me, but Old Gun was watching over his shoulder. Watching me.

Everything about this situation screamed *Walk away now*. It was tempting, but I knew that look. These men were targeting *me*. If I did that, they might just put a bullet in the back of my head, and I wouldn't see it coming.

Cross the street and walk on? Maybe. On the other hand, they struck me as the kind of people who would blast away at their target across a busy road. Too risky for civilians around me.

Call for backup? Absolutely. But first, I had to get off the X, and there was only one way to do that.

I kept walking.

Eyes fell on me, flitted away, and looked back. My heart pounded, sending fresh waves of adrenaline through my blood. My mouth dried. My hands threatened to clench. I breathed, walked, looked around, keeping the duo and the car in the edge of my view. I pretended to sip from my Platypus bottle, and smoothly pulled the zip of the main compartment of the runner's rig. Just partway through, just enough to prep for a draw without exposing the gun.

The two Hispanics stepped off, sauntering towards me. Young Gun on my left, Old Gun on the right, spreading out to occupy the sidewalk.

Game time.

"Yo *ese*. How's it going?" Old Gun said.

I held my hands out. "Sorry, I'm busy right now."

As I talked I widened my steps and angled off, circling around him, keeping to his outside.

"Hey, we just need directions. How do you get to the metro from here?"

"I don't live around here. Sorry," I replied.

The Hispanics kept turning, facing me as I completed my half-clock turn. Behind them, the Ford's doors popped open. Two more Hispanics stepped out.

I pointed at the newcomers.

"Hey, are those your friends?" I asked.

Their eyes widened. Their faces paled. Young Gun glanced at his partner.

"Get him!" Old Gun ordered.

They clawed for their shirts, hands racing for their waistbands.

I Amped.

Stepped into Old Gun and chopped my left forearm into the side of his neck, stepped off to Young Gun and flicked my fingers across his eyes. He screamed, recoiling from me, left hand going for his face—

Right hand already on his gun.

My right shin was pressed against his, my foot wedged behind his own. I seized his right wrist with my left hand, the back of his head with my right. Pulling him down, twisting his skull up and out, I dropped my weight into his shin.

He fell.

Next customer. Old Gun was turning into me, his hands a blur. I swung around, left palm going for the small of his back, but all I got was the back of his elbow, spinning him back around. I shot my right palm into his temple, grabbing and twisting his skull, kneed the back of his leg, and wrenched him down, crashing his head into the sidewalk.

"*Mierda!*"

The two guys who had stepped out of the car were running towards me. One was unarmed. The other had an AK-47.

I turned and ran.

The Kalashnikov stuttered in a semi-auto spray and pray. Passersby screamed. Shrapnel peppered my legs, a cloud of dust erupted from the wall ahead of me, a bullet whined past my ear.

Cars and street lamps buzzed violently. My skin tingled, my hair stood on end, and the taste of metal flooded my mouth.

I leapt and covered my ears.

Lightning flashed the world to white. Thunder roared behind me. The pressure wave slammed into my back.

My vision swam. My ears rang. My feet hit the ground and I kept running, rounding the corner.

The civilians hadn't gotten the good news yet. A few were standing around, gawking. Cars filled the road, frozen at a red light.

A guy wearing a massive set of earphones bopped away to blaring K-Pop, walking obliviously towards me.

I grabbed his shoulders.

"Heeeey, whaaaat the—"

"THERE'S A SHOOTING BEHIND ME!" I screamed.

"Whaaaaat?"

I ripped the headset away.

"SHOOTING BEHIND ME! TAKE COVER NOW!"

Men screamed in Spanish. I shoved the civilian towards the nearest car and ran.

There was a cherry-red coupe parked by the road. No one inside. I vaulted across the hood, planted myself behind the front wheel well, reached into my rig, pulled my Glock, breathed.

My heart thudded in my ears. The aftermarket stippled grip strips bit into my palm, rough and reassuring. Footsteps pounded and horns screamed. I gritted my teeth and pushed through the noise, listening for—

"Where the fuck did he go?!"

I peeked around the hood.

Three shooters. The one with the AK leaned out and side-stepped in a tight circle, slicing the pie. A second man peeked low around the corner, exposing only his face. The third guy, Young Gun, stood above the second man, bracing himself against the wall with one hand, extending his pistol with the other.

These guys were trained.

As that thought flashed through my head, the front sight of the Glock, crisp and clean and clear, found the chest of the man with the AK. I rolled the trigger, once, twice, shot him twice more in the head. He plopped face-down in a blood spray.

"Behind the red car!"

Young Gun fired, spraying rounds my way. Bullets punched through glass and metal, showering me in fragments. I ducked. A tire exploded, rocking my ears. I glanced to my left, saw a suddenly-empty street. No cover, and the air crackled around me.

Move or die.

Headphone Man was curled up behind the body of a black Ford sedan in front of me. The doors offered barely any protection against bullets, but there was no time to educate him now. Keeping my head down, I sprinted to the Ford, metal buzzing all around me, blew past Headphone Man, and slid to a stop behind the engine block.

"Hey! What—"

Lightning blasted from the sky. Thunder pounded my head like a sledgehammer, wiping out my hearing.

Gritting through the pain, I popped up, saw Young Gun swiveling in place, trying to track me, while the unarmed guy, the Prime, sprinted to his fallen friend. I trained my sights on Young Gun, saw his eyes gape open and his mouth drop as he realized where I was, and fired.

The bullet caught him in the hand. Brick dust blew up in his face, and he screamed, staggering out of cover, shielding his face. I rolled the trigger, and my next round punched through his open palm and into his head.

I turned to the last man, dragging his buddy by the collar with his left hand, right hand hidden from view.

"Drop the weapon now!" I yelled.

My skin prickled. Static danced down my spine.

DANGER DANGER DANGER

I hammered him twice in the center of mass, raised the sights, saw his face, fired twice more.

He slumped over his friend's corpse.

My ears ringing like church bells, I reloaded my Glock. Approaching the corner, keeping well away from the wall, I checked on the shooters. Their bodies twitched, spilling gore from their shattered heads, still unaware that they were already dead.

Weapon ready, I cleared the corner. The last *sicario* was sprawled across the sidewalk, arms and legs splayed open, completely motionless.

I scanned. A few cars sat abandoned on the street, their doors flung open and their occupants out of sight. Next to me, the lightning strike had blasted a massive smoking hole in the hood of a black

Taurus. Civilians curled in balls or hid behind cars, lamp posts, and doors.

Sounds whistled through my battered ears. Someone whispered into her phone, pleading for the police to come. High above in an apartment, a baby wailed.

No more threats.

I stepped down my Power. Breathed. Covered the remaining body and walked up to him.

Old Gun was utterly still, his eyes rolled up in his head, his arms splayed out. His handgun lay a foot away from his empty hands. I checked for a pulse. None. I pressed my fingers to his nose. No breath.

I patted myself down, looking for blood. I'd picked up a few small cuts on my exposed calves. Must have been struck by shrapnel, but nothing important. I washed the wounds with my water bottle, then Amped my natural healing factor.

The wounds clotted over before my eyes, and in moments, vanished. My ears warmed up, and sound flooded back in. People whimpering and crying, someone whispering into her phone pleading for the cops to come, a baby wailing high above me.

I never openly advertised my healing factor. Never let the world know what you're truly capable of.

Sirens screamed, just a block away. A woman shrieked in pain. A child cried. I unloaded my gun and set it down. Took out my badge and concealed carry permit, placed them next to my weapon. Took out my phone.

Called 911.

9

AN INNOCENT MAN

P rimes arrested in Halo City were transported to Central
Police Station, the only station in the city equipped to handle
terrorists and Primes. I'd placed more than a few people in
the maximum security holding cells in the basement. This was the
first time I saw a cell on the inside.

Three blank white soundproofed walls. A white-painted steel
door twelve inches thick, with a food port at hand height and a
viewing slit at eye level. A dome camera on the ceiling, positioned
right above the low bench bed. Across the bench, a stainless steel
sink and a toilet bowl.

But that wasn't everything.

Hidden slots in the walls and ceiling housed microwave emitters,
tear gas sprayers and stun grenades. The moment the duty sergeant
spotted a Prime acting out of hand, he would hit the panic button.
Tear gas would flood the room, the stun grenades would detonate,
reinforcing bolts would crash down, and the microwave emitters
would cook the detainee. The microwaves wouldn't kill him; it would
merely make him wish they did.

Activists had decried the design as inhumane—but only if it were
used to house ordinary humans. When used to hold people who

could turn themselves invisible, melt metal with a touch or emit life-leeching fogs, it was merely the absolute minimum required to prevent escape.

Even so, a truly dedicated Prime could still escape. I just had to Amp to the max, tear the door off its hinges, and step out of the cell before the security systems kicked in. No guns were allowed down here, so overpowering the guards would be a piece of cake. Then I just had to run out the door, and I'd be home free.

On the other hand, I was an innocent man. And as an innocent man, all I could do was wait until something happened.

After calling 911, I explained what had happened to the dispatcher and waited for the first responders. When they brought me to the station, I made one phone call under the watchful eye of half of the on-duty cops on site. Then they threw me into the cell, where I lingered in limbo.

The hours dragged on. No one came to me, no one checked in on me. I sat on my bench, half-closed my eyes and meditated, breathing out the vestigial stress in my muscles and rehearsing what I had to say later. Once the food port opened to admit a tray of something that nearly qualified as food and a set of plastic utensils. After I finished the meal the port opened again, and I returned the tray.

That was the one interaction I had with anybody. I returned to my meditative state and sank into silence.

An eternity later, words emerged from the depths of my mind.

THE GREAT WHEEL *revolves*
   Crushing the six realms
   Under cosmos-spanning rims.

BLOOD LUBRICATES *it*
   Bone nourishes it
   Flesh fuels the furnace at its heart.

                    .   .   .

Blow out the flame within
Fill the world with inner light
Watch! The Wheel halts.

But only for you.

I SMILED and shook my head. The wheel revolves, indeed. And even if it you find a way off, there are still so many people trapped within. How could someone help them? How could someone *not* help them?

Soft footsteps approached my door and stopped. I opened my eyes just as the vision port slid open.

"Detective Song, you awake?"

"Yes," I replied.

"Your counsel has arrived. We can begin your interview."

"Let's do it."

The food port opened.

"Place your hands through the food port."

I did. Cold steel handcuffs bit into my wrists. The door slid open, revealing four beefy cops clad in heavy cell extraction suits. Two of them fastened heavy shackles to my ankles. The other two joined the cuffs to the shackles with a metal chain.

"Let's go," the leader said.

Two of them grabbed my arms and led me down a narrow hallway. The others walked behind me. They brought me to the interview room, where two people awaited.

One of them was Will Dawson.

"Adam!" Will said, rising to his feet. "Are you okay?"

"I'm fine," I replied.

This was an off-duty shoot, but I was being treated like a suspect. Perhaps it was simply an overabundance of caution, but it didn't hurt to have a lawyer in my corner.

Will turned his gaze on the cops. "Why is my client shackled like a terrorist?"

"Sorry, Counselor," the detective said. "It's standard procedure."

"You will release him right now," he demanded.

"I can't do that. The shackles are for everyone's safety."

"He's a police officer, and he's been completely cooperative. He's not some hardened criminal, is he?"

"It's alright Will," I said. "They have to do what they have to do."

Will grunted and sat back down.

I joined him and Amped, just a little bit, enough to effortlessly swing my manacled hands up on the table. The detective's eyes narrowed. He'd gotten the message.

"Let's get started," I said.

"*After* the security team leaves," Will said.

The detective waved them out. As they left, I reduced my power to baseline levels.

"I'm Detective John Clements," the interviewer said. "Internal Affairs. Before we begin, are you feeling well?"

"As well as can be," I said.

"Why did you place my client in a cell?" Will demanded. "Why was he locked in there for hours?"

"Sorry," Clements said. "We had to secure the scene and evidence, sort out witness testimonies and verify his identity. Shootings like this can get messy."

Will shot him a withering look. Clements ignored him and briefed me on post-shooting procedures. It was pro forma, and we all knew it, but he had to dot the i's and cross the t's. He set his recorder on the table, stated the date, time and location, and introduced everyone around him.

"You are Detective Adam Song, a Prime with the codename Amp, correct?" he asked.

"Yes," I said.

"Detective Clements," Will interrupted, "my client's identity is protected under the Prime Privacy Protection Act. All references to his name must be scrubbed from the interview. From here on out, you shall refer to him exclusively as 'Amp.'"

"So noted, Counselor," Clements agreed. "Now, Amp, please tell me exactly what happened during the shooting earlier today."

I walked Clements through the sequence of events. As before, this was just the initial interview, to establish the basic facts of the case. The Inquisition would examine my full statement later.

I talked and talked and talked, stopping only to sip at a proffered glass of water. Will chipped in, asking for clarifications and occasionally intervening on my behalf. When all was said and done, Clements pursed his lips and tapped his fingers against the table.

"Let me see if I have this straight," he said. "You were returning home from your morning run when you saw a suspicious car and two suspicious individuals outside your front door."

"Yes."

"Why didn't you leave?"

"I felt that if I turned around, they would have shot me in the back."

"How do you know this?"

"Their body language. When Young Gun saw me, his eyes locked on to me. Then he quickly turned away and talked to his partner, who angled himself to continue observing me. It felt to me that they were targeting *me*, specifically. If I'd turned around, they might have just shot me there and then."

"You were at the end of the street at that time, as I recall. You couldn't just turn to your left and make your way down the road?"

"I was tired. By the time my brain kicked in, and I realized what I was looking at, I was past the point I could safely turn away."

"Uh-huh," Clements muttered. "So why did you walk up to those guys?"

"My plan was to identify myself as a police officer and ask them what they were up to. But they beat me to the punch."

"You didn't think about calling for backup?"

"My phone was in my rig. If they saw me reaching for it, they could have drawn down and shot me before I could react."

"You're a Prime," he said accusingly.

"Detective, what are you implying?" Will asked.

"Amp, did you think of using your powers to prevent the situation from escalating?"

I shrugged. "I tried. Nothing came to mind. My powers don't make me invincible, and the bad guys chose to initiate the ambush."

"You had no other choice but to brace the shooters?" Clements asked.

"That's right."

Clements tapped his fingers again. "To continue the summary, after the suspects initiated the ambush, you knocked down the first two suspects, then ran away. Meanwhile, the shooter with the AK fired at you, while a Prime threw a lightning bolt."

"Yes."

"You rounded the bend, pushed a civilian to safety, drew your weapon and took cover. The bad guys then sliced the pie around the bend. That was the moment you chose to engage."

"Yes."

"Why didn't you run away?"

"I'd spent all my energy training at Grand Park. After that last sprint around the corner, I was gassed."

Clements raised an eyebrow. "You're a Prime, and you work in STAR, but ran out of breath?"

"My client's powers do not extend to instant recovery from exhaustion," Will said. "It sounds like you're expecting too much from him."

Clements shrugged. "Very well. Amp, when you shot at the suspects, were they firing at you at that time?"

"No, but they had their guns up," I replied. "It was clear they were still hunting me. I felt my life, and the lives of everyone around me were in danger."

"And that's why you fired."

"Yes."

"First responders noted one suspect with gunshot wounds to the hands and face. The hand shots would have disabled him. Why did you keep shooting?"

"That guy was leaning around the corner. The only target I had was his arm. After taking the shot, I didn't know if he'd dropped his weapon. I didn't see his weapon falling, and I didn't have time to stop and look. I only saw him stumbling out of cover. I shot him again in the head, but he must have gotten his other hand up at the last second."

"Freak occurrence?"

"Sounds like it."

"But you didn't check if he was still armed after you took the hand shot."

"Detective," Will interrupted. "My client was in a life-or-death situation. He was exchanging fire with three gunmen. At that time, two of the threats were still active. You can't possibly expect him to take the time to see where the other gun went. That would have exposed him to greater danger."

I nodded. "I didn't see what happened to the hand until it was all over."

"I see." Clements leaned in, his eyes boring into mine. "Detective Song, the last man you shot was unarmed."

"He was also a Prime who could throw lightning bolts."

"Did you have positive confirmation of his powers?"

"Yes. While running from the ambush, someone threw lightning at me. During the gunfight, someone flushed me from cover with another lightning bolt. He had to be the same guy."

"When you shot him, he was unarmed and dragging his friend behind cover."

"He was preparing to zap me."

"How did you know?"

"My skin was tingling. That's a warning sign of an impending lightning strike."

"That's it?"

"What else do you want?"

Clements rubbed the bridge of his nose. "You have to understand, from my perspective—from the public's perspective—you shot an unarmed man. The more evidence we can use to prove he was a Prime, the better it looks for you."

I didn't blame him. Everyone knows what a supervillain looks like. He strides down the street, casually flinging powers around, scaring the wits out of everyone in sight. But that's how amateurs work. A professional would hide his powers until the last moment, when his target can't escape.

"The smoking holes don't count as evidence?" I asked.

"At this moment, all we have are eyewitness testimonies. And yours. We will, of course, look for videos and other evidence, but if you can think of any more, it would help."

I shook my head. "I don't have anything more for you."

"So you shot the Prime because you sensed an impending lightning strike?"

"Yes."

"All right then."

We covered the final moments between my 911 call and the arrival of the first responders.

"Were you aware there were injured people nearby?" Clements asked.

"Yes," I replied.

"Did you help them?"

"I wanted to, but I didn't have any medical supplies on me, and the first responders arrived a few minutes after I hung up. How did they get there so fast anyway?"

"You got lucky," Clements said. "There was a patrol car just a couple of blocks away when you called 911."

When the cops arrived, they cuffed me, confiscated my gear, and stuffed me in the backseat of their car. The senior officer grabbed the first aid kit and went to work, while his partner worked the radio and kept an eye on me.

I would have volunteered to help, but once in cuffs, you're treated as a bad guy, actual or potential, and I didn't want to do anything that might be misinterpreted.

After a few more questions, Clements leaned back and said, "That's all I got for you for now. Personally, I don't see any reason to charge you, but you still have to talk to the DA's office.

"I'm surprised the DAO hasn't sent anyone yet," Will remarked.

Clements shrugged. "They said their team will be delayed, so we should conduct our own interview first, and they'll speak with Amp separately."

I shook my head. "Someday, I'll be done with interviews, right?"

The men chuckled tiredly.

"Someday," Clements said. "For now, I'm going to make arrangements to release you. Once you're out, you can set an appointment with the DAO. But we will have to keep your weapon and ammo as evidence."

"Understood," I said.

Clements recited a few more scripted sentences, closing the interview, and turned off his recorder. Then he leaned into me.

"By the way, you never heard this from me, but you gotta watch your back."

"What do you mean?"

"This 'ambush' as you called it. Did you think something was off about it?"

I nodded. "It had all the hallmarks of a hit."

"Bingo. I never told you this, but we've ID'd the shooters. They're all former US Army, now El Trece *sicarios*. We've linked them to at least six hits across the country."

"Son of a bitch..." I whispered.

Members of El Trece and other gangs enlisted in the military to receive training, gain experience, and access weapons and explosives. The ones who stayed in supplied their *carnales* with hardware, the ones who got out passed on what they learned.

"Hold on," Will said. "If the men waiting outside my client's apartment were El Trece *sicarios*..."

Clements nodded. "El Trece knows who you are and where you live, Amp. You've got a bullseye on your back."

10

THE HURT LOCKER

I'd known it was a hit. I had plenty of time in the holding cell to reach that conclusion. Clements' words merely confirmed my suspicions.

The guards returned me to the cell after the interview, but I wasn't a believer in sitting around and doing nothing. As the wheels of the bureaucracy ground away, I thought hard and deep about my next steps.

The military uses METT-TC to plan operations. Mission, Enemy, Terrain and weather, Troops available, Time and Civilian considerations. My mission was to ensure security for myself and those around me. The enemy was El Trece. Terrain and weather, Halo City in the opening days of summer.

Troops available: myself, plus whoever I could convince to help.

Time and civilian considerations weren't as important. El Trece would keep coming at me until their leaders got bored or had something more pressing to take care of. Civilian considerations hadn't changed since I joined the force: the safety and security of nearby civilians, how they would perceive my actions—and how the law would view my actions.

I sat and pondered until the guards came for me again. No shackles this time, but they brought me back to the same interview room. Will was waiting. So were the Two Sams, Conway and Franks.

"We keep seeing each other," I said.

Sam Cho scowled. "That's my line."

"We're already investigating your previous shooting," Byrd said. "The brass decided to throw this one at us too."

"Sorry for doubling for your workload."

Franks chuckled. Cho palmed her face and looked away, but her shoulders shook with barely-constrained amusement.

"We're going to need a full statement from you," Conway said, her tone brisk and businesslike. "Detective Clements already gave us your initial statement. We just need to set an appointment for the follow-up interview."

"Tomorrow morning, HCPD HQ," I said. "Nine o'clock?"

Everyone agreed.

"That should be everything," Byrd said. "You're free to go."

Will smiled. "The four of you came down here just to set an appointment with my client?"

"And to take over the case from Clements," Byrd said.

"Did Clements tell you that my client is at risk?"

"Yes. We have alerted Central Station, and they will step up patrols around your home."

"That's it?" Will asked. "My client is being targeted by a vicious street gang, but you're just going to 'step up patrols'?"

"Easy there, Counselor. The hitters are all dead. Until we have evidence that there exists a continuing threat, that's all I can justify."

"Someone hired those hitmen. There's your threat."

"Yes, but until we know who, there's not much I can do."

"I'll manage," I said. "Do I get an escort?"

"Yes. We can assign one for you."

"I can make my own arrangements, thanks."

Byrd looked at me skeptically. "I'll have to sign off on it. And justify it in my report."

"I know a few Primes willing to take a personal contract. That good enough for you?"

He blew out his cheeks and adjusted his frameless spectacles. "That'll do."

Back upstairs, I retrieved my things, sans Glock and magazines, plus receipt. I parted ways with Will at the exit, then made my way to a nearby cafe.

Over a cup of tea, I made a series of calls.

The first was to James Moss, informing him of tomorrow's interview.

The second was to Halo City's most reputable self-storage company.

The third, and fourth, were to Danny Gonzalez and Thomas Crane.

The last was to a priest.

As I waited, I enjoyed a cup of green tea and read the news on my phone. The protests were still headline news, still going strong. I studied photos and footage of the crowds, examining faces and clothing and props and other indicators.

The protesters were divided into two blocs. The major one was almost exclusively Hispanic, dressed in rough street clothes, holding up signs and shouting at the building. The minor bloc, situated on the right side of the plaza, was more cosmopolitan, dressed in brighter and more expensive clothes.

It wasn't a clean demarcation, but their signs betrayed their memberships and their causes. The ones from El Barrio were all handmade, proclaiming their identity and their grievance: *JUSTICIA POR SOFIA Y EMMANUEL, JAIL AMP NOW, BROWN LIVES MATTER.* The other group's signs were printed on high-vis glossy paper, their banners emblazoned with logos.

NO KILLER CAPES. NO JUSTICE NO PEACE. NO EXCUSE FOR PRIME BRUTALITY.

El Barrio on one side, Cape Watch on the other. Hard young men and boys swam through the crowd, wearing the distinctive green bandanas and jackets of El Trece.

An unholy trinity if there ever was one.

REACT was still staring down the protesters. Uniformed police stood watch nearby. But there was no kettling, no attempt to isolate the protesters. They could come and go as they pleased, receive supplies and reinforcements at will.

The protests had hit the international news, and a small army of reporters were ready to broadcast anything REACT did to the world. Perhaps the brass believed that the protests would burn themselves out, and that any action to accelerate their dispersal would backfire on the PD.

It might even make sense, except that I was still the target of the mob, and the brass still hadn't reached out... to me...

Lightning jolted through my brain.

I was a walking civil liability suit. Why hadn't *anyone* spoken to me yet? At the very least, Public Relations would have prepared me to fend off the media and the crowd, and the brass would have sat me down to figure out what to do next.

And why hadn't Public Relations released the helmet cam video?

I checked my mail. Nothing from the brass. Just a pro forma mail from Public Relations advising me to say nothing to the press and direct all inquiries to their office. Somehow, some reporters had gotten ahold of my police email address and flooded it with requests for inquiries. I spammed all of them.

The lack of official contact wasn't the only thing wrong with the picture. After an OIS, if an officer's weapon needed to be retained as evidence, it was standard practice to discreetly issue a replacement. In my previous shootings, my supervisors either gave me one of their personal firearms or helped me draw a loaner from the armory.

I'd used my issue Glock 19 in my last shoot. The serial number was on file, and I'd mentioned it to Clements. Yet no one had given me a replacement weapon or authorized me to draw a new one.

The only indication that the PD cared about my well-being was a promise to step up police patrols around my home and an offer for an escort, and that came from Sam Byrd. Not the brass.

There was only one explanation: someone on the top floor was playing politics.

And I was the target.

This was familiar ground. I was used to working alone, isolated from the wider community, with minimal support or none. First as a boy, then a Marine Raider, I had never had much in the way of social support.

It was time to look after myself.

I scoured the news, looking for intelligence on the protests, gang activity, anything relevant to my situation. Once again, I was front and center.

The three Halo City newspapers ran three different-yet-similar fluff pieces on the Ruiz family, completely papering over their connections to El Trece while emphasizing Ricardo's youth and skin color.

The *Halo City Herald* published a short article describing this morning's shooting. The first line read: *Prime police officer Amp shot and killed four heavily-armed gunmen in Chinatown this morning.* The last line went: *Amp is presently under investigation for another unrelated on-duty shooting.*

Editorials on the *Halo Examiner* and the *Halo Daily Post* argued for tighter controls on Primes and police use of force. Of course, they mentioned the protests and last week's shoot, and of course, they ignored the self-defense aspect. The former also detailed my history of violence in the police force and wondered if I were out of control.

There was still no helmet cam footage.

Halo City had fallen a long way. The emergence of superpowers brought both crisis and opportunities. Eager to distinguish itself from Silicon Valley, the captains of the local industries transformed the city into a hub for superpower research. The city government followed their lead, passing a slew of measures designed to encourage Prime immigration and resettlement. Soon, billions of dollars and thousands of Primes flowed into the city, sparking a golden age.

Somehow, when I wasn't looking, the winds of fortune had turned against Primes. I was simply the latest victim of historical and political trends.

Politics is never personal until it happens to you.

Shortly after I drained my tea, a man entered the cafe. He wore an anonymous gray suit that perfectly matched the bland clothing civilian city employees favored. He seemed in his late forties or early fifties, and his blonde hair was thinning, but looks were deceiving.

His face was a blank mask, a complete absence of presence that, to the right eyes, betrayed the predator beneath. He dipped his head ever so slightly as he passed through the door, expanding his peripheral vision to cover both sides of the doorway, and as he approached his ice-blue eyes darted from side to side. He walked with a smooth, rolling gait, betraying a lifetime of training, and I knew that under his deliberately oversized clothing was a body trained and hardened for war.

"Adam," Tom Crane said, sitting at my table.

"Tom," I replied. "Hope I wasn't interrupting anything."

He smiled. "It's all good. I needed to get out of the office anyway."

"Did you get the things I asked for?"

"Yup. They're in the trunk of the car."

"Thanks."

Tom cocked his head at the glass door. "So, you've really pissed off El Trece this time."

I sipped my tea. "Yeah."

"Something's fishy about this."

"How so?"

"HCPD puts down a few El Trece animals every year, right? But have you *ever* seen protests of this scale?"

I shook my head. "No. But then, I'm a Prime. Cape Watch *always* turns out when a police Prime kills someone these days."

"True," he said, "but Cape Watch doesn't usually reach out to El Barrio. They target a different demographic. Diverse, progressive youths with time and money to burn."

He pronounced the last sentence like a string of blasphemies.

"I think El Trece mobilized their supporters and their *carnales*," I said. "Ricardo Ruiz is a shot-caller. He might have the juice to do something like this."

"He organized a protest, reached out to Cape Watch, and put out a hit on you. He must be some shot-caller."

"We don't know if he put a hit on me."

"He's got the motive. And we both know El Trece repays blood with blood."

"That's true. I'll need to check with the Intelligence Bureau, see what they say about him."

"That's a good idea," he replied.

A few minutes later, Danny showed up. He was in full REACT kit: ballistic helmet, plate carrier laden with gear, holstered Glock on a duty belt plussed-up with extra magazines. All he lacked was his carbine, and that was probably stored safely away.

"Hey, Tom, it's been a while," Danny said.

"Right back at ya, Speedy," Tom replied.

Danny sniffed. He'd long ago given up trying to correct anyone who used it.

"Did I take you from anything important?" I asked.

"Nah," Danny replied. "As far the brass is concerned, a citizen flagged me down asking for help. I can't refuse, can I?"

Tom grinned. "Ever Officer Friendly, ain'tcha?"

Danny puffed up his chest. "Of course, 'mano. I dunno about you, but I gotta work for a living."

We shared a moment of laughter.

Phantom, Aegis, Amp. They don't make very many like us anymore. Unlike so many Primes out there, we weren't born with our powers. We had to earn our places in a world ruled by supermen, and earn them again when destiny elevated us to their ranks.

There were some fifteen thousand known Primes in Halo City, and probably another fifteen thousand that weren't registered. Most were amateurs and small fry. The moment they registered themselves with the HCPA and completed their mandatory training and certification modules, they hit the streets and went trolling for trouble, utterly unaware that T&C wasn't meant to prepare them for the real world—it was merely a political compromise.

Low-level superheroes subsisted on small stipends or floated from contract to contract, hustling every day to make ends meet, ceaselessly promoting themselves in a never-ending quest to secure corporate sponsorship or crowdfunding. Their services came cheap, those who didn't work pro bono, but their tradecraft was nonexistent, and few bothered to upgrade their skills. Most of them had nothing going for them but their powers. Every time a superhuman showdown led to serious collateral damage, third-rate Primes were almost always involved.

There was no way I could bring amateurs into this. I didn't need the lawsuits and criminal charges that came with reckless use of powers, and I sure as hell didn't need a supervillain tracking me down through an amateur.

The big fish, the top ten percent who had secured sponsorships, *probably*, but not definitely, had the skills I needed. I knew many of them on sight. But if you take the king's shilling, you do the king's bidding. If they had to choose between fulfilling a personal contract or answering the demands of their paymasters, you could count on them to protect and serve the corporate interest. Couple that with the protests and I was confident very few Primes would be interested in helping me.

In the end, you can only count on your own.

Superpowers are no substitutes for tradecraft, tactics, and proper equipment. Regular humans had been killing superhumans for the past three decades and counting. Powers gave you an edge; they did not make you invulnerable. And guns were superpowers.

Aegis, Phantom and I made this truth a part of our lives. Instead of relying on our powers to see us through, we built our bodies and brains, and schooled ourselves in critical skills, the way warriors did before the age of Primes.

Sure, Danny gained his powers before joining the HCPD, but his were only good for helping him reach a hot zone. In his ghost form, he couldn't touch anyone, much less take down a suspect. Once on site, he had to count on skill, speed, aggression, and surprise to see him through. And if he got careless or unlucky, if someone shot or stabbed him before he had a chance to deploy his powers, he was as mortal as everyone else.

Danny might have been a civilian once, but he had long ago transformed himself into a full-fledged gunfighter. He was one of us now.

We married old school tradecraft with new age powers. We were adept with guns, blades, powers and empty hands in equal measure. We were the gunfighter kings of the streets. All the Primes of Halo City would tremble at our approach, and no mere mortal could stand in our way.

"We're burning daylight," I said. "Let's get going."

We TREATED my return home like a tactical operation. In a very real sense, it was.

Tom and Danny drove around the block, checking for surveillance and unwanted attention. I rode shotgun in Tom's car, looking for anything out of place.

A crime scene unit was working the block and had taped off the sections of the street where the bodies had fallen. But the technicians didn't impede access to my apartment proper.

Anywhere else in Halo City and there might have been a few curious onlookers. Here in Chinatown, nearly everybody in the vicinity scurried away, their gaze averted.

No one acted out of place. No one looked at us. We parked across the street and geared up.

Danny got out of his car, grabbed his SIG Virtus and stood watch by the door. Tom took off his jacket, revealing an empty custom-molded polymer holster at his hip, then pressed his fingers to a discreet fingerprint reader.

A leather-lined box between the front seats popped open, revealing a small vault made of heavy-gauge steel. The door faced me, and I couldn't look inside, but the scent of gun oil and metal wafted into my nose. Tom reached in and drew a Glock 34.

A gunsmith had worked over this Glock, turning a factory-spec workhorse into a glamorous stallion. Pronounced cocking serrations ran down the elongated slide. A micro red dot sight sat just behind the ejection port. The original sights had been replaced with aftermarket tritium sights. A miniature flashlight hung from the accessory rail. Knowing Tom, I had no doubt the grip had been sculpted to perfectly fit his hand.

"Fancy gun," I said.

"Thanks," he replied, slipping it into his hip holster.

"Sponsored?"

"Ashford Precision offered us a steep discount in exchange for endorsement and advertising. They're calling it the Aegis Special."

"Must be nice. Is that weapon unloaded?"

He grinned.

"Absolutely," he said, inserting a pair of spare magazines into his magazine pouches.

"Riiiiight..."

He reached inside the vault again and removed an ultra-compact AR-15. For a second I thought it was a unicorn, a true short-barreled rifle, illegal for almost everyone in the state who wasn't a law enforcement officer to own, until I noticed that the stock was merely an arm brace.

"See? *This* pistol is unloaded," he proclaimed.

The weapon was a pistol. It was chambered in a rifle caliber, based on a rifle platform, and sported a super-short barrel, red dot sight, and flashlight, but thanks to its arm brace it was legally classified as a pistol.

"Yeah, yeah," I replied. "You got your permit?"

He dangled a green card in front of my face. "Here you go."

The card stated that Thomas Crane was a registered security guard, authorized to openly carry pistols, long guns, assault weapons, and high capacity magazines while on duty.

"Keep it close," I said.

"Yes sir, officer, whatever you say."

Tom pocketed the card, then grabbed a pair of magazines held in a two-mag clamp and slapped the right-hand mag into the weapon.

"Is that weapon a custom job too?" I asked.

"Yeah. LWRCI's Six8 pistol, the latest iteration, customized to our specifications."

Famous superheroes got paychecks and Gucci gear. Everyone else had to do without.

"Must be nice to have sponsored gear."

"Capitalism, my friend." He racked the charging handle. "Be back in a bit."

Tom stepped out and crossed the road, scanning in every direction. The lab techs alerted on him, but Danny smoothed things over with them. The Primes stacked on the front door of my apartment and made entry. They would sweep the floors one by one, looking for unwanted visitors. I would have preferred a lower-profile operation, but my address was already known to the bad guys, and Tom didn't have a concealed carry permit.

In lieu of going invisible, we were sending a message: *mess with me and you'll have hard cases all over you.*

Long minutes later, my phone vibrated. It was Tom.

"All clear," he reported.

"Roger that," I replied.

Danny stood on the roof and watched the street. Tom strolled out of the apartment, his Six8 slung around his neck. I met him at the trunk of his car. He popped the trunk, revealing a pair of large plastic storage boxes and another pair of empty gym bags. Stacking one box atop the other, I shouldered the gym bags, grabbed the boxes and followed Danny inside. The receptionist goggled at us as we came in.

"Mr. Song?" she asked. "What's going on?"

"Just clearing out my stuff," I said.

"Do you need assault rifles for that?"

Tom grinned. "It's only a pistol, ma'am."

She blinked, dumbfounded.

"Did you see any strangers head upstairs?" I asked.

"No, no one. Why? Is something wrong?"

"Just being safe."

We headed up to my floor. All quiet so far. I set my load down and checked my telltale, a paperclip wedged in the hinge. Still intact.

Tom wordlessly handed me his Glock. I pointed it at the floor and eased back the slide, saw brass winking back from the exposed chamber. Tom positioned himself on the hinge side of the door, while I took the knob. I unlocked the door, and he slowly edged it open, scanning for tripwires, mercury switches, or other unpleasant surprises.

Once the door was fully open, Tom stepped in, weapon shouldered, and I followed.

The entrance hallway was clear. Tom held position and whispered, "Check the closet on the left."

I peeked inside. Shoes and other odds and ends. I shone my flashlight, looking for tripwires.

"Clear."

We took three more steps, stopping just before the bathroom.

"Going right," Danny whispered.

"Go."

I opened the door to my bathroom. Together, we swept the tiny room.

"Clear," I reported.

We headed back out and flowed into the living space. Everything was where I had left them this morning. We checked the closets and cabinets and balcony.

"Clear," I reported.

"All clear," Tom said. "I'll stand watch outside," he said. "Do what you gotta do."

"Thanks."

I returned the handgun and changed into a set of fresh clothes. Gunfighter clothes. Gray shirt, olive cargo pants, battle belt, Bates tactical boots, and escape and evasion tools secreted all over my person. With this set-up I could go anywhere in Halo City and disappear.

I opened my closet and reviewed my clothes. They were sorted into two main piles, home wear and tactical. I threw the former into a storage container, picked through the latter and put away out-of-season and tactically inappropriate clothes.

I ended up with six shirts made of Merino wool, three cargo pants, seven sets of socks and underwear, and my favorite Arc'teryx jacket, all of them in dark or neutral earth colors.

And one set of police uniforms. Just in case.

I brought out my bags. At first, I considered my USMC-issue rucksack with attached assault pack. A legacy of my service, it was large enough to carry everything I needed, and was already set up for extended missions.

But with its distinct camouflage pattern and PALS webbing, it was too high-viz for this mission. The rucksack went into storage too.

I chose what I liked to think as my general purpose set. The main pack component was a large 72-hour pack, fitted with wide, comfortable shoulder straps and compression straps. My secondary was a flatpack. When completely compressed the flatpack was almost entirely flat, yet at a moment's notice I could unzip the gusset zippers and transform it into a full-sized 24-hour pack. I took off the harness of my runner's rig and lashed the kit bag atop the backpack, then buckled the flatpack to my main pack.

The three-pack arrangement offered me almost as much storage space as my rucksack in a low-viz setup. Colored in ranger green, with no obvious logos or external webbing, the packs presented the image of a backpacker or a hiker.

I had long ago staged tools, food, and medical supplies inside the bags, stored in pockets and accessory pouches mounted on internal webbing. I double-checked everything, threw in a Dopp kit, and stuffed my clothes, laptop, peripherals, and other odds and ends inside the bags.

With the essentials set, I turned to weapons.

Where most homes had a TV, mine had a gun safe. A large one, sufficient for the weapons I'd collected over the years. Opening it, the scent of gun oil and lubricant invaded my nose. A familiar smell, not unpleasant.

Guns greeted me. AR-15s and AK-47s and more exotic rifles, pump-action and semi-automatic shotguns, pistols large and small. Smaller shelves held ammo cans, cleaning supplies and spare parts. See-through pouches mounted on the door carried standard capacity magazines—15, 16 or 17 rounds for pistols, 30 rounds for rifle calibers —and the odd extended magazine just for kicks.

Short swords and axes and knives hung from loops in between and under the pouches. They were all live blades, purchased mostly for fun, but occasionally useful when life took me to the hills and forests at the city's edge.

As a bona fide law enforcement officer, the state's so-called assault weapon laws and concealed carry restrictions didn't apply to me. The contents of the gun safe would give local politicians paroxysms and force activists into foaming fits. Once when I'd showed a date what I stored inside the safe, she stormed out and never spoke to me again. I didn't care. Every man had to have an obsession, and this was mine.

El Trece wanted a fight. If they came for me, I intended to oblige.

Every weapon in my main safe served a purpose. Precision shooting, home defense, close quarters battle, plinking. I set the pistol safe next to the main safe and contemplated my options.

Pistols first. I needed lots of bullets, reasonable accuracy, and absolute reliability. And should I have to give them up to the police, they wouldn't be guns I would miss.

The answer was Glock. Ugly, simple, functional, battle-proven and cheap enough. I'm not a fan, but they would do.

I wore my other Glock 19 on my hip, a Glock 26 on my left ankle, and two spare G19 magazines fitted with +5 base pads in my magazine pouches.

I fitted a second Glock 26 with a VanGuard holster, clipped it to a Raven Concealment PocketShield, and stuffed it inside my left front jacket pocket. Two spare G26 magazines, both with +1 base pads and secured to another PocketShield, went into my right jacket pocket to even out the weight.

A PocketShield was a deceptively simple device. A flexible skeletonized polymer platform in the shape of a shield, it allowed the user to carry small items without betraying their presence. I looked in a mirror, and all I saw were slight bulges the size of wallets and phones.

Knives were next. I selected a pair of Delica Wharncliffes and clipped one each to a pair of Pocketshields. For tactical situations, I preferred fixed blades to folders. But it was illegal to conceal a fixed blade in the state, and I didn't want to advertise my kit.

To the left-hand PocketShield I added my flashlight and Leatherman multitool; to the right I fastened my Shinobi koppo-cum-keychain with paracord. Both platforms disappeared into my front pockets, leaving ambiguous bulges indistinguishable from phones or wallets.

I had a single long gun bag. Gray and discreet, but it would only hold two weapons at a time. I examined my arsenal and considered my choices.

Against an enemy of overwhelming size, the best defense was invisibility and mobility. If I had to engage El Trece or their allies, it would be from a vehicle, in an urban environment, or in close quarters. They would come to me with superior numbers, and the answer was superior firepower and mobility. I needed something lightweight and compact with a large ammunition capacity. Two somethings.

My first choice was my first AR-15. Not the neutered version compliant with state law; this was a true rifle that carried Eugene Stoner's grand vision into the new millennium.

Shortly after joining the police, I had argued long and hard for special permission to buy so-called assault weapons. For years the brass said no. After becoming a detective, they begrudgingly allowed me a couple. When I gained my powers and joined STAR, all resistance melted and asking for permission was simply pro forma. The first thing I did was to ship in a bunch of high-end parts and assemble my own carbine.

My Frankengun was semi-auto only, with a 14.5-inch barrel fixed with a permanently-pinned 1.5-inch flash suppressor, to avoid legal hassles. But in every other respect, it was the equal of many top-tier AR-15 models—and only cost half as much.

My second long gun was a shotgun, a Mossberg 500 FLEX. It was the first firearm I'd ever purchased, a present to myself on my twenty-first birthday. Adorned with quick-release levers and fittings, the Mossberg could be quickly configured for different mission profiles in a matter of seconds.

Its main drawback was its magazine capacity. Five shells plus one in the chamber. But that was with traditional shells. I'd loaded the Mossberg with Aguila minishells and attached an adapter to the loading port. With each minishell a mere one and three-quarters of an inch long, I could stuff nine shells in the tube. If I needed more than ten shotgun shells for a single engagement, it was time to go to pistols or, more likely, it would be the end of the world.

All my minishells were slugs. With three times the mass and velocity of a 9mm bullet, a minislug would do a number on anyone. As a bonus, I could pull off a hostage rescue shot without worrying about pellet spread.

I loaded up my gun bag with my weapons, accessories, ammo and cleaning supplies. I still had a bit of space left, so I jammed in even more ammo. On top of the gun bag I placed a small messenger bag filled with shotgun shells. Next to it, I placed my martial arts training bag.

The holy trinity of combat was to move, shoot and communicate. With the first two sorted, I moved on to the last.

I'd stashed a half-dozen burner phones and SIM cards in my closet, none of them used. Among them was a Nullphone, the most secure smartphone in the world. Running on a proprietary Android-based operating system, it was designed from the ground up for maximum security and armed with a suite of security and encryption software. No one had the number for that phone, and with a burner app I could easily generate fresh numbers. I'd bought them all shortly after the Morgan Arts Center incident, saving them against the day when a supervillain or gangbanger decided to take a swipe at me.

Today was that day.

I powered down my personal phone, tossed it into a storage box, and pocketed both my Nullphone and police-issue smartphone. The other burner phones went into the backpack.

With the essentials secured, I moved on to my other kit.

My plate carrier and helmet hung from the side of the safe. They'd go into storage too. Armor was for bad luck, not bad tactics. I wasn't going to war; I was trying to avoid a fight. If I had to go to guns, I wouldn't have time to put on armor.

But the plate carrier was set up for an AR, and it was convenient for staging AR-15 mags. I folded up the carrier and tried stuffing it into the backpack. No dice. It was too large.

The plate carrier was a two-part setup, a Haley Strategic chest rig mounted on a Mayflower plate carrier. I peeled off the chest rig and mated it to the original H-harness. Now it fit snugly in the backpack.

The top shelf of the gun safe held other odds and ends. Passport, bank statements, Social Security card, certificates from a half-dozen firearms training institutes. And a pair of thumb drives sitting on a sheet of paper.

They weren't ordinary thumb drives; they were my cryptocurrency wallets, holding half of my life savings in digital assets. The paper listed my emergency passwords and mnemonics.

I hid the wallets and password paper in my pack. The documents went into the storage boxes.

I stuffed the remaining guns and ammo into the two empty gym bags Tom had brought. My handguns and so-called assault weapons went into one bag, the remaining long guns in the other. After some creative juggling, I managed to stuff the larger blades into the bags. The smaller ones went into the storage boxes. When I was done, every bag and box was filled to bursting.

There was one last thing I hadn't touched yet. The Box.

Everyone who ever served has a Box. Mine was an olive green footlocker, bought surplus, emblazoned with the gold Eagle, Globe and Anchor of the Corps, parked next to my main safe.

Inside the Box was the detritus and keepsakes of years: old

uniforms, faded but still fitting; certificates and paperwork and files from so many schools and too many bases; two copies of my DD214, one redacted, the other complete; challenge coins in custom cases; boxed-up flags, one of them still rust-red with old blood; photographs I couldn't hang on the walls; citations for medals I wouldn't wear.

Everything inside the locker was a memory I couldn't discard. My time in the Corps was the best of days, the worst of days, the glory days. Days of pain and blood and sweat and tears and laughter, days when unceasing agony piled on until it felt like a mountain of knives in my back and bricks on my bones, days when it seemed the world had ended in ice and fire and smoke and blood, days that made everything I'd done worth it.

After leaving the Corps, nothing I'd done came close. Not in the police, not even in STAR.

The Buddha said that attachment was the root of all suffering, and inside the locker there was only an ocean of hurt. But I couldn't discard it. I couldn't walk away from the days that had made me.

I placed the locker atop the storage containers, then stepped back and thought about the things I needed and the things I'd packed. I wouldn't be able to come back here, not for a long while. As far as possible I had to take everything I needed with me. I was almost done but...

I thought again about the *Shoninki* and the six essential tools of the ninja. I wasn't a ninja, but essentials were essentials. I rummaged through my things and made up for my deficiencies.

There. Done.

I couldn't take everything with me. The washing machine, the futon, the furniture and other bulk items couldn't come with me. But I could live without them. This was only a temporary situation.

"I'm finished!" I called out.

Tom sauntered in. "Finally."

I shrugged. "Only got one pair of hands."

Tom called Danny down from the roof. I passed off some of the shoulder bags to them, then donned my multi-pack, Amped my strength, and picked up the boxes. It was like picking up a cloud.

Back downstairs, the receptionist gaped at us again.

"Are you... what *are* you doing?" she asked.

I flashed her my most winsome smile.

"Moving stuff around."

"You look like you're moving out."

"I'll be back."

11

SANCTUARY

Walking away was easy. I'd spent my entire life walking away from something. But doing it in a way that wouldn't burn the people around me took some planning.

We drove to a self-storage unit in downtown Halo City, where I put down money for a three-month contract. It wasn't cheap, but the place was as secure as a civilian facility could be. Exterior fence topped with barbed wire, security cameras, biometric access controls, and a security guard on duty 24/7. Shame the guard wasn't armed.

I insisted on buying my own padlock though. A huge Stanley Hardware padlock, with a shielded shackle, anti-drill plate, and anti-pick pins. Short of destroying the lock, there was no way to defeat it —at least, not without risking unwanted attention.

As Danny stood watch outside, Tom and I moved my stuff inside my unit. The sum of my worldly possessions—two storage containers, two gym bags, the martial arts bag, the hurt locker—fit inside a room half the size of my sleeping space. That might not be a bad thing.

Just before we left, I gave Danny and Tom the number for my Nullphone. Danny resumed his patrol, while Tom dropped me off at the nearest car rental agency. I told the saleswoman that a drunk driver had crashed into my car yesterday. Fortunately, I wasn't inside when it happened, but the car was completely totaled, and I needed a replacement posthaste. She was only too happy to offer me a sea-blue Ford Fiesta. I topped off the tank at a gas station and headed back to Chinatown.

The guerrilla must move amongst the people as a fish swims in the sea. And if the enemy had a place he wouldn't touch, all the better.

El Trece were animals. They peddled drugs to kids and recruited them out of high school as mules and killers. They smuggled contraband and illegal immigrants across the border, then forced men into sweatshops and women and children into brothels. Every murder they planned was public and savage, teaching everyone to fear them. For all that, there was one place they would never, ever, desecrate.

The Church.

There were two ways to leave El Trece. The first was to die. The second was to join a church. For decades, churches have led community outreach and rehabilitation programs among the poor, the disenfranchised and the street animals of Halo City.

Anyone who tired of The Life could walk through the church doors and find sanctuary. Even the most black-hearted among El Trece wouldn't dare touch anyone born again in the light of the Holy Spirit. If only because killing churchgoers was bad optics.

Regardless of why they refused to attack a church, I could use it against El Trece, and find some sanctuary myself.

The evening sun painted the sky the color of burnt sienna. Traffic snarled up like it always did this time of the day. Inching past the Civic Center, at the border between Chinatown and Koreatown, I saw the spire.

A spear composed of intricate columns and tipped with a cross, the spire stabbed at the sky and towered over the neighborhood. Just beside the spire was the Church of the Immaculate Heart of Mary.

There was much to admire here. The Neo-Gothic aesthetics, the rich stained glass, the crosses carved from rich, deep wood, the alabaster statue of Mary in the courtyard just in front of the church. Best of all, the spire offered clean lines of fire all around, and the brick walls were thick enough to stop rifle bullets.

Off to the side of the church, there was a single-story white-painted building. It was the clergy house, one-half administrative office and one-half living quarters. I parked my car and stepped through the blue glass double doors.

The reception area was small but cozy. Magazine stands next to the entrance held copies of the church's newsletter and Catholic magazines. A potted plant in the corner gave the room some life. A young Vietnamese woman, her hair tied up in a bun, sat behind the front desk. She smiled as I approached.

"Detective Song!" she said. "Hi!"

I smiled back. "Hi, Anna. Please tell Father Joshua I'm here."

"Of course. Please, sit, sit."

Setting my bags down, I sat in a well-worn leather couch. Anna picked up her landline and dialed a number from heart.

"Hello? Father Josh, it's Anna. Detective Song has arrived. Yes, of course." Hanging up, she turned to me. "The Father is on his way."

"Thank you," I replied.

"Do you want a drink?" she asked. "We have tea and coffee."

"Tea please."

She made her way to the pantry in the corner. "No milk or sugar, right?"

"That's right. You still remember, eh."

"Thanks!"

She placed a teabag in a cup and filled it with hot water. She placed it on a saucer and served them to me with both hands. I stood and accepted the drink in the same way.

"Thank you," I said.

"You're welcome!" she beamed.

I sipped at the brew. Black tea, commercial grade, nearly tasteless. But I wasn't above accepting drinks when offered.

Anna returned to the table, typing away at a computer. I

wandered around the room, reading the posters and notices hung on
the walls, all the while keeping an eye on the doors.

Two men entered the room, both dressed in black cassocks and
clerical collars. One was short and middle-aged, an ugly scar running
across his right cheek. The other was taller and younger, his skin
fresh and taut.

I bowed to them. "Father Josh, Father Matthew. Thank you for
coming. It's good to see you again."

They bowed back.

"Adam," the older priest, Father Joshua Park, said, "the pleasure is
all ours."

"How did your surgery go?" I asked.

He grinned. "Perfectly. Look."

He held up his right hand and wiggled his fingers, every motion
accompanied by a subtle whirring almost inaudible to everyone
but me.

"It's just like the real thing," he continued, "complete with tactile
sensors."

"Congratulations!" I replied.

"Thank you. And thank the Lord also."

During my patrol days, and later in the Asian Gang Unit, I established contact with many community leaders in my beat. It was part
of the HCPD's policing strategy, to forge strong ties with the public
we served and to keep a finger on the pulse of the neighborhoods.
Among my early contacts were Father Joshua Park, his curate Father
Matthew Nguyen, and Matthew's younger sister, Anna, the church's
administrator.

Some forty years ago, Joshua Park fell in with the Ghost Killers, a
small-time Asian-American gang that roamed these streets. He
dropped out of school, his family chased him out of his home, and he
almost became a statistic.

One summer evening, while he and his crew were having dinner
at a local noodle store, a rival gang entered the establishment. Both
sides exchanged stares, then harsh words, and escalated to gunfire.

When the dust settled, three people were dead and four more

wounded. Only the innocent had died that night, a waitress and a couple that got caught in the crossfire. Young Joshua had caught three bullets to his right arm and shoulder.

The rounds had pulverized tissue, bone, and nerve far beyond the ability of modern medicine to patch up—and back then, there were no Primes to save the day. By the time he was discharged from hospital, he could barely move his right arm, much less grasp anything. And he was right-handed.

After long, long years of prison time, physical therapy and soul-searching, he dropped out of his old crew and found his way to the Church of the Immaculate Heart.

Over the next few decades, he served on overseas missions, went to seminary, then worked his way back here, to the church that had saved him.

Here he was now. The last I'd heard from him, his congregation decided to give him a special birthday present by crowdfunding a prosthetic arm. It was next-gen cybertech, coated with synthetic skin, filled with miniature ultra-precise servos and sensors and nerve interfaces, and controlled by a brain implant.

"How's it working out for you?" I asked.

"It's perfect," Josh declared. "I just need to re-learn how to use my right hand all over again."

"I heard it's a difficult process."

"Yes, but one of my flock has connected me with a cybernetics specialist in Halo City General Hospital. One of the best. I visit him once a week, and he says I'm making a lot of progress."

As he spoke, Father Josh idly twirled and rotated his arm and wrist and fingers, as though they would go still forever if left to idle.

"Marvelous," I said. "What about you, Father Matthew? How are things?"

"Good, good," he said. "Father Josh has been letting me handle prayer services and workshops by myself. It's been a challenging, but enlightening, experience."

"He's got a lot of potential," the parish priest said, beaming.

"Thanks," the curate said shyly.

"How are things with you, Detective?" Father Josh asked. "I heard on the phone you had some important matters to discuss."

"I do, but they are strictly confidential," I said.

"Is it of a spiritual or secular matter?"

"Sp..." I corrected myself. "Secular."

"Well, Anna has been handling confidential church correspondence for the past two years now." His eyes sparkled. "Besides, you can surely trust a Catholic priest to keep secrets, yes?"

I downed a mouthful of tea. "Fair enough."

I told the three of them about El Trece, about the hit earlier this morning, and my current situation.

"I think it's a revenge hit," I concluded. "Until this affair blows over, I'd like to stay in your church."

"I'm glad you're safe," Father Josh said.

"Thank you," I replied.

"I—" Father Josh began.

"Why do you want to stay here?" Father Matthew interrupted. "What about your relatives?"

"El Trece are... ruthless. If they can't get at you directly, they will go after your friends and family. I can't drag mine into this."

"There are plenty of motels, aren't there?" Anna asked.

I grinned. "Motels charge rent. A church doesn't."

Everyone laughed heartily. Even Father Matthew.

"More seriously though," I said, "I'm still the subject of a police investigation. *Two* investigations, actually. I need a fixed address where the HCPD can reach me, and I have more confidence in the security of your church than a motel."

Father Matthew's eyes bored into mine.

"Don't the police have facilities for you? Like witness protection?"

"I'm not a witness to anything. I don't qualify."

I had my own suspicions about the police brass, but I wasn't going to reveal them to outsiders. There was only so much you could confess to a priest.

"This is most... unusual," Matthew said.

"Indeed," Father Josh said, "but given the circumstances we'd be happy to help."

"Father?" Matthew began.

"*Detective* Song has done right by us. It's only proper to do the same."

In my time in the Asian Gang Unit, I'd busted a few gangsters who had harassed his churchgoers. Father Josh had been fully cooperative with my investigations, and he was pleased with the results.

What goes around comes around.

"Thank you," I said. "I don't mean to impose on you but..."

"Don't worry," he said. "We have a guest room in the back. Please, stay as long as you like."

"Father, there are gangsters after him," Father Matthew said.

"El Trece won't dare to attack a church," I said. "They have *never* attacked a church."

"There's a first time for everything."

"Matthew, Jesus stood up to an empire and gave his life for all mankind," Father Josh said. "How can we call ourselves Christians if we are afraid of mere street thugs?"

Father Matthew bowed. "I apologize."

"It's nothing to apologize for," I said.

Father Josh smiled at me. "Feel free to stay. You're always welcome here."

"Thank you. I'll make it up to you. I promise."

Father Josh held both hands up. "No, please, *we* are the ones making it up to *you*."

The guest room was austere. There was a small bed in the corner, under a simple wooden crucifix. Next to the bed was a small nightstand and a plain plastic lamp. A closet faced the bed. Light streamed in through a window on the far wall. As I inspected the room, I found a small Bible in the nightstand. That was all.

But it was enough.

I set my bags down, then followed Father Josh on a guided tour. There was a communal bathroom down the hall, shared by everyone in the house. A storeroom filled with junk. A kitchenette where we could prepare light meals. In exchange for letting me stay, I promised to help keep the pantry and fridge stocked. It went down well with the priests. In gratitude, they gave the password for the church's public Wi-Fi network.

Returning to my room, I contemplated how someone might try to kill me. It wouldn't be too complicated. Kick down the door, burst in through the window, pepper the bed with bullets. The closet wasn't large enough for me to hide inside, and rolling under the bed and waiting to die was not an option.

I reinforced the door with a firefighter wedge. Sturdier than a regular rubber wedge, it would keep the door chocked and buy me time to respond to an intrusion. I drew the curtains across the window, then hung a noisemaker to the latch. It looked like a simple wind chime, but the moment it moved it would kick up an unmistakable metallic racket.

I staged my shotgun inside the closet. At such close quarters, I was better off using my bare hands or a knife, but if an attacker had friends, the gun would even the odds. The carbine was for an Alamo moment, or if I had to fall back to the main church building.

Now that I was reasonably secure, I pulled out my phone and switched it on. Emails rushed into my inbox. Confirmations of my appointments with the Inquisition and Dr. Murphy. James Moss promising to show up. Administrative matters, all of them unimportant.

Which itself was an important clue. The brass *still* hadn't reached out to me. In my previous shootings, the leadership and the media relations staff always contacted me within 48 hours. But in the past week, all I'd heard from them was pro forma emails. Even Sergeant Oliveira and the rest of the team would have contacted me, had IA lifted the sequestration order.

It must be the protests. With so much publicity, the brass would be too busy covering their asses to care about a mere cop. In the halls of power, politics always came first.

As always, you can only count on your own.

With that in mind, I called Jim Wilson.

"Who's this?" he asked.

"Adam Song. I got a new number."

"Ah, okay. What's up?"

"I won't be able to attend classes any time soon."

"That rarely happens."

"I heard through the grapevine that El Trece has me in their sights. I've been advised to lie low for a while."

"Damn. Sorry man. Anything I can do to help?"

"Not now. But El Trece might come sniffing around the community center for a while."

"If they do, I'll give 'em a lesson they'll never forget."

I smiled despite myself. "Be sure to let the cops in on the fun too."

"Of course. But listen: if you need help, any kind of help at all, just call me and I'll come running."

Warmth rushed through my chest and up my face.

"Thanks," I choked.

"No problem, brother. Times like this, we gotta stick together."

I took a moment to compose myself, then called Shi Shifu. He was teaching the evening gongfu class, so I left him a voice mail in Chinese.

"This is Song Gao Yang. I've been informed that the El Trece street gang is targeting me. Don't worry, I'm taking security measures, and I'll be fine. However, they may visit the temple with bad intentions. Please be on the lookout for any suspicious activity, especially aggressive or dubious-looking Hispanic males with tattoos of the letters 'ET' or the Latin numbers for 'thirteen.' El Trece also prefers green clothing, especially green bandannas. If you see anyone who fits the profile, call the police immediately."

One last call left. A surge of resistance rose within me. I didn't want to do it, but it had to be done. I centered myself in the moment, breathing deep, allowed the feeling to pass, and called my parents.

ANOTHER EVENING, another late-night meeting over dim sum. This time, Tom met me outside the entrance. Dressed in his sharp gray suit, he looked more like an executive than Halo City's premier bodyguard, which no doubt was the point of his sartorial choice. I found him wearing a wide smile.

"What's so funny?" I asked.

He gestured at the gun free zone sign. "Really, Adam?"

I shrugged. "It's their property. Are you armed?"

"It's illegal to carry a concealed firearm without a permit."

And no one without connections to City Hall or the HCPD ever got a permit in Halo City. Not even Primes.

"In other words, you're armed."

"Not with a gun, Detective."

The staff was expecting us. The maitre'd ushered us into the back, past empty tables and employees cleaning up after a long night. My family awaited us at a table in the far corner.

My parents were here, Father in his chef's uniform, Mother in a bottle-green dress. Aaron, too, and next to him was his wife, Julie.

Aaron had done well for himself. After high school, he went to university and earned a degree in business administration, with a specialization in hospitality. He came home to manage the business side of the restaurant, allowing Father to focus solely on cooking, his one true passion. Aaron immersed himself in the local community and met Julie Ng, daughter of a local curtain contractor. Eight years of marriage and two children later, they still radiated genuine happiness, their eyes sparkling in the light.

Sometimes I wonder if Aaron had drawn the better hand in life.

We exchanged greetings, me in Cantonese, Tom in English, then made some small talk and placed our orders.

"De, you're not cooking today?" I asked.

"I want to see how our assistant chef will do today," he replied.

"Is he any good?" Tom asked.

"He is... acceptable."

Aaron smiled. "He thinks Ron can take over the kitchen."

Father snorted. "He still has a long way to go. He puts too much sugar, too little salt, sometimes he leaves the food on the pan too long..."

I turned to Tom. "He's only this nitpicky if he thinks his employee is worth the energy."

"*Aiya*, don't be so mean to *Ah De* lah!" Mother said.

Tom chuckled. "I understand where you're coming from. In my company, we're always hardest on the new guys, especially those with potential."

"What do you work as?" Julie asked.

"I represent an executive protection and security consultancy company," he replied. "Aegis Security Group."

"Is that like a bodyguard?"

He smiled neutrally. "Yes. But I also help clients harden their security and assess potential threats."

"Aegis Security..." Aaron said. "Is that the company founded by the Prime named Aegis?"

"Yes."

"Ah. What's it like to work with a Prime?"

Tom's smile remained. "Aegis is a pro. He's got decades of experience in the military, and that's before he gained his powers and became an executive protection specialist. We've protected some of the world's highest-profile personalities, and I'm proud to say we have never lost a single client."

"What's your role in the company?" Father asked.

"I interface with clients and manage assignments. Occasionally I go out into the field as a team leader."

"Aegis isn't coming today?"

"He prefers I handle the business side of matters."

Like me, Aegis kept his identity masked. But without the force of law backing him up, he relied on more traditional operational and personnel security measures. Sometimes that meant talking about himself in the third person.

"But we are here to talk security?"

"Yes."

"Why?" Mother asked, pointedly looking at me.

"I have reason to believe that El Trece is gunning for me," I said slowly, "and they will be targeting you."

My parents went quiet.

"Who's El Trece?" Julie asked.

"A Hispanic street gang that aspires to become a cartel," Tom replied.

"Why are they targeting you? What did you do to offend them?"

"El Trece has an honor code," I said carefully. "If you kill one of theirs, the survivors are required to kill you in return. I shot one of their members some time ago, and now I heard that they are sending hitmen after me."

She covered her mouth. "That's horrible!"

"*Yen zha*," Father muttered. *Scumbags.*

"Will you be alright?" Mother asked.

"I can see to my own security measures, but they might come after you instead." I looked at Aaron and Julie. "They might also target Oscar and Sophie."

"*Ham ga can*," Father swore. *May their families die.*

"Yeah, that's how El Trece works," I said. "If they can't find you, they'll go after your relatives. You need to upgrade your security."

"Is that why Tom is here?" Mother asked.

"Yes," Tom said.

The waiter chose that moment to lay out the dishes and tea. My family paused to sample the food. Half a beat later, Tom mimicked them, expertly using his own chopsticks.

I picked up a *siu lung bau*, brought it to my lips and bit down. Hot, rich broth flooded my mouth. I sucked down every last drop before chewing on the meat and vegetable filling.

"This *shaomai* is magnificent," Tom said, referring to a steamed pork-filled dumpling topped with prawns and mushrooms.

"You mean the *siu mai?* It's too salty," Father pronounced.

"Really?" Tom wondered.

I tried it myself, dipping it in soy sauce.

"It's not bad," I said.

"*Aiya*, this late at night shouldn't eat too much salty food. Not good for health. Ron needs to know when to adjust the seasoning."

Mother simply smiled and shook her head.

Father looked back at us. "What kind of security upgrade are you thinking about?"

"My company has a safe house at the outskirts of the city," Tom replied. "It's heavily fortified, with alarms and an intrusion detection system, and a security team nearby. You can stay there until the situation blows over."

"This is too much," Aaron said. "The kids are still in school."

"El Trece won't spare children."

"What about Adam? Doesn't he need it more?" Mother asked.

"I've made my own arrangements," I said. "I'll be fine. But now we're concerned about you."

Father frowned. "You want us to, what, just stop work, pack up and move to the safe house?"

"That's the ideal, yes."

"Cannot."

"What are your concerns?"

"Loong Moon is our life. It's our home. Everyone lives upstairs. If we leave now, our life is over."

"It's only a temporary measure."

"For how long?"

"Until El Trece stops looking for you."

Aaron shook his head. "Mr. Tom, allow me to explain. In the F&B business, profit margins are tight. We're operating at a profit margin of six and a half percent. We must support a family of six on that income, including two children. If we just pack up and go... I don't know how we can survive."

"Is the danger really so serious?" Father asked.

Tom looked at me and raised an eyebrow. I steeled myself with a sip of tea.

"El Trece sent killers after me this morning."

The women recoiled.

"They did WHAT?!" Aaron demanded.

"*Yau mo gau cho!*" Father exclaimed. *Are you kidding?*

I raised my hands.

"I'm okay, everything is okay, but I can't talk about it. It's an ongoing investigation. But yes, the threat is real."

"But so far they're only after you," Mother said.

"Better to be safe than sorry," Tom said.

"We didn't give in to Tin Fo," Father said. "We won't give in to El Trece."

Tin Fo was the triad that claimed ownership of Chinatown. Where El Trece reveled in brute force, Tin Fo preferred infiltration, subversion, and subtlety. What passed for subtlety among the triads anyway.

"I busted the Tin Fo gangsters who tried to drop by," I said. "But I can't protect you from El Trece now."

"Why not?" Julie demanded.

"After a shooting, an officer is placed on admin leave, then on desk duties," I replied.

"I could station an armed guard outside the restaurant 24/7. How does that sound?" Tom asked.

"People will talk," Aaron said. "They'll wonder why we need protection. They'll say that it's too dangerous to come here, and we'll lose business."

"Let me be frank," Tom said. "That gun free zone sticker is not going to stop El Trece. The only language they understand is violence."

"They are gangsters, not terrorists," Father said. "They won't just come in and shoot the place up."

"Yeah, yeah," Julie said. "I know this sounds racist, but I have to say this, okay? This is Chinatown. Hispanics don't come here often. Those who do stand out everywhere they go. If El Trece comes, we can see them coming."

"If they come, we can call the police," Mother added.

"The police take between fifteen to thirty minutes to respond to a call," I said. "Plenty of time to do lots of damage."

"Yeah, but it's not like they're targeting us now, right?"

I swallowed some tea and forced my fists to unclench. "If they do, the police won't respond in time."

"But they're supposed to save us," she insisted. "You're a cop, you should know that, right?"

"When they do arrive, it'll be all over," I said.

"How about this," Tom said. "We have armed security officers running patrol routes nearby. I could ask them to swing by your place while out on patrol and report any suspicious activity or persons."

"The police can do that, right?"

"This is in addition to police patrols," Tom said.

"That's... acceptable," Aaron said.

"How much does it cost?" Father asked.

"Don't worry about it," Tom replied. "It'll only add a few more minutes to the patrol routes; it won't cost us anything. It won't be right to charge you."

"Thank you very much."

Tom smiled. "No worries."

"Just one last thing," I said.

"What is it?" Father asked.

I slid two burner phones across the table.

"These are new phones," I said. "I saved my number in them. From now on, use only those phones to contact me."

"That's a bit much, isn't it?" Julie asked.

"Only if you don't have gangsters after you."

The mood chilled. But at least they accepted the phones. And supper ended amicably. Once outside the restaurant, outside the earshot of the staff, Tom sighed.

"They're stubborn, aren't they?"

"They're civilians," I said. "Civilians who grew up in low-crime authoritarian cities. They've never had to seriously think about their personal protection, and they've never had to interact with the police."

"That makes our lives more difficult."

"And shorter."

He chuckled. "Ain't that the truth?"

In this line of work, you aren't just saving people from monsters in human skin. You're saving people from themselves. Normalcy bias is the norm, and common sense isn't common.

"If El Trece knows who I am, where I live, it won't take much for them to find Loong Moon," I said.

"Yeah. I'm going to take a personal interest in this case."

"You're going into the field too?"

"Of course. If my ASOs see something suspicious, they'll let me know. I'll contact you too, and we'll coordinate our response."

"Sounds like a plan," I said.

My police-issue phone vibrated in my cargo pocket. Unknown number. I picked up the call but waited for the caller to speak.

"Is this Detective Adam Song?"

"Who's asking?" I replied.

"This is Detective Derrick Duran, HCPD Arson and Explosives. Are you Detective Song?"

"Yeah. What's wrong?"

"Your house has just been torched."

12

DECLARATION

By the time I returned to my apartment, the fire was out. The firefighters were packing up, but the scent of acrid smoke lingered. Bright yellow fire tape cordoned off the street. Cops patrolled the edges of the scene, keeping away bystanders and gawkers.

I left my vehicle a block away from the site and covered the rest of the distance on foot, watching the passers-by and cars around me. There was the usual crowd of gawkers, but they were all looking at the fire scene, not the roads and sidewalks. No spotters or sicarios.

The windows of my apartment had been blown out, the balcony and external wall blackened with ash. Tongues of soot licked at my neighbors' windows. I couldn't look inside my apartment from here, but already I knew the damage was total.

Picking my way through gawkers, my badge held high, I found the fire line. A patrolman directed me to Detective Duran, standing by a nearby streetlamp.

"Detective Song," Duran said by way of greeting. "Awfully sorry this happened to you. But at least you're safe."

I nodded. "Thank you."

"It must be a difficult time for you," he continued. "Are you ready to answer some questions?"

I wouldn't say it was difficult, but glancing up at my apartment again, I felt a hollow pang in my chest. I'd lived in that home for a bit over a year now. It was gone now. But I'd stored everything important to me in a secure location, I still had a roof over my head, and I was still alive. What few things I'd lost was immaterial.

"Go ahead," I said.

Taking out his notepad, he began with a list of pro forma questions. Where I was earlier this evening, whether anyone lived in the apartment and if there was anything valuable inside, and if I had any enemies.

"El Trece," I said. "They've got the motive and manpower to do this."

"El Trece?" Duran asked, clicking his pen. "What happened?"

"I shot a shot-caller last week, shot four more gangsters this morning."

"You shot..." Duran's eyes narrowed. "You're Amp?"

"Let's not go spreading that around."

"Understood." He scribbled into his notebook. "Damn, Amp, if they tracked you down, there's a massive leak in our security."

"You can say that again."

"We found a torched car in the parking lot too. I'm guessing it's yours."

"Got a picture?"

He took out his phone and showed me a photo. There was nothing left of the car, just a blackened, burnt-out wreck resting on patches of melted rubber. Even the license plate was melted off. But the wrecker sat in the same spot I'd parked my Honda last night.

"It's mine," I said.

"I'm sorry, man."

I clenched my fists. I'd bought that car after leaving the Corps. Second-hand and cheap, but I'd refurbished it over the years, and it ran just like new. It was...

I breathed in. Breathed out.

It was gone. As surely as yesterday was gone, I could never bring it back. Remaining attached to it, and my home, was pointless. It was just a tool, a nonliving thing of some sentimental value. Shock, anger, grief, it was all natural, but there was no sense being overly attached to something that could no longer work.

A thought flashed through my head. The opposition knew my address and my car. What else did they know?

"You all right?" Duran asked.

"Yeah, just... trying to come to grips with it."

"I understand completely. Is your house and car insured?"

"Yup. I kept the insurance policies in storage."

"That's something, at least."

"I've got a question for you."

"Fire away." He winced. "Sorry."

"Don't worry about it. Normally, the HCFD investigates fires, doesn't it? A&E only gets involved if the FD suspects criminal involvement. Why did they call you up?"

"There's no 'suspecting' criminal involvement in this case. We *know* there's an arsonist."

"How?"

"When the perp made entry, he vaporized the hinges and the lock of the front door and kicked his way in. It's like he took a thermal lance to the door."

"Bad guys don't normally carry that kind of kit around."

"Exactly. Once he stepped in, he melted the security cameras. *And* the control hub in the main office. We're not sure how he did it; we're hoping we can pull something off backup. If there *is* a backup."

"Is anyone hurt?"

"No, thank God. The night receptionist was on a bathroom break when it went down. She called 911. The firefighters evacuated everybody else safely."

"That's a relief."

"Absolutely. The receptionist stayed put in the bathroom until the FD rescued her. During that time, the suspect must have gone upstairs, did what he did, then came out and torched your car before leaving. We're still canvassing for witnesses and videos, but when the firefighters arrived at your door, they found this."

He showed me another photo. Seven black words seared into the wall next to my front door.

AMP

WE ARE COMING FOR YOU

XIII

"Son of a *bitch*," I whispered.

"That's not the worst part," Duran said.

"What is?"

"The words were burned into the wall a half-inch deep."

"Blowtorch?"

"Or a Prime."

THE FIRST TIME I faced a Prime, I was a freshly-minted Recon Marine, finally acknowledged as a life form slightly more useful than a boot. As the newest guy in the company, brimming with too much testosterone and too little common sense, I was raring to prove myself.

The world obliged.

The state formerly known as the Islamic Republic of Iran was on the verge of meltdown. Decades of resentment against the ruling theocracy boiled over into street protests and bank runs. Things came to a head when a retired Prime publicly unveiled herself and sided with the protesters. When the regime sent troops to arrest her, violence broke out.

The unrest rapidly spread throughout the country. The Supreme Leader and his mullahs mobilized the military and police to crack down on the demonstrations. But many of the rank-and-file, and many officers, defied their superiors and threw in their lot with the protesters. For every military and police Prime deployed against the people, two more defected to serve the people.

What began as widespread protests erupted into civil war. As the world watched, all eyes turned to the Strait of Hormuz. Twenty percent of the world's petroleum passed through the narrow Strait; if the regime closed the Strait, the results would be disastrous. The oil must flow, and only the United States could guarantee that.

The President deployed a carrier battle group and a Marine Expeditionary Brigade to the region. Their mission was to keep the Strait of Hormuz open. Naturally, our presence angered the regime, and the myriad of enemies we had made over the past two decades who called the Middle East home.

A week before we were due to arrive, regime loyalists closed off the Strait, citing 'self-defense against invasion'. They were trying to buy public support by rallying them against an external aggressor.

It didn't work.

The might of the most powerful Navy on Earth fell on the Strait. Warplanes flew night and day, unleashing hundreds of tons of ordnance on the woefully under-armed Iranian military. Cruise missiles pounded military installations deeper inland. Swarms of anti-ship missiles and anti-missile missiles filled the air and sea with fire and smoke. Submarines dueled in the depths of the sea and assassinated warships. As the battle raged, many Iranian ships suddenly switched sides, joining the Americans against the loyalists. A hundred hours later, nothing remained of the loyalist Navy.

But it was only the beginning.

As soon as we took control of the Strait, the second wave of attacks began. Anti-ship missiles launched from mobile launchers and aircraft. Suicide swarms of small, fast boats packed with explosives. Divers with limpet mines. The regime couldn't hope to match us in a straight-up fight, so they fought the war of the flea, making themselves too small, too agile and too ubiquitous to destroy all at once.

Day and night, they harassed us, occasionally drawing blood. On bad nights, I could still remember flowers of flame blossoming over oil-blackened waters, the never-ending screams of klaxons, the steady drumbeat of M2 machine guns mixing with the high-pitched liquid tearing of Phalanx autocannons as they belted out walls of lead in a last-ditch attempt to intercept incoming boats and missiles, and the explosions when they failed.

We weren't going to sit there and take everything they could throw at us, of course. The boats and rocket launchers and divers had to come from somewhere. It was up to the Recon Marines to find them.

On the morning of the seventh day in-theater, my six-man team was inserted into Iran. The brass suspected that the enemy had a forward operating base in a village by the coast. Our mission was to observe the village for signs of enemy activity.

Infiltrating the area just after midnight, we set up within a sea of grassy sand dunes a couple of kilometers out, set up long-range lenses and watched the village. I saw armed soldiers wandering the streets and enforcing a night-time curfew, and in the daylight, I saw more soldiers keeping order on the streets. But there was no sign of boats being laden with explosives, divers readying for a combat mission, or rocket launchers preparing for sudden salvoes.

As the sun set on the third day, a hot, dust-laden wind swept across our position, kicking up clouds of sand. Soon, the sand cloud hid the town from sight.

We dug in, covering our noses and mouths with shemaghs. For hours we lay in place as the sun-baked sand scourged our exposed skin.

Then, through the clouds, I saw movement.

Soldiers. A company of them, advancing slowly and cautiously. They kept low to the ground, trying to hide behind the sand, but here and there the clouds parted for a moment, long enough to betray their positions. And their intent.

We remained in place and stayed quiet. Darkness fell, and the heat of the day surrendered to a bone-deep chill. Yet the sandstorm continued unabated, and the soldiers continued to close in on us.

They were almost invisible to the naked eye, but with our night vision and thermal imagers, we tracked their progress through the storm.

It wasn't a patrol. They were creeping up on us, setting up a deliberate attack. As the maneuver platoons closed in, another platoon broke off to prepare their heavy weapons.

Somehow, they knew we were here.

We let them come. Once they were a half-klick out, the team leader, Staff Sergeant Herrera, sent out the word: prepare to engage.

As the slack man, I carried the team's M249 Squad Automatic Weapon. Through my night sight, the world was colored in shades of brilliant green and inky black. Six bright green beams played across the forward edge of the enemy line. Infrared aiming lasers. And still the soldiers kept coming.

A hundred meters out, Herrera whispered a single word.

"Fire."

Gunshots crackled in the dark. I set the M249 to full auto and hosed down the kill zone with six-round bursts, left to right, right to left. Blazing tracers stabbed into the night, and as they vanished men gargled and screamed.

"Break contact! Break contact!" Herrera shouted.

We fell back, one pair at a time, laying down covering fire in the enemy's direction. No taking chances, not this deep in enemy territory.

The enemy pursued. Automatic fire gnawed at our heels. Mortars and rockets spiraled wildly into the dark. The sandstorm they had used for concealment now hid us from their sights.

We fired and ran, ran and fired, hammering the enemy with rapid aimed fire, short bursts, the odd M320 grenade. I shot at movement and muzzle flashes, keeping up a steady stream of fire. We had no air support, no artillery, nothing but what we had on hand. I aimed carefully and made my shots count.

Finally, the Iranians gave up the chase and halted to lick their wounds. We faded into the desert.

We were compromised, and the mission was scrubbed. Herrera called for an emergency extract. We marched to the landing zone, dug in, and awaited the helicopter.

After the heat of the day and the vigor of the firefight, the night chill was a welcome relief. For all of a second, until my sweat cooled against my skin and leached the warmth from my body.

We huddled together and waited. I didn't think any of us slept that night.

As rays of orange light streaked across the brightening sky, I heard the distant whipping of chopper blades. Looking up, I saw a tiny dark dot, zooming in towards us. A USMC Huey, come to pick us up.

The mission should have ended there. For a moment I allowed myself to relax.

Suddenly, powerful winds swept through the world. The Huey lost control, dropping into a death spiral. A wall of razor-sharp dust slammed into our position, tearing at clothes, ripping at exposed flesh. I pressed myself low, shielding my face with my shemagh. Sand grains blasted my goggles and scoured my ears. The wind whipped off my boonie hat.

And I bled.

At first, I didn't realize what I was looking at. It was as if a hundred paper cuts suddenly appeared on my uniform. On my arms, my legs, my thighs, my face. I blinked, and all at once blood oozed from the wounds and my nerves screeched in an infernal symphony of pain.

I fell to the ground, curling up in a ball, fighting the urge to scream lest I inhale the deadly dust. Blood-curdling cries rang out around me—the sounds of men dying.

Looking up, I saw a dark figure walk through the dust storm. It was as though the dust flowed around him, leaving him completely untouched. He sauntered towards us, as though he hadn't a care in the world.

Unseen knives sliced my face and arms. The uncanny wind shredded my gloves and ripped at my naked hands. I forced myself to stay still, to grit my teeth and force down the pain.

The figure came closer, closer, closer. Peering through the dust, I saw the G3 cradled in his arms.

I sprang up and stitched him up from chest to face.

The winds abruptly died. Dust fell like ultra-fine snow, drifting through the air. The world went quiet again, but through the ringing in my ears, I heard men cursing and grunting.

I inspected the body. The sand seemed to drink in the blood, revealing long, lean limbs and a curvy silhouette. A woman. What was left of her.

I wanted to forget what the SAW did to her face. I couldn't.

We'd taken two dead that day. Wind-razors had slashed their throats and arteries. Everyone had been slashed up, their uniforms running red with blood.

We grabbed our dead and ran. Injuries be damned, we had to move, or the rest of the Iranian Army would come with us. But every movement, no matter how slight, was agonizing, as though a thousand fire ants were chomping down all at once. As the sun rose it baked us under its unrelenting glare.

Wonder of wonders, the Huey had survived. The pilots had pulled out of the spiral at the last second and crash-landed a few miles away. By the time we got to them, the crew had managed to jumpstart the engines. We hauled aboard and got the hell out of Iran.

Much later, through informal channels, I learned that the woman was a Prime, a member of the Basij with the gift of wind manipulation. Her callsign was Samiel. The Iranians had exalted their Primes to near-mythological status, and killing one was a psychological blow. Her death sent shockwaves through the local garrison, contributing to their eventual desertion.

That day was a day of many firsts. The first time I'd gone to war. The first time I'd scored a confirmed personal kill. The first time I'd lost brothers in arms.

That day, I learned that with enough firepower, even Primes could die.

THIRTEEN YEARS and a gulf of blood stood between Samiel and me. She was only the first of many Primes I'd encountered and neutralized. After my time in the Corps, especially in the Task Force, having Prime hitmen after me was no longer a novel experience.

But having a Prime *sicario* with the courtesy to leave a declaration of war was new and... amusing.

After answering Duran's questions, I drove back to the church, thoughts tumbling and turning in my head. Professional killers don't leave warnings for their victims. They just set up the kill and execute. This guy was either an amateur or someone had ordered him to leave the message, and my money was on the latter.

El Trece knew where I lived. They failed the first time, so they sent a heavy hitter after me for a second try. If I were at home, the *sicario* would burn down the apartment with me inside it. Public, dramatic, brutal, exactly in line with El Trece strategy. If I weren't in, the hitter would burn down the apartment anyway and leave his message, attempting to rattle me and flush me out into the open.

Not a bad plan, but it counted on a target who would blindly react to their maneuvers. The simplest response to a provocation like this is do nothing.

More precisely, do nothing the enemy expects.

Back at the church, I discovered that the clergy office was empty, and the priests had turned in. I packed my guns and walked the grounds.

It was a quiet night. A peaceful night. There was no smoke here, no fire, just the chirping of crickets and the deep purring of passing cars. As I circled around the church, I noted the layout of the structures, the positions of security cameras, and potential vulnerabilities.

The cameras covered the doors to the church and the clergy house, but not the windows, and most definitely not the front gate. The gate itself was locked but scaling the fence would be a trivial exercise. The fence posts were simple metal spears aimed at the sky, joined by three bars running parallel to the ground. They were only slightly taller than me.

Straightaway I could see four ways to breach the fence. Mundane humans could simply climb over, using the crossbars to support their feet. To prevent impalement, they could throw a thick mattress on the spikes. Primes could cut the fence with their powers, jump over it, or walk right through it. And there were no guards.

I walked the neighborhood, studying the stores, the traffic, the grid-like layout of the roads and alleys. I identified a convenience store, a hardware shop, eateries, and, just two blocks away, a gun store. I logged them all in my mental map.

Back inside the clergy house, I took a long, cold shower, then sat at my desk and war-gamed multiple scenarios. How I would breach the church given so much time and resources, how I would defend against such an attack, the equipment I needed to mount a successful defense, the people I needed to rope in.

El Trece's resources were, in comparison to mine, nearly limitless. Sure, there might be a bona fide supervillain after me with the power to wield fire—but it didn't mean there weren't more, with different powers. Many small-time rogues had pledged themselves to some gang or other, including El Trece, and carved out their own little fiefdoms. Optimizing a defense against pyrokinetics was useless against someone who could walk through walls.

Awareness and invisibility. These were my main strengths. El Trece couldn't target someone they couldn't find, and if I saw an attack coming, I could respond to it appropriately. I needed to establish an early-warning system, fallback plans, evacuation routes.

When I checked the clock again, it was well past midnight. Fatigue weighed down my eyes, and I still had work to do in the morning. The moment my hair dried, I flopped into bed and dreamed of oily smoke and unquenchable flame and a torn-up woman under the desert sun.

It was still dark when I awoke. I cranked out five hundred Hindu push-ups, a thousand Hindu squats, twenty handstand push-ups, and three-minute front and back and side bridges. After a quick shower, I dressed in my best clothes and headed out.

The moment in my car, my Nullphone rang. The call came from the burner I had given my family. I answered immediately.

"Adam, it's Aaron. We have a problem."

"What is it?" I asked.

156 KAI WAI CHEAH

"The phone's been ringing non-stop. Every time we pick up, some woman shouts at us in Spanish. Julie says she's swearing at us, swearing to kill us, that sort of thing. And she keeps repeating herself, exactly the same way."

"It sounds like a robocall."

"A what?"

"A robot programmed to harass someone over the phone. It calls a target every second or so, and when he picks up it delivers a prerecorded message."

"*Mo gao chor...*" Aaron sighed. "That's not all. There's tons of spam in our inbox. Something like two thousand spam mails, last I checked."

"El Trece's harassing you."

"How do you know?"

"Who else has the motive?"

He grunted. "Why would they do it?"

"They're trying to flush me out. They burned my house down last night, and now—"

"They *what?* Burned your house down? What the hell?"

"I'm okay. I wasn't in it at that time, and I've already stored away everything I need. Now listen, expect things to get worse. They'll probably make a run at Loong Moon soon. They might even come after you, Julie or the children next. You *must* step up security."

"I will," he promised. "What do I do about the robocalls and the spam?"

"Disconnect your phone, ignore your mails and lodge a report with HCPD Cybercrime."

"We can't do that. Our suppliers and our customers need a way to reach us."

"Look, if the robocall program is still active, they're not going to reach you anyway. As for your inbox, if you want to maintain it, you'll need someone to watch the screen and mark spam full-time. At least until Cybercrime can give you better advice."

"Okay. Thanks. You be careful, okay?"

"You too."

Driving past City Hall, I saw a hundred and fifty-strong mob swarming the entrance. Holding up signs and banging pots and pans, they chanted slogans in English and Spanish.

No justice, no peace, no killer police!

Killer Primes off our streets!

Justicia!

The protests were spreading throughout the city like a metastasizing tumor, agglomerating in the vitals of the body politic. The radio said other protests were planned downtown and in the barrios, scheduled to run through the day.

The original demonstration outside HCPD HQ had overflowed its old boundaries. Clusters of brightly-colored tents and islands of cardboard sheets covered the park. The protesters were up and about, linking arms and revving up for the morning hate. It reminded me of slime mold growing on dead wood.

This wasn't a protest anymore. This was an occupation.

With my registered vehicle slagged, I couldn't enter the underground parking lot. Instead, I parked a block away, donned my cap and jacket, and walked into the building in plain view. Nobody stopped me. Nobody even recognized me.

My attorneys were in the cafe waiting for me. Over coffee I briefed them on last night's shenanigans. Moss was outraged, Will a smidgen more. But in the end, it hadn't changed our fundamental strategy one bit. Once we were set, we headed up to face the Inquisition.

We returned to the same interview room we used last time. It was set up the same way, too. The Two Sams on one side of the too-small table, Conway and Franks next to them. We took our seats, and the interview began.

"What weapon did you carry before you left your home?" Cho asked.

"A Glock 19," I replied.

"Personal or issue weapon?"

"Personal, but authorized for carry."

"Was the weapon concealed?"

"Yes. I placed it in my runner's rig. It's worn across the chest."

"Your pistol was loaded with a high-capacity magazine at that time," Byrd said.

"*Standard* capacity magazine," I insisted.

Byrd shrugged. "By state law, any magazine capable of holding more than ten rounds is a high-capacity magazine. No amount of wordplay will change that."

I shook my head. The politicians had lied about 'high-capacity magazine' so many times it became the truth.

"It was loaded with a fifteen-round magazine," I said.

"Why did you use a high-capacity magazine?" Franks asked.

"It was my issue magazine," I said.

"As a law enforcement officer, Detective Song is exempt from the city's magazine restriction laws," Moss said. "As I'm sure you know."

Franks ignored the barb. "What ammunition did you load your magazine with?"

"Department-issue jacketed hollow point bullets."

This way, no one could accuse me of using extravagantly lethal bullets. As though such a thing existed for handguns.

We walked through what I did before the shoot, focusing on my training. Moss and Will objected vociferously to their questions about my exercises, arguing that they were irrelevant to the matter at hand. The Two Sams, in turn, argued that it was necessary because I had claimed I was exhausted at the time of the shoot. In the end, I divulged the details, just so they would stop arguing in circles.

"By the time you returned home, you were exhausted," Cho said. "That was when you saw the subjects. Correct?"

"Yes," I replied.

"Tell us what you saw."

I did. As best as I could.

"Why did you choose to brace the subjects when you were exhausted?" Byrd asked.

"As I told Detective Clements, I felt that if I tried to walk away, they would have shot me in the back."

"How did you know that?"

"The micro-expressions on the younger guy's face. The way he locked on to me, hardened his eyes and quickly looked away. It's a tell of someone targeting you."

"Where did you learn to read body language?" Conway asked.

"In the Police Academy. Then, on the streets, I saw it first-hand in suspects who decided to fight instead of complying."

There was also the Task Force, where I'd first applied my training, but no one here needed to know about it.

"You have plenty of experience fighting people?"

"What are you implying?" Paul demanded.

"I'm just establishing how much street experience he has."

"It's all on my record," I said.

"Very well," she said. "We'll check that."

The questioning proceeded, with the inquisitors interrogating my every move during the pre-fight interview, the moment the subjects drew their weapons, the chaos that followed.

"Amp, you threw the first two subjects to the ground," Conway said, "and you killed one of them."

"Yes," I said.

"With your bare hands."

"Yes."

Her eyes narrowed.

"Do you have any martial arts experience?"

"Yes. I've studied Southeast Asian martial arts for the past eight years, and I'm an assistant instructor at the Southeast Asian Martial Academy."

"Were you aware that the techniques you employed were potentially lethal?"

"Yes."

"But you used them anyway."

"The situation justified lethal force," Moss interrupted. "It doesn't matter if my client used a gun or his bare hands."

Conway pursed her lips. "Very well. After you took the subjects down, what happened next?"

"I saw two more armed men step out of their vehicle," I said.

"That was when you chose to run around the corner," Franks said.

"Yes. Let's not forget they were shooting at me and throwing thunderbolts my way."

"Noted. You took cover behind a car engine and drew your weapon. The subjects followed you, and you chose to engage."

"Yes. I felt that my life, and the lives of those around me, were in danger," I said.

"Why didn't you keep running?"

"I was exhausted."

Franks frowned. "You fired ten shots, and you hit everything you aimed at. Good shooting for someone who's exhausted."

"In the military, I learned how to shoot accurately when I was out of breath. STAR training did the same drills."

"You hit someone in the *hand* while you were out of breath." Franks smiled skeptically. "How is that possible?"

"I used my power to stabilize my hands and line up the sights."

Byrd leaned in. "If you could use your power to improve your aim, why didn't you use it to run?"

"Detective, are you saying that a police officer should run away when confronted by armed gunmen?" Paul demanded.

"The Supreme Court has ruled that police officers have no duty to act, on or off duty," Conway said.

"My client had no choice but to defend himself," Moss interjected.

"If your client were a normal human, I'd agree," Byrd said. "But Detective Song is a Prime with superhuman abilities. He is on record as having Olympian levels of speed and agility, second only to the Prime named Phantom. Detective Song, why didn't you attempt to flee the scene?"

"The rifleman had an AK-47," I said. "Effective range of three hundred fifty meters, muzzle velocity of some seven hundred and fifteen meters per second, give or take a few. Lightning travels at the speed of light. Even with my powers, I can't outrun a bullet or a thunderbolt. I had to take cover, and by the time I got there, the shooters were covering the street. I couldn't run away. If I had broken cover, they would have opened fire, endangering the civilians behind me."

"The shooters hit three people in the crossfire," Cho noted.

"And I stopped them from shooting more."

"Your powers sure make it awfully convenient," Byrd said.

"Detective Byrd," Paul said in a dangerous tone, "did you just make a prejudicial remark against my client?"

"That wasn't my intent. But from where I'm sitting, it looks to me that Amp fell back and laid an ambush for the shooters."

"My client has already established that he was in fear of his life," Moss said. "The use of deadly force is justified. His tactics in the exercise of deadly force are irrelevant to this interview."

"Counselor, an ambush implies *homicide*," Byrd said. "Yes, I know, by any reasonable standard this would have been self-defense. But Detective Song, being a Prime, will be held to even higher standards."

The specter of necessary force raked its claws down my spine. The investigators and the DDA were trying to see if I'd set up circumstances that required lethal force—thus violating policy.

"Detective Byrd, there was no cover on the street," I said. "I had to fall back to a better position. Or are you implying that I should have just stood there and let myself get shot?"

"Fair enough," Byrd said.

The interview dragged on and on, the investigators and the DDA trying to wear me down, quibbling over the tiniest of details. Like Clements, the Two Sams pointed out that the lightning Prime was unarmed, and Moss stated that department policy allowed for lethal force against any Primes who unlawfully used a power against a person, regardless of whether they had a weapon at the time. It was as much a contest of stamina as it was of wits. Hours after I stepped into the room, the Inquisition finally ended proceedings.

"Thank you for your cooperation, Detective Song," Byrd said formally.

"You're welcome," I said. "How's the investigation into my other shooting going?"

"It's still ongoing," Cho said. "We can't talk about it. But we're treating it as a separate case."

"What about you two?" I asked, turning to Conway to Franks. "The DA put you up to this too?"

Conway went completely still for an instant.

"I can't comment on that."

The quartet was already investigating me. It only made sense for them to handle this shooting too. But I couldn't help but wonder if there was more to it than this.

I slipped out of HCPD HQ the same way I entered, then spent the rest of the morning and most of the afternoon filling out the insurance paperwork.

The HCFD's report was sobering. My apartment was completely destroyed. Even the gun safe, allegedly fireproof, hadn't survived: the locking mechanisms were so badly warped, the safe was useless. Just as well I'd moved out everything I needed. I hadn't lost anything. Just my home.

As I worked, I glanced at my inbox. Three thousand spam mails and counting. No doubt if I'd turned on my personal phone, the robot would keep calling until the phone ran out of juice. I steeled myself to banish the spam to the junk mail folder, then caught myself.

El Trece already knew my personal email address. Keeping the address made no sense. Better to patch the chink in your armor than to hold on to what's already lost.

I opened a new email address on Protonmail and spent an hour migrating my accounts. After a quick write-up to Cybercrime to report the spam campaign, I checked my work inbox.

I had one email. A flowery, eloquent mail commiserating with my current problems and wishing me well, delivered from no less an august personage than the Chief of Police himself. I might have been touched had I not already had four similar emails already, all of them written almost the same way.

At the end of his mail, Chief Charles Anderson invited me to come to his office to discuss the next step. Anderson always did this for every officer who survived an OIS. I called his executive assistant and arranged for a meeting tomorrow morning.

In the evening, I went to see Dr. Murphy to talk about the shooting all over again. I was getting tired of having to talk about the same thing the same way so many times. But it had to be done, and I'd rather get it over and done with as soon as I could.

When her interview was over, Dr. Murphy said, "You sound exhausted. Have you been sleeping well?"

"Not much," I admitted.

"It's been a rough week," she said sympathetically.

I sighed. "Yeah."

"I'm surprised you're taking it so well."

"Oh?"

"Between the stress of a shooting, the harassment, and the possibility of being on an El Trece hit list, most people would show signs of distress by now."

I shrugged. "Exercise and meditation works wonders."

She chuckled. "I bet. But I can't help feeling there's a lot you're not telling me."

"Oh?"

She smiled. "There's that 'oh' again. You're playing your cards close to your chest, holding everything in while probing for intentions."

"It's been a long day," I said.

"Have you gone back to the temple?" she asked.

"It's not safe to do that."

"But it's safe to take refuge in a church?"

"I'm known to frequent the temple, but not the church. And El Trece doesn't attack churches."

She smiled, resting her chin on her hand. "So it's good tactics?"

"Yes."

"Was it safe to come here?"

"It's an acceptable risk. I'm required to speak with you before I'm cleared for duty, so I have to be here no matter what. And before coming here, I made sure you weren't under observation, and I wasn't being followed."

"This sounds so... strange. I know I'm a civilian, but none of my clients ever said anything like that before."

"Have your clients ever been in a situation like mine?"

"I guess not. But from the way you're talking, you make it sound as if you have plenty of experience with personal security and countersurveillance."

"I *am* a police Prime. A high profile target. If I don't see to my own security, I'll have the scum of the world chasing me."

"They already are."

"Yup. Rough days are coming."

She nodded. "I hope things blow over soon."

"Me too."

They wouldn't, of course. If anything, this had only begun. All I could do was ride it out, all the way to the end.

13

THICK FACE, BLACK HEART

T he Office of the Chief of Police occupied the top floor of HCPD HQ. From this lofty position, he could peer down on the city he protected, or at least the neighborhood. As I entered, I saw the chief waiting behind his desk.

"Ah, Adam," Chief Charles Anderson boomed. "Come, sit."

I crossed the floor of his expansive office. The thick blue carpet absorbed the sound of my footsteps. To my left, a collection of leather sofas and couches surrounded a gleaming oak table. On my right, a dozen metal chairs surrounded a conference table. Bookshelves filled with heavy tomes lined the walls.

The man himself sat behind an enormous wooden table, peering from between two monitors. Anderson had rocketed through the ranks for the past thirty years, paying his dues in Patrol before moving on to increasingly prestigious posts. As Assistant Chief he'd publicly supported the Mayor and District Attorney during their election campaigns, and as a reward he received the top job.

Anderson had come a long way from the street. His face was ruddy and fleshy, with heavy jowls sinking to his chin. His dress blues were sharply-creased, adorned with five silver stars on both lapels. On his left breast, he wore a gold shield and a colorful salad bar denoting his many commendations. As he stood to shake my hand, I saw a slight bulge over his belly, and in lieu of a duty belt laden with gear, he wore a dress leather belt.

"Good morning Adam," he said.

"Morning Chief," I said.

"Did you have any trouble getting here?"

"Not really."

Meeting the chief in civilian clothing was too informal, even for a Prime, but wearing my blues was a great way to get recognized and stopped on the street.

Per my regular practice, I parked my car a block away and made my approach on foot. But this time, I carried a uniform in my backpack. I entered HCPD HQ right in front of the protesters, changed in the locker room, and headed up.

"These have been terrible times, haven't they?"

I nodded. "Yes, sir."

"Two shootings, six deaths, a protest, and now I heard your house and car's been torched, and someone's been harassing you and your family."

"Yes, sir."

"Terrible. Just terrible," he repeated. "How are you holding up?"

"Pretty well, all things considered."

"Good, good. I read the reports from Doc Murphy, both of them. She says you're unusually stable and composed despite everything that's happened to you."

"I don't think she meant it in a bad way."

He smiled. "No, she didn't. She said you're fit for duty. Do you agree?"

"I'm ready to get back into the thick of things, sir."

"Easy there, cowboy. I'm afraid there's a lot of hoops you'll have to jump through."

After an OIS, an officer is relegated to desk duty for a spell. At least until after IA and the DAO concluded their investigations.

I was reconciled to this fact already. And yet, there was something about his voice and his phrasing that didn't sit right with me.

"Let me guess: I'll have to drive a desk for a while," I replied.

"You got that right." Steepling his hands, he leaned into me. "I was thinking of assigning you to the Intelligence Bureau. The Intelligence Operations and Analysis Section needs an experienced cop, someone like yourself."

The Intelligence Bureau gathered and analyzed information on crime trends and incidents across the city, disseminated it to the rank and file, and supported ongoing investigations.

"You want me to work as an analyst, sir?"

He nodded vigorously. "Exactly. You've got time in patrol, in detectives, in STAR, and you're also a Prime. You'll bring a unique perspective to Intelligence."

Another red flag. Most of the analysts in the Intelligence Bureau were civilians, while sworn officers handled investigations and intelligence-gathering activities. Only two kinds of cops served as analysts: those with a head for numbers and talented at pattern recognition, and those sentenced to exile from the street.

"I'm not sure if I'm a right fit for the position," I said.

"Why not?" he asked.

"I don't have any relevant work experience in research or analysis positions. Just about *all* my time was spent on the street. Plus, I don't have a degree—at least, not a relevant degree."

Right out of the Academy, I pursued a four-year criminal justice degree in night school. The Detective Bureau called me up for a recruitment interview soon after I'd earned the paper.

"Don't worry about that," he said. "Everybody's got to start from somewhere, yes? And you've got lots of time on the street. I'd rather have someone with street experience than a degree."

"What exactly does being an analyst entail?"

"Come with me a second, will you?"

He got up from his desk and ambled to his window. I followed.

"See that down there?" he asked, pointing.

From here I had a bird's eye view of the plaza and the surrounding streets. An army of protesters formed thick blocks stretching across the plaza. Small tent towns were scattered among them like brightly-colored islands in a roiling sea. More protesters arrived, strolling across the plaza to join them. From way up here they looked like ants.

Blue-uniformed cops formed a loose line in front of them, keeping them away from HCPD HQ. But now there were even fewer of them than before. There was just a thin blue line between the protests and the main entrance. There were no cops monitoring the wings of the police formation, managing traffic, or patrolling the plaza.

"What do you see?" Anderson continued.

"A protest," I said.

"A protest," he repeated. "Well, that's certainly the street-level view. But from way up here, it's more than just an ordinary protest.

"Crime has evolved. Yes, there'll always be the small-time crooks and crews roaming the streets, but once we start talking about gangs and criminal syndicates, the picture becomes complicated. We know —not suspect, *know*—Ricardo Ruiz organized the protest after you shot his son last week. He reached out to Cape Watch, the media, and other activist groups, and he's still doing it. Now there are protests outside City Hall, and there's talk of a larger demonstration later this week. Why do you think he's doing this?"

"To build up his own image and discredit the police," I replied. "Especially the Primes who serve on the force."

"Excellent. But *why?*"

"To drive a wedge between the community and the police, so they will be more likely to support him—and El Trece. This would also give El Trece breathing room to continue their illegal activities."

He smiled broadly. "Well done! That's the same conclusion the analysts reached."

"Thank you," I said.

"Crime and politics are becoming increasingly intertwined. Technology today allows people to organize, to act, to make their voices heard. Gangs like El Trece are making full use of social media to manipulate do-gooders and ordinary citizens into turning against us.

They're hollowing out the city so they can continue their criminal enterprises without police interference.

"From street level, a crime is a crime. But from way up here, crime is a complex, multifaceted phenomenon, one that has ramifications across the city and the nation. We need someone like you to help us keep abreast of the gangs in the city and figure out what they're up to."

"Someone like me, sir?"

"Exactly." He turned to me. "Before joining the HCPD, you were a Marine, right? Some kind of special forces operator?"

"Yes, sir."

"You were deployed in combat?"

"Yes."

"You must have seen the same phenomenon overseas. Terrorism, crime, politics, and business all wrapped up in one messy ball, so tightly intertwined you can't tell where one ends and the other begins."

"I was at the tip of the spear," I said slowly, "but I've seen a few things that support that conclusion."

In the Philippines, the Marines told me of how terrorists ran legit businesses to earn income and launder their funds the way gangs did. In the Middle East, the difference between a farmer and a fighter was whether it was planting season or after harvest season. In Mexico and South America, criminals terrorized the police and used military tactics to carry out high-profile robberies and hits.

In Dark Net forums and on the news, everybody learned from everybody else, both merchants and customers in a grand bazaar of violence.

"I can believe that," Anderson said. "My overseas counterparts tell me they have a devil of a time trying to figure out if some gangs should be treated like terrorists, or if terrorist organizations should be treated like gangs. I don't blame them.

"We've seen gangs like El Trece up their game over the past decade. I understand the shooters who attacked you on Monday showed signs they were trained. That's bad business all round. Left unchecked, El Trece will run rampant across Halo City. We can't let that happen."

"That's why you need me as an analyst?"

"Yes. You have that perspective we need to monitor and pre-empt El Trece. And..." he shook his head. "To be honest, some of the analysts are, shall we say, stuck in an old paradigm. To them, a gangster is a gangster, a terrorist a terrorist, and never the twain shall meet. We need to shake things up. We need you."

He was smooth. Confident. But he was trying too hard.

The first time I'd met the chief, it was after my first shooting. He was polite, but somewhat distant; he asked after me, then ordered me to serve a spell in the Records and Identification Division while the investigation ground on to its inevitable conclusion.

My other post-shooting meetings played out the same way. Asking after well-being, then reassignment to a section that was at least tangentially related to my experience. But now, he was glad-handing me, treating me as a near-equal, trying to sell me on the idea on becoming an analyst.

Something was wrong.

"Sir, there are some complications I need to sort out."

"What are they?"

"El Trece is still gunning for me."

His expression melted into a frown. An exaggerated frown, his lips pressed into a tight comma.

"El Trece really has it in for you, don't they?"

"Yes, sir."

"Well, in Intelligence, you'll be working here, answering directly to me. That should keep you well away from them."

"They tracked me down once. I need to see to my personal security."

"Indeed. You said you're living in a church now, yes? Is it secure?"

"Reasonably secure, but I can't stay there forever."

He nodded. "Well, if you need secure lodging, just let me know. In the meantime, I've assembled a task force of detectives to investigate the shooting and any potential security leaks on our side. We'll find the shot-caller who put out the hit on you."

He was good. He kept his face stony and his eyes on me. But he was a liar.

Ten stories down, there was a protest aimed at me, one of the few active-duty Primes in the HCPD. A protest that he himself had said was organized by an El Trece shot-caller. Days after the protest, El Trece took a shot at me, and when that failed, they burned my house down and harassed my family and me to send a message.

Even the densest cop could clearly see that I'm on an El Trece hit list. Yet Anderson was nonchalant about it all, as though assassins and arsonists and robocalls were minor nuisances. He had spent more time trying to convince me to become an analyst than to assure me of my safety. He was hiding something.

"Thank you," I said. "However, I need to see to my family's security too."

"I understand completely. El Trece is infamous for targeting those close to their would-be victims. How long do you need?"

I shrugged. "Hard to say, sir. Security operations are complex, after all."

"I see. Well, you're still on administrative leave, and you don't have to report for duty until... let's say next Monday. Does that work for you?"

"I might need more time."

"If that's not long enough, just let your supervisor know. But we'd really like to get you into Intelligence as soon as possible."

"It sounds urgent."

"Oh yes. El Trece is into a lot of activities. Narcotics, gunrunning, human trafficking, armed robbery... We need a mind like yours on the case as soon as possible."

"Understood. I'll make the necessary arrangements, and I'll check in when I can."

He grinned. "That's the spirit, Amp. I look forward to seeing you around here more often."

"Same here, sir. Just one last thing."

"Shoot."

"I still need a replacement pistol."

"Oh, you won't need much of that around in Intelligence."

"I'm *still* a cop, sir."

His face went blank. For a moment I feared I'd insulted him. Then he chuckled.

"Dedicated to the end, I see. Well, I'll write up a memo authorizing you to draw a gun from the armory. How's that sound?"

"Fine by me, sir."

I left his office, pondering his words, and the hidden intent behind them.

Unlike most other sections in the HCPD, there were only two degrees of separation between the analysts and the chief. He was trying to get me off the street, put me in the one place where he could keep an eye on me all the time.

But he couldn't outright order me to become an analyst. He had the power to do that, certainly, but as a Prime, it would be a waste of my talents and we both knew it. He had to secure my buy-in, get me to willingly work there instead of finding an excuse to get out on the street or to wiggle out and be re-assigned elsewhere.

But what's he trying to achieve? What does he get by taking me off the street?

The political philosopher Li Zong Wu argued that to conceal your will is to be thick, and to impose it on others is to be dark. To succeed in life, one must present a thick face to the world, creating an image of complete shamelessness, and exercise one's will with a black heart filled with ruthlessness. Anderson was, without a doubt, doing just that.

But two could play this game.

14

RECONNAISSANCE

There was no way I was going to take the chief at his word. I took the elevator to the ground floor and made my way to the Special Operations Bureau. Tucked away in the hallway between the STAR office and the motor pool was the gun cage.

The gun cage was the SOB's private arsenal, usually frequented by the gunfighters of STAR, REACT and SIS. Manned day and night by a small pool of armorers, I knew all of them on sight—and they, in turn, recognized me.

Today's duty armorer was Officer Steven Williamson. A student of the gun, he'd pursued armorer certification training the second he left the Academy and helped me put my Frankengun together.

I found Steve at his usual post, manning the desk behind the counter. He reeked of gun oil, and the light reflecting off his bald pate reminded me of an egg.

"Morning, Steve," I said.

"Hey, Adam. Been a while since I saw you here," Steve said.

I shrugged. "Admin leave. You know how it goes."

"The shootings?"

"Yeah."

"Good shoot. You ask me, those perps had it coming."

"No doubt about that."

"The brass cleared you for the street yet?"

"Nope. I'm not due to report in for work until Monday."

He smiled. "But you're here because you miss me so much right?"

"Just your guns."

"Hah. I bet you love guns more than you love women."

"If you maintain your weapon, it won't let you down. Can't say the same for people."

He laughed. "Ain't that the truth. So. What'd you come down here for?"

"I need a new pistol. IA took mine, and I haven't received a replacement."

His lips curved upside down. "No shit? Why not? Aren't you supposed to get a replacement after the shoot?"

"Beats me. No one, not even Sergeant Oliveira, gave me a new gun."

He shook his head. "That's a breach of policy. A major one. I'll have to write this up. Someone's head is going to roll."

"Yeah, you do that. But right now, my holster's feeling awfully light."

"Of course. What can I get you for?"

"G19."

"Aw, come on! It's the most boring gun we've got."

The HCPD had authorized a half-dozen pistols for carry, plus variants of those models. I was proficient with all of them. Nonetheless...

"Boring is good. Boring is reliable." I paused. "If I had to take a pistol to a gunfight, I'd pick boring."

He caught the look in my eye.

"Expecting trouble?" he asked quietly.

"Lots."

"Need a long gun to go with that? I know they haven't given you a replacement carbine."

STAR officers were authorized to check out long guns and store them at home, if they had approved gun safes, to better respond to call outs. However, long guns taken as evidence weren't usually replaced; Steve had told me once that there were too few spares to make it possible.

I shook my head. "I just need the Glock. And three mags."

"Right then. One Glock 19 coming up."

He disappeared into a back room, which held the armory proper. Minutes later, he reappeared with a basket.

"Here ya go," he said. "One Glock 19 and three magazines."

I signed them out, and he slid them through a slot next to his counter. I slipped an empty magazine into the Glock and holstered it, then filled my pouches with the spares.

"Thanks, Steve."

"No problem. Now, if you'll excuse me, I've got asses to kick."

"Go get 'em."

Ammo was stored separately from weapons. I headed to the magazine down the hall, drew a box of ammo, and carefully loaded my weapon and magazines.

El Trece had declared war on me. I couldn't ignore them anymore. But before fighting a war, you need to know what you're up against.

I headed to the team room and found it empty. No surprises there. I powered up my desktop, checked my mail—nothing of note—and hit the police database.

Created and maintained by the Intelligence Bureau, the database stored everything ever known about crime and criminals in Halo City. To a much lesser extent, it also contained information about supervillains, terrorists and other threats present in the city, state, and nation.

El Trece's dossier ran to dozens of pages, cross-referencing studies and findings from police agencies and federal law enforcement across America. I prepared a cup of coffee and settled into my seat.

Six and a half decades ago, in a low-security state prison, thirteen gangsters formed a pact. Since then, the gang exploded across the state, recruiting extensively from poverty-stricken barrios and illegal immigrants. El Trece quickly made alliances and business deals with other ethnic gangs, rising to prominence shortly after the turn of the millennium.

Narcotics was El Trece's bread and butter. They bought cocaine wholesale from the cartels across the border, then smuggled the drugs in by air and sea and shipped them across the nation. As demand and market share increased, they moved into growing marijuana, operating meth labs, and importing narcotics from Asia to diversify their supply.

Once the narcotics pipeline was in place, El Trece's business expanded into human trafficking and smuggling. Using the same narco-trafficking routes and equipment, they brought in contraband and illegal immigrants, including Primes. More ruthless cliques kidnapped illegal immigrants and put them to work in sweatshops and brothels.

Over the years, El Trece had steadily expanded their business, making full use of their smuggling network. These days they were into illegal guns, money laundering, gambling, fraud, extortion, contract killing, and lately cybercrime.

A decade ago, El Trece made a bid for supremacy. In a week of blood and fire, they launched an all-out offensive in Little Mexico and surrounding satellite communities, aiming to crush their rivals. As the crime wave engulfed the city, REACT, STAR and patrol officers went into overdrive, responding to dozens of shootings and stabbings and drive-bys every day. Danny made his bones there, stepping into no less than three shootings. For a few tense days, it seemed the Mayor would call in the National Guard. Fortunately, the HCPD and the city's Primes got the situation under control and cracked down hard.

But the damage was done. El Trece had destroyed their rivals or forced them into submission. Now they were the unchallenged rulers of El Barrio.

For all that, El Trece wasn't a monolithic group. It was composed of dozens of affiliated cliques, many of them deadly rivals. El Trece infighting wasn't uncommon, usually over turf or respect, and green-on-green killings weren't unheard of. We'd have smiled at it had they not taken innocents with them in the crossfire.

The closest El Trece had to leaders were the shot-callers of the cliques. While they were all nominally equal, many strove to be the first among equals. Factionalism was rampant in El Trece, with alliances forged and faked and fractured every day.

El Trece was also split between the Primes and the mundanes. Many El Trece Primes in Halo City were outsiders, brought in as heavy hitters during the days of rage. Most of the mundanes, by contrast, were long-term residents. While a significant number of the Primes had been taken off the streets, the ones who remained tended to be far more aggressive and expansionist than their regular counterparts.

Among the major factions in El Trece were Calle and Cielo. Calle, or 'street,' was the old guard, oriented towards street-level crime and traditional ways of making money. The Cielo faction were the young blood, their ambitions reaching for the sky, eager to adopt the tactics of the cartels and expand into new avenues for illegal income. Where Calle used violence to settle beefs and defend their businesses, Cielo was far more aggressive, actively targeting rival gangs and the police.

The factions didn't necessarily oppose each other all the time either: Cielo pushed for war and did the strategizing, while Calle funded operations and pulled in muscle and materiel through their pipelines. However, specific cliques aligned with each faction usually feuded with each other, and it was an open guess whether Calle and Cielo were officially at each other's throats.

As if *that* wasn't complicated enough already, there were plenty of smaller factions organized along personal loyalties to shot-callers, or to specific streets and geographic locations that served as the clique's home base. Cliques could be part of multiple factions at once, dropping in and out as their leaders decided.

El Trece was a swirling chaotic mess of fluid alliances, double-crosses, and low-level internecine warfare. But no matter their beefs, they were blood-bound to band together against all outsiders. Their sense of honor had driven them to victory over their rivals a decade ago, but now...

I walked around the office, framing my thoughts.

Up to this point, I'd assumed all of El Trece was after me. But what if it were only one faction, one clique, or even one man? The Calle faction was much more reluctant to fight the police than Cielo —it took loads of negotiations and concessions and browbeating before they finally supported the crime campaign—and I didn't see them organizing a hit just because a Prime happened to shoot a shot-caller's son. That sort of thing happened all the time in El Barrio, and if they spent their days settling scores they wouldn't be making money.

The situation reminded me of the Middle East. There was an old Arab saying that went, 'me against my brother, my brother and me against my cousin, my brother and my cousin and me against the world.' Perhaps this saying also applied here. And if so, I could isolate Ruiz's clique, the only clique with a motive to target me...

I needed an expert. Someone with street knowledge, someone who knew the ground in El Barrio, someone whose insight wasn't captured in the Intelligence Bureau's Report.

Fortunately, I knew someone who might know that someone.

THE DETECTIVE BUREAU was spread out over multiple floors, each specializing in different fields. The Bureau office on the third floor was earmarked for the Gang and Narcotics Division, and its associated subunits.

Scarcely anyone who worked here was in uniform. I exchanged greetings with the detectives who knew me and wound my way to the entrance of GND. Past the front door, I met a familiar face, accompanied by an unfamiliar one.

"Wah, Adam!" Robert Low said. "*Lei mo sei ah?*" *You're not dead yet?*

In English, it might have been a threat. In Cantonese, it was merely a familiar, if rude, greeting.

"Of course," I replied. "I hit the gym, go to the range, get in training time... You should try that sometime. Who knows, maybe you can finally catch someone without needing to call for backup."

Low guffawed, folding his hands over his ample belly.

"That's what you STAR boys are for," he said.

"I'm still a detective, you know."

"You should come by more often. We miss you."

"I do my best." I nodded at the other man. "New guy?"

"Yes," the rookie said. "Ken Zhou."

"Ken's been with us for three months," Robert said. "He's smart, works hard, he's going places."

During the oral board interview, the recruiters from the Detective Bureau were especially impressed with my ability to speak multiple languages and my familiarity with Chinese culture. Once I got the nod, I was assigned to the Asian Gang Unit.

The AGU specialized in tackling the panoply of Asian gangs in Halo City and assisted regular detectives and uniformed officers when they needed insight into Asian culture. Within the AGU there were smaller subdivisions, with Rob and me going after the triads. Rob, despite his physical shortcomings, taught me everything I knew about detective work.

Rob and Ken made a strange pair. Rob was short and squat, his cheap suit bulging at the seams, his face broad and open. Ken was tall and lean, towering over me, dressed in a sharp tailored suit. His eyes are sharp and narrow and hungry, drinking in everything around him. It was a bit like looking at a teddy bear standing next to a wolf.

"What are you doing here anyway?" Rob asked. "STAR is on the first floor, ya know."

"I'm looking for a subject matter expert on El Trece," I said. "Know someone like that?"

"Sergeant Jose Garcia," Ken replied. "He's in HIDTA Squad One."

HIDTA meant High Intensity Drug Trafficking Area. There was a half-dozen of them scattered throughout Halo City, almost all of them owned by El Trece.

"Thanks," I said.

Rob beamed. "What'd I tell you? He's going places, that kid. Knows everybody in GND by now."

Ken smiled shyly. "Thanks."

"What'd you need to know about El Trece anyway?" he asked. "Got a beef with them?"

"It's the other way around."

"The other..." Rob's eyes narrowed. Behind them I saw the gears turning in his mind.

"What's wrong?" Ken asked.

"Last week, we had an OIS," Rob said carefully. "On Monday there was another. Is this related?"

I nodded.

Officially, Rob didn't know I was a Prime. All he knew was that a bit over a year ago, I had to take medical leave out of the blue. When I recovered, I was fast-tracked for STAR try-outs, and soon after that, the HCPD announced a new Prime in the force. He never explicitly stated what he knew or what he thought he knew, and I returned the favor by not telling the brass.

Rob smoothened his pale green tie. "Well, then. Speaking of El Trece, I've heard something you might be interested in."

"What's that?" I asked.

"Tin Fo is pissed at El Trece."

"What happened?"

"The Monday shooting. Four El Trece hitters went into China-town to hit someone, but got hit instead. There's an unofficial agreement among bad guys that if they want to do a hit on someone else's turf, they need to clear it with the owners. It's only good manners, right?"

I nodded. "Right."

"Word on the street is that El Trece didn't get permission. They simply sent in their shooters and went blasting away on Tin Fo turf."

"That would make Tin Fo lose face," I mused.

"Big time," Rob confirmed. "It shows that Tin Fo can't control their own territory, and that El Trece doesn't respect them."

"Will there be reprisals?" I asked.

He shrugged. "Who knows? The El Trece shooters didn't get their mark, and they've all been iced. That might be enough to satisfy the Dragon Head. But if not, I expect he'll order a pushback. Maybe some

El Trece shot-caller gets beaten up, or a crack house gets burned down. Nobody dies, at least not on purpose, but Tin Fo will show their strength."

"Won't that escalate?" Ken asked.

"Maybe. Reprisals have to be carefully calibrated, yeah? There's got to be just enough violence to say, 'Respect the rules and don't mess with our turf', but not so much that El Trece feels they gotta go to guns. Even then... all it takes is one hothead to start a shooting war."

"We need to stay on our toes," I said.

"Oh yeah. You be careful out there, okay?"

"You too."

As the duo left, I pondered the meaning of Rob's words. El Trece was huge. Impossible for any one man to fight. But if I could turn another gang against them...

I shook my head. What the hell was I thinking? There are rules and laws now, laws I've sworn to uphold, and I could not walk away from that.

My Task Force days were buried in the past. They had to remain so.

15

CARA

I made a few inquiries around the GND office. Garcia was out on the street, but I managed to call him and set up a lunchtime meeting. Nothing formal, I assured him, just a fellow dick needing some input on a tricky case.

As I waited for lunch to roll around, I returned to the church and found the Nguyen siblings in the office. After brief greetings and small talk, I explained my situation to them.

"I feel kind of awkward just staying here without contributing," I said.

"It's no problem," Father Matthew said. "You can stay as long as you like."

"At least let me help you with security," I said.

"What do you mean?"

"I could help you keep an eye on things while you're not around."

"Well..."

"That sounds wonderful," Anna said. "I keep telling Father Josh to hire a night guard, but he says the cameras are enough."

"Criminals are getting bolder by the day," I said.

"Yeah." She sighed. "We've had two shootings in the neighborhood in two weeks. I don't know what the world is coming to."

"Exactly. So how's this: give me access to your security cameras, and I'll help you keep watch in the evenings. And whenever I'm around."

"Sounds good," Anna said.

"I need to tell Father Josh," Father Matthew said, "but I don't see any problems."

"Where's he now?" I asked.

"He's ministering to one of our flock at Memorial Hospital. I'll talk to him when he gets back."

"Great. Oh, and do tell him that, with his permission, I'd like to install wireless cameras around the perimeter."

"Well... we don't exactly have a budget for more cameras."

"I'll pay for them," I said. "I was going to buy them anyway. It's the least I could do."

His face brightened. "All right then. I'll let Father Josh know."

That went a lot easier than expected.

I set off again at half-past eleven. During the drive to the meeting, I plotted what to say and, more importantly, what not to say. It wasn't the first time I'd had to conceal the truth from people nominally on my side. It didn't make it any easier.

Marie's Cafe was an unassuming greasy spoon a stone's throw away from the HITDA of Feliz Hills. It was a cramped establishment, with a long narrow counter on to my left, an assortment of tables to my right, and in between an aisle barely wide enough to squeeze through. It reminded me of a yakitoriya, a traditional Japanese eatery specializing in grilled dishes.

The second I stepped in, the sound of sizzling oil filled my ears. A young man manned the counter, greeting me with a tired smile. Behind him, an aged woman deftly handled a frying pan on an ancient cooktop. Grease and fat filled my nostrils. The tables were all occupied, the patrons tucking into an eclectic mix of tacos, chops and burgers.

I spotted Garcia straightaway. Seated at the far table, he stood out from the others. His boots were placed flat on the floor, his hands resting in his lap, his eyes sweeping the establishment. He wore a heavy jacket not unlike mine, though his was made of real leather. I'd never seen his face before, but I pinned him as a cop straightaway.

"Sergeant Garcia?" I asked.

He smiled thinly and stood to shake my hand. "You must be Detective Song."

"Pleasure to meet you. Did you wait long?"

"Nah. Just got here myself."

"Thanks for going out of your way to meet me."

"No problem. It's been a boring paper day anyway." He handed the menu to me. "Go ahead and place your order. I've already made mine."

"I've never been here before," I said. "Got any recommendations?"

"Marie makes a fine beef taco."

I don't eat beef. My parents never did, and passed on that practice to me. It was a Buddhist thing, actually Mahayana Buddhist, but I never got around to tasting the forbidden meat anyway. I ordered a fish taco instead. When I returned to the table, Garcia was all business.

"So," he said, "what do you need help with?"

"On Monday, El Trece attempted a hit in Chinatown," I began.

Garcia smiled. "But Amp hit them back. Man, that was some fine shooting. I'd love to shake his hand."

I smiled back. "I agree. But anyway, the hit's got the Tin Fo triad riled up, and I'm trying to understand why."

"Why what, exactly?"

"Chinatown's a long way from El Barrio. Why would the hitters go all the way there?"

Garcia stroked his chin. "Just so we know where you're coming from, what's your stake in this case?"

"I'm gathering intelligence on gang activity. I'm tracking Tin Fo in particular, and this thing with El Trece doesn't look like your everyday gangland shooting."

If Garcia checked up on me, he would learn I was assigned to Intelligence, and with my track record, it only made sense for me to start working the streets now. Perhaps the chief's assignment was a blessing in disguise.

"It's not. It was a hit, plain and simple."

"Oh?"

"They attacked Amp outside an apartment complex, and Amp was described as off-duty and wearing jogging attire. What else could it be?"

My heartbeat spiked, but I nodded along.

"El Trece tracked Amp to Chinatown and tried to hit him at his home," I said.

"Got that right. They sent in heavy hitters too."

"You know the shooters?"

"Yup. Christian Alvarez, Manuel Velazquez, Alex Desoto, Roderick Cortez. They're not a clique, more like an independent crew operating under the auspices of a larger clique. Ex-military, all of them. Cortez was a Prime too, with the power to throw around lightning bolts.

"Word is they met in the brig before they were dishonorably discharged. After they got out, they worked as *sicarios*, beating, stabbing or shooting whoever in El Trece pays them to."

"They're freelancers?"

"Sorta. They only take contracts from within El Trece, but they might do hits for outsiders if one of their *carnales* brokers it."

"Do they have a beef against Amp?"

"Not that I heard of. I think someone paid them to do it."

"Who?"

"I've got my theories." He looked at me. "But what do you think?"

"Amp killed some El Trece big shot last week, right? Seems like someone's taking revenge."

"Bingo," he said.

The man from the counter interrupted us, placing our food at the table. Garcia had gone for a massive breaded fried cutlet with generous helpings of potatoes, tomatoes, and lettuce. My plate held three huge fish tacos, also fried, slathered with mayo.

The fish was excellent, just the right mix of springiness and juiciness. The vegetables and mayo and the meat were an exquisite combination of crunch and cream and savoriness. I made a note to come back if I could.

"Who do *you* think did it?" I asked.

"Ricardo Ruiz, of course. The father of the guy Amp killed. No one else has the motive, and the hitters I mentioned earlier work directly for him."

I expected that answer.

"I read he was a 'local businessman' and 'community organizer'," I said.

Garcia doubled over laughing, but there was a bitter edge in his laughter.

"Man, a joke like that's gonna give me a heart attack."

I should point out his choice of sustenance would likely do him in first, but it probably wouldn't be polite. Besides, under his jacket and cover shirt I saw an iron-hard physique earned through dedicated training and constant use.

"What's he really do?" I asked.

"More like, what's he not do. He's got a finger in every pie. Narcotics, guns, prostitution, you name it, he does it. He runs a large clique with smaller sub-cliques that focus on different operations."

"Like subsidiary companies."

"Exactly. He runs his clique like a business."

"I guess that's where 'local businessman' comes from."

"You got it. He keeps his hands clean these days, keeps himself distant from the street. He's remade himself as a *cara*."

"A what?"

"A *cara*. It means 'face.' The upper echelons of El Trece want to rebrand themselves. Not just as street thugs, but as 'businessmen.' Hence the *caras*. These guys don't look like lowlifes. They are clean-cut, dress and speak well, don't have visible tattoos, many of them even have a good education. They run legit businesses, give to charity, all that good stuff. In fact, the *caras* are eclipsing the old guard and becoming the de facto leaders of El Trece."

"Hence 'community organizer.'"

"You got it. Everybody in El Barrio knows Ruiz is dirty, but since he goes to church, gives people jobs and so on, they'll turn a blind eye. And those outside El Barrio don't know better." Ruiz sighed. "Those bastards. They're taking a leaf from the cartel playbook down south."

"I heard they're planning to become a cartel themselves."

"Yup. They're starting here, in Halo City. They're testing new businesses, new strategies, new approaches to doing business and politics. If—or when—they take off, you bet El Trece elsewhere will follow suit."

"Where can we find Ruiz?"

Garcia raised an eyebrow. "What's it to you?"

"Me?"

"Yeah. I've been doing all the talking so far. No offense, but what's this got to do with your investigation into Tin Fo?"

Some cops were so steeped in professional pride, they viewed all outsiders with suspicion. Garcia must be one of them.

I was this close to stepping on a tripwire. I bought a bit of time by drinking some water.

"This hit in Chinatown might cause a beef with Tin Fo. If it does, we'll need to stamp it out before it ignites into a shooting war."

He laughed. "Don't you worry about that. The hitters got hit themselves. It just makes El Trece look weak."

"I heard the shooters didn't clear the hit with Tin Fo. What's up with that?"

"Maybe they were sitting on time-sensitive intel. Or maybe Ruiz just wants to handle everything in-house. He's canny like that, you know."

"What'd you mean?"

"Amp killed his boy. To show his strength to everyone else in El Trece, he has to take revenge. But he can't let anyone else outside his clique do it for him, especially since he's a *cara* and a shot-caller with a rep.

"If Ruiz sent his shooters to kill Amp and succeeded, he'd gain a lot of standing among his own. Even more so if he did it without Tin Fo permission. It makes him look like he's got *cojones*, see?"

I nodded. "But if he cleared it with Tin Fo..."

"Sure, it'll be nice and proper-like, but he won't get that rep boost. He might also have to give something up in exchange for that favor, something he doesn't want to concede. Given that both El Trece and Tin Fo will benefit if he removes a superhero from the streets, there wouldn't be any repercussions from Tin Fo if he succeeded."

"But he failed."

"Gangsters intrude on each other's turf all the time. This isn't anything different, even if the target this time happens to be a cop. A Prime cop at that. Maybe there'll be a beef, but it won't boil over into a shooting war."

"I see." I finished a taco. "So Ruiz had nothing to lose but everything to gain if he pulled it off."

"Exactly."

"There's one thing I don't get, though."

"What's that?"

"Why is Ruiz still walking the street?"

Garcia sighed, shaking his head. "El Barrio loves him. If we pick him up, we won't hear the end of it."

"Politics, huh?"

"You got that right. We need an airtight case against him. Evidence, witnesses, the whole nine yards. And even if we do have a case, we still have to find him first."

"You don't know where he is?"

"He disappeared. He's stopped visiting his usual haunts, and none of my CIs know where he is."

"He must have a vulnerability somewhere."

"Maybe..." Garcia sipped at a glass of water. "Say, you're being real inquisitive about El Trece for a detective who's covering the Triad beat."

I shot him a winning smile. "It's just my nature."

He scoffed. "C'mon, pull the other one. Why are you really here?"

I sighed and raised my hands in mock-surrender. "Promise you won't tell anyone?"

"Depends on what you gotta tell me."

"You know Amp is our golden boy. Brought in a lot of villains, stellar record, made the PD look good."

"Our literal supercop."

"Exactly. And now there's a bullseye on his back. The brass is getting anxious. They don't want the supercop getting shot."

"That'll be embarrassing."

"Absolutely. Shortly after the Monday shoot, a message comes down from the chief through informal channels. He says he wants to nail the shot-caller who called the hit on Amp. He's setting up a secret task force, answerable only to him, to handle that case."

"You got the tap?"

I nodded. "The hit happened in Chinatown. I was already investigating the El Trece-Tin Fo angle, so they brought me in too. But since we're already talking about El Trece, I figured, why not ask you about Ruiz too?"

"You could have told me that earlier, saved me a lot of time."

I spread my arms. "Sorry, man. Chief says the task force is classified. He doesn't want the media, and therefore El Trece, learning about it. If we can bust Ruiz for the hit, it's a win-win for us."

"That's going to be a real tough proposition if you ask me. Ruiz has been underground since last week."

"I've been told you're the department's subject matter expert on El Trece."

He chuckled. "Naw, not really."

"But you have an idea how to find Ruiz, right?"

He poked at his food. "Maybe."

"Tell me."

He looked at me and raised his eyebrow in a silent question.

"Hey, we're on the same team, right?" I continued.

He snorted. "Right. So. What do you know about how an El Trece clique is set up?"

"Pretend I don't know anything."

He cleared his throat. "Every El Trece clique has a fundamentally flat hierarchy. There may be smaller subordinate crews within the clique, but, at least on paper, everyone's equal."

"Except the shot-callers."

"Yup. Every clique has two leaders. The big fish is the *primero palabra*, the first word. Ruiz is the *primero palabra* for his clique. After the *primero* is the *segundo palabra*, the second word. So far as I can tell, Ruiz sets strategy and policy for his clique, while his *segundo*, Adrian Vargas Chavez, handles day-to-day operations.

"For such a flat structure to work, they have to rely on man-to-man relationships. But the clique has hundreds of members, divided into multiple groups. To enforce his will, demonstrate his power and meet his smaller fry, Ruiz collects taxes every week. In person."

"In person?" I repeated. "We know this, but we can't bust him?"

"Believe me, we tried. On his tax runs, he carries no contraband on his person, and neither do his bodyguards. We can't bust 'em for carrying cash around."

"But they're armed."

He pursed his lips. "Of course they're not. They're only carrying utility knives, screwdrivers, rubber mallets, tire irons, stuff you need to fix up your car."

"All perfectly legal, huh."

"Of course. But anyway, Ruiz hasn't been seen doing his tax runs lately, and he didn't tell his *carnales* where he went. Which makes him so hard to track down."

"But someone's been collecting taxes for him, right?"

"Right. This morning, my CI said that Chavez collected last week's taxes, and said that for the foreseeable future, he'll continue collecting taxes on the big man's behalf. Same schedule, every Friday."

"And Chavez might know where Ruiz is."

"Maybe so, but Chavez joined his boss in hiding too. All I heard is that he's been seen making the rounds in Feliz Hills."

"But he'll show his face when he goes to collect taxes."

"There's that," he said. "What, you're planning a stakeout?"

I grinned. "Nah, it's just for my report. I've got more important things to do."

He grinned back. "I'm sure you do."

16. Feliz Hills

THE INTELLIGENCE BUREAU database management system was astonishingly detailed. If you knew how to work the antiquated system, navigate between databases, and draw relationships between people of importance. I'd heard the PD had contracted with an external company to upgrade and integrate the databases with the rest of the city. It couldn't happen soon enough.

Parsing through the databases, I identified El Trece dope dealers affiliated with Ruiz's clique. I sifted out those with no known addresses and those whose addresses could not be confirmed, then those with active warrants, leaving me with a handful of names.

Of those that were left, most were listed as being 'suspected' of narcotics offenses. I got rid of those without prior convictions, then zoomed in on those based in Feliz Hills.

There was only one man: Alberto Torres.

Torres was small vegetables. He was a street-level dealer, not quite prominent enough to warrant the immediate attention of STAR and GND, but not so clean the HCPD could ignore him. His last major contact with the cops was three months ago. An honest citizen spotted him working the street and called the police on him. Unfortunately, his buddy Alfonso Martinez spotted the cops coming, and Torres dumped his dope. When the patrol officers finally caught up with the duo, they found nothing illegal on them.

Torres and Martinez weren't formally part of El Trece, they'd never been jumped in, and they didn't sport gang tats. But El Trece couldn't ignore freelancers operating on their turf. They imposed exorbitant taxes on Torres, much higher than their own taxes for regular members, in exchange for granting him and his crew permission to do business in Feliz Hills.

Naturally, someone had to collect those taxes.

I found a spy store and purchased a GPS tracker. Roughly the size and shape of a hockey puck, its battery would last for a week, and it could be adhered to any reasonably flat surface.

I spent the rest of the day cruising around Feliz Hills, learning the lay of the land, keeping an eye out for Torres. Once the district was a prosperous middle-class neighborhood, but sometime in the past couple of decades, the good people moved out and the gangs moved in.

Green graffiti was everywhere, occasionally covered by other tags from smaller rival gangs. Litter drifted across the pavement. As with Franklin Boulevard, many of the streetlights in the rougher parts of the district had been shot out. Security grilles were as much a part of the landscape as the omnipresent graffiti.

The few people I saw on the street were regular people. A dog walker, a cluster of high schoolers, a husband-and-wife duo pushing a pram. But once I drove past a gang of youths congregating outside a dark two-story home, dressed all in green, their hands near their waistbands, their eyes empty and soulless. One of them couldn't have been older than twelve.

I located Torres at the same spot he'd been picked up, a crossroads near a derelict apartment block. He did his business in a nearby parking lot, standing nonchalantly around his car. Martinez hung out near the apartment, acting as both tout and lookout.

I circled around, parked three blocks down the road and scooted over to the passenger seat. Seated like this, it would appear as if I'm merely waiting for a friend to return to the car. I dug out my camera, binoculars, and journal, and recorded everything I saw.

Torres and Martinez had a clear division of labor. Martinez hustled on the sidewalk, approaching passers-by and likely marks, and guiding them to Torres. Torres handled the actual transactions. In between customers, Torres paced the parking lot and worked his phone, making three or four calls an hour. Perhaps he was hitting up his regulars, suppliers, and friends.

They were doing okay, for small-time drug dealers. They pulled in four or five transactions an hour, half from passers-by, half from people who just drove up to them. They were careful to conceal what they were selling, but once I caught a flash of white powder in a sealed plastic baggie.

When dusk fell, Torres and Martinez packed up and drove off. I stayed where I was for a little longer, then departed.

Torres and Martinez were still in the life. That meant they still owed El Trece taxes. Sooner or later the taxman would come for them. The question was where.

I had two nexuses to work from. The crossroad where they did business and Torres' home. The home seemed more likely. At the street level, drugs were a cash-only trade. Anyone would be nervous carrying large amounts of cash to a hand-off. At least, anyone without protection or legitimacy.

Torres' listed address was a mile away from his workplace, a three-story low-rise apartment stretching from one end of the street to the other. Open-air corridors and stairwells granted access to street-facing doors and windows. I could see anyone coming in and out, but they could see me too.

I parked four blocks down the street, watched, and waited.

As the sun grew low and shadows fell across the street, traffic picked up. Ordinary people were rushing home, eager to get indoors before the street animals came out to play.

But El Trece was already here. A young man wearing a green bandanna left the apartment, swaggered down the street, and met a small group of similarly-dressed youths. Their vibes were jovial and casual, a group of friends out and about, but I had no doubt that things would change later tonight.

I was the only Chinese male in sight. While my car was cheap and moderately old, like most of the ones here, it had no tinted windows. A few passers-by glanced at my car as they passed, sometimes making a double-take. I spread a map over my lap and hid my gear underneath, occasionally frowning down into the paper.

In my peripheral vision, I saw a black man approach my car from behind. He held a dog leash in one hand, a poop collector in the other. Probably an average upstanding Joe—most bad guys don't care to pick up after their dogs.

The dogwalker rapped his knuckles against my window. I lowered it a fraction, just enough to hear him.

"Whatcha doing here?" he asked.

"Waiting for a friend," I replied.

He frowned at me and at the map on my lap. "And just what are you and your friend doing here?"

"Just picking up and dropping off packages."

"You don't look like no courier to me."

"Ever heard of Magic Carpet?"

"What's that?"

"Well, you've heard of Uber and Lyft?"

"Sure. Is this something similar?"

"Yeah. Magic Carpet is like Uber, but for package deliveries. We make a few bucks doing deliveries, and help people save on shipping through the mail or a courier company."

"That sounds neat."

The dog appeared at my window, propping itself on its hind legs, smiling at me and letting its tongue fall out.

"Down!" he said, turning to his dog.

The dog went down.

"Cute dog," I said.

"Thanks," he said. "Gets too friendly when talking to strangers though."

"Better friendly than aggressive."

"Except in this 'hood. There's gangbangers about. Don't stay too long, 'kay? This ain't no place for outsiders."

"Got it. Thanks."

The dog walker jogged off.

I didn't know if he'd come back, but I was confident he wouldn't rat me out to El Trece. If he wanted to, he would have gone straight to them instead of speaking to me. I stayed in place and continued watching.

The greatest enemy of long-term surveillance, after being made by the target, was boredom. I kept myself alert with stretches and twists and rotations, going slow and smooth, minimizing my profile. As people came and went I studied them and played mind games, extrapolating their life stories from their clothing, their gait, their facial expressions, everything I could observe. I tracked seemingly inconsequential details, from the number of cars on the road to potential El Trece members. Whenever I felt fatigue set in, I moved slow and breathed deep, flooding my lungs with cool air.

Just after half past six, Father Matthew texted me. Father Josh had approved my request to help with security. Anna sent me an email informing me that I now had access to the church's camera network, and explained how to use the app that coordinated the security system.

The Nguyens and Father Josh had placed their complete faith in me. Cheered by that thought, I resumed my lonely watch.

Full dark fell. The evening rush passed and the streets cleared out. Young men in El Trece greens and young women in scanty clothes strutted down the sidewalks. I slunk low in my seat, keeping out of sight.

At a little past nine, Torres returned. He parked his car in front of his apartment and headed upstairs. A half hour later, I decided he wasn't coming out, and headed home myself.

Tomorrow, the real work would begin.

16

THE BORROWED KNIFE

I bought sandwiches for dinner and returned to the church. Inside the church office, I configured the security set-up. Fortunately for me, they used a popular commercial security suite, one that could be scaled up or down to suit the user's requirements. After downloading the app on my Nullphone and my laptop, all I had to do was install compatible hardware, register them on the app, and I was good to go.

When I was finally done, I packed my gear and went to bed. My alarm woke me at four. I chased away early-morning bleariness with a punishing routine of high-intensity bodyweight exercises, then washed off the sweat and fatigue with a mixed shower.

I stepped out of the bathroom just in time to see Father Josh shuffle out of his room in his pajamas.

"Morning Adam," he said.

"Morning, Father."

"You're up early."

"Things to do and places to be."

"Of course. Would you like to join us for breakfast?"

"No thanks. I'm headed out."

I wasn't sure what Catholic priests did so early in the morning. But I knew what I had to do.

I topped off the gas tank at a 24-hour gas station and bought a large bottle of water and a selection of sandwiches. I raced through the dying night, reaching Feliz Hills just before rush hour. Cruising around, I saw Torres' car still parked where we had left it.

I slid into position four blocks away and waited.

Slowly, the neighborhood awoke. The street animals had slunk back to their lairs, and the regular joes were reclaiming their streets. Working stiffs shuffled to their cars and bikes, a news carrier expertly tossed newspapers out of his truck with extreme precision, a woman dared to jog the streets alone.

I recognized a few of those faces from yesterday. It didn't seem like any of them knew me. I wondered if the dog walker would show up. I hoped not; I couldn't use the same excuse on him.

Torres remained indoors, no doubt sleeping the sleep of the mildly wicked. Being a drug dealer must have its benefits. Choose your own hours, keep all your income, build a solid rep as the neighborhood go-to guy for good times; and all you need to worry about is people ripping you off, the police rolling in hard, or El Trece demanding their dues.

At nine o'clock, a cherry-red Ford with tinted windows drove up to the tenement. Three men got out, one of them carrying a duffel bag. As they scanned the road, I kept my head down and pretended to play with my phone. When my sixth sense said I was clear, I raised my camera and zoomed in.

Two of them were huge and stout, with massive muscles, thick necks and powerful trunks. These weren't pretty body bodybuilders; they had trained for pure strength. Tattoos swirled down their exposed arms and up their necks. One guy had a huge handlebar mustache, the other boasted a tattoo of a skull on his neck. Sandwiched between them, the last guy was practically a mouse. But he moved with confidence and authority, and the muscle trailed him. I snapped photos, but all I got were their profiles.

Come on, look this way, don't be shy...

As if in response, the bag man turned and said something to his *carnales*. I got a clean full-on photo of his face.

He was in his late thirties, maybe early forties, but the street adds years to a man's face. He had shaved himself bald but sported a thick mustache that flowed into a scraggly beard that covered his neck. He was dressed in a loose shirt and pants, almost like a civilian, but faded blue ink peeked out from his collar and cuffs. His eyes were cold and dark and empty.

Adrian Vegas Chavez.

They climbed the steps to the second floor, their backs to me. Chavez knocked on Torres' door. Moments later, Torres opened the door and greeted them with a bright, if nervous, smile. After a brief exchange, Torres invited them inside.

Digging into my backpack, I donned a pair of cotton work gloves and grabbed my tracker. I ripped off the adhesive backing, donned my baseball cap and a pair of sunglasses, and got out.

I approached the car, scanning as I went. I caught a few glances but no hostility. I was a stranger, yeah, but I walked as if I belonged here, as if I had business to do. Nobody challenged me or paid me any undue attention.

Five feet away from the target vehicle, I made out the silhouette of a man seated in the driver's seat.

My heart thumped. My hands warmed up. But I was committed, and my danger sense remained silent.

I kept walking, closing the distance. The driver didn't recognize me, or maybe he was simply looking the wrong way. I stopped just behind the car, bent over and re-tied my shoelaces. I looked for witnesses—*clear*—and brushed my hand against the rear bumper, sticking the tracker on the inner side.

I got up and crossed the road, casual as can be. No shouts, no challenges, no tails. I walked round the block on foot at an easy pace. By the time I returned to my vehicle, Chavez's car was gone. I powered up my Nullphone and checked my GPS tracking app.

A bright blue dot appeared on the map. Chavez was in motion.

I drove at a casual pace, keeping one street behind and parallel to the El Trece car. I recorded every stop, adding it to my database. Most of them were residential addresses; the rest were workshops, bars, a restaurant. Now and then I eyeballed the target, just to make sure they hadn't peeled off the tracker and placed it on another vehicle.

This was illegal as all hell. I needed to obtain supervisory approval and a court warrant to plant a GPS tracker on a suspect. But that would take way too long, weeks at least, and I had no desire to sit around and let El Trece take a swing at me again.

The alternative approach was to tap into the city-wide surveillance camera network. Capable of scanning a million faces and license plates a second, I could track anyone in the city so long as they stayed within range of a camera. But to do that, I needed to submit a request in writing, and with the shenanigans from the top floor, I wasn't sure if it would be approved.

Or that it was a good idea to let the brass know what I was doing.

At a quarter past four, the car returned to Feliz Hills, going deep into the suburbs, and went still. It remained stationary for a half hour. Maybe that was the hideout.

I rolled down the street, slow enough to study the street, not so slow I'd be noticed. This was the nice part of town. No graffiti, no gangsters, not even litter. Just long lines of trees and small homes lining the street. They didn't even have security grilles.

The GPS led me to a two-story home with attached garage. No sign of the car in sight, but the garage shutter was closed. A bear of a man sat at the front porch watching the street. He wore a jacket to conceal his tattoos, but I recognized him straightaway. Skull Throat, one of Chavez's bodyguards.

Got you now, Chavez.

ON SATURDAY I watched the phone. The targets stayed stationary for most of the morning. When I did a drive-past, a new guy was seated outside the main door, glaring at all and sundry. I wasn't sure, but I suspected he was Chavez's driver.

I kept a low profile and waited.

In the afternoon, the car moved again. I followed it to a parking lot near a pizza place just outside Feliz Hills. I stopped the car nearby, just in time to see Chavez and his crew enter the restaurant. I stayed outside and subsisted on cold sandwiches and warm water.

At 1427 the gang left the restaurant and returned home. I did the same. Safely ensconced in my room, I typed out a contact report, crafting a story for my intended audience.

A confidential informant called me and claimed that he saw one Adrian Vargas Chavez, the *segundo palabra* of an El Trece clique, at the pizza restaurant at 1315 hrs. I hustled over to perform a hasty stakeout, and shortly after my arrival I spotted Chavez, and his crew leave the establishment. I continued monitoring the subjects and tracked them to a possible hideout in Feliz Hills. I took photographs of the subjects, fed them to the database, and discovered active warrants on them. As a professional courtesy, I am now forwarding my findings to the appropriate investigation team, and should they choose to act I would be perfectly willing to assist.

I kept my tone professional, but the unspoken request was clear: I did a favor for you, so let me help with the arrest.

I sent that report to Sergeants Garcia and Oliveira, and cc'd it to a few friendly supervisors in STAR and GND. Now the action was all nice and legal, just Supercop Song acting on his own initiative to locate a dangerous criminal, while leaving room for everybody else to swoop in and claim the glory.

Leaving the tracker in place was risky. But department policy held that STAR handled all narcotics and gang-related warrants in the city, without exception. Oliveira would bust his chops to ensure his team got the call to take down Chavez, and knowing him, he would invite me for the ride. And if his efforts failed, I had juice of my own.

Once the raid went down, it wouldn't be too difficult to 'examine' Chavez's car and surreptitiously remove the tracker.

Sunday passed in peace. I wasn't a fan of crowds, so I stayed in my room during the church service and caught up on the news. At the top of the hour was the Anti-Amp protests, *still* going strong. No longer content to make noise outside City Hall and HCPD HQ, the protesters were now marching down the roads and clogging the arteries of the city.

Didn't these people have to work or something? How were they able to keep a protest like this going on for a week?

As if that wasn't bad enough, Cape Watch and their allies held sympathy protests in other cities across the nation, the largest being in Serenity City, still recovering from the latest Prime showdown.

Cape Watch fueled the protests with a fresh lie: I had killed an unarmed person. Never mind that he threw lightning bolts at me. In America, being shot while unarmed automatically made you an innocent victim.

The shootings must have touched a raw nerve in the psyche of the American people. Primes were supposed to be the brightest and best of humanity, but too many of them had used their powers in the service of greed, wrath and the other cardinal sins. The aftershocks of the Serenity City calamity were still reverberating in America, and my shootings had merely amplified them.

The protests weren't about me. Yeah, the shootings had catalyzed them, but ever since Primes appeared in the world, there had always been a vein of fear and envy and naked anger bubbling under the surface of polite society, waiting to explode into life. After I'd pulled the trigger, all that ugliness came pouring out in the streets.

I was only one man. There was only so much I could do. The only option I had left was to let the Public Relations Office do their thing and keep my head down until it was safe to come back up again.

In this spirit, I stayed inside my cell, reading the books I'd saved on my Kindle and maintaining my equipment. After morning Mass, when the last of the churchgoers had left, I headed out to pick up security hardware.

Wireless cameras to monitor access points. Intrusion detection sensors for windows and doors. An external hard disk drive dedicated to storing the take from the cameras. After lunch, I returned to the church, mounted the cameras and sensors, and walked the priests through on their proper use.

Back in my cell, I practiced my repertoire of techniques, modifying my footwork and angles and weapons to accommodate the enclosed space. Eventually I called a break, did my laundry and checked my inbox. Garcia sent me a brief thank-you note, promising to follow up on the tip. I wished him good luck.

One of the first Chinese proverbs I'd learned was *jie dao sha ren*. Kill with a borrowed knife.

El Trece was huge. Taking them head-on was impossible. I didn't have the manpower, resources or firepower to do it. But the HCPD had. I just had to point them at the right target.

Monday morning was clear and cool and crisp. It had rained overnight, and the world gleamed with a fresh wet coating. I ran around the neighborhood, familiarizing myself with the layout and the rhythms of the street.

Per my usual practice, I dressed in my civilian best and drove to my preferred parking garage a block away from HCPD HQ. Looking out, I saw a small sea of tents cover the plaza. Fully half of the plaza was overrun, in blatant violation of city ordinances.

Uniformed cops walked the perimeter of the tent town, helpless to prevent its expansion. REACT officers in riot gear stood at the ready nearby, unable to act. Journalists and bloggers and reporters trained cameras and tablets and phones at the cops and the protesters, eager to capture the smallest provocation, the slightest misstep.

This was a naked challenge to the legitimate authority. But if the cops moved in now, they would open themselves to accusations of police brutality, lawsuits, and more protests.

The brass probably thought it was best to let them be. At least until the costs outweighed the benefits. I powered up my police-issue phone and checked my inbox. There was a new message from Garcia.

THE ADDRESS *you gave us is empty. Chavez must have flown the coop.*

17

INSIDE GHOST

My breath caught in my chest. My heart pounded in my chest. I sucked down a breath, calmed myself down, and checked the timestamp. Garcia had sent the mail at 0338. Four hours ago. Maybe he was still up. I dialed his number.

"Who's this?" Garcia grumbled.

"Adam Song, HCPD," I said.

"Oh, hey there," he said, his tone lightening. "You got my mail?"

"Yeah. Tough luck."

"It happens, man. Sure you didn't spook them?"

"Nah. They were completely oblivious to my presence. Didn't even take any countersurveillance measures."

"I see. It seemed to me they cleared out in a hurry last night."

"What did you see?"

"Whole lotta nothing. There wasn't anyone on guard duty at the front door. I had to double-check the address, see if I got it right."

"Did you look inside?"

"Yup. I walked up to the front door and shone a red light through the living room windows. There was no sign that anyone lived there. Just cheap furniture and a small TV. No clothes, no cups, no signs of life.

"I took a chance and checked the garage too. The door was unlocked. I lifted it just a fraction, peeked inside, and saw nothing. No cars, no tools, not even an oil stain."

His actions toed over the line of legality. Just saying it was admitting to a crime. He was a cowboy. Just like me.

"I still have a couple of guys watching the house," he continued, "and when the neighborhood wakes up they'll canvas the place. But if you ask me, the birds have flown the coop."

"Damn," I said. "We must have just missed him."

"Yeah. He might be playing a shell game, moving from one safe house to another."

"We can't underestimate him, huh."

"Damn straight. But anyway, I appreciate you taking the trouble to find him. If you hear from your CIs again, be sure to let me know too, okay?"

"Sure thing."

The good guys didn't always win. Sometimes they fell in battle. Other times the bad guys escaped. One day Lady Luck smiles on you, the next day she blesses your target instead. This sort of thing happened all the time.

But there was one other possibility Garcia hadn't mentioned: corruption.

I powered up my Nullphone and checked the tracer app. The device was still online, currently broadcasting from just outside a motel. Scrolling through the menu, I viewed the device's movement history.

A bright blue line cut through the map. I touched the blue dot, and a call-out appeared, stating the moment in time the tracer was at that spot: 1747 hours.

I ran my finger down the line, watching the clock roll back. The tracker had zigged and zagged through Halo City, stopping only once at a gas station. The driver had made the turns at random intervals, as though he were trying to throw off a tail, and now and then he drove in complete circles. I continued tracing the line, following it all the way back to Feliz Hills. Back to the house I'd identified. The time-stamp said the car moved off at 1632.

Fourteen minutes after I'd sent my mails.

Lightning crackled through my chest. I paced the length of the parking lot, sucking down fresh air, forcing myself to coldly and rationally examine the implications.

Cops were as human as everyone else. As fallible and as prone to vice as everyone else. Corruption was as old as crime.

However... this alone didn't prove there was a dirty cop in the department. It was so circumstantial it wouldn't stand up in court. Hell, it was the fruit of the poisonous tree. Since the tracer had been planted without a warrant, it was illegal and inadmissible in court.

I needed more information. And to do that, I needed time and space.

I infiltrated HCPD HQ through a side entrance this time. The protests had grown even larger, almost filling the entirety of the plaza. Whatever it was they were doing to stoke the flames, it must have worked. It was too dangerous to enter through the front now.

I changed into my uniform blues and headed to the top floor. This time, I made my way to the Intelligence Bureau. It was a warrens of short corridors and private offices surrounding a central command center, but eventually I found the office of Captain Anna Hopkins. The door was open, and she was slouching behind her table, frowning at her screen.

Standing at the threshold, I knocked on her door.

"Good morning, ma'am," I said.

Hopkins looked up from her desk. Her dirty blond hair was tied back in a severe bun, shot through with gray and white. Forests of fine lines streaked through her face, and no amount of makeup could hide the bags under her eyes. Then she smiled, and for a second twenty years fell away.

"Good morning. You must be Detective Song."

"Yes ma'am," I said.

"Pleased to meet you. Come in."

I sat at attention by her desk. In my peripheral vision, I saw a framed family photograph. Hopkins, her husband, and a teenage daughter who looked like a younger version of her, all smiling at the camera.

Hopkins chuckled. "Come now, Detective, there's no need to be so formal around here."

I relaxed a fraction. "Yes, ma'am."

She laced her fingers. "The Chief told me you've been through two shootings in the space of a week. I can't begin to imagine what it's like."

"I survived. I wasn't even scratched. It could have been a lot worse."

She nodded. "I like that attitude. I've been on the force for twenty-two years, and I've never had to fire my weapon outside the range."

"May it continue to remain so."

"Indeed. I hope Internal Affairs and the DA's office clear you soon."

"Thank you."

She leaned in. "To business. The Chief said he wants you in Intel Ops & Analysis for the time being, and that you seemed eager to get back to work."

"Not anymore."

She seemed taken aback. "Why not?"

"I'm on an El Trece hit list."

"So I heard. Those animals. But don't worry. Intel Ops & Analysis is a safe assignment. You won't have to kick down doors or expose yourself to hostile situations."

"I'm not afraid of danger, but my family is at risk."

"How so?"

"My informants told me that El Trece is on the warpath. They can't find me, so now they're targeting everyone close to me."

She nodded. "We can make arrangements. Increase police patrols, keep an eye out for El Trece in the area. How's that?"

"Ma'am... I've got to be straight with you."

"Sure."

I had plenty of excuses prepared. But the family photo, positioned next to her keyboard, told me the best one to use.

"They sent professional killers after me. Military-trained. And at least one, possibly more, are Primes. That tells me they're deadly serious. They're not going to send a B-team after my family; they'll send their best. They're not going to stop.

"Increased patrols are fine and good, but unless a patrol unit is nearby, they won't be able to respond in time. And, well, my parents are hippies."

"Hippies?"

"They don't have guns. They don't even like guns. Their idea of security is to install a CCTV camera and security grilles, and even that took a lot of convincing. Now I need to sit them down and tell them their world has turned upside down."

"It can be difficult dealing with... well, civilians."

I nodded. "I need to look after my parents, brother, sister-in-law, niece and nephew. I've got to audit their security, hire a close protection detail, plot secure routes... it's going to be extremely time-consuming."

"You're going all the way for them, aren't you?"

"They're family."

"Of course. But what I meant was, do you have to do this much?"

"Ma'am, are you aware of my status in the HCPD?"

She glanced out the door and lowered her voice. "As a Prime?"

I nodded. "If you do, then you know if bad guys target a Prime, they won't do it half-cocked. They'll send heavy hitters. I need to bring my A-game, and I can't do that while I'm driving a desk."

"I understand. Do you need to take leave?"

"Yes. I've got six weeks' leave stored up."

I rarely use vacation time. I think I've only ever used it to attend specialist training schools when I'm off the clock.

"Excellent. How's this: I'll put you in for a week of leave, and if you need more time off, just let me know."

"That sounds great. Thanks."

"No problem. Family comes first."

AFTER SORTING out the necessary paperwork, I changed into civilian clothing, donned light disguise and went shopping.

Sandwiches. Bottled water. A replacement tracker, just in case. Last of all, I changed cars again, this time picking a dull gray Honda. When I checked my phone again, there was still no movement. I couldn't tell if they enjoyed sleeping in or if they were lying low. Or if they had discovered and removed the tracker.

I had to get eyes on the target.

La Luna Motel was like any other motel. Painted a cheery yellow, it was a two-story complex arranged like a 'U' around a central parking lot. A large sign proclaimed free air conditioning and Wi-Fi, and the best rates in town.

The parking lot was packed, but there was no one in sight. My first drive-by yielded no results, so I drove in and occupied the lot farthest from the entrance. I hustled to the main office, tensing up my abs and shoulders.

A corpulent young man sat behind the counter, staring intently at something below eye level. Frenetic pop music and Japanese dialog scratched at my ears.

"How can I help you?" he recited monotonously.

"I need to use a bathroom," I said.

He pointed down a hallway, eyes still glued to the screen. "Over there."

"Thanks."

I did my business, then walked out, loosening my muscles and straightening my back. Keeping to the shade, I studied the parking lot, as though looking for my car.

There. Tucked away in a corner was a bright red Ford. I Amped my sight, just a little, and read the license plate.

It was Chavez's vehicle.

I climbed into my car and drove off. Peeking in the rearview mirror, I saw no sign of angry gangbangers.

This phase had gone smoothly enough. But you can't ever underestimate your opposition.

I drove a couple of blocks away and popped into the first cafe I saw. I ordered a cup of jasmine tea, paid up front, and watched the tracer app.

To outside observers, I was just a guy enjoying a drink while playing with his phone. A completely ordinary sight in Halo City. As a bonus, the tea was excellent.

Chavez's car remained still. I drove off again, ensconced myself in an underground parking lot, and waited.

At half past noon, the car moved again. I drove off immediately, keeping one eye on the road and the other on the screen. Chavez moved in steady, straight lines, and I mimicked him, staying one street away.

The car made one last turn and came to a rest. I sped up, cleared the block, and parked on the opposite street. I lifted my binoculars just in time to see Chavez and his three-man crew enter a diner. I leaned back and waited.

Fifteen minutes later, I was sure they were still inside. I watched the street for a while longer, until I saw a couple of young men enter the joint. I counted to three hundred and called Garcia.

"Who's this?" he mumbled sleepily.

"Adam Song, HCPD. Did I just wake you?" I asked.

"Yeah." He sighed. "What's up?"

"You're not going to believe this, but my buddies just spotted Adrian Chavez."

"What?!" he exclaimed, instantly awake.

"My buddies just spotted Adrian Chavez."

"I know, I mean, how?"

"Hell of a thing. They went to Maria's Diner on 88th Street for lunch, and the moment they walked in, they saw Chavez and his crew. There's four of them, Chavez included. If you move fast, you can find him."

"I... Damn, man, that's incredible. Tell your friends to keep an eye on Chavez. I'll mobilize my team. Once we arrive, we'll take over the stakeout from there."

"Got it."

I hung up. Ate my sandwiches. Drank my water. Waited.

Twenty minutes later, the El Trece gangsters left the diner. Chavez was playing it cool, but his bodyguards were on edge, puffing themselves up and scanning in every direction. The second they were inside the car, they rocketed down the road.

I checked my phone. The gangsters shot down narrow streets and made hairpin turns, keeping just under the legal limit. They circled round and round and round, occasionally making abrupt U-turns and driving off in a random direction. These were extremely aggressive countersurveillance moves, designed to flush all but the best and most well-equipped wheel artists.

There was only one conclusion: someone had tipped them off.

Someone within the HCPD.

I SHADOWED the gangsters a while longer, following them back to their motel. When I was sure they were holed up indoors, I fell back to the church.

Both hands firmly grasping the wheel, breathing long and slow and deep, I turned my thoughts entirely to the present. There was a hollow psychic ache throbbing in my heart, a bitter taste at the back of my throat, an iron tension gathering in my jaws and shoulders. The blast of the air conditioner grated at my ears, the sunlight lashed my eyes, and the pseudo-leather of the steering wheel was unpleasantly slick.

I breathed, relaxed, focused.

I had no evidence. That was the crux of the matter. All I had were two separate observations of Chavez and his crew fleeing a location after I had alerted Garcia. I had no definitive proof that there was a dirty cop feeding information to El Trece, or at least Chavez.

But there was no other possible explanation for Chavez's behavior. Only the guilty and those with secrets to hide drive the way he did, so soon after I had informed Garcia. The evacuation from the first safehouse might simply have been part of a shell game, but not the flight from the diner. When Chavez received the alert that the cops were on him, he must have kept his men in line, made them finish their meal and do nothing that would further raise suspicions. That would explain why they took so long to leave, and their subsequent flight.

Was Garcia dirty? Or his team? Or supervisors? Or all the above?

At this stage, it didn't matter. The important part was that I didn't know anyone in the department I could trust to take care of El Trece for me. Especially on an unofficial basis. I couldn't even officially pass on my suspicions about a dirty cop either; the warrantless tracer practically guaranteed that any investigation using this angle would die in the womb.

There was also the problem of the brass. I had no reason to believe Anderson and his senior leaders were acting in good faith. They violated post-OIS protocol by not replacing my pistol, and they did not make any arrangements to protect the family of a cop known to be on an El Trece hit list. The assignment to Intelligence felt like an attempt to bury me. Maybe the brass was hoping the protests would die a natural death if I didn't appear on the papers for a while. Maybe I was being set up. I didn't know which.

One of the many Chinese terms for 'traitor' was *nei gui*. The literal translation was 'inside ghost.' An apt description. I couldn't hit back at ghosts I couldn't see, but everywhere I went I felt their claws digging in my back.

I couldn't trust the system. I had to rely on myself. And those I could trust.

My phone vibrated in my pocket. Garcia. I pulled over and answered the phone.

"Hey Song, I'm on site," he said. "Where's the suspects?"

I'd forgotten to close the loop with him earlier. Just as well he'd called.

"They got away," I replied.

"Got away? How?"

"I decided to head over to the diner in case my buddies needed backup. The moment I arrived, Chavez and his crew drove off. I tried to follow, but he must have spotted us. He pulled a number of aggressive countersurveillance moves and shook us off."

"Son of a bitch." Garcia sighed. "Well, nothing we can do."

"Sorry," I said.

"No worries. There's always a next time."

Garcia's emotional responses sounded genuine. On the other hand, his caginess during my initial meet was perplexing. Was he defending Chavez then? Or merely his own turf? I couldn't tell.

Paranoia gripped me. I fired up the security app and checked the cameras and sensors. No signs of suspicious activity. But from now on, I had to check the sensors before returning to the church. Just in case.

Back at the Church of the Immaculate Heart, I returned to my cell in the clergy house, fired up my laptop and opened my word processor. I touched my fingers to the keys, but no words came. What the hell was I supposed to do, write a report about my suspicions on corruption in the HCPD based on an illegal investigation? That would just get IA on my case and leave the true criminals untouched.

But I couldn't walk away. This wasn't right. More importantly, I couldn't just sit here and wait for El Trece to try again.

But what could I do?

I thought about it, then opened my word processor and typed.

Calvary

THROUGH BLACKENED *smog clinging to the blasted earth*
  Illuminating moonless skies and naked clouds
  At the farthest end of distant Calvary
  The empty cross blazes bright

                                    . . .

I CHUCKLED. This place was getting to me. Maybe some fresh air would do me good.

Outside, it was mid-afternoon in Chinatown. Teenagers and children were returning home, steadying themselves to tackle the mounds of homework and tuition and extra credit assignments that awaited them, occasionally ducking into nearby stores for a brief respite. A private bus rumbled down the road, filled with Caucasian and Mediterranean tourists. At the far end of the block, right across the road, was a store selling hero memorabilia. T-shirts and mugs and hoodies of the most famous Primes in the world.

I spotted an advertisement on a giant billboard. It showed the Jade Empress and Justice Di standing side-by-side, her in her trademark turquoise cheongsam, him in a tailored suit and hat. The words 'CITADEL DESIGN' floated next to her face, and beneath that was the company's motto: Glamorous, Relentless.

I shook my head. Protective clothing had gone high street. I remembered a time when the tactical industry served a small niche, military and law enforcement, and bona fide superheroes. Today everybody wanted to wear the same clothes superheroes did, never mind that most of them didn't lead the kind of lives that required stab-proof and bullet-resistant armor capable of masquerading as high fashion.

It wasn't necessarily a bad thing. At least until rogues get their hands on body armor indistinguishable from street clothes.

My feet carried me back to the church grounds. I was still in no mood to return to my room, so I passed through the main doors of the basilica.

Blessed silence enveloped me. Mass was long over, and there were no other programs scheduled for today. Wandering down the nave, I had only statues of saints and angels for company. I didn't recognize most of them, but there were so many, one for every column running the length of the walls. Paintings of other holy men and women flanked the statues, labeled with brass plaques. Stained glass windows reproduced key scenes from the Bible: the Sermon on the Mount, the Passion of the Christ, the temptation of Eve.

The chandeliers overhead granted the nave a rich golden radiance, emphasizing every exquisite detail of the artwork around me and throwing the high ribbed vault ceiling into sharp relief.

The light drew my eye to the altar, a white granite table covered in a cloth of deep purple velvet. A pair of tall, lit candles stood on the ledge. Behind both altar and candles was the crucifix.

Mounted just above eye height, the giant cross loomed over the pews, visible even from the entrance. I sat at an empty pew in the front row and studied Jesus on his cross. His head was lowered, his crown of thorns ensnared deep in his flesh, yet his face was a mask of complete serenity. He gazed down at me in mute judgment.

"What am I supposed to do now?" I asked.

Jesus said nothing.

I laughed. What else did I expect? This was an inanimate carving, not the man himself. An anchor for believers to ground and direct and proclaim their faith, but not a sentient being capable of answering my questions.

I sighed.

"Is something the matter?"

My heart slammed into my chest. My left hand flew to the Glock in my jacket pocket. Glancing behind me, I saw Father Joshua Park down the aisle. I'd been so preoccupied I hadn't heard him coming.

I couldn't let that happen again.

"Oh, hello Adam," he said.

I released my pistol and breathed.

"Hello, Father Josh."

"I heard you sighing. What's the matter?"

I couldn't think of an answer. Not yet. I pursed my lips. Held the space. Breathed.

"Well..." I began.

"Yes?"

"I've been thinking..."

"You do a lot of that."

We chuckled. The priest sat down next to me with a soft groan.

"Getting old," he muttered.

"Age catches up with everyone."

He smiled. "It does."

I leaned back and continued staring at Jesus. Jesus stared back. Father Josh said nothing.

"I have a question about the Bible," I said, finally.

He smiled. "Ask away."

"There's a passage that goes, 'render unto Caesar the things that are Caesar's, and unto God the things that are God's. Correct?"

"Yes. Mark 12:17."

"What does it mean?"

He laughed. "That's a deceptively complicated question, with many answers."

"What's yours?"

"Well, we need to understand the context first. The chief priests, the teachers of the law and the elders of Judea wished to entrap Jesus, so they sent some Pharisees and Herodians to ask if they should pay the imperial tax to Caesar. Jesus called them out on their hypocrisy and asked for a coin. When he received it, he asked them whose image was on the coin. They said it was Caesar's. Jesus told them to give back to Caesar what belonged to him, and give to God what is God's.

"To me, this passage says that a good Christian should obey both the lawful secular authority and the authority of God. Per Dan 2:21, God removes kings and sets up kings, so secular authority flows from God. Thus, obedience to Caesar is obedience to God, and defying Caesar is also defying God."

"What if Caesar can't enforce his laws?"

"Why do you ask?"

"Hypothetical question."

"Hypothetical?"

"Yes."

He raised an eyebrow and stroked his chin.

"Speaking from a Christian perspective, we are required to obey God's law. Whether Caesar can enforce his laws is immaterial."

"But you have to obey Caesar anyway?"

"Yes…"

But he sounded doubtful.

"What if Caesar's actions break the laws of God?" I asked.

"Then God will surely throw him down in time, as He did with the Caesars of Rome. As for Christians, they are not obliged to obey Caesar's laws whenever they contradict with divine law." He paused. "And yet, should Christians choose disobedience, they must still recognize the authority of Caesar, and accept what punishments he metes out."

"In other words, there is a higher law from which all secular laws must flow."

"Ideally, yes."

"Does it also mean that any secular authority that defies divine authority must be disobeyed?"

He shifted uncomfortably in his seat. "Well… yes, if they also ask you to defy God."

"I see."

I wondered what Shi Shifu would say if I'd asked him the same question. There was no supreme God who laid down the law, but all sentient beings were bound by the principle of karma. A ruler who was not morally upright, did not serve his citizens, and fostered discord and ill-will among the people would surely bring about his own downfall.

But someone would have to be the agent of his karma.

"Did that answer your question?"

"Yes."

"I'm surprised you asked a question like that."

"Oh?"

"You strike me as a pragmatic man, if I may say so. Someone more concerned with practical than spiritual affairs."

I said nothing.

"It sounds to me that you're thinking deeply about something you should do," he continued.

"I guess I should go to church more often," I said with a smile.

He laughed. "Fortunately, you're living next to one."

Jesus gazed down on me in silent judgment. The angels and the saints joined him. I stared back at them. They didn't respond, of course. They couldn't.

My phone rang. Thomas Crane.

"Amp, we have a problem," he said.

"What is it?"

"One of my ASOs spotted a suspicious vehicle outside Loong Moon."

18

IMMEDIATE ACTION

"Wait one," I said.

Rising, I rushed out of the nave, phone pressed against my ear, hand at my Glock, scanning for threats. In the relative sanctuary of the transept, I asked, "What happened?"

"My ASO was rolling by Loong Moon when he saw a gray van parked across the road from the restaurant, facing traffic. He stopped his car nearby and approached Long Moon on foot. He went inside, introduced himself, and when he walked out he used the opportunity to study the van.

"He saw two Hispanic males seated up front, observing the restaurant. They quickly turned away as he looked at them. As he returned to his car, the van rocked slightly. He called it in straightaway."

There was someone inside the van. No doubt about it. It was a classic rookie mistake—but sometimes even veterans make it.

"Where is your ASO now?" I asked.

"Just around the corner. He's stationary and awaiting further instructions. He wants to know if he should call the cops."

That would be the smart move. But I thought of the words burned into the wall next to my apartment, and Clements' speculation that a Prime did it. If ordinary patrolmen chanced upon a Prime criminal...

"I *am* a cop," I said.

Tom laughed. "That's why I called you. How do you want to play it?"

"I'm going down to check it out."

"Roger. Need backup?"

"Yes."

"Got it. I can be on site within twenty minutes."

"Copy that. We'll meet at Tang's Emporium. It's at West Hill and Clancy, a block south of Loong Moon."

"Gotcha."

"Need a gun?"

"I have my own."

"Need a *long* gun?"

Silence for a moment.

"No," he decided. "You keep yours. I'll use my powers if things go hot."

"Roger. See you in a few."

I rushed to my cell. Threw open my closet door. Considered my options.

My first instinct was to play it like a traffic stop. But I was a target. If the van were filled with El Trece hitters, moseying up there was a great way to eat a faceful of lead.

But if *they* thought I was bracing them with nothing more substantial than what I was carrying...

I grabbed my gun bag. My AR-15 was inside, locked and loaded, ready for action. I threw on my chest rig, zipped my jacket over it, and slung the gun bag over my shoulder.

As I left, I met Father Josh at the entrance of the clergy house.

"Where are you going?" he asked.

"Just taking care of business," I replied.

THE DRIVE to Tang's Emporium took just under ten minutes. I pulled up right outside the shop and waited. A few minutes later, a green Chevy rolled up right behind me, and the driver stepped out.

Tom Crane. Today he was dressed almost like me, a gunfighter trying to be a gray man, wearing low-pro garments in earthy tones laden with hidden pockets. Instead of a jacket, he wore a green long-sleeved synthetic shirt, emphasizing the swell of his powerful arms, and he carried his custom Glock 34 openly on his right hip.

Grabbing my bag, I got out to greet him.

"Tom," I said. "Thanks for coming out here."

"No problem," he replied. "Expecting trouble?"

"Can't hurt to be prepared." I gestured at his pistol. "Isn't that provocative?"

"I'm on duty, and I have all my paperwork with me," he said, grinning like a wolf. "I'm not looking for trouble, of course, but if they shoot first..."

Shaking my head, I said, "I'll do the talking. Just stay beside me and back me up as needed."

"Gotcha. If things go south, get behind me and take cover. I'll put my shield up."

"Sounds like a plan."

We sauntered down the street, just a pair of men out and about on a sunny day in Halo City. I rested my right hand on my bag, pinching the zipper with thumb and index finger. Nobody spared us a second glance. The passers-by were too absorbed in their phones to notice Tom's firearm.

"That's the suspect vic," Tom said.

In the middle of the road, in front of a jewelry store and right across the street from Loong Moon, was a gray four-panel van. The kind of van I'd used for stakeouts in another life. The rear doors sported a pair of windows. I tried to peer inside, but the sun glared off the rear bumper and into my eyes.

I donned my sunglasses and scanned. Civilians ambled down the sidewalk, focused entirely on their affairs. No danger vibes from them.

More cars lined the road to my left. Wordlessly, Tom moved up on my right. The implication was clear: if things went bad, I'd go left immediately. I needed the cover more than he did.

The van shifted on its suspension. My pulse quickened.

"Movement inside the vic," I warned.

A dark shape popped up at the window and quickly ducked back down.

"I think someone just looked out," Tom said.

The doors flung open.

Four men, two with AKs, two with pump-action shotguns, aimed at us.

"CONTACT!" I yelled.

I lunged to my left, ducking behind the trunk of a car. Tom squared off and extended his arms.

Shotguns roared. AKs chattered. Aegis grinned.

Small metallic objects floated in front of his face. Bullets and buckshot, suspended in mid-air.

I unzipped the bag, tore out the AR-15 and brought it to my shoulder. Aimed down the red dot sight, rested the blazing scarlet circle on the nearest threat—

A fist of living flame filled my optics. A wall of heat seared my skin and hair and eyes. Wincing, I ducked.

"AAAAAAAAAAAAAAAH!" Tom screamed.

He was wreathed in flames, burning like a human pyre.

"TOM!" I screamed.

Covering his face, he dropped to the sidewalk and rolled back and forth.

"Adam! KILL THEM!" he yelled.

I peeked out. A fresh barrage of gunfire drove me back. Bullets whistled past my ears, skipping off the road and pavement and slamming into engines and tires. I kept low, placing the engine block between my body and the shooters. I switched shoulders and peered out the other side of the car. No shot. I scuttled out a couple of inches, brought up my carbine—

"FUCK YOU!" Aegis roared.

Cold fear gripped my guts. My muscles locked up. My blood chilled. My fingers froze. What was I doing there? How could I hope to fight a Prime and three more—

I exhaled sharply. Inhaled. Screamed my lungs out, expelling whatever it was that had sunk into my veins.

My head cleared. I popped up and aimed.

The van sped off, doors flapping in the air. I tracked it, red dot seeking the driver, thumb clicking off the safety, finger taking up first pressure on the two-stage trigger, finding the moment of resistance just before—

No.

The van turned a bend and disappeared.

I lowered my weapon.

The sickeningly sweet scent of cooked pork flooded my nostrils, mixing with the nauseating odors of melting polymers.

"Tom! Are you okay?" I demanded.

"No! Adam! Fuck! I'm burning!"

Tom was still rolling back and forth, still covered in flames. I pulled off my jacket and swatted his body. Flames scorched my hands, smoke ripped at my nose. One last flap, and the fire was out.

"Is it over?" he asked.

"I... My God..."

His hands were charred and blackened. Ugly red and yellow patches covered spots in his torso where the flame had burned through. The flesh and skin of his face was a melted ruin, exposing the pale bone beneath. His eyes were...

"I can't see!" Tom shouted.

"Stay put!" I replied. "I'm going to call for help."

Looking around, I saw a large black man hustling over. He looked at Tom and skidded to a stop.

"Jesus *Christ!*" he said. "What happened?"

"He's been burned," I said. "Listen, I need your help. Go to the Chinese restaurant across the street and ask for clean towels and warm water. *Not* cold water; it must be warm."

"Got it."

As the man rushed off, I grabbed my phone and dialed 911.

"Adam..." Tom whispered.

"Don't worry," I said. "I gotcha."

"911 Emergency, how can I help?" the dispatcher asked.

"This is Detective Adam Song, calling in an attempted murder with superpowers."

"Go ahead, detective. What's your location?"

"Tang's Jeweler's. West Hill and Wilkins. There were six suspects in a gray van. Two up front, four in the rear. The ones in the rear have automatic AK-47s and shotguns. One suspect in the rear is a Prime, a pyrokinetic.

"Suspects were loitering opposite Loong Moon Dim Sum restaurant. Security guard called in me and the Prime Aegis to investigate. Suspects opened fire on us and wounded Aegis. Aegis has severe burns all over his body. Suspects have fled the scene."

"Copy all that. Are you okay?"

"Yes. But I'll need an ambulance for Aegis."

"Got it. How badly is he injured?"

"His arms and everything above his knees are covered in burns. Full-thickness burns, down to the bone."

"Okay. Is anyone else wounded?"

I paused, looked around. The streets had emptied out. No screaming, no crying. Aegis was sucking it all in, his teeth gritted.

"No other casualties in sight. But there may be more."

"Okay. Did you get the suspect's license plate number?"

"Yeah," I said, and read it out.

"Got it. Do you have a description of the suspects?"

"Negative. All I could tell was that they were Hispanic males. All of them."

The black man hustled across the street. Aaron was right behind him, hauling a huge bucket of water.

"I'm going to apply first aid," I added. "I need to hang up now. But I'll stay on site and update you if necessary."

"Understood."

Aaron set the bucket down. "Adam, what happened?"

"Aegis was burned," I said. "Help me sit him up."

Sweeping away a lake of fallen projectiles at our feet, Aaron and I dragged Aegis over to a nearby car and propped him against the wheel. The black man set the bucket next to us. Mr. Tang popped out of his jewelry store.

"Is everyone okay?" he asked. "Anyone need help?"

"We're good here," I said, "but could you look around and see if there's anyone else injured?"

"Okay!" Tang said and sprinted off.

Turning to Aegis, I said, "Aegis, talk to me. Can you breathe? Any pain?"

He gasped. "Yeah. Bit hard to breathe. Can't see much. Getting cold."

"Got it. Hang in there." Looking at the other two men, I said, "His wounds are going to swell. We need to take off his boots, belt, rings, and necklace."

As Aaron and the other man stripped off Aegis' boots, I unbuckled his belt and carefully removed it. The belt held his holstered Glock and three spare magazines, all of them burned and melted. It was a small wonder the bullets hadn't cooked off.

"Who the hell did this?" the black man wondered.

"A rogue," I said, checking Aegis' fingers.

"A what?"

"Local term for supervillain. You're not from around here, are you?" I said, carefully extracting Aegis' burnished wedding ring from his left hand.

"I'm from Sante Fe." He sighed. "This was supposed to be a business trip."

"Welcome to Halo City," Aegis wheezed.

"What next?" Aaron asked.

"We need to cover the burns. You got any towels?" I asked.

"They're soaking in the pail," he said.

"Excellent." I paused for a second, checking Aegis' feet. No burns. "I need you two to help dress Aegis' fingers. Wrap all of them with the towels. But keep the fingers separated.."

As the men worked, I rolled up my pants, exposing my ankle-mounted first aid kit. I donned a pair of bright blue nitrile gloves, then grabbed a packet of combat gauze, tore it open, and soaked the gauze in water.

The fabric was impregnated with chitosan beads. Once exposed to fluid, they would expand and stick to each other, forming a gel that served as a two-in-one hemostatic agent and burn protector.

The working surface of the gauze turned slick. I pulled it from the water and wrapped it around Tom's charred throat. He moaned in relief.

"That feels better," he said.

"His fingers... are... stuck," Aaron remarked, disgust leaking through his voice.

"Don't separate them," I said. "Aegis, can you still breathe?"

"Yeah," Tom whispered.

I tied off the gauze and placed my fingers just under his nose. His breathing was rapid and shallow. I pressed the back of my hand to his forehead. The skin, what was left of it, was cool and clammy.

Shock was setting in.

"We need to cover the rest of his wounds," I said. "Help me take off his shirt."

The men held his arms up. Sirens howled in the distance. I pulled his shirt up and immediately felt resistance. I grabbed my multitool from my chest rig, unfolded the scissors, and began cutting away at the thick material.

"My God..." Aaron whispered. "Adam, why are you dressed for war?"

"Blame the people who did this."

I cut off Tom's sleeves, then removed large swatches of fabric from the shirt, careful to cut around the material embedded in his skin. I ripped open my spare gauze packet, soaked the gauze, and handed the roll to Aaron.

"Wrap this around his body," I said. "You can also use the leftover gauze from around his neck."

As the men worked, I continued cutting off his clothes, exposing his thighs. They were as badly burned as the rest of him. I reached into the pail for more towels and—

A thought struck me.

"Shit!"

"What's wrong?" the man from Santa Fe asked.

I'd forgotten one important thing: hypothermia. Without insulation from skin and clothing, and with wet dressings wrapped around his body, hypothermia could quickly set in.

I paused for a breath. I didn't have any more gauze packets. The towels were all soaked. The EMTs were coming. It was a pleasantly warm day in Halo City, and the water was room temperature.

We were committed. And Tom was a fighter.

"Wring the remaining towels dry before you apply them," I said.

We covered Tom's arms and thighs with the remaining towels, and elevated his arms above his heart. As soon as the EMTs got here, they had to be able to quickly remove them. I kept up a running dialogue with Tom, keeping him alert while monitoring the quality of his breathing. The sirens inched ever closer.

At last, we were done. Tom was covered head to toe in towels and gauze, the fabric quickly turning red and pink. I didn't have anything else on hand to help him.

"What now?" the Santa Fe man asked.

"Guide the ambulance as it comes in. Aaron, help me elevate his legs. I've got his arms."

The men scrambled to work. Aaron grimaced, grabbed Tom's legs and lifted them as high as he could. I dragged Tom's gun belt next to me, then moved my gun bag beside it, and held his arms up.

"Adam," Tom whispered.

"Yeah, I'm here," I said.

"Stay..."

I held his hand. "I'm here."

"Don't..."

"I'm not going anywhere."

We stayed where we were until the medics came.

19
_____

IT ONLY TAKES ONE SIDE

I'd been here too many times to count. Seated outside an
operating room, covered in dust and blood, weapon close at
hand, waiting for the doc to pronounce his verdict.

The first time was off the coast of Iran. After the showdown with
Samiel, the dust off chopper sent us to a hospital ship. I was the only
one in the team who could still walk. Everyone else—the living,
anyway—was rushed to the trauma center. After I was treated, I
wandered the hall outside the OR, half-catatonic, sand spilling from
my boots and uniform, until a nurse finally sat me down and told me
to wait.

Half the team made it. The rest died.

Since Iran, there'd been so many more visits. A few were state-
side, after a training accident or off-base incident. Often, they were in
Germany or Japan or other, more austere facilities in the furthest
corners of the world. Sometimes I was the guy in the OR, doped up to
my eyes; more often I was the guy outside, sometimes alone, sometimes with others, waiting for the doc. The only difference now was
that I was at Halo City General Hospital.

A plainclothes detective took my statement in the waiting area. I hadn't fired my weapons, so I'd been allowed to keep them after a quick field test. I didn't know if it were a blessing or a curse.

If only I'd gotten rounds downrange faster, if only I'd gotten the AR in the fight sooner, maybe if I'd gone for the Glock instead, Tom would be fine.

And yet, if El Trece tried another pass in the hospital, I'd be ready for them.

Maybe I should have shot up the van. Killed the driver, worked the body of the van, closed and destroyed the enemy. Exactly the way I would have done in the Raiders, in the Task Force. They wanted to play with the big boys, they'd get what was coming to them.

But that would have been murder. This was America, not some third world hellhole. The rules of engagement here were different, and the consequences of every trigger pull far weightier.

And yet...

I shook my head. I was thinking too much. Regret poisons the soul. What's done is done, learn what you must, and roll with what you have left.

All I could do was hold space, breathe, and wait.

Nurses walked past me. I breathed. Civilians moaned and complained and shouted. I looked, saw no threat, donned my earplugs, and breathed. An old man with a pair of cybernetic legs whirred and clunked past. I breathed. Around me, men stared into smartphones, women held their faces in their hands, children fussed and played. I breathed. The scent of disinfectant filled my nose, a thousand smaller sounds clawed at my ears, my clothes dried against my skin. I breathed.

The double doors opened, revealing a tall black woman in green surgical scrubs. She took off her mask and walked up to me.

"How's he doing?" I asked.

She smiled. "He'll make a full recovery."

"Good work, Angel," I said.

She was Angela Dawson. The other half of the Dawson power couple, and arguably the more famous half. She wasn't in public service, she wasn't a cop or a warfighter, she was just a trauma surgeon.

And a Prime with the power to heal any injury with a mere touch.

"Thanks. But honestly, you kept him alive long enough for him to get here."

"Just did what I could."

She was trying to make me feel better. Burns this severe had a fatality rate close to a hundred percent. The only way to guarantee survival was to have a healer like Angel on standby.

"How's he doing now?" I asked.

"We'll have to keep Tom under observation for the next twenty-hours, but I don't foresee any complications."

"As always."

She smiled. "I do what I can."

"Can I see him?"

"Not right now. Healing places a great toll on the body. You could come see him tomorrow."

"Got it."

Peeling off her cap, she shook loose a head of short, kinked hair. She was in her mid-fifties, but her face was still smooth and her sweat-slicked hair still dark.

"What happened to Tom?" she asked.

"Someone hit him with a fireball."

"A fireball? But I thought he could produce shields."

"Electromagnetic shields. Maybe it doesn't work on heat."

The HCPD file on Aegis noted his ability to generate and manipulate electromagnetic fields so powerful they could stop bullets in mid-flight. But he wasn't invulnerable. The fireball proved that.

And now, thinking about that sudden wave of fear, the way the van suddenly sped off when the shooters had us on the ropes, I wondered if there were more to Aegis' powers than he openly admitted.

"Looks like Aegis isn't so invincible after all," she said.

"He stopped the rounds when it counted. That's the important part."

"Yeah." She gestured at the empty chair next to me. "Mind if I sit here?"

"Go ahead."

She slumped into the seat, pressing the first phalanges of her index fingers into her temples.

"Long day?" I asked.

"Every day is a long day," she said.

Her power was incredible, but so was the toll it took. She claimed she could only heal up to ten patients a day. Less, if the wounds were especially grievous or complicated.

It didn't stop her from writing her own checks.

"I appreciate you coming down to help."

She flashed a smile. "Anything for Aegis. And don't worry about the bill; I'll take care of it."

"Thanks. You're a real angel."

She laughed. "Just part of the job."

A little girl wandered up to her, clutching a teddy bear in one hand and a book in the other.

"Um..." she began.

"Hi sweetheart," she said. "Is something wrong?"

"Are you Angel?" the girl asked.

"That's right."

The girl held up the book. "Could we have your autograph?"

"Sure thing."

Angel signed the back cover in a clear, confident hand. The girl beamed.

"Thanks!"

"My pleasure. Is there anything else you wanted?"

"Well..." The girl hid her stuff behind her back and fidgeted. "Granddad is in surgery. Doctor say it's a heart attack. Can you... can you make him well again?"

"I'll make sure he gets the best care possible."

"Thank you!"

The girl pranced off, hugging her bear and book. Her mother beckoned her over, and her father favored Angel with a smile.

"Does this happen often?" I asked.

"All the time." She continued massaging her temples. "Everywhere I go, people keep asking me for autographs."

"Must be nice to be appreciated."

"I just do what I can."

I chuckled. Behind the mask of humility was a pragmatic businesswoman.

Angel ran a private practice downtown. Exclusive clinic, appointment only, catering to the rich and famous. Her power wasn't limited to trauma; she could heal any ailment, no matter how stubborn or allegedly incurable. Celebrities and politicians and executives all over the world routinely booked her services. Her fees were astronomical, but all her patients walked away in the pink of health.

She regularly did charity cases too. When a first responder is injured, when a mass casualty event occurs in Halo City, when the plight of a diseased person makes international news, she offers her help. Free.

By sharing her power with the world, she became the most famous Prime in the city. She was so popular among the religious crowd, if she were Catholic, the Pope would have to seriously entertain the possibility of having her declared a saint. As if that wasn't enough, in between bookings, she organized charity drives to support medical research.

Her latest being the gala at the Morgan Arts Center.

It was her show from start to finish. She had found the beneficiaries and the sponsors, tapped her network of friends across the country, and browbeat the media until they gave her favorable press coverage. Her husband dutifully showed up, the moon to her sun. For protection, the Dawsons hired Aegis and his hand-picked team of specialists.

Then the terrorists hit.

That was a goat-rope from start to finish. Or, at least, it could have been. When my team arrived, we intercepted two gunmen fleeing the scene, panicking and screaming for their lives. We yelled at them to stop, one guy raised his weapon, we put him down with a barrage of aimed fire, and his buddy surrendered. Inside, we rushed to the sound of gunfire and neutralized the bad guys pinning Aegis down.

But still...

I closed my eyes, dredging the depths of my brain. The first threat I saw was leaning out behind a glass display, aiming at Aegis. I put two in his side, saw him fall, moved on to the next. That guy was fleeing, his weapon clenched firmly in his hands, sprinting right towards us.

Oliveira yelled at him to stop. He swept his weapon at us. I shot him in the head.

But in the final moment before the trigger broke, I saw that his face was a rictus of fear.

Angel. Aegis. Will. Plutarch. Myself. Our lives had collided at the Morgan Arts Center and had remained intertwined since. Sometimes I wondered if someone up there was amusing himself. Or if there was a grand plan in motion, one I couldn't begin to comprehend.

"You're pretty quiet today," Angel said.

"Just thinking."

"About?"

"Karma."

She laughed. "Karma. I expected nothing less from you."

"Thank you."

"Thinking about the protests?"

"Sometimes."

"Don't let the haters get you down. There'll always be people out there who hate us. Who hate what we do."

"They are annoying."

She smiled. "What you do comes back to you. Spread the love and love comes back. That's how karma works, doesn't it?"

"Essentially."

Angel had a gift everyone could love. My power was suited only for destruction. I'm pretty sure I couldn't do what she did. But maybe some principles were universal.

I stood, dusting myself off. "Thanks for helping, Angel, but I've got work to do now."

"Me too. See you when I see you."

"Give Will my regards."

Her face flattened. Her eyes darkened. Her lips went still. A microsecond later, she posed a smile.

"Sure, I'll do that."

She lied.

But so had I.

IT ONLY TAKES one side to fight a war.

It only takes one side to lose it.

A cold fire burned in my chest. As I drove out of the hospital, I breathed it out, breathed out the venom of anger and rage and sorrow and fear, leaving behind a thick face and a blackened heart.

The tracker was still merrily broadcasting Chavez's location. They had moved out of the motel, settling into a two-story apartment in Balboa Park. Another low-middle class neighborhood, quietly going to the dogs. I had made the mistake of going to the cops and expecting them to take care of Chavez. Twice. Shame on me.

There won't be a third time.

When I returned to Loong Moon, it was almost closing time. Despite the late hour, there was still a long queue outside, eager to get in before last orders. I cut to the front of the queue, still reeking of ashes, gun bag slung around my shoulder. The maître d' tried to stop me, until I gave him my name.

"I won't be long," I said. "I just need to speak to my family."

"They're busy," he said hesitatingly.

I showed him my badge. "There was a shooting here earlier today. I need to talk to them."

The maître d' hurriedly showed me inside, taking me to a small table. He left me a menu and an order sheet. I set them aside and waited.

Moments later, my brother appeared. My parents followed in his footsteps.

"Adam!" Aaron said. "You're back!"

I nodded. "Yeah. Is everyone okay?"

"Yes. No one else was injured. What about Aegis? How's he doing?"

"He's fine," I said. "Angel treated him. He'll make a full recovery."

"Thank God."

I gestured around the restaurant. "Still open for business?"

"We won't close," Father said stiffly. "Not for gangsters."

"You didn't hire extra security either."

"But the customers…" Aaron began.

"Almost got shot," I said. "Look, Aegis is in hospital because we didn't step up our security. We can't let them happen again."

"You brought them here!" Father exclaimed.

I clenched my fists. Breathed. Relaxed.

"What do you mean by that?" I asked.

Father shoved past Aaron.

"You shot that gangster. Now they're coming after you! It's your fault!"

Mother clicked her tongue and patted his arm. "*Aiya,* that's—"

"I didn't have a choice," I said evenly.

"Bullshit! You bring trouble to us, and you tell me you didn't have a choice?" He jammed his finger into my chest. "You tell me—"

I grabbed his hand with both of mine and twisted sharply into him, at the last second pulling in my elbow to avoid his chin. He gasped, suddenly stumbling. I caught him and stood him back upright.

My mother's jaw dropped. Aaron held both hands up. My father looked up at me in sudden fear. Diners around us stopped and stared.

Silence.

"Adam…" Aaron said.

"What's done is done," I said. "I'm not here to blame anyone or to argue with you. I don't have time for that. But the fact remains that El Trece set up an attack outside Loong Moon, and Aegis is down. You must take the threat seriously."

Aaron crossed his arms. "Adam, you shot—"

"I know who I shot," I said. "That doesn't matter now. El Trece doesn't care. You are on their hit list too, and no amount of blaming or complaining will change that."

"But—"

"Shut up," I snapped.

He shut up.

"Here's what's going to happen," I said. "You will close the restaurant and leave town. Immediately."

"We can't do that," Mother said. "Not possible!"

It wasn't impossible. She had merely given up before considering the option.

"If you won't do it, then you must hire armed security," I said. "You need to protect the restaurant, the children when they go to school, and yourselves when you're out."

"That's... it's not that bad, right?" Aaron asked.

"Aaron, are you fucking kidding me?"

He recoiled. "But—"

"But they almost killed Aegis right across the road! You saw it yourself! When will you take the threat seriously? When they throw a firebomb through the door? When they shoot up the place? You're lucky they didn't kill anyone today. But tomorrow? The day after?" I shook my head. "Either close the restaurant and leave the city, or hire protectors. Your choice. But understand this: El Trece is coming for you."

"Get out," Father said.

"*De*," Aaron began.

Father pointed at the door. "Get out!"

"If you need me, you know how to contact me," I said.

I turned and walked away.

"Wait!" Aaron said.

"What is it?" I demanded.

"Where are you going? What are you going to do?"

"What I must."

I left the restaurant and drove off.

Normalcy bias was a bitch. But that was civilians for you. After a lifetime of stability and security, suddenly having gangbangers at your door shakes things up and threatens your way of life. It's tempting to simply dismiss the threat, downplay the risk, and point the finger at someone familiar, someone you know you can accuse without blowback. It's so easy to take that option.

We'd played out this script so many times before. The first time I admitted I'd killed someone to my family, they reacted with shock and horror and indignation. Good people don't kill anyone, after all. Violence is always evil. Eventually, I learned that it was best to say nothing to them, or failing that, as little as I could get away with.

But not this time.

My father's words were a scorching brand. My mother had said nothing, like she always did, and my brother acted exactly the way I'd expected him to act. It was the same old shit as before. The same refusal to adjust to reality and get on with the program, the same bullheaded belief that if you just keep doing what you were doing, things would always go your way. Things had changed now, whether they accepted it or not. If they refused to adapt, well, I couldn't save their asses anymore. It's not worth the heartache.

At least I knew where my family stood.

The fault line between me and them was as wide and deep as ever. In the end, I had to do things my way.

As I always did.

20

MIZU NO KOKORO

In the Raiders, then in the Task Force, we spent days, weeks, months on preparations and rehearsals. We never rushed a job if we didn't have to. The higher the stakes, the more careful we were. We accounted for every possibility, trained for every contingency, readied backups to backups to backups. Should something go wrong—and something *always* went wrong—we would know exactly what to do. Or improvise accordingly.

The first thing I had to do was establish just how much the enemy knew and what assets they could bring to bear. After a fitful night's sleep and a hard hour of bodyweight training, I drove to Bright Moon Temple. I took the usual precautions, finding no surveillance teams or suspicious vehicles. By the time I was done, morning meditation was over, and a small group of Asians were filing out of the entrance.

I found Shi Shifu crossing the courtyard, making his way to the main hall. As I approached, he peeked over his shoulder and smiled.

"Gao Yang," he said. "*Ni hui lai le.*" *You're back.*

He was the only man in Halo City who used my Chinese name. Not even my family did. Not anymore.

I cupped my fist at chest height and bowed. "I apologize for being so abrupt with my last message."

He returned the gesture. "It's completely understandable."

"Have you had any trouble?"

"Not at all. Aside from the occasional tourist or sightseer, no Hispanics have come by. There's no sign of suspicious people or activity either."

"That's a relief. But the danger hasn't passed yet."

"I heard of the shooting at Long Men Restaurant. Was that El Trece?"

Long Men was Loong Moon in Mandarin.

"Yes."

He shook his head sadly. "That's terrible."

"They had a Prime with them. Someone who can manipulate fire. Have you seen or heard of anyone like that around here?"

"No. But we'll keep an eye out and take appropriate measures."

"*Ni xinku le.*" *You've worked hard.*

"Not at all. If anyone's been working hard, it's you."

"Really?"

"It's written on your face," he said. "You must look after yourself, okay?"

"Okay."

I followed him into the worship hall, where the trinity of Buddhas awaited on the wooden altar. Bhaiṣajyaguru offered no medicine for the wounds of my past, Amitabha issued no illumination for the future, and Shakyamuni stayed silent on my present.

But then, these were only statues, and nothing more.

Shi Shifu lit a trio of joss sticks for the figures. I followed suit. He bowed his head in smooth, fluid arcs, as regular as a metronome. I kept still and focused my thought.

May my friends and family be safe from harm, and may the evil receive the fruits of their karma.

We placed the joss sticks in the brazier outside the hall, then pressed our palms at our chests and bowed to the statues once more.

"Thank you for accompanying me," Shi said.

"You're welcome."

"I sense you have a question."

He wore a gentle smile, but his eyes seemed to penetrate deep within me, punching through mere flesh and bone to see the spirit beneath.

"I've been thinking about karma," I began.

"Ah, karma. Such a simple, yet a complicated concept."

"Indeed. I understand that every action, no matter how insignificant it may seem, generates karma."

"Correct. Every action carries consequences. The only way to avoid creating karma is to do nothing."

"You can't escape your karma, can you?"

His eyes glinted. "There is one way."

"How?"

"To attain enlightenment before the fruits of your karma ripen."

"That's impossible for me. At least in this lifetime."

He laughed. "Ah, but you can at least walk just a little further down the path."

"I'm trying."

"Hence the questions on karma."

"Yes. I remember you said once that if an action generates both good and evil karma, they do not cancel each other out."

"Yes. The fruit will ripen, and you will experience the good and the evil."

"Is there any way to reduce the evil karma?"

He chuckled. "An interesting question. And a complex one. Do you have an example?"

"As a detective, I'm required to use force to subdue noncompliant suspects. If the suspect presents a lethal threat, I may have to use deadly force."

"Why do you use force?"

"To stop the suspect."

"Why do you stop him?"

"To prevent or stop violence. To protect others. To uphold the law."

"And why do criminals use force?"

"To harm others. To rob, rape, kill, and to avoid facing justice."

"Your intentions are different from the intentions of a criminal. That makes all the difference."

"How so?"

"Your intent motivates your actions. The intent you send out through your actions comes back to you, yes? While violence is always regrettable, the blowback of violence with the intent of preserving life is less severe than violence with the intent of taking life."

"I'm not sure I understand."

"Allow me to illustrate. In a previous life, the Buddha was the captain of a ship, named Great Compassionate. One day, five hundred merchants boarded his ship on a journey to the Jambu Continent. But hidden among the merchants was a bandit, who intended to murder everyone aboard and steal their possessions.

"The deities of the sea revealed to Captain Great Compassionate the identity and intentions of the bandit and explained that if the bandit slew the merchants, all of whom were on the verge of becoming Buddhas, he would surely suffer in the great hells for eons. The deities asked Captain Great Compassionate to find a way to prevent the bandit from suffering in the great hells.

"For seven days Captain Great Compassionate meditated on the matter. He decided there was no way to protect the merchants but to kill the bandit. Yet if he alerted the merchants, they would fly into a rage and murder the bandit with angry thoughts, and go to the great hells themselves. The captain decided the only solution was to kill the bandit himself."

"Wouldn't that cause him to go to hell?"

"Indeed. But Captain Great Compassionate accepted that he would bear the pain of suffering in the great hells, sparing both the bandit and the merchants from suffering. Thus, with a heart filled with compassion, he slew the robber himself.

"Through this act, the merchants would awaken, the robber was reborn in a world of paradise, and Captain Great Compassionate shortened his existence in Samsara by a hundred thousand eons."

Samsara was the cycle of life, death, and rebirth.

"It's rather esoteric," I said. "How would killing with compassion spare you from suffering?"

"If you kill with anger, the anger returns to you. If you kill with compassion, compassion returns to you also."

"It's... It's pretty difficult to feel compassion for your enemy."

He tapped his temple.

"Hell resides here, in the mind. But so too does Paradise. If you act in anger, you see only anger. If you act with compassion, you see only compassion."

"What if you act without feeling?"

He laughed.

"A few years ago, I met a Zen monk from Japan. He was a part-time monk, and a part-time martial arts instructor. He said that samurai trained to be calm at all times, to do only what was necessary, especially at the moment of killing."

"If you send out calm, you receive calm?"

"Essentially, yes. Any blowback—mental, emotional and spiritual —will be minimized. Strive to keep your mind like still water."

Mind like still water. I'd heard that before. In MARSOC, and later the Task Force, we brought in martial arts experts and neuroscientists to help us perfect the art of killing. Among the former was a *koryu* specialist who had studied the classical samurai battlefield arts and translated them to modern-day applications.

He used the term *mizu no kokoro*. By setting aside all emotion, you can see the solution to the problem in front of you. Indeed, he instructed us to view all threats and critical incidents as nothing more than problems to be solved, problems whose solutions were visible to he who could perceive them with a still heart.

I didn't know if I could develop compassion for the enemy. But inner calm... it was something I could do. Something I could continue to train.

"It feels... odd, talking about killing with a Chan priest."

He laughed. "Life, death, and rebirth is part of our jurisdiction. So, too, is killing."

"I'd expected you to say I should refrain from violence."

"I am a priest, you are a policeman. We have different dharma and thus different standards of behavior. I must follow the five precepts and two hundred and twenty-seven rules, you are only encouraged to adhere to the five precepts."

Dharma meant many things. Here, it meant the duty one is expected to perform, in line with universal law.

"Lucky me."

"I wouldn't say that. I couldn't begin to imagine what it's like to take a life."

I'd never told him I'd killed anyone before. Yet he gave me a look filled with knowing, understanding—and acceptance.

"May you never know the sensation."

"Thank you."

THE MORNING HAD BARELY BEGUN, and already the waiting room of Halo City General Hospital was overflowing. Every chair was taken, and knots of people clustered along the walls and corners. A pair of harried-looking nurses ran the reception table, processing patients as quickly as they could. Sirens howled and babies wailed and phones rang and buzzers chimed. The overhead TV blasted a breaking news report about a showdown between Primes an hour ago near the port. I stuffed earplugs into my ears, filled my lungs with the scent of antiseptic and made my way to reception.

Producing my badge, I asked for Aegis' room. It was a gamble; Primes who needed medical attention were usually checked in under their real names, unless they had registration cards with privacy hold privileges.

Tom did, in fact, have such a card. The nurse gave me directions to the Burn Intensive Care Unit. I dodged doctors and patients and a surgical team en route to the Burn Center, and in the ICU I saw a cop standing guard outside Tom's room. I showed him my badge, and he let me in.

Tom had the room all to himself. Dressed in a light blue gown, he lay comfortably on his bed, wired up to trees of monitors and clear fluid packs. His skin was a fresh shade of pink, the flesh regrown, and when he opened his eyes they were the same shade of cold blue.

"Morning, Tom," I said.

"Morning, Adam," he replied, his voice strong and clear.

"How are you feeling?"

"Weird. It's like a thousand spiders crawling all over me at once. Their legs are on my skin and *inside* my bones and flesh. But I feel energized. Powerful, even, more powerful than ever before."

"You seem to be doing fine."

He chuckled. "'Fine'? Hell, I'm feeling *great*. Like I could jump out and run a decathlon and do it all over again tomorrow. I'm getting cabin fever just lying here."

"Angel says you'll make a full recovery."

"She told me the same thing. The docs think I can be discharged by the end of the day."

"That's wonderful."

"It is. If you'd come later, you might have missed me."

"Guess I got lucky."

"That's right. But all the same, thanks for dropping by. And for getting me here."

"No problem. You generated your shield when El Trece began shooting, so that makes us quits."

"For now."

We shared a knowing chuckle.

"What's next for you?" he asked.

"El Trece isn't going to give up. I need to take countermeasures."

"You're going freelance?"

I shrugged. He chuckled.

"They might try to hit Loong Moon again," I said. "Once you're out of here, could you talk to my parents and try to convince them to hire armed security?"

"Have you spoken to them?"

I sighed. "It didn't end well. They're stubborn. And they're civilians."

"Thought so. Will you be coming with me to speak to them?"

"I've got a lot to do... and I don't think it's wise to show my face around there again. El Trece, you understand. They might have spotters in place."

He snorted. "Really?"

"Really."

He held my gaze for an instant.

"Well, what the hell. I'll go talk to them. But if you're not around, I can't promise you anything."

"That's fine. Thanks."

"No problem. But Adam? This is war. Plain and simple. You're not going to win this by staying on the defensive forever."

"I don't plan to."

RETURNING TO THE CHURCH, I retreated to my room, dug out my laptop and inserted a special thumb drive. This one was loaded with the latest distro of Kali Linux, an open-source operating system optimized for computer security. Including offensive security.

I fired up Tor, then connected to a browser-based Virtual Private Network. The Onion Router directed Internet traffic through a world-wide network of relays, concealing the user's location from network surveillance or traffic analysis. The VPN would tunnel the user's data through its own servers, masking its origin. Used together, with the right security precautions, I was a ghost in the digital sea.

I visited a Dark Web website, hosted on the Tor architecture, careful to type every single letter from memory. The address took me to a software repository filled with a curious collection of software tools. I downloaded the ones I needed, then plugged my police smartphone into the laptop.

The smartphone used an in-house app to grant access to the Intelligence Bureau's databases. The app wasn't listed anywhere, but the enterprising hacker can easily sideload it into a Nullphone, especially since both phones were based on versions of the Android operating system. I copied the app's APK file to my computer, then transferred it to my Nullphone and opened the file on the phone.

As the Nullphone installed the app, I booted a database hacking tool on my computer and pointed it at the Intel app. The software went to work, deploying algorithms and tools to sniff out and test passwords.

There was always an admin account, and there was always a master password. My own access was limited to the areas I was cleared for, and for what I had in mind, I didn't want to use my phone and account.

As the program chipped away at the database's defenses, I scoured the Dark Web and updated my electronic arsenal, uploading the latest versions of the tools I've stored. A quarter of an hour later, I was done—but not the program.

Computer hacking wasn't like the movies. There wasn't anything I could do but wait patiently for the program to run its course.

I wasn't a cracker, but I knew a few dance steps and recognized some tunes. In the Task Force, we were expected to go anywhere and do anything in pursuit of our targets. As the world grew increasingly digitized, our mission sets expanded into seizing and downloading protected electronics—or sneaking into places, accessing or laying down devices, and slipping out without a trace. Our training covered a broad spectrum of fields, ranging from traditional infantry field-craft to more esoteric fields, computer science among them. I still maintained a healthy interest in the art, in case I ever had to use it again.

When the Intel app was installed on my Nullphone, I called Marc.

"Yo Adam," he said. "How are things?"

"Peachy. And you?"

"It's all good. No sign of El Trece."

"You sound disappointed."

He laughed. "Who, me? I'm not looking for a fight, Detective. Honest to God."

We shared a chuckle.

"I've been getting rusty," I said. "Lack of practice. Got time in your schedule for private lessons?"

"Not interested in a regular class?"

"It's safer this way. Besides, there are a few things I'd like to cover with you."

"What kind of things?"

"Things we don't normally cover. For a *civilian* class."

"Ah. Well, I'm free today from three to five thirty at my place."

"Excellent. See you then."

My computer hummed away. I sat on my bed and accessed the Intelligence database, reading up on El Trece, looking for updated information on key players. There was still nothing on Ricardo Ruiz's current location—or, for that matter, on his current criminal activities beyond 'suspicions' and 'hearsay' and second-hand sources. All the same, I took copious notes on El Trece. Now and then I consulted the tracker and recorded where Chavez went, looking for patterns of life.

I spent lunch with Fathers Josh and Matthew. The senior priest had a little difficulty handling a knife with his prosthetic arm, but he persevered, carefully slicing his steamed fish. We kept conversation light and easy, focusing on their daily routine, upcoming church events, the latest goings-on in the neighborhood.

Up until the moment Father Matthew said, "I read about the shooting at your family restaurant."

"El Trece," I said. "No doubt."

"It's confirmed?" Father Josh asked.

"Officially, no. But the shooters were Hispanics wearing El Trece colors."

The priests sighed as one.

"Was anyone hurt?" Father Matthew asked.

"A security officer. But Angel healed him, and he's as good as new."

"Thank God."

"And Mrs. Dawson," Father Josh added.

He had a slight frown on his face. It seemed he didn't like referring to her by her nickname.

"Will El Trece come here?" Matthew asked.

"Not likely," I said. "Chinatown isn't their turf. I don't think they know I'm here. Even if they do, they wouldn't dare attack a church."

"I wish I had your confidence," the younger priest confessed.

"Do you have security guards at your church?" I asked. "Other than myself, that is."

"Not regularly," the older priest said. "We have a group of volunteer security guards, but they're unarmed, and they are only deployed during Sunday mass."

"You might want to consider looking into standing up a full-time security team," I said.

"*Armed* security?" Father Matt asked.

"Of course."

"This is a house of God…"

"And thus, a prime target for evil," I replied.

Father Josh stroked his chin. "Thank you for your suggestion. We'll take it under serious consideration."

Meaning: we won't stand one up. Yet.

I returned to my room after lunch. The laptop was still humming away, the cracking tool still pounding away at the database's defenses. I grabbed my phone and checked the *Halo City Herald*.

2 HCPD Officers slain in ambush.

I sprang to my feet. A curse leapt to my lips, but I stifled it in time. Instead, I read the article.

An unknown assailant attacked a pair of cops in broad daylight. Two patrol officers had reportedly pulled over by the road to do paperwork when the suspect approached them. Eyewitnesses say he opened his hand and produced a ball of flame. The fireball engulfed the victims and slagged the car. The suspect fled the scene.

The two officers were pronounced dead on arrival at Halo City General Hospital.

He was a Prime. The same Prime who attacked me yesterday.

And when Primes were involved, STAR would get the call.

I called Sergeant Oliveira on my police phone. Sequestration order be damned, this was too important to let slide. He picked up after a single ring.

"Have you heard about this morning's ambush?" I asked.

"Yeah. Great timing. I was about to call you about that."

"What's up?"

"The brass issued a BOLO for one Alberto Leon Mendez. He's an El Trece heavy hitter, an unregistered Prime from Juarez. His street name is 'Bombero,' 'Fireman' in English. As you might have guessed, Mendez's circus trick is to generate and control fire. He's like a living flamethrower."

"I've seen his power up close."

"When?" He paused. "Ah, right, you mean the drive-by at Long Moon."

"You heard about that?"

"The whole PD's talking about it, 'mano. You alright?"

"Yeah. But Bombero burned Aegis. He's still in hospital, but he'll be discharged tonight."

He whistled. "Consider yourselves lucky you survived. His victims usually don't. The Federales say Mendez is connected to at least thirty murders on both sides of the border. His specialty is burning up the bodies until there's nothing but ash."

"Great way to destroy evidence too."

"Absolutely. Bombero is in Halo City now, which makes him our problem. This guy is a hard case. He's participated in firefights against the Mexican military, helped El Trece clean house in Halo City ten years ago, and rubbed out more than a few cops. Between you and me, I don't think he's the surrendering type."

"It sure sounds like it. Do we have any specifics on Bombero's powers?"

"Nothing. He was a street kid, never tested at a hospital or institution or whatever. All we have are speculations based on what the Federales fed us, and some decade-old reports. But there is one thing, though."

"What is it?"

"Word has it he developed his powers when he was twenty. About ten years ago. And he's *not* a first-gen or new-gen Prime."

"No way," I said. "How's that possible? Second- and third-gen Primes manifest their powers by puberty. Twenty is too late in the game for a power to show up."

"Damn if I know. Maybe it's just bullshit."

"Maybe it is. Do we know why El Trece sent this guy after me?"

"My guess? You took out some of their *sicarios*, so now their *jefe* is sending in Bombero to finish the job."

Violence breeds violence. Death begets death. Such is the way of the world.

"I don't rate a personal security detail?"

"That's the thing. You should. We keep telling the brass you should have a PSD. We'd volunteer to do it, even. But they keep telling us no. We don't have the resources, manpower, bullshit like that."

"Politics?"

"Has to be, brother. They say you're a Prime and you can take care of yourself, but come on. They're hiding something. I can taste it. I wish we could help, but the brass has us running the streets serving warrant after warrant. We just can't back you up."

"Don't worry about me. I can take care of myself. But you and the guys, you gotta stay safe."

"Thanks. Oh, and before I forget, how did you learn about the ambush?"

"The news."

"Oh. Well, there's a small detail we asked the media to keep secret. Not that it will be secret much longer."

"What is it?"

"Bombero burned a message into the sidewalk before he left. It goes, *Amp, we are coming for you.*"

THIS WASN'T my first time being hunted by a Prime. It still sucked. But now, I had a single advantage: Bombero didn't know that I was hunting *him*.

I downloaded Bombero's file from the police database. It was an expanded version of what Oliveira told me, incorporating surveillance photos and a write-up from the Federales.

Bombero was huge. A walking man-mountain, the dossier estimated him at six foot four, two hundred and seventy pounds. His clothes strained to contain his bulk, much of it pure muscle. No visible tats, which marked him an outlier among the El Trece lifers. He wore a thick beard in one photo, a trimmed mustache in another, and was completely clean-shaven in a third. What all three photos had in common were his broad, puffy face; his nose, broken and healed crooked; and tiny, beady eyes.

Fighting him would be like taking on a bear. It was easier to call in an air strike or snipe him from a mile away, and, more importantly, much safer. He would be running the same calculations on me, no doubt, thinking about the powers I possessed and how to counter them.

A few months after joining STAR, the brass told me to put up a show for the media. Community relations, they said, to show the public what I could do and to foster stronger ties with the local news. I obliged.

I blazed around a running track, easily breaking the state's track records for baseline humans. I pulled a 250-ton metro train down a track without breaking a sweat. I leapt entire buildings in a single bound.

But I didn't reveal my other powers.

I had to assume Bombero knew everything about what I'd revealed to the public, both my powers and my prowess with firearms and martial arts. He might know or guess about my enhanced reflexes too. But I hadn't breathed a word about my danger sense or accelerated healing to anyone. They were my hidden aces for a situation just like this.

Bombero would set up a situation that would allow him to use his power at close quarters while denying what he knew about mine. I had to do the same to him. It's a game of ambush and counter-ambush, and the only question was who would do unto the other first.

In the afternoon, I drove to Marc's home. He lived in an apartment building in the Port district, just a stone's throw away from Wilshire Community Center. I did my usual security drive-by and found nothing to be alarmed about, and found him standing by the front door.

Approaching him on foot, I asked, "Been waiting long?"

"Nah. Just came down myself." He peeked both ways down the street. "No uninvited guests, eh?"

"Not today."

"Shame. Today's lesson could use more volunteers."

Marc lived in a spacious four-room apartment on the eighth floor. His wife, a pretty blond in her mid-thirties, was in the kitchen, and prepared water for us.

The living room was already laid out for training. Soft gray rubber mats covered the warm parquet. A massive bag of training weapons sat at the edge of the mat. A humanoid training dummy stood by the window.

"This time is now your time," Marc said. "What would you like to cover today?"

"Close quarters combat," I said.

He smiled. "Excellent."

We began with empty hands. Working from the clinch, we explored takedowns, strikes, defenses and, most importantly, how to fight to a draw or retain a weapon, be it a knife or pistol.

From empty hands came knives. We practiced quickly diagnosing and dealing with incoming bladed threats, especially the infamous grab and stab, better known as the prison shanking.

Halfway through training, Marc's children returned home. Two daughters and a son, all of them in junior high. He called for a break, long enough to greet them with a sweaty squirming hug, and sent them on their way.

Having re-acquainted ourselves with familiar tools, we moved on to something more exotic: the Shinobi koppo.

An evolution and re-imagining of the Japanese yawara, koppo and the te no uchi, to the untrained eye it was simply a titanium tube with a keychain on one end and a paracord loop on the other. I'd wrapped a length of paracord around the shaft of my Shinobi, creating a retention loop large enough for two fingers.

I'd punched holes through sheet steel and plywood with the pocket stick. With a sharp tug on the main paracord loop, I could unfurl the paracord and deploy it as a garrote. The paracord itself was tied to the keyring cap. I could unscrew the cap and use it as a throwing weapon or a distraction.

The Shinobi was an obscure weapon, deceptively simple to use, but mastery demanded a lifetime of study. Even now, so few people had heard of it that I was confident nobody would recognize it until it was too late.

The stick was for striking, breaking, distracting and throwing, the long cord for capturing, deflecting, locking and strangling. We ran through some applications, testing and fine-tuning techniques, exploring principles of motion. Striking with the stick was similar to knife and stick work, but the garrote demanded knowledge of flexible weapons.

We finished with flow. He fed me random attacks, and I responded with the appropriate counter. Initially, he allowed the counter to land, but as we progressed, he countered the counter and fed me another strike. We moved through long, medium and short ranges, employing many of the concepts we had covered today, going faster and faster and faster, acting and reacting faster than conscious thought, until we were in full-blown sparring mode.

No time to think. Just act. Strike and block and counterstrike and dodge and jam and clear and move and strike again. We moved as fast as we could but took the power out of our blows. One last exchange and he jumped out of range.

"Time," he said. "Great work, Adam. You actually hit me a couple of times."

I shrugged. "You got in what, four or five hits for every time I tagged you."

He patted my shoulder. "You're getting better. That's what counts."

"Thanks."

I packed up and put away the gear while Marc prepared for his evening class.

"How much do I owe you?" I asked.

He held his hands up. "Don't worry, man. You're an assistant instructor now. You don't have to pay any dues."

"You sure about that?"

"Come on, you know my word is good."

I smiled. "I guess I'll see you more often, then."

"That'll be great."

He escorted me downstairs. At the front door, I showed him a photo of Bombero.

"How would you fight him?" I asked.

"Who's he?"

"Hardcore *sicario*. Six-four, two-seventy pounds, at least thirty murders to his name. Oh, and he's a pyrokinetic Prime."

"You kidding me?"

"No."

"You're really asking me how to fight him?"

"Yes."

He shook his head.

"Just shoot him."

22. No Turning Back

AFTER DINNER, I killed time driving around Halo City, contemplating my current situation.

All my life I'd tried to follow the rules as best as I could. From my childhood days in Hong Kong, primary school in Singapore, then junior high in America, rules defined my life. So long as I stayed within them, I was a model, upstanding student.

Then in high school, a group of bullies decided to pick on the foreign brothers who wrote and spoke funny. When the fracas was over, everyone was suspended. Myself included, just for daring to defend myself.

They called it zero tolerance policy. I called it ass-covering.

Instead of getting to the truth, my parents sided with the school, chewing Aaron and me out for getting into a fight, and grounding us semi-permanently. Fighting was for bullies, not for good people. That was the moment I knew that some rules and laws existed only for the convenience of those in authority.

When I was finally allowed to leave home for 'errands' and 'study sessions' and 'exercise', I conducted a guerrilla campaign of my own and made sure those bullies would never touch us again.

After enlisting in the Marines, I had to teach myself to follow the rules again. Discipline, regimentation, meticulousness, to survive in Boot, and later in Recon, you had to be at the top of your game, keep your nose clean, and immediately spring into action the moment you receive an order.

Then came MARSOC, and the Task Force, where I learned once again how to break the rules to get the job done. This time, not through trial and error, but with the guidance of some of the finest spooks and warriors in the nation.

The moment I received my honorable discharge, I exchanged my Marine greens for police blues. Once again, I had to toe the line, but this time as an enforcer of the law, not just a subject.

Now the law had failed me. There were still good cops in the PD, but the brass was more concerned with protecting themselves than the rank and file. El Trece was after me, but going after them through regular means was impossible. Once again, I had to break the rules.

Life is cyclical. We the sentient are trapped in an endless loop of eternal recurrence, and even your next life won't free you from it. You can't run from karma. All you can do is endure, and work to free yourself from self-inflicted snares.

Damn if I knew how to do that now. Short of renouncing the material world and becoming a priest, anyway.

In the end, all I could do was find a way to survive.

Chavez's car had remained stationary for the past few hours. When I drove by the beacon, I saw a two-story home with an attached garage, just one of two dozen along the road. No sign of the red Ford; perhaps it was inside the garage. But seated at the front porch was a large Hispanic male, one of Chavez's ever-present bodyguards.

That was all the confirmation I needed.

I parked four blocks away, grabbed my binoculars, and began my surveillance.

For all of ten minutes.

An old woman, dressed in a pink nightgown, stormed out of her home and stamped towards my car, her hands on her hips. She rapped thunderously on the passenger window. I opened it just enough to admit her voice.

"Just who the hell are you?" she screeched.

"Excuse me?" I asked.

"Who are you, and what are you doing here?"

"My partner's out making a delivery. I'm just waiting for him to come back."

"Bullshit!" she screamed, spittle splattering across the glass. "I had my eye on you when you came here! I saw you sitting for ages without doing nothing! What are you, some kind of pervert?"

"Ma'am, I'm just—"

"Get out of here! I called the po-lice! This is a nice neighborhood! We can't have perverts like you hanging around!"

I rolled up the window and drove off.

The finger of Murphy strikes again. A damn shame that old lady didn't turn her attentions on the gangbangers. But hey, this was a nice neighborhood, and gangsters don't come here. The ones who do are too dangerous to be trifled with. Better to save your ire of people who you know—or *believe*—won't harm you.

Story of my life.

In the morning, right after breakfast, I returned the rental car. Two hours later, I had a new one, a bottle green Toyota with a hybrid gasoline-electric engine.

I spent the day in my cell in the clergy house, taking more notes on the enemy, studying maps, practicing and refining some of the more useful techniques I'd learned. My cracking tool was still hammering away at the police database, looking for a way in.

When I had done everything I needed to do, I sat on the bed, closed my eyes, and fell into a meditative state. Unbidden, words flowed from my being.

Hundred Fathoms Deep

Dueling sharks
    Circling
    In blood-maddened waters
    A hundred fathoms deep.

Eyes hazed in crimson
    Fins flick against flesh
    Tails brush against scale
    An explosion of muscles
    A frenzy of teeth.

Scavengers and predators and bottom-feeders
    Rush for the sudden feast.
    Morsels drift soundlessly into endless black
    A thousand fathoms deep
    From lightless abyss

The kraken rises.

I COMMITTED the words to my computer and smiled. Why be a shark when you can be the kraken?

At half past five, I prepared for battle.

This job was illegal as all hell. If a weapon tasted blood today, it had to disappear. I locked my Glocks away, leaving only my Spydercos and my Koppo.

The drive to Feliz Hills was long and easy. My traffic app told me how to avoid the worst of the evening rush. A quick drive-by confirmed that Torres and Martinez were at their usual spot, Martinez enticing customers at the cross-junction, Torres waiting by his car in the nearby parking lot.

I left Feliz Hills, drove into an underground parking lot, turned off my Nullphone and removed the battery. Unlike just about every smartphone on the market, the Nullphone had a removable battery, the better to prevent unwanted surveillance. My keys, mounted on a quick-detach ring, went into a jacket pocket. I donned a baseball cap and a pair of display glasses and drew a large mole on my left cheek. Finally, I donned a pair of flesh-colored latex gloves. As far as most witnesses were concerned, I was now a new man.

I returned to Torres' turf. Traffic was light, and passers-by didn't notice. My heart pounded in my chest and temples, and the faux-leather steering wheel flexed under my hands. I breathed, relaxed, kept my power at the baseline.

When the derelict apartment appeared in sight, doubt stabbed my heart. Was this the right thing to do? Did I have to do this? I could still drive away, abort this mission, fade back into obscurity.

I purged those thoughts with a breath.

These men had poisoned too many people with narcotics. They had sowed the wind, and I was the whirlwind.

I slowed to a stop near the pavement. Alfonso Martinez bounced over to me, smiling brightly, waving his hand. I checked my mirrors, saw no carjackers incoming, and lowered the window slightly.

"Yo, buddy!" he said. "How you doing?"

"I'm okay," I said guardedly. "What are you doing here?"

"Me? I'm a salesman. I've been doing business here for years, and it looks to me you could use a pick-me-up."

"Really, now?"

"Yeah, yeah, you look like you've got a monkey on your back, if you know what I mean."

"It's been a tough week."

"Exactly. But don't worry, man, we've got exactly what you need to smooth things out and make it all go away."

I smiled. "Does it come in powder or pills?"

"Both, buddy. Whatever suits you."

"Sounds good to me. Whatcha got?"

"Go around the corner in the parking lot. My buddy Alberto will take care of you. You'll see him by his car."

"Thanks."

I followed Martinez's instructions, pulling into an empty space in the parking lot. Once again, my heart slammed into overdrive. Cold sweat gathered in my palms and armpits. I spent a moment breathing, finding calm.

I was committed. No turning back.

I got out of my Toyota. Torres was sitting on the hood of his car, his arms crossed. The vehicle was pointed at the exit, ready for a quick getaway. Sauntering over, I greeted him with a smile and a wave.

"You Alberto?" I asked.

"That's right," he said.

His eyes scanned my face. Darted to my hands, my pockets, neck, looking for clips, exposed weapons, mics, anything that suggested I was a cop.

"I'm looking for a bit of spice. Your buddy said you could help me out."

He grinned, uncrossing his arms, and slid off his car.

"Sure, man. What are you looking for?

"Special K. Got any?"

"Yup. How do you want it? Snort, shot, or pop?"

"Shot."

"How many shots do you want?"

"Five."

"It's twenty-five bucks per shot. Works out to a hundred and twenty-five in total." He paused and squinted at me. "But you're a new customer, am I right?"

"Right."

"Excellent. You get the first-timer discount. Hundred bucks. How's that?"

"Good deal."

"Great! Stay right there; I'll go get the dope."

He turned around, quickly making his way to the back of the car. I took a casual look around. A few people walked past, all of them studiously ignoring the parking lot. Torres popped the trunk and checked for witnesses, then reached in.

I dropped to a crouch, slipped my hand into my pocket and palmed my Shinobi. Sliding my fingers through the retention loop, I approached the car—

The key ring rattled against the shaft.

Damn. Overlooked that. I capped the Shinobi with my thumb, smothering the ring against the tube, and ghosted down the right side of the car. Gravel shifted under my boots, a metal zipper opened noisily, and plastic rustled. Reached my left index finger into the paracord loop and unfurled the cord to its full length. I choked up on the excess cord, crossed my arms and rounded the corner.

Torres stepped away from the trunk and looked at me.

"Hey, I said—"

I kicked him in the groin.

He doubled over, his breath spurting out. Stepping off, I threw the cord around his neck and pulled my arms apart.

He jerked, eyes bulging, hands rushing for his throat. I jammed the Shinobi into his flesh and pulled him down.

His hand shot out, catching himself as he fell. I went down with him, keeping up the strangle as I circled around, planting my knee on his back. He wheezed and coughed and flailed and went still.

"Hey! What the fuck are you doing?!"

Martinez. He was stepping around the car, left hand pointed at me, right hand hidden behind his back.

Releasing the cord, I stepped away from the unconscious dealer and Amped.

Now Martinez was slow, slow as molasses. His teeth were bared, his eyes dark and blazing, his left hand reaching for my face. I still couldn't see his right hand. I studied the distance between us, watching every step, slipping my left finger into the paracord loop and pulling it down to find the bight.

He leapt.

Seized my lapel.

I pinned his hand to my chest, dropped low, and whipped my Shinobi through a sharp 'U.' The titanium tube struck his locked arm. Bone broke. Flipping my hand around, I speared the keychain end into his rib and rammed the other end into his thigh.

His leg buckled, his grip faltered. Peeling off his hand, I dragged the paracord around his arm and pulled him into me. He stumbled. I spun in and crashed my elbow against his temple. He went completely slack. Reversing my momentum, I wrapped the cord around his throat, cradled his head, then spiraled in and dumped him on the ground.

Stepping away from him, I looked all around. No witnesses. I freed the Shinobi and checked for signs of life. He was out cold, but breathing. Thank God.

Torres was slowly regaining consciousness, trying to pick himself up. Stepping down my power, I ran up to him and kicked him in the side.

Ribs crunched under my boot. Torres yelped, rolling onto his back. I toed him onto his belly and sat on his back.

"Who... the hell... are you?" he gasped.

I grabbed his left arm with my free hand and wrenched it behind him. He yelped and tried to squirm away. I pinned his hand against his spine and reached for his other arm, but it was too far away.

"Give me your right hand!" I ordered.

"Are you... a cop?"

I slipped my fingers into his exposed right armpit and jammed them hard into the flesh. He yelped and jerked his arm. I grabbed his wrist, joined his hands together and pinned them with my knee.

"The fuck... are you doing?" he asked.

"Shut up," I replied.

I reached into a jacket pocket and removed a zip tie. He squirmed, and I dug the point of the Shinobi against his neck. He jerked away with a sharp yelp, and I tied his hands behind his back.

"I'm sorry, man, I'm sorry!" he whined. "Don't kill me! You can take the drugs! The cash! Everything! Just don't kill me!"

"You wanna live, you keep still and shut up," I said. "Understand?"

"Yeah, yeah, understood!"

I secured Torres' ankles with another pair of zip-ties, then rolled him on his uninjured side.

"What the—" he began.

"Stay still and shut up."

I patted Torres down, producing a wallet, a cellphone, a set of car keys, and a folding knife. I stashed everything in my jacket.

"You can't just—"

I kicked him in the side. "Shut up."

He shut up.

Stepping away from Torres, I turned my attention to Martinez. He was conscious, but all the fight had been beaten out of him. I zip tied Martinez in the same fashion as his buddy, placing him on his side to prevent involuntary asphyxiation, and searched him too.

This time I found only a wallet and a phone, but there was a screwdriver nearby. I confiscated everything, stuffed the paracord back into the Shinobi with my pinky, and returned to Torres' car.

A large black duffel bag rested inside the open trunk, partially unzipped to reveal a half-dozen smaller plastic grocery bags. One of the bags, marked with a bold black 'K' had been untied. Inside were bottles filled with clear fluid.

I tied up the plastic bag, zipped up the duffel, and hauled it over my shoulder. Tossed the car keys into the trunk and shut it. Sauntered over to Torres and knelt over him.

"You know who I am?" I asked.

"No," he whispered.

I ground my boot against his broken ribs. He shrieked.

"You sure?"

"Yes, yes!"

Interesting. Was Ruiz keeping his campaign in-house?

"You know people in El Trece?"

"No, no, I—"

"Shut up. How do you think I found you?"

"I don't work for El Trece! I just—they just sell me dope, that's all!"

"Go tell your friends in El Trece they messed with the wrong people. Tell them never to go back to Chinatown again. Otherwise, Tin Fo will come after them. Hard. Got that?"

"Yeah, yeah, I get it!"

"Message ends."

One last scan. Passers-by glanced at us and scurried away. This was El Barrio. No one would take photos or videos. No one would call the cops. Not if they knew what was good for them.

Even so, I pulled my cap low over my face and walked away.

21

THE DARK OF THE NIGHT

Torres was small fry. Nothing he said would reach the ears of a shot-caller. But better he thought I was sending a message than to guess what I was really after: his drugs.

I picked out the ketamine and placed it in the passenger footrest, and slung the duffel bag and the rest of the drugs into a random collection of dumpsters.

The recovered wallets were stuffed with receipts, cards, coins, and cash. I took the money and tossed everything else into another dumpster.

The screwdriver had been sharpened to a fine point. The knife was a cheap Chinese clone, with a flimsy lock and a wobbly blade. I had much better gear than this crap. They, too, went into yet another dumpster.

The op had gone well, all things considered. But Martinez had surprised me. If he'd had a gun instead of a knife, it would have ended badly. I couldn't allow that to happen again. I was flying solo now; I didn't have someone to watch my back. I needed to maintain constant situational awareness.

Live and learn.

I checked the tracer. It was still going strong. Chavez had driven around the city now and then, but he always returned to his safe house. That made things a lot easier.

In a supermarket, I bought a bundle of one-use-only insulin needles and a carrying case. Back inside the car, I filled the syringes with ketamine, stuffed four inside the case, and dropped the case into a jacket pocket.

After a quick dinner, I checked and cleaned my kit, and headed to the target neighborhood. This time, no suspicious old women came running out of their homes to drive me off, and no cops rolled around sniffing for trouble. I set up three blocks down the street from Chavez's safe house and broke out my binocs.

The driver was on guard duty. He was bopping his head to a tune I couldn't hear, occasionally fiddling with his phone. I couldn't afford such distractions. I simply logged everything I saw and waited.

As the evening deepened, the good citizens of the neighborhood returned home. Cars pulled into garages. Lights turned on and went out. A jogger wearing a massive set of earphones ran past my car, completely oblivious to my presence.

Every two hours, the guards changed shifts. The lights were all on, but the curtains were drawn, and I couldn't see past them. All three of Chavez's men took turns watching the house, but the man himself didn't stand guard.

I still had hours to go before I could move. I kept myself limber with slow stretches and small movements, relieved myself into an empty water bottle, and crafted life stories for the people I'd observed to keep my mind sharp. Whenever I found my mind wandering off, I breathed deep, brought myself back to the present, and carried on.

At two in the morning, I drove off, making one last drive-by past the target house. The guard seemed bored out of his mind, but he still tracked my car as I moved past. The lights were all off, and there was no other sign of external security in sight.

Once out of sight, I made a sharp right turn and parked my car by the curb. Gulped down some water. Pulled on a pair of tactical gloves and a black balaclava, and donned my flatpack. Steadied myself with a breath.

Stepped out of the car.

The night was cool and silent. A soft breeze carried the scent of dry earth and fresh flowers. No passers-by. I sauntered down the street, casual as can be, just another inhabitant enjoying an early-morning stroll. As I walked, I counted off the houses, moving up behind the—

A dog barked.

Whirling to my right, I drew my knife and—

No. The dog was safely contained behind an imposing metal gate. It barked away, jumping about on its legs, pressing its face up against the grilles, but it couldn't reach me.

I eased away from the gate, the dog woofing at my back.

As soon as I was clear, I spent a few moments breathing, calming down, returning my knife to its pocket. I kept walking, just in case someone had heard the dog.

Six houses later, I stood before a small two-story home. I looked left, right, up, down, behind me. No witnesses, no cameras. The dog went silent.

I ran.

Across the concrete sidewalk, across the mowed grass of the far yard, past the house, through the backyard, and vaulted over the rear fence.

I landed softly on my feet and scooted over to the nearest corner. Breathed. Looked. Listened.

The scent of dry earth and cheap cigarettes filled my nose. But there was no sound, no motion.

I took a second to recall where the guard was seated, then sneaked over to the other corner. Lifting my foot an inch off the ground, I glided a step forward. Rested my toes on the grass, then the ball of my foot, and last of all my heels, letting the soles capture what little sound I made.

I ghosted to the other corner and peeked out. All clear. I drew my Shinobi, extended the paracord loop to its full length, and approached the front side of the house.

Leaning around the corner, I saw a large male sitting on a lawn chair next to the door, backlit against a street lamp. His arms were crossed over his chest, his feet planted squarely against the ground. He shifted his head left to right, watching the street.

He was alert. Pity he was looking the wrong way.

I looked up and away from him, keeping him in my peripheral view. Looking directly at someone triggers a primordial instinct that alerts him to your gaze. Breathing slowly, deeply, I crossed my arms, forming a loop of cord, and slowly approached him.

One step. Two steps. Three. Four. Five.

I pounced.

Throwing the loop over his head and around his throat, I dug the point of the Shinobi into his clavicular notch, seized the paracord with my left hand and jerked my arms apart.

His fingers clawed uselessly at the cord. As he struggled, I pressed my cheek against his skull and brought up my left forearm. He flailed for my face but found only my forehead. With a final burst of strength, he scrabbled at my right fist. My glove repelled his fingernails. The Shinobi was too deep and too small to snatch away. I kept up the pressure, squeezing tighter, tighter, tighter—

He went limp.

He was done. The strangle had closed off his carotid for a few seconds, long enough to completely shut him down. Any longer would risk death. I eased off the pressure and laid him on the ground face-down. Placing my knee on his back, I looked for more threats. There were none.

I checked his pulse. His carotid jumped against my finger. I opened my syringe case, grabbed a syringe, popped the cap, stuck him in his neck, and hit the plunger.

Ketamine takes about thirty seconds to kick in. A human usually recovers from a choke in ten. Right on the dot, the driver began to stir. I sank in another choke. This time he couldn't resist, and went out like a light. I counted off the seconds, and when he recovered again I sent him back to sleep.

The third time was the charm. He remained still, lost in a twilight state. I ziptied him, then patted him down and recovered a wallet, a phone, a Glock 17 pistol and a set of keys.

I wound my right hand through the long paracord loop, wearing the cord on my shoulder. As I scanned around me, I unloaded the gun and cleared the chamber. Retrieved a trash bag from my flatpack and tossed the wallet, phone, weapon, magazine, ejected bullet and spent needle into the bag. Stowing everything away, I pressed myself against the left side of the front door and listened.

Silence. I tried the door. Locked. I tested the appropriated keys. Two tries later, the lock gave way.

Stowing the keys in a pocket, I drew my flashlight in my left hand. Fitted with a red filter, it provided illumination without degrading my night vision. I Amped just a little, boosting my hearing, then opened the door and stepped through.

No light. No movement. No sound. I placed myself on the right of the door, clicked on the light and scanned.

Dead ahead, at the far wall, a large dining table and a half-dozen seats. Next to the table, there was an open door. On the right side of the dining room, another doorway. Sofas and couch and TV to my right. Opening to my left.

Someone snored upstairs. He sounded like a freight train. He could wait; I had to clear the ground floor first.

Scanning both ways, I entered the dining room. The first door led to the kitchen. Past that was the laundry area and a small washroom. A door led to the back yard. No one around. I backed up and entered the other door. This one took me to the garage.

The red Ford occupied the garage, facing the door. Tools and workbenches lined the walls. I felt around the rear fender and found the GPS tracker. I turned it off and stored it in my flatpack. I headed for the door and—

Footsteps.

I positioned myself next to the door. Turned off the light. Listened.

The footsteps receded. Glass tinkled. A tap ran. Silence. The tap ran again. A heavy weight rang against metal. The footsteps grew louder, and headed past the door.

Taking the cord in my left hand, I stepped out into the dining room. A large dark shape shuffled to the front door. One, two, three steps and I was on him. I kicked out the back of his knee, looped the garrote around his neck and pulled.

"What the—"

I dragged him back a couple of steps, taking away his balance, and sank in the cord. He tried to speak but only a strangled sound emerged. Seconds later, he was out.

I hit him with ketamine and prepped the strangle. He revived, I strangled him, he revived again, I strangled him again. Half a minute later, he was mumbling incoherently to himself. I ziptied him, dragged him into the garage and patted him down. Phone, wallet, and a battered Ruger handgun.

I secured the paracord around my shoulder, stored the loot in the trash bag, then went back out and carried the first guard back inside, setting him down next to his buddy. It wouldn't do for a passer-by to see the downed guard and call the cops.

Back in the living room, I went left. A short hallway led to a staircase and another room. The room was a home office. No people inside, but there was a huge blue duffel bag on the floor. I could examine that later, once the house was clear.

I headed upstairs. A room straight ahead, another to my right, two to my left. The snoring came from the room in front of me. I readied my syringe in my right hand, paracord loop in my left, and entered.

A figure lay on the bed, snoozing away. I trained my flashlight away from him, closed one eye, and turned it on. Red light washed the room. I saw a large man half-covered by a blanket, his muscular chest exposed. I turned the light back off and stowed it. Ghosted over to the bed, both eyes open, and injected him in the neck.

The snoring ceased. He took a sharp breath and sat up.

"What—"

I threw a loop of cord around his throat and yanked both ends.

His voice died with a soft wheeze. I jammed the Shinobi into him and drove him down into the bed.

"Get—off—"

He writhed. Kicked. Wriggled. He reached around and tapped my shoulder, but I wasn't letting go. Not until he was done. He struggled for a moment longer, and went out.

Cloth rustled against something. I held still and listened. Wood bumped softly against wood. I waited.

The subject woke up.

He fought once more, pushing hard against me. I grounded my weight and kept him down, grinding the Shinobi into his deltoid. He summoned a final burst of strength, *almost* sitting up, then plunked back down on the bed.

I waited again. Listened. Nothing.

The man moaned. But remained still.

I rolled him on his side and zip tied him. Stowed the needle. Stepped out of the bedroom and listened.

Nothing again. I Amped up just a bit more and heard breathing from the sole room to my left. I approached the open door, slowly, carefully.

Paused.

The breathing didn't quite sound right.

Cold fingers crawled down my spine. Something was wrong with this picture. Through the open doorway I saw a slice of the room. Just the bed and empty space.

But the breathing didn't come from the bed.

Flashlight in my left hand, I sliced the pie, stepping slowly in a semicircle, clearing the room inch by inch from the outside. I stepped in front of the open door and—

Nothing.

But the breathing remained.

Inside the room. To my right.

Raising the flashlight high, I crouched. Burst into the room. Swung right. Clicked on the light.

A man stood by the wall, aiming a pistol at the door. He flinched away from the light, covering his eyes with his left hand.

Chavez.

He fired.

Light blazed across my sight. The muzzle report hammered my ears. A bullet whizzed past. I rushed him, angling off from his weapon. Rising, I whirled my arms around, captured his gun arm and pulling it down into a rising elbow.

Bone crunched. He yelped in pain. The pistol clattered at my feet. He spun into me, and I instinctively raised my elbow. His fist caromed off my arm. I went low, stabbing him in the belly, driving him against the wall.

He shuddered. His legs went weak, his body bowed forward. I worked the cord around his neck, jammed the Shinobi into his back, and yanked.

His good hand grabbed my sleeve. He held on tight for a moment. He gurgled. And just like that, he fell into me.

I gently guided him down, placing him face-down against the floor. Kneeling against his spine, I dialed down my power, set the flashlight on the floor and aimed it at the ceiling, pocketed his gun, and grabbed more zip ties. I breathed slowly and regularly, bringing my muscles back under control, and secured his wrists. He groaned. I dug my knee into the small of his back and rammed my elbow into his upper back.

"Don't move," I said.

He jerked, trying to throw me off. I dropped my elbow into his lats. He gasped in pain.

"Don't move!" I said.

"What... what do you want?" he whispered.

"Are you Adrian Chavez?"

"Who's asking?"

No time to play nice. The gunshot would have woken the neighborhood. I ground my knee into his spine, jogging his injured arm. He cursed. Loudly.

"Are you Adrian Chavez?" I demanded again.

"Yes! Who the hell are you?"

I altered my accent, adopting the Mandarin-influenced pronunciation patterns of Singaporean English.

"I work for Tin Fo."

I exaggerated the Cantonese pronunciation, reverting to the tongue of Hong Kong and the rhythms of Singapore.

"Who? The triad?"

"Yes."

"*Pendejo!* You broke my arm! I can't—"

I worked the Shinobi into his temporomandibular joint.

"Ai ai ai ai ai!"

"Shut up and listen," I ordered.

He shut up.

"Last week, you hit someone in our turf," I said. "This week you sent a Prime to cause trouble. What the hell are you thinking?"

"I didn't do it!"

"Who did it?"

"I... I can't say!"

"*Pok gai!*" Die in the street! "You think I'll just let you go, issit?"

"I—"

"Shut up! If you don't tell me now, I'm just going to keep asking your people until they do."

"What's your beef, man?"

I kneed his arm. He swore. Loudly.

"I ask the questions, not you," I said.

"You know who I am, you know who I'm with," he said, panting. "You kill me, my *carnales* are going to come find you."

I laughed. "You make trouble for us before. We're not going to stop until we settle the problem."

"It's just a small beef, right? We can talk it out!"

"Start by telling me who you work for. Then we can talk."

"It's..." he sighed. "Ricardo Ruiz."

"Ruiz sent the shooters and the Prime to Chinatown?"

"Yes!"

"Why?"

"What's it to you, man?"

"*Tsat tao!* The cops are running all over Chinatown and making life difficult for us. When life is difficult, the Dragon Head calls me. Me, I decide whether to kill you or not."

"Look, you know the hit failed. We don't need to go to war over this."

"Maybe. Why did Ruiz send in his *sicarios*?"

"To kill a cop. A Prime. He goes by Amp. You must have heard of him."

"Why does Ruiz want to kill him?"

"Amp killed his son. He wants revenge. You can understand that, right?"

"Revenge? Are you trying to fight a war with the cops?"

"Ruiz can't *not* seek revenge. If he doesn't, he'll look weak. You're in the life, you know what I mean, right?"

"What about the Prime at the restaurant? Does he have something to do with this hit on Amp?"

"Yeah. The restaurant belongs to Amp's family. Amp showed up, and our guy tried to kill him, but Amp brought backup. Another Prime. The hit failed, and no one died."

"Are you still planning to kill Amp?"

"Like I said, man, we have to. It's the rules."

"Why didn't you tell us about the hit?"

"It's... complicated."

I jammed the Shinobi into the side of his neck, just enough to establish dominance.

"Bullshit. Tell me why you didn't inform Tin Fo."

"Amp was a detective in the Asian Gang Unit," Chavez said through gritted teeth. "We thought that... if we went to Tin Fo... he might have heard about the hit."

How did they know that about me?

"You never thought to tell us?"

"We were going to, after it was over."

"Too late. AGU is cracking down on us, and it's your fault. Someone has to clean up the mess."

"Look, look, we can talk about this, right? Your Dragon Head, my *jefe*, we can sit down and talk things through."

"It depends on what you say to me. How do you know so much about Amp?"

"We... I can't say."

Time was running out. I increased the pressure on his neck and arm. He jerked, screeching in pain. I eased off a little and allowed him a second to catch his breath.

"You say you want to talk things through with us, but you won't tell us how you found Amp? How should we trust you?"

"We followed Amp, all right?"

I laughed.

"You think I'm stupid issit? We have eyes everywhere in Chinatown. If a spic steps on our turf, we'll know straight away. How did you really find him?"

"We—" he sighed. "We have hackers. They hacked into the police database and downloaded his dossier."

My heart stilled. My breath caught in my chest. I forced myself to speak.

"So you know everything about Amp?"

"Everything that's on the dossier. Name, age, address, next of kin."

"All of El Trece knows this?"

"No, no, just our clique."

"Why?"

"Revenge is personal. We can't have someone outside the clique take care of it for us."

"So this is how you know where Amp stayed."

"Yes."

"And also how you know where his next of kin lives."

"Yes."

"All this is just your boss looking for revenge against Amp."

"Yes. Look, we don't want to fight with you, okay? You can keep your turf. We just want Amp. We can work things out."

"Really. Where is your boss?"

"I don't know."

"You want to play this game again?"

"No, really, I don't know! He didn't tell me where he went. He just said he's going dark for a while."

"Then how do you talk to him?"

"Calls or texts. But since this started we never met face-to-face."

"What about the Prime? What's his name?"

"Bombero. I don't know him, not even his real name, and I have no way of contacting him. He only answers to *el jefe*."

Damn it. I thought I'd be able to reach Ruiz or Bombero through Chavez. Ruiz was smart, and his operational security was tight. This was a dead end.

One last thing to do. I produced the syringe case from my jacket.

"Hey, what are you doing?" Chavez asked.

"None of your business. What's your role in all this?"

"Me? Nothing much. I just help *el jefe* run the business."

"Like a manager?"

"Yeah, yeah, like a manager. I'm nobody important. Not important as him."

I set the case next to him and retrieved a syringe. "All things considered, though, maybe I won't have to kill you."

Hope entered his voice. "Really?"

"Your boss and my boss can talk it out. We're just following orders."

"Yeah, just following orders," he agreed.

I popped the cap of the syringe.

"I've got a message for your boss," I said. "You can do that for me, right?"

"Yeah, yeah. What's the message?"

"Don't drop the soap."

I jammed the syringe into his neck. Hit the plunger. Set it aside.

"What the—"

I tightened the cord around his throat and choked him out. He recovered, and I choked him again. When I was sure he was done, I threw him on the bed.

Searching Chavez's bedroom, I found his wallet, keys and a bunch of cell phones in a grocery bag. Everything went into my rapidly-bulging flatpack.

I checked the rest of the rooms on the second floor. The dressers were stuffed with clothes and personal effects. I didn't have time to sort things out, but perhaps the police would. I did, however, take the snoring man's pistol, hidden under his pillow.

I retraced my footsteps, looking for any evidence I might have left behind. Back inside the home office, I examined the duffel bag.

Cash. Bundles and bundles of cash tied together with rubber bands.

I shouldered the bag and continued my hasty search. If someone had called the cops, I had maybe five more minutes until they came. I had to be out in two.

The subjects I'd drugged and dumped in the garage were still insensate. I tested the recovered keys on the car until I found the one that worked. Popping the doors, I rifled through the car.

There was nothing of interest. Nothing except a rubber mallet, a tire iron and a pair of screwdrivers. Everything you need to fix a car or end a life.

I powered up the phones and checked the call history. Four of eight had been used before, as far as I know. I kept the used ones, grabbed the nearest phone and dialed 911.

"911 emergency," the dispatcher said. "How can I help?"

"I saw a man break into a house," I replied, switching into a Hispanic accent. "I think I heard a gunshot."

"Understood. What's your location?"

"I— Oh, damn, he's looking this way!"

I tossed the phone into the car. If no one had called the cops earlier, this would guarantee a response.

I unlocked the front door of the house and left it wide open. Walked down the street, fighting the urge to run, and breathed deep.

I returned to my car, my heart still pounding in my chest. I fired up the engine and drove off into the night.

Mission complete.

22

COPS, GUNS AND MONEY

I slept well.

None of my unquiet dead visited me in my dreams. Actually, I didn't dream at all. I simply hit the sack and closed my eyes, and when I opened them again it was morning.

The last time I'd slept like that, I was at war.

I awoke at my usual time. Bad thing about sharing your home with others, they'll notice your habits and deviations from them. The last thing I needed was to drag them into my business. They didn't deserve it.

After morning training and breakfast with the priests, I retreated to my room and counted the spoils of war.

First were the weapons. The Glock 17 and Ruger were functional, but barely so. Their barrels were coated with carbon, and their internals were bone dry. Maintenance was never a strong suit among criminals.

The other two pistols were in better shape. The snoring man's gun was a Glock 22, an older generation with finger grooves, but it was clean and functional. The last weapon, Chavez's pistol, was an oddity, a Smith & Wesson Performance Center Military and Police pistol. No way the M&P was bought on the open market; this was a race gun, with bright red fiber optic sights, aftermarket rubber grips, a ported barrel, and a miniature holographic sight. This had to be stolen.

The guns had to go. I had plenty of weapons already, and there was someone out there who wanted his S&W back.

I flipped through the wallets. The cash went into my wallet, of course, and the cards into the waste bin. I photographed the drivers' licenses too and tossed them into the bin.

I contemplated the phones. Having more burners would be nice, but if the numbers were compromised, it wouldn't do me good. In the end, I elected to discard the used phones and keep the rest.

Finally, I counted the cash in the duffel bag.

Most of the money was organized in neatly-stacked bricks. But the gangsters had also randomly tossed money into the pile without counting or sorting them. I sighed, broke up the bricks of cash, spread the notes out on the floor, sorting them by denomination, and counted them by hand.

It took a *long* time. But when I was done, I found myself sitting on just over fifty-five thousand dollars.

Cash was king, and cash was troublesome. I couldn't leave the money in the cell; that was just asking for trouble. But I couldn't bank all of it either. Banks had to report transactions that exceeded ten thousand dollars—or multiple rapid transactions of smaller amounts.

As I pondered what to do with the money, I checked my laptop. And smiled.

I was inside the police database.

The first order of business was to create a dummy profile. Michael Bosch, civilian employee, assigned to the IT Division. He was a database administrator, not a cop, but he was the guy the cops relied on to maintain the police databases. He needed administrator rights and complete access to every police database. I mocked up his background, education history, address and next of kin. Then I scoured the Internet, found a stock photo of a male model, and uploaded it into his profile.

When I was done, paranoia gripped me. If the cops raided my

safe house, confiscated everything here and compromised my devices, what would they find? Enough to convict me.

I had to protect myself.

I went back to my secure website on Tor. Uploaded the AFK of the database app on the repository and Bosch's details, deleted the app on my Nullphone, and wiped the histories and caches of my browser and tracker app. The tracker alone would raise eyebrows, but it wasn't illegal to own.

I wiped down the guns, magazines, and bullets. Retrieved a plastic bag from the kitchen and did the same to it. I stowed the weapons and ammo in the bag and carried the duffel bag to my car. Returned to my cell and considered my options.

After what I'd done, there'd be blowback from El Trece. The only question was whether I'd have to fight it or evade it. In the end, I loaded my gun bag with my shotgun, grabbed my shotgun ammo bag, and stowed both in the trunk of my car. The Mossberg was loaded, in contravention of state law, but my badge conferred legal immunity.

I stashed the criminal guns under a bench in a park, then got on my Nullphone and submitted an anonymous tip on the HCPD website. The website promised the cops would act on the information immediately and keep my identity secret, and gave me a tip number.

I wanted to keep eyes on the weapons until the police picked them up, but that could take hours, and I still had work to do.

Driving around Halo City, I bought a half-dozen gift cards from every major retailer. I deposited a random amount of cash in each card, ranging from a hundred and fifty to three hundred, just enough money to be useful without raising red flags.

After that, I hit a string of cryptocurrency ATMs. Crypto money laundering was the boogeyman of the modern banking sector, and companies that operated crypto ATMs were required to obey a stringent set of anti-money laundering regulations. Transactions over seven hundred dollars were recorded, and the customer had to present and verify his ID.

At every stop, I bought between five hundred to six hundred and fifty dollars' worth of cryptocurrencies. Wherever possible I chose privacy-centric coins, but I also bought legacy coins: Bitcoin, Litecoin and their respective forks.

I opened new wallets for these purchases, then routed the funds through cryptocurrency mixers and into fresh wallets. I lost a bit of money along the way, but better safe than sorry.

Crypto money laundering was more anonymous than traditional methods, and far easier for individuals to perform, but it carried its own risks. To continue laundering the rest of the funds, I'd have to spread out purchases over days, weeks, months, changing up details to avoid triggering AML tripwires. The value of crypto fluctuated daily too, sometimes even hourly. If I were unlucky, when the time came to cash in, I might end up with much less money than I'd invested.

But that was all right. The value of crypto trended upward in the long term, and there wasn't much I could do about it anyway. The key was to only invest as much money as I could afford to lose.

During my travels, I made a brief stop at Bright Moon Temple, long enough to offer incense and stuff two hundred dollars into the donation box. Earning a bit of extra karma couldn't hurt.

I dumped the rest of the cash and the gift cards in storage, keeping a few hundred for walking-around money.

I spent some of it a gun store to buy a shotgun brass catcher. It was a clunky box designed to be strapped over the ejection port, capturing expended shells as they were fired. Excellent for keeping firing ranges and hunting grounds clean, and to avoid leaving behind forensics evidence.

Shotguns were smoothbore weapons. Without rifling, recovered slugs or pellets could not be conclusively traced to a specific shotgun. Tool marks in the barrel might link a projectile to a specific weapon, but a hard training session and a good scrub with a steel wire brush would introduce reasonable doubt. The only other way to trace a shotgun shell were extractor and firing pin marks on the spent shell. Which could be recovered by the shooter.

Which wasn't to say shotguns were completely untraceable. A

recovered sabot could tell an investigator what kind of ammo was used, and the batch number. Deposits on the barrel could be matched to a pellet or a slug. More tests would reveal the powder and manufacturer.

If I ever had to use a shotgun for an unsanctioned op, the spent shells had to go. Arguably even the barrel and the ammo box. But I could re-use the gun. *If* I stored it so securely the cops couldn't find it.

Of course, this was the final option. In case there was no way to neutralize Ruiz and his goons through other means.

I also bought three shotgun dispensers. Shaped like a rifle magazine, each dispenser could hold six shells. If needed, I could swap my AR magazines for the dispensers on my chest rig, and I was good to go. I had no desire to lug around the ammo bag on an op if I could avoid it.

I had lunch in a taco place. Fatigue caught up with me soon after. My head pounded too much to think straight, and I didn't have much to do today. Back at the church I dropped a couple of hundred dollars in the poor box, loaded the shotgun dispensers with fresh minishells, lay my head down, and awoke in the late afternoon.

The news reported my exploits. In the middle section of the *Halo City Herald*, a small article reported the police responding to a home invasion call only to find four trussed-up men, all of them members of the notorious El Trece street gang. The police refused to speculate what, exactly, had happened. Buried near the bottom, a tinier story mentioned a robber ripping off a drug dealer and his accomplice in a ghetto. Coming up next, the latest in celebrity antics.

The paperwork in the police database told a different story. All four El Trece gangsters had lawyered up and said nothing. Without any illegal items on site, there was nothing the cops could use to charge them. However, there were outstanding warrants on all of them. It was their third strike, and they were all going to prison for twenty-five years at least. Further, Chavez had snapped his right elbow and fractured his left hand, and needed advanced medical care.

Too bad.

In his report, a detective noted that the alleged home invasion might be payback from a rival gang, siccing the cops on El Trece. Criminals usually didn't do this, not unless they felt their targets were so powerful and so malicious it was worth violating their informal code of honor.

The recovered guns made their way into the evidence room. The race gun was indeed reported stolen six weeks ago. If it weren't connected to a crime, it might be returned to its rightful owner eventually.

If my tip had led to an arrest, I'd be eligible for a reward. Then again, I was still technically a public servant, and ineligible for one. You can't have everything.

I spent the rest of the day studying El Trece, focusing on Ruiz's clique. Decentralized groups like El Trece were highly resilient; simply removing the leader wouldn't disrupt the group for long. There was always someone else waiting in the wings to take over a splinter faction. Even if I found Ruiz and removed him from play, it might not spell the end of the beef. Should Ruiz go to jail, there would always be someone willing to make a name for himself by taking on his old boss' debt. A Prime like me is always at the top of every two-bit punk's hit list.

In the Raiders, then the Task Force, we found a different way to fight. Leaders are only powerful insofar as they could get things done. Without the ability to deploy men and material, they were just useless mouths. Organizations existed to serve the needs of its members, clients, and patrons. Take out the people who facilitated and executed operations, and the organization would crumble.

Someone had to liaise with other gangs and smooth over deals. Someone had to source for trusted suppliers and distributors. Someone had to launder the money, keep the books, make sure everyone up and down the chain got his cut. And when things went wrong, when someone reneged on a contract, when a rival gang stuck their noses where they didn't belong, when a cop dropped the hammer on the wrong man, someone had to pull the trigger.

Take these guys out, and *el jefe* would be isolated. Once isolated, he becomes vulnerable. Once vulnerable, he can be taken.

I studied Ruiz's files and his known associates. His police file was heavy on background detail and light on current information. A second-generation gangster, he had roamed the streets of Halo City and raised hell wherever he went. After his first strike, he took an extended vacation in Mexico and popped up on the DEA's radar. His second strike took him to a medium-security prison, where he learned at the knee of his seniors. When he stepped out, he had apparently turned over a new leaf.

He lasered off his visible tattoos. Opened legit businesses and charities with money that seemed to materialize out of nowhere. Started a family, showed his face in church, spoke up on behalf of the community. His rivals mysteriously disappeared, and their cliques fell into his orbit. Inside a decade, he went from *carnal* to *cara*.

Ruiz had come a long way from the street. With plenty of underlings to do his dirty business, there was little the HCPD could pin on him. The Intelligence Bureau tried to map his relationships, at least, but it wasn't a crime to be friends with criminals.

The map itself was mostly incomplete. There was Chavez, now off the street. A couple-dozen others, some in prison, some dead, some missing. Of the remainder, a few were marked with key roles—*sicario*, treasurer, in Bombero's case a Prime—but there were many blanks in the organization. I wouldn't be surprised if El Trece's pet cop or cops had a hand in hiding names and activities.

All the same, I worked with what I had, making notes on Ruiz's circle of friends.

I had dinner with the priests, then continued working on the notes. I matched names and addresses to my map, studied the terrain with open source imagery, looked up local demographics and crime rates and a hundred other relevant factors.

It was just like old times, prepping for ops in the cesspools of the world. But this time I was alone, and I was breaking all the rules.

Not that I had any other choice.

At a quarter to ten, my police phone rang. Oliveira.

"Amp," he said gravely, "we have a problem."

THIS WAS GETTING AWFULLY FAMILIAR.

My heart slammed into my chest. My fingers and feet went cold, my mouth dried up. I licked my lips and said, "Hold on a second."

I locked the door, drew the curtains, bought a moment with a breath, and returned my phone to my ear.

"What's wrong?" I asked.

"It's Shane. Bombero abducted her."

"*WHAT?*"

"Woah, easy there."

I sucked down a breath. "Right. Tell me what happened."

"At twenty-one hundred, a live stream popped up on all the major social media sites. It showed Shane, tied to a chair in a room. A masked man on the screen held up her badge and her driver's license and said she was a cop.

"The man snapped his fingers and produced a ball of flame. He touched it to her, and..."

I sighed.

"Yeah," Oliveira said. "I'll spare you the details, but they're torturing her live on the Net. Slowly. It's... it's bad. You don't know want to know how bad."

"Why are they doing this?"

"Every ten minutes, Bombero turns to the camera and calls you out. He said, 'Amp, if you call yourself a hero, come and rescue her.' Well, he didn't exactly say 'her,' but I'm sure you know what he really said."

"He's baiting me. First my home and the car, then the restaurant, then the cops he burned..."

"Yeah. He can't find you, so he wants to draw you out."

My blood boiled. My heart rampaged in my chest. I clenched my fists.

Breathed.

Released.

"Still here, Amp?"

"Yeah," I said. "Do we have anything to go on?"

"Well, the good news is, we've traced the address. The horror show is in Franklin Heights. They didn't even bother trying to hide from us."

"It's a trap," I said.

"Exactly. Which is why I want you with us."

"I'm still off-duty."

"You're still STAR-qualified. The only Prime in the city who can run with STAR. We both know it's a trap, but if anyone can help us reverse it, it's you."

"What about Danny?"

"Speedy's good, but this is STAR business. We kick the door, REACT backs us up. You with us?"

There was only one answer.

"Yes," I said.

"Excellent. Don't worry about kit. We'll take extras for you in the BearCat. Just get over here, and we'll sort you out."

"Understood. Text me the address."

I hung up and dressed up.

Flame resistant shirt and pants. Gloves. War belt. Boots. Badge. Oliveira might be bringing extra kit, but you can only count on the things you bring to the fight. As I stuffed my balaclava into my pocket, my police phone rang again.

Unknown number. But coming so soon after Oliveira's call, I had a bad feeling about it. I activated my voice recorder app on my Null-phone and answered the call on the speaker.

"Detective Song, this is Chief Anderson."

I knew it.

"I heard Sergeant Oliveira asked for your help to participate in a STAR operation," Anderson continued.

"Yes," I said.

"Are you going?"

"I have to."

"'Have to'? Interesting choice. Why do you say that?"

"A police officer has been kidnapped. We do not abandon our own."

"An admirable sentiment. But don't worry. STAR and REACT are on the way. Your presence is no longer required."

"It's a trap. There's a rogue—"

"Yes, we are aware of that," Anderson interrupted. "STAR and REACT have been briefed and equipped accordingly."

"Sir, among all the officers in the HCPD, I have the most experience with rogues. I have to be there."

"Phantom will take your place."

"He's not STAR qualified."

"But he *is* a Prime, and he is in REACT. Detective, I know you're upset, but we must be rational about this. Bombero wants to draw you out into an ambush. We can't give him what he wants."

"We can reverse the ambush—"

"Yes, but your presence is not required for that. REACT is containing the scene as we speak. Bombero has nowhere to run. It's time for you to stand down. We can take it from here."

Something didn't add up. Anderson wanted me to stay well away from the scene. Why? Two police Primes are always better than one, especially with a rogue involved.

"Sir, why don't you want me to deploy?"

"It's too dangerous. They're expecting you."

"C'mon, sir, STAR has handled more complex cases than this."

"Detective, overconfidence kills. We've already lost two officers this week. We can't lose another."

"You'll lose more if I'm not there. Look, in my uniform and gear, I'm just another STAR officer. I can't be pinned down, I can't be tracked, and I can't be identified. That's the whole point of going masked, isn't it? If I go masked, Bombero won't even know I'm there until it's too late for him."

Anderson sighed.

"Detective... *Adam.* You are currently the subject of two ongoing

Internal Affairs and DA Office investigations. It is against policy to deploy you in the field when you haven't been cleared."

"Sir, is it also against policy to *not* issue a replacement weapon after a shooting? Why did I have to jump through hoops just to get a new pistol?"

"Detective—"

"And speaking of policy, *Chief*, everyone in the department knows I'm on an El Trece hit list. Me and my family. Why aren't we under police protection?"

"Detective! You will not speak to me like that!"

"Chief, all I'm hearing from you is that you think I'm a liability. Not a cop."

Anderson remained silent for a moment.

"Adam, I know you're upset," he said. "It's been a long week. We can talk about guns and additional protection when you come back in. But right now, I need you to stand down. We are not giving you to El Trece."

"Chief—"

"I didn't call you to argue with you. Do *not* deploy. Sergeant Oliveira has already been informed of my decision. If you do deploy, you will be subject to disciplinary measures. Am I clear?"

"Yes."

I turned the phone off and chucked it aside.

This was... unbelievable. I knew Anderson was a politician, but this? I never thought a cop could stoop this low. I needed a good, long chat with my lawyers in the morning. And perhaps mail the recording to a sympathetic journalist.

But for now, Shane had been kidnapped, and Bombero was on the loose. El Trece would be waiting in ambush. The only question is what shape the ambush would take.

Policy said I shouldn't deploy. There were many good reasons for that. But divine law superseded secular law. And when I wake up tomorrow, I had to live with what I had done. And hadn't done.

Detective Adam Song, alias Amp, couldn't deploy. But Adam Song, former USMC and Task Force, could.

23

GO WITH GOD

I wished I had my gear. Body armor, Virtus, Glock, all the tacticool tools a self-respecting operator needed to operate operationally. But there was no time to dash to storage and pick it up. I had to work with what I had.

I loaded my pockets with my tools, clipped my flatpack to my chest rig and swapped out the AR magazines for the shotgun dispensers. I grabbed my Mossberg 500...

It was still in its baseline configuration. Too long and too unwieldy for close quarters. And the ejection port was uncovered.

Fighting down the urge to swear, I replaced the stock with a pistol grip, exchanged the full-length barrel for an 18.5-inch, and strapped on the brass catcher.

I patted myself down one last time, checking my kit, my knives, my flashlight, my Shinobi, my entry tools. My backpack held medical supplies, a change of clothing, food, a water bottle. Everything was set.

Stepping out the door, I saw Father Josh in the hallway. He gave me a once-over and raised his eyebrow.

"What's wrong?" he asked.

"Call out," I replied. "I have to go."

He crossed his arms, his artificial limb whirring slightly.

"Call out? What do you mean?"

"A cop is in danger. I need to go."

He nodded and stepped aside. "Go with God, Adam."

I rushed to the parking lot and jumped in my car. Hit the gas and raced to Franklin Heights.

As I navigated the neon-lit roads, I pondered the situation. Something was wrong wiht this picture.

Why did Bombero set this up? He would know that we knew this was an ambush and would take no chances. Once the police lock down a site and send in STAR, there's no escape. The only variable is the final body count. If he had survived the narcowar in Mexico, he would know that. Once found and fixed, a threat *will* be finished.

Bombero was a monster, but he wasn't insane. He wouldn't hunker down and wait for STAR to come and kill him. He gained nothing from it. He wasn't some jihadi out to take as many infidels as he could with him; he was a predator, a survivor, a *sicario*. He was here to kill me *and* get away clean.

Maybe he felt confident he could blow through the STAR team and the police cordon with his powers. Not out of the realm of possibility; the most powerful Primes were walking weapons of mass destruction. Maybe he had planned an ambush, one we wouldn't see coming. Again, not impossible; he must have learned many tricks south of the border.

Maybe it was both.

Five minutes later, I saw a set of blue and red lights flash behind me. I sighed, pulled over, and readied my badge.

A fresh-faced patrolman appeared at my window and shone his flashlight into my face. He was young, barely in his twenties. Before he could say anything, I lowered the window.

"Sir, do you know how fast you were going?" he asked.

"Off-duty officer," I replied. "I'm responding to the callout at Franklin Heights."

He blinked. "Uh... I need to see your badge, please."

"It's in my left hand. I'm going to raise it slowly."

"Go ahead."

I lifted my hand, forcing myself to move slow and steady. He scrutinized the badge and nodded.

"I could escort you to the scene," he offered.

"Thanks," I said. "Let's go."

Lights and sirens blaring, the patrol car raced down the city streets, clearing me a path. The driver was far more reckless than I was, tearing down streets and highways at top speed, but I wasn't complaining.

We stopped at the outer cordon. Police cruisers and motorbikes parked haphazardly across the street. REACT officers, decked out in helmets and armor and carbines, sealed off the streets with traffic cones, tape, and their bodies.

I jumped out of the car, waved goodbye at the departing patrol car, and donned my gear. Radios chattered, people whispered and shouted orders, civilians peeked out and popped back behind cover. As I stuffed my earplugs in place, a petite REACT officer hustled over.

"Sir, you can't be here!" she shouted.

I held up my badge. "Off duty officer. I'm here to help!"

She looked at the shotgun, my get-up, and back at the gun.

"That's not standard-issue HCPD equipment," she said.

"A cop's been kidnapped and tortured, a rogue is out there waiting in ambush for us, and that's what you're concerned about?"

She adjusted her weight ever so slightly, blading her posture.

"Anyone can flash a badge."

"This is my personal kit. I can show you my ID. It's in my wallet, right thigh pocket."

"Go ahead."

Slowly, I reached for my pocket and produced my ID card. She stared hard at it, her eyes flicking back and forth between the card and my face.

"All right, Detective Song. I apologize, but we're on high alert."

"No worries. What's the situation?"

"We're drawing a perimeter around 32 Franklin Heights. REACT has the scene locked down, STAR is en route, and patrol officers are evacuating surrounding residents." She paused. "At least, up until a few minutes ago."

"What happened?"

"Snipers with semi-auto rifles, situated within the target building. They're shooting at whoever tries to approach or leave the scene."

"Shit. Did any heroes try to help?"

She sighed and shook her head.

"Wild Cat and Miss Midnight showed up about ten minutes ago. We told them to help with the evacuation, but those idiots tried to l. The moment they stepped out on the street, snipers opened up on them."

I sighed too. "Amateurs."

"Yup. They took a couple of rounds each. But Wild Cat managed to drag Miss Midnight back to the perimeter. EMTs evacuated them just before you arrived. Now, our orders are to prevent all Primes from interfering. They can help with the evacuation and with perimeter security, but they must not cross this perimeter."

"No one else made entry?"

"We're waiting on the BearCats. Until they get here, we can't cross the kill zone."

"Who else is downrange?"

"We've got unis and taxpayers trapped in the neighboring units."

The former meant uniformed cops.

"Right. I'm going in. Call in my presence for me."

"What? Are you nuts?"

"Yes."

I pushed past the REACT perimeter, the cop yelling at my back, and headed down the empty street. My blood sang, my power surged, my muscles tensed. I stopped at the corner and peeked out.

This part of town was reserved for housing projects. A row of blocky eight-story brick buildings stretched down the sidewalk, interspaced with tiny grass courtyards and crowded parking lots. Patrol cars flashed blue and red in utter silence, their headlights aimed to illuminate the windows and doors. Shadows moved furtively in the distance, small knots of civilians escorted by lone cops.

So much for a silent perimeter. The flashing lights alone advertised that we were on to them. The bad guys would be digging in, preparing themselves for a fight.

And where the hell was STAR? This was a rapid deployment. The BearCats should be shuttling back and forth, shielding the civilians, while the teams stormed the building.

Someone had screwed up big-time. Call it friction, fog of war, sheer bad luck, the only thing that mattered was that Bombero and his clique would be preparing themselves for their final stand.

"What the hell are you doing?"

It was the petite cop again, rushing towards me, her partner right behind her. The other REACT cops held their ground but watched us, maintaining the perimeter.

"Preparing to make entry," I replied.

"You're *loco!* Get back to the perimeter!" she said.

In for a penny, in for a pound. I sucked in a breath.

"Officer, I'm a police Prime. My callsign is Amp."

The two cops exchanged a look.

"No. Way," her partner said.

"Yes way," I said. "You can confirm with Dispatch later, but right now, I need your help."

"Hold up," she said. "Why are *you* here? Aren't you with STAR?"

"Chief Anderson told me not to come."

"What? Why?"

"I'm being investigated for a couple of shootings."

"That's *bullshit!*" the other cop exclaimed.

"Yeah. But look, there's at least one rogue in there torturing a cop, and he's got plenty of friends with him. I have to go."

"Come on, this is suicide," she said.

"Look, the bad guys are forcing STAR to roll in hot. They will see STAR coming. Once the BearCats arrive, they will execute the hostage and ambush the STAR team. You want that?"

"Hell no," they both said.

"Exactly. If I go in solo, they won't see me coming. I can rescue the hostage and neutralize the rogue. But to do that, I need your help. You with me?"

"Yeah. What kind of help do you need?"

"Two things. First, either of you got a flash-bang?"

"Yup," the other cop said.

"Good. I'm going to the neighboring unit, 33 Franklin Heights, but I need a distraction. On my signal, toss the flash-bang on the road and cover me. I'll be going in. The moment I'm clear, fall back to your perimeter."

"Got it. What's the other thing?" she asked.

"Don't tell anyone I'm here."

"Why?"

"Do you want the Chief and IA riding you?" I asked.

"*Hell* no," they said in unison.

"Exactly. Just say something like you're covering an EMT or whatever. But I have to go in now. You ready?"

"Let's do this," she said.

She knelt by the corner, readied her Virtus, and whispered into her radio, letting everyone know they were covering an EMT's approach.

Her partner produced a flash-bang and stepped up. On my signal, he pulled the pin and tossed the banger with all his might.

The distraction device sailed through the air. I closed my eyes and covered my ears. Tremendous light and sound blasted in my head.

"GO!"

I Amped.

Ran.

A rifle cracked. Gunfire strobed in the night. I pumped my legs and kept running. Bullets ricocheted and spattered into metal and concrete and asphalt. The REACT cops opened fire. I kept running.

The door of 33 Franklin Heights swung open. A cop peeked out.

"What the—"

I slowed down, holding up my badge.

"HCPD! LET ME IN!" I called.

The cop stepped aside, and I burst through the open door.

I was in a narrow hallway packed with civilians. They stared at me with fearful expressions, clutching children and backpacks and phones and wallets and keys.

Next to the door, the cop wiped his forehead with his right hand, his Glock in his left. His nametag read 'DuBois.'

"Damn, man, you were *fast,*" he said.

"Thanks," I said, and sucked down a breath.

"Who the hell are you, and why the hell did you come here?"

I gulped down more oxygen.

"I'm here to help," I said.

"Help? How? Without the BearCat, we're not going anywhere."

"Don't be so sure about that."

DuBois shook his head. "Where you from?"

I held up my badge. "Off duty officer. How bad is the sniper fire?"

"Comes and goes," he said. "But it's been picking up over the past few minutes. Man, you were lucky."

"It's just harassing fire," I said. "My guess is, some gangbangers are slinging lead downrange just to let us know they're there."

"Yeah, well, they got us pinned down," DuBois replied. "We can't shoot back either. Captain told us to hold our fire."

Without clear targets, it was too easy for rounds to go wild and strike an innocent.

"Whatchu doing here anyway?" a civvie asked. "Now you stuck in here with us."

I smiled and held up my shotgun. "I'm STAR. I'm going to give the bangers a taste of their own medicine."

Smiles spread through the civilians' faces.

"Go get 'em!"

"Yeah, kill them all dead, you hear?"

"Stop those motherfuckers before they kill more people!"

"That's the plan," I said. "Is there roof access?"

"Yeah, but the door's locked, and no one has the key," a woman replied.

Fortunately, locks couldn't hold me back.

"Gotcha. Everyone, please make way."

The crowd parted. As I turned to go, DuBois called out. "Hey, wait."

"Yeah?" I replied.

"The radio said you were an EMT."

"Bad guys could be listening in."

"Ah. Where are you going?"

"I need to assess the area first. Once I find a good overwatch position, I'll update you."

"You need backup? We've got a few more cops upstairs evacuating the area."

"No, thanks."

"Got it. Stay safe out there."

"You too."

I dashed up the stairs, encountering a couple of fleeing civilians. I kept my badge high and my weapon clear of their hands and kept running. On the eighth floor, I met another cop. Her name tag read 'Peterson.'

"Is the top floor clear?" I asked.

She squinted at my badge and nodded. "Yeah. We evacuated everyone downstairs."

"Excellent. I can take over from here. You go down and help the others."

Her eyes narrowed. "What are you planning?"

"I'm going to see if I can deal with the snipers."

"That's not department issue kit."

I sighed. "You're not the first one to say that. Look, I'm off duty, I grabbed what I had on me, and here I am. Let me help."

As if on cue, more shots rang out. Peterson flinched.

"I don't know about you, but I'd rather engage that shooter with a long gun," I added.

"The snipers aren't on the roof, and from where we are, we don't have an angle on them."

"Then I'm going in."

"You? All by yourself? How?"

"I'm Amp."

She did a double take. "You? Amp? *Really?*"

"Really. Look, we don't have time to argue. There's a hostage inside the objective building. I need to get her out before STAR arrives, or the bad guys will execute her. Just let me through."

"How do I know you're Amp?"

"Who else in the PD is crazy enough to do this?"

She pursed her lips. Swallowed. And stepped aside.

"Don't make me regret this," she said.

"I won't. And one more thing."

"Yeah?"

"I was never here."

"What do you mean?"

"IA and the DAO is investigating me for a couple of shootings. The Chief told me to stand down and not respond to this call."

"What? Why?"

"Politics. I'm ready to face whatever they can throw at me, but you, if you want to stay in the force, don't tell anyone I'm here."

She swore softly under her breath.

"Politics." She sighed. "Well, I'm not going to stop you."

"Thanks."

"And Amp?"

"Yeah?"

"Good luck."

"Thanks."

Two more flights of stairs and I was at the roof access. The lock was a cheap piece of junk. For a second I readied myself to kick the door open, then I realized that if there were bangers on the roof or near the top floor windows of the objective, they would hear me coming.

Instead, I broke out my lock pick set and went to work. Half a minute later, the stiff tumblers yielded and turned. I donned my balaclava and opened the door. Shotgun ready, I stepped out to the sound of rotors.

I ignored the sound for now and swept the roof. Clear.

Looking up, I saw red lights flash in the night sky. Helicopter. Police or news, I couldn't tell just yet.

As if on cue, a massive white spotlight blinded me. I looked away from the glare, shielding my eyes.

Police aviation. Had to be. If I were truly unlucky, there'd be a sniper or STAR team aboard, wondering just who the hell was on the roof.

Slowly, deliberately, I released my Mossberg, fished out my badge and held both hands up and out to the light.

Searing blue light played across the cockpit. The helicopter juked away.

Laser. I looked away, blinking hard. The windscreens of HCPD helicopters were coated with anti-laser films, but the film only protected against green lasers. Someone had done their research.

STAR wasn't coming in from the roof. But I could.

Lowering myself to the prone, I crawled to the parapet. Five meters of empty space separated me from the objective. Shadows flitted past lit and curtained windows on the upper floor. Flashing fingers of red and blue light streaked up from the street, accompanied by a chorus of whooping sirens.

STAR was here.

Two BearCats barreled down the street, approaching the objective. Gunfire rang out. Undeterred, the armored cars kept coming, screeching to a halt right outside the front door. Officers popped out of the roof hatches and laid down covering fire with their suppressed carbines.

STAR operators filed out of the BearCats. The shield operators oriented their shields high, scanning for threats, while the assaulters covered the windows.

"Five-Oh! Five-Oh!" someone yelled.

A burning bottle fell from a window. It shattered against a shield, spraying burning fluid everywhere. A couple of cops broke ranks, dropping and rolling, extinguishing their burning clothes. Someone screamed, so loudly I could hear it from here.

For a second the assault stalled. Then the remaining cops stacked on the door. The point man booted the door and the teams piled in. A pair of roof gunners clambered out of their vehicles and raced to the wounded.

It was over. STAR would clear the building floor by floor, find Shane, and end the madness. Despite what I'd said to the REACT cop, I was sure El Trece wouldn't execute Shane. They weren't terrorists, and they had to be sure I was there. So long as I didn't show my face, they would keep her alive...

Then again, I still had a bad feeling about this. Bombero was still unaccounted for. And come to think of it: maybe he hadn't revealed the true scope of his powers.

No more time for hesitation or analysis. I had to go in.

24

NECESSARY FORCE

Under more regular circumstances, to access a roof, we would rappel from a helicopter or deploy an assault ladder. Here, all I had to go on was my gift.

It had to be enough.

I stepped back from the edge.

Amped.

Ran.

Arms swinging, legs pounding, I sprinted for the edge, pouring every last bit of power into my muscles, and jumped.

I soared. Gravity lost its grip for a moment. Air rushed past my ears.

I fell.

Braced.

Landed.

Covering my head, I threw myself to the side, bleeding off the excess energy. The concrete slammed into my calf, my thigh, my butt, my lats.

That hurt. The contents of my pack dug into my back. I'd jumped higher than I expected. But nothing felt broken. I picked myself up, grabbed my shotgun—

Gunfire. The thunderous crash of a shotgun, the low-pitched crack of an AK, the harsh metal swats of suppressed Virtus carbines. STAR was running into resistance on the lower floors.

"HELP! OVER HERE!" a woman screamed.

Shane.

"I'M OVER—"

Her voice cut off.

Damn it.

She was one floor below me, at the rear of the building, somewhere near the middle.

I raced for the roof. Reaching the edge, I unbuckled my chest rig and rifled through the flatpack. My hand closed around a coil of aramid fiber rope and a metal tube. I pulled them out.

Four claws lay folded against the tube. I unfolded and fixed them in place. Tested the carabineer connecting the rope to the device. Uncoiled the rope.

It wasn't a tube. It was a grappling hook.

I lay prone, grabbed the parapet and eased myself into clear space. Looking down, I saw columns and rows of windows. No security grilles.

There were two more BearCats at the street, parked outside the rear entrance. A pair of cops stood near the vehicles, scanning for threats.

They'd be looking for snipers and runners. Not someone climbing down the wall. If I timed it right, went fast enough, they wouldn't shoot me.

Probably.

Each row had four pairs of windows, generously spaced from their neighbors. Shane's voice had come from the second pair of windows from my right. They were both closed and curtained, but light leaked through the glass.

A situation like this required a harness, backup carabineers, an anchor man, proper rappelling gear, the whole nine yards. The gunfire chased all thoughts of proper procedure from my head.

I repositioned myself above the right-hand window. I fastened the rope to my belt with a carabineer, anchored the hook against the parapet, and tossed the rope down the side of the building. It unspooled as it went, extending for a hundred feet. Gripping the rope, I lowered myself down the side of the apartment.

My gloves bit into the high-friction fiber, holding me in place. I positioned my legs to the side of the rope, then reached down with my left boot, hooked a length of rope, and swung my left foot above my right, trapping the rope in place.

Now secure, I walked my hands down a few inches. Released the trapped rope, straightened my back, and recaptured the rope.

I went down, down, as quickly as I dared. More gunshots erupted, but none were aimed my way.

My boots brushed against a window. Keeping my left hand on the rope, I retrieved a spring-loaded glass breaker from a utility pouch, pressed it against the glass, and squeezed the trigger.

The tempered glass shattered inwards. Taking the rope in both hands, I pushed off and swung into the window.

Glass raked my sleeves and pants and face. Momentum carried me to the ground. My boots skidded off the floor. I dropped into a crouch, released the rope and scanned.

I was in a cramped kitchen. Through the doorway, I saw a video camera mounted on a tripod in the living room.

"What was that?" a man said.

"Go check it out!" another male ordered.

I unclipped myself from the rope. Dashed to the side of the door. Drew my Shinobi. Slid my fingers through the retention loop.

Amped.

A youth stepped through the door, AK awkwardly held against his shoulder.

"What the—"

I shot in low, trapping his foot, seizing his left arm, slamming the Shinobi into his knee. Bone crunched. Pulling him into me, I struck him in the belly, ribs, sternum, feeling bones flex and crack. I flicked my hand up, fingers raking his eyes, and as he shrieked I grabbed his head, twisted it anticlockwise, and drove his temple down into my knee.

He went silent.

"Andre! You okay?"

I dumped him on the floor, grabbed his AK-47, held it up to the light, and retracted the charging handle. Brass winked back at me.

"Oi, Andre! What the hell happened?!"

AK high, Amping my reflexes, I pivoted into the living room.

Gunman, AK-47 held low. Camera. A woman tied to a chair. I snapped my sights on the threat.

"Drop the weapon!" I ordered. "Do it now!"

His eyes widened. His jaw dropped.

"DROP THE WEAPON!" I boomed.

He dropped the gun. Unbidden, he went to his knees and raised his hands.

"Don't shoot, man! I surrender!" he shouted.

I penetrated deeper into the living room, flowing along the left-hand wall, scanning for threats. To my left there was a bedroom door. The main door was closed. Halfway down my wall, there was an opening. A ragged hole smashed through the thin material.

What the hell?

As that thought flashed through my head, a man stepped through the hole.

"Enrique, what's going on?" the newcomer asked.

Swiveling to the newcomer, I clicked down the safety. One notch, *two* notches.

"FREEZE!" I shouted.

He spun around.

He had an AK-47.

I hammered him twice in the chest. He staggered away, and his face disappeared from my sights. Lowering the weapon a fraction, I caught movement in my periphery and turned to Enrique.

He was looking up at me. His hands were on his AK.

"Don't—"

I shot him in the head. Once, twice.

I switched to the newcomer. He groaned softly, a blood bubble forming on his lips. His upper chest twitched.

I double-tapped him in the face.

Scanning, I found no more threats.

I reminded myself to breathe. This AK had a three-position switch. It was capable of full-auto fire. El Trece had brought out the big guns for this job.

I slung my rifle and peeked through the hole in the wall. Saw more holes in more rooms, extending clean through to the other side of the building.

Mouse holes. The gangsters had tunneled through the walls, facilitating rapid movement through neighboring apartments. In the Mid East, militants used them to evade and ambush attacking troops.

El Trece had brought that tactic home.

All at once I saw Bombero's plan: draw in STAR, use the mouse holes to flank and ambush the team, then attempt a breakout. Hell, if he and his homeboys dumped their guns and gang flags, they could pose as civilians and escape.

He's not getting away. Not this time.

I powered down, kicked the camera aside, and examined the woman. Shane.

She was...

Most of her clothes had been cut off. What was left were smoking black patches. Zip ties bit into her ankles, fastening her to the legs of the chair. Her arms were tied behind her back. Angry red blisters and charred patches covered her thighs and torso. Skin sloughed off her face, revealing tendon and bone.

Bright blue eyes gaped at me.

"Who...?" she whispered.

I held a finger to my lips and drew my Spyderco. She gasped. I shook my head.

Kneeling, I cut the ankle ties. Stepped around her and cut her hands free.

"Can you walk?" I whispered.

She wobbled to her feet.

And crashed back down with a pained grunt.

"No," she replied.

Men shouted in Spanish.

"They're coming... for you," she translated.

"Stay here."

"Wait!"

I put the knife away and Amped a little bit, just enough to enhance my hearing. Hurried footsteps charged down the corridor outside, congregating at the front door. I positioned myself to the right of the door, positioned my Mossberg by my side, and pressed up against the wall.

Someone pounded the door.

"Rico! *¿Estás bien?*"

I held up my left palm.

The door lurched into me. Men charged into the room. My hand arrested the door's movement for a moment, then the swinging arm swung the door closed.

Four threats. All of them had their backs to me.

I Amped.

Lunging to the nearest gunman, I raised my right hand and buried the Shinobi into his crown. A soft, wet crunching sound filled my ears. I retracted the weapon, spiked his shoulder for insurance, and kicked him towards his buddies.

The three shooters turned, orienting towards their buddy. In an instant I saw force vectors and angles, saw that the flying corpse would stumble past the closest threat and temporarily shield me from the other two.

I angled off, pouncing on the next customer. His eyes widening, he turned to me, bringing his weapon up slowly, so slowly. I took careful aim and spiked the back of his gun hand. The delicate bones crunched under unyielding titanium. Seizing his elbow, I stabbed the ring end into his throat. Ricocheted off and hammerfisted him in the temple. His body slackened. I pulled him into me and stomped his ankle, then hacked my forearm into the side of his neck, shoving him towards his buddies.

The body careened into the closer of the two remaining threats. I stepped off, raising the AK. The threat pushed the body away, clearing my line of fire, and I double-tapped him in the chest. I swiveled right, looking for the other guy. My sights rested on his torso. I fired one two three four times, and he went down.

All four threats were down. I shot all of them again in the head.

"What did you do?!" Shane screamed.

This wasn't police work anymore. It ceased being police work when El Trece brought in Bombero, blasted holes in the walls, issued assault rifles to their *sicarios*, and ambushed cops.

This was war.

I hustled over to her. She shrank away, eyes wide with fear.

"I'm here to get you out," I said.

"Adam?"

"Plenty of Adams in the world."

I snaked my arm through her armpit and gripped her torso. Skin and flesh crinkled and peeled against my glove. I helped her up on her feet and made for—

DANGER DANGER DANGER

I looked up.

The bedroom door flung open, revealing two men with AK-47s.

I raised mine with one hand and blasted away. Shane shrieked. The leading gunman collapsed. The other scooted behind cover. Still mashing the trigger, I led Shane through the mouse hole.

We entered another living room. No threats. I set her down against a wall.

The new threats must have come in from another mouse hole, one that connected to the bedroom. Crap. I'd lost count of how many rounds I'd fired, and I needed more.

The corpse propped against the mouse hole was wearing a chest rig. I grabbed him, dragged him in and placed him on his back. He had a cheap Chinese chest rig with three magazine pouches. I popped the closest pouch open, reached in, and grabbed an AK magazine.

"ADAM! WATCH OUT!"

I looked up just as two AK-armed gunmen entered through the mouse hole on the other side of the room. I clicked the safety down a notch, indexed on the closer one's center of mass and held down the trigger.

The rifle went cyclic, kicking out rounds at full-auto. Riding the recoil, I tracked the AK to the right, Amping my strength to dampen the recoil, counting the rounds, one two three four five—

CLICK

The threats slumped to the floor. One was on his knees, looking stupidly at his wounds, the other had fallen out of sight. I rammed the fresh magazine against the mag release lever, kicking the empty mag out into clear space, slapped the new mag in place, reached over the receiver and worked the charging handle, aimed at the threats and shot each of them in the head.

A tongue of blue-white flame roared through the hole. I jerked away from it. Shane screamed incoherently. When the fires passed, I saw a black greasy spot where the man I'd shot once was. The sweet scent of cooked pork wafted into my nose.

"AMP! YOU'RE DEAD!"

Bombero. He was right next door.

Screw this. Taking him head-on was suicide. I scooped up Shane, opened the door—

DANGER DANGER DANGER

Sun-hot flames flooded through the main corridor. I jumped back and dropped to the floor. A tendril of fire washed into the apartment whipping back and forth, singing my hair and back and clothes. I lay atop Shane, shielding her as best as I could, the shotgun and the rifle compressing my ribs. She closed her eyes and gritted her teeth.

The air grew hot and stale. My lungs shrank, the strength fled from my limbs. Suddenly I felt the floor falling away from me, the world spinning round and round.

I kept low and breathed deep. I just had to hold on. Bombero needed to breathe too.

The fires retreated. Smoke and ash coated my face. A ferocious roaring filled my ears. A wall of flame blocked off the exit. Someone barked an order in Spanish.

And footsteps approached the mouse hole.

Rolling over on my back, I readied the AK. A young man, short and scrawny, clambered through the hole, bleeding profusely from a graze across his temple. I keyed on his hands, saw an AK-47, fired, stitching him up from belly to sternum to throat to head.

I sat up and fired two shots at the left side of the hole, two shots at the right, blowing out clouds of dust and shrapnel. Bombero yelped a curse. Through my sights, I saw clean tunnels where the bullets had punched through the thin wall.

I picked up Shane with my left arm and dashed for the other mouse hole, blindly firing behind me, the Mossberg slapping against my thigh. Staggering into the neighboring apartment, I saw a massive scorch mark on the far wall, and a river of flame rushing past what used to be the front door.

Nowhere to run.

My danger sense shrieked. I kicked in the nearest door and found an empty bedroom. I set Shane on the floor and—

White flame surged through the mouse hole. I covered her again, protecting my head with my hands.

A handful of heartbeats later, the fire ceased. Much shorter than last time, and the tongue of flame hadn't reached the bedroom. Maybe Bombero was getting tired. Or maybe he was trying to lure me out. Rising to a knee, I Amped my hearing.

Footsteps.

Breathing.

He was sneaking towards the mouse hole.

Dialing down my power, I raised the AK. Aimed. A dark shape filled my sights. I snicked off the safety—

—The target moved—

I fired a rapid four-shot string.

Bombero let loose a prolonged cry.

I trained my sights on the mouse hole. Blood speckled across the opening. I got up and...

Paused.

Amped.

I heard Bombero's breathing. Smoothly and deeply and regularly and quietly.

This wasn't how a gravely wounded man breathes.

Keeping low, I angled off from the mouse hole. Pressing the butt of the AK against my shoulder, I brought my right hand to my left, gripped the Shinobi with the fingers of my left hand, and gently eased my right hand free from the retention loop. I took the pocket stick in my right hand and tossed it through the mouse hole.

It clattered against the floor.

Fresh flames roared.

I took the AK in both hands and clicked up the safety lever and fired at the wall.

The 7.62x39mm rounds ripped through the thin sheetrock in a blizzard of white dust. Aiming low, I swept from right to left, left to right, riding the muzzle from ankle to knee to hip—

CLICK

I tossed the empty AK aside, took up my shotgun and entered the room.

Bombero was lying on the ground. My rounds had damn near blown off his right leg and left arm. Blood soaked into the floor. He groaned in pain. He was done.

I trained the shotgun on his face. He grinned through a mouthful of bloody teeth.

"You're a cop," he whispered. "You can't... kill me."

He was right. If a cop pulled the trigger now, it would be murder, plain and simple. At its heart, the job was to save lives—even the life of the suspect. The suspect decided how much force must be used, not the police officer.

But I wasn't a cop now.

"You—"

I fired.

Stepping back, I scanned. Reloaded. Listened. Breathed. No more threats.

Smoke scratched my throat. Fires blazed all around me. Coughing and wheezing, I recovered my Shinobi. Looking out the corridor, I saw small fires choking off the ends of the cramped passage. Bootsteps echoed in the confined space. The STAR team was coming up.

"No go! No go! The door is burning!"

"Get the fire extinguisher over here!"

STAR could finish the job.

I returned to Shane. She was a bloodied, burnt bundle in the corner, far from the flames. She looked up at me, her chest heaving, her eyes pleading.

"He's done."

She blinked. Nodded.

"STAR is on its way. I'm going. I was never here."

"You can't—"

I ran.

Past Bombero's remains, past the bodies I'd left in my wake, past the glass and debris and who knew what else. I returned to the kitchen.

The rope was still there, still intact. Thank God.

I grabbed the rope, carefully hoisted myself out the window, and climbed up.

Sirens continued wailing. The helicopter was orbiting the scene once again, lighting up the world with its spotlights. As I hauled myself up on the roof, I heard a distinct whistling.

A gray cloud coalesced in front of me, taking the shape of a man. A cop in a ballistic helmet, body armor, and SIG Virtus.

Danny.

25

WHAT WE GOTTA DO

P hantom aimed his carbine at me. I kept my hands at my sides.

"Hands up!" he shouted. "Down on the ground!"

"Shane O'Neil is downstairs!" I said, hamming up my quasi-Hong Kong-Singapore accent. "Third apartment from this corner!"

"Down on the ground NOW!" he ordered again, approaching me.

"She's barely conscious and covered with third-degree burns. She needs to be evacuated *now*."

Danny stood still, his carbine still trained on me.

"You know how the game is played," he said. "I need your cooperation."

A spotlight swooped past, and in the brief illumination I saw the camera attached to his helmet.

"Get down on the ground *now*," Danny ordered.

"I can't do that, Phantom."

He glared at me. I glared back.

He sighed.

Marched towards me, carbine raised.

"Oh come on!" I said.

"We gotta do what we gotta do."

He walked robotically, his limbs unnaturally stiff and extended.

"Show me your hands," he said.

I kept them low.

He stepped into range.

"Show me your—"

I slipped out, grabbed his carbine and twisted.

He threw *himself* off the ground, landing with a heavy thump. I kicked him in the torso, making sure to catch him on his rifle-resistant trauma plate. He grunted loudly. Kneeling, I wrested the camera free from the helmet and crushed it under my boot.

He curled up on the concrete and went still. I retrieved the grappling hook. Running to the edge of the roof, I folded the claws and coiled the rope around my arm.

Amped.

Jumped.

I landed heavily on the other roof. Unzipped my bag and dumped the hook and rope inside. As I zipped up, Peterson burst out the door.

"Hey!" she shouted. "Dispatch says there's a suspect up here!

I pointed at Danny.

"He was right there!" I replied. "He took down Phantom, then set down some kind of grappling hook and rappelled off the side of the building!"

"You didn't help?" she demanded.

"Phantom was in my line of fire! I couldn't shoot him too!"

She opened her mouth. I cut her off.

"Look, I'm going after him. Call it in."

I barged past her and charged down the stairs. Along the way, I removed my hat and balaclava, stuffing them into my pockets. Holding my badge up high, I rushed past the cops on station and out the front door.

I kept running, past a squad of officers rushing to the front door, past the assembled BearCats, past the corner. Near the STAR line, a group of civilians jumped out of a BearCat. Keeping my shotgun low, I blended into them, catching my breath.

A pair of unis led the civilians to a group of waiting ambulances. I readied my badge. As they turned to me I held it up.

"Off duty officer," I said.

He turned his flashlight on me.

"Man, you look like you walked through hell. What happened?"

I looked down. Dark patches covered my clothes and rig. Blood dotted the heavy fabric. Not enough to signify an injury. I hoped.

"I'm fine. Look, I've got first aid supplies in my car. I'm just going to get 'em."

He gave me a once over. Sure, I looked terrible, but I was on my feet and still breathing. No sense getting a medic to waste time looking me over when there are others who needed medical attention.

"Yeah, sure, go ahead," the cop said, waving me past.

I sauntered to my car, patting myself down. The heavy fabric of my clothing had taken the worst of the flames. They were singed in many places, but I didn't feel any injuries. I hoped.

The press had arrived. Media trucks and civilian cars choked off the street. Journalists swarmed the sidewalk. A thin blue line of unis held them back. I jumped into my car and drove off.

Nobody stopped me.

THE NIGHT WASN'T OVER YET.

Five blocks away from the scene, I parked my car and examined myself more thoroughly. My sleeves and pants were scorched and torn in several places, but there was no bleeding. My gloves and balaclava were materially intact. The fire-resistant material had held.

My flatpack had fared worse. Much of the outer material had melted and bubbled, leaving ugly blisters. One of the two zippers were gone. Must have been burned off. The pack was still usable, but I needed to replace the...

Scratch that. The clothes and the flatpack had to go. The Shinobi too; it was covered in blood and tissue.

I changed into fresh clothing, stuffed the burnt clothes and Shinobi into the flatpack, then buried the pack in a large dumpster.

The shotgun had to go into cold storage. I had to assume the fired slug could be traced to the weapon. In hindsight, I should have finished Bombero with someone else's gun, or with my boots, but it was too late.

I drove to the self-storage facility. Safely inside my storage unit, I unloaded, disassembled and cleaned the shotgun, scrubbed the barrel with a steel wire brush, then wrapped it in heavy grease paper, retrieved my shovel and carried it to my car.

I drove outside the city limits. I followed the highway north, then headed down a series of narrow winding dirt roads. The drive was long and dark and lonely. Once I saw an owl perched on a branch, training wide unblinking eyes on me, as if seeking out my secret sins. Then I flashed past and no other animals approached.

The road took me to San Miguel National Forest. Taking the shotgun, I ventured deep into the woods, keeping to hiking trails. Insects chirped and called all around me, but none showed their faces. Branches and bushes rustled, betraying the presence of larger animals, but none approached me. Once I heard whispering overhead, and I looked up to see a solitary bat gliding through the night.

My route took me up a small, unnamed hill. Through a break in the trees, I saw the lights of the city.

Halo City was gorgeous by night. A blanket of stars spread out before me, white and red and green and gold. Brighter lights highlighted the towers and skyscrapers of the financial district. The city radiated a faint white glow, blurring the line between earth and sky, a broken halo of manmade light.

Halo City.

I chuckled. I was getting sentimental. The city lights were all false stars, their visage cold and unblinking. Despite the lights, dark shadows crawled across the city deeps. Many people wouldn't be going home tonight. Many mothers had lost their sons, many wives their husbands, many children their parents. A tragedy, sure, but this time next week the headlines would have moved on. Cops and gangbangers, citizens and politicians, everyone would keep doing what they were doing, adjusting or not as their whims dictated.

Come this time tomorrow, there would be another robbery, another rape, another murder. There were child molesters and hired guns and rogues still at large. Somewhere out there, crooked cops, criminal hackers, and Ricardo Ruiz still slept in peace, sure and certain that the HCPD wouldn't touch them, that the real cops would be too busy trying to recover from this disaster to chase down the real criminals.

Halo City? More like Hollow City.

I dug a hole in the soft earth, buried the shotgun, captured GPS coordinates of the location with my smartphone and committed the numbers to memory.

During the drive home, I thought about the op. In the moment of truth, the old tactics, techniques, and procedures had come roaring back, like ghosts reaching out from beyond the grave.

The brass might convince themselves that they had persuaded me to join STAR, but the truth was, I would have joined anyway. STAR was fundamentally a life-saving organization. The mission was to preserve life—even the lives of the suspects. It wasn't just a tactical unit; its secondary mandate was search and rescue.

During a critical incident, be it a terrorist attack or a superhuman showdown, STAR would escort firefighters and medics through the warm zone, and penetrate the hot zone to protect and evacuate the innocent. After a decade of taking lives, I thought I could turn my new talents to saving them.

I was, and am, an idiot.

You can't run from what you've done. Your deeds brand your soul forever, irrevocably molding you, *changing* you. Even if you try to walk away, you can't throw off the weight of your past.

But what I did to Bombero wasn't murder. It was necessary.

He was a monster and had to be put down. There were only two ways to safely arrest a noncooperative Prime: sedate him or wreck him so thoroughly he couldn't fight back. I'd heard that a Prime up in Serenity City had developed a device that could nullify powers, but that tech hadn't propagated down here. If I'd left Bombero to STAR, the second he could walk again, he could burn his way free and kill more innocents. The only way to prevent that was to kill him first.

I could shoulder the karma of his death.

Back inside the city limits, a dull ache gathered in my muscles and temples. I breathed hard and deep, forcing myself to carry on. I returned the shovel to storage, then checked my map.

I had to lose the car too. Its presence would have been noted at the scene. Eventually, it would point back to me. I'd need to drive it into gangland, park it somewhere conspicuous with the doors open, and walk away. Someone would claim it inside a minute.

After that, I'd have to report it to the police and the rental agency, figure out a way to square it with tonight's events, hope they wouldn't dig too deep...

I stopped myself.

I was overthinking this. There was nothing on my person or in storage linking me to any of the deaths tonight. Sure, the car established my presence there, but so what?

I told everyone present I was an off-duty officer. That was the truth. Nobody had seen me jump the roof and make entry. Not even the police chopper. If it had, the pilots would have sounded the alarm, and the cops in the building would have swarmed me.

To the world, I was just a police Prime doing my duty, responding to a call out and supporting my brother officers the best I could. If Chief Anderson wanted to punish me for that, he would have to explain to the public why he told a Prime to stand down when a rogue was wreaking havoc. The recording would keep his mouth shut.

I should be fine.

I hoped.

By the time I returned to the church, it was a quarter to five. I staggered into the clergy house and took a long hot and cold shower. Blood and dust and grime sluiced down the drain. When I was completely clean, I stepped out.

And almost bumped into Father Josh in his nightgown.

"You're back," he said.

"Yeah."

"How did it go?"

"Score one for the good guys."

He smiled. "Excellent."

I yawned. "I need to hit the sack."

"Yes, please. You earned it."

I lurched into my room. Dried my hair. Collapsed on the bed.

DARK, nebulous shapes haunted my dreams. Formless masses danced and twirled to the soundtrack of rhythmic gunfire. My eyes snapped open, and I heard a heavy knock on my door.

"Adam!" Father Josh called. "You have visitors."

I slid out of bed, massaging my eyes and temples, and checked my phone. It was just past noon.

The priest knocked again.

"Adam?"

I opened the door. "I'm up."

"Excellent," Father Josh said. "They're in the office."

"Can this wait? I need to brush my teeth."

"They said it's urgent."

I sighed. "Fine."

I followed him through the office doors.

Anna Nguyen sat stiffly at her desk. Father Matt stood nervously in a corner, his hands laced in front of him.

In the middle of the room were the Two Sams.

They stood at an angle away from the door. Sam Byrd, dressed in a sharp black jacket, blue shirt, and dark pants, rested his right hand on his hip, slightly parting the outer garment, his eyes mournful behind his glasses. Sam Cho was wearing a gray pantsuit, standing in a similar posture, her badge hanging off her belt.

Through the window glass, I saw a BearCat parked by the road.

"Sam Byrd and Sam Cho," I said. "What's going on?"

"Adam Song," Byrd said formally, "you are under arrest."

My heart stopped.

"What?" Anna exclaimed.

"Impossible!" Father Josh blurted.

Ice flushed through my veins. My vision narrowed into a gray tunnel. I breathed, and my heart restarted.

"Detectives," I said, "you're going to have to be more specific than that. What are the charges?"

"Six counts of homicide and two counts of deprivation of rights under color of law," Cho said.

My head spun. My legs tensed. Had they traced last night's killings to me? Was this—

Wait.

Color of law?

That was the deliberate deprivation of a person's rights using the pretense of legal authority when no such justification existed. That didn't apply to the shootout at Franklin Heights, did it?

Father Josh wrung his hands, his motorized joints whining softly.

"Homicide? Impossible!" he declared.

"Could you be more specific about the charges?" I asked.

"You killed Sofia Vega, Emmanuel Ruiz, Christian Alverez, Manuel Velazquez, Alex Desoto and Roderick Cortez," Byrd replied. "The first two deaths occurred while you were acting in an official capacity."

They were arresting me for killing the six gangsters I'd shot in my last two OISes.

Not the deaths of Bombero and his clique.

This explained why the brass had abandoned me. They must have decided to throw me to the wolves, and they couldn't be seen treating a potential criminal with any kind of favor.

They had kept their mouths shut all the way to the moment the Grand Jury returned a true bill. I hadn't seen this coming. Hell, I didn't even *think* I'd be arrested. I didn't do anything wrong, much less anything against policy.

I sighed.

In relief.

"Adam, STAR is just outside," Cho said. "They wanted to do a dynamic takedown, but we convinced them to give you a chance. There's no need to wake up the neighborhood, no need for any drama. Just come with us quietly."

I could fight this arrest. But not here. Not now.

"Do what you gotta do," I said.

26

UNMASKED

I n the secure custody suite, time ceased to hold any meaning. Day and night was reduced to the dictates of the burning bulb overhead, so bright it chased away all shadows. There were no visitors, no guards, no cellmates to pass the time with, only the unblinking gaze of the camera on the ceiling. Meals were the only way to track the passage of time.

On the bright side, I managed to brush my teeth and wash my face.

I did the only thing I could do.

I sat.

Waited.

Breathed.

Well after the third meal, the lights abruptly snapped off. I climbed on the bench and stared into darkness and breathed. Unbidden, words swam from the depths of my subconscious.

CAPTURED *lightning*
 Suspended in fragile glass
 Crackles brilliantly

. . .

I CLOSED my eyes and went still.

Presently the lights flashed back on. I opened my eyes. Stretched. Cranked out hundreds of push-ups and squats, dozens of hand-stand pushups, and concluded with side and rear and front bridges held to the count of three hundred.

I took a quick cold shower, then changed into my only other worldly possession, a spare bright orange jumpsuit.

And waited.

Breakfast came. Two slices of wholemeal bread, with two small packets of margarine and jelly. A dull yellow mash that might be eggs. A scoop of dry oatmeal and a packet of milk.

I consumed everything. It was barely edible, but I had to keep my strength up. I washed everything down with water from the tap. The food slot opened, and I returned the meal tray.

Meditated.

A lifetime passed.

A voice boomed from the ceiling speaker.

"Adam Song!"

I opened my eyes.

"You have a visitor," he continued. "Stand up now."

I stood. The food slot opened.

"Turn around and place your hands through the slot."

I complied.

Strong hands snapped handcuffs around my wrists. The heavy door opened and a quartet of burly guards in riot gear entered the cell. Wordlessly, they slapped shackles on my ankles, grabbed my arms, and marched me out of the cell.

Will was waiting inside the visitor room. His face was haggard, but his suit was sharp. He favored me with a smile as the guards sat me down, cuffed me to the security bars, and warned me not to do anything stupid. The moment the guards left, Will spoke.

"I'm sorry I got here so late, Adam. I was held up in court yesterday. By the time I got your message, it was past visiting hours."

"The important part is that you're here now," I said. "I appreciate you dropping by."

"It's the least I could do." He steepled his fingers. "Adam, I'm not going to lie to you. This is going to be an extremely difficult fight."

"How bad is it?"

"This morning, while I was driving here, the DA announced your arrest. Live on television, radio and the Net. He says you were a rogue cop who 'hid behind his badge' and 'abused the people's trust' to 'play the role of judge, jury and executioner.' He told the press all about your previous shootings, your prior service in the Marines, and how you killed every criminal you shot. The media is lapping it all up."

"That's funny," I said. "It wasn't too long ago when the media lauded me for stopping rogues and terrorists."

"Fame is a fickle mistress. And it only gets worse."

"How?"

"The DA says he is going to prosecute you himself."

I absorbed the news in silence and contemplated the implications for a moment.

"This has gone political, hasn't it?" I asked.

"Yeah. My gut says he's doing all this to appease Cape Watch and their pet protesters."

"And score political points with his father."

The current DA, Stephen Carter, was the son of Mayor Patrick Carter.

"Not just his father," Will said. "The City Council, the police chief, and commissioner, the media, they're all part of the Carter Machine. If they decide destroying someone will build them up, they'll do it without a second thought."

"I'm just the latest victim?"

"Yeah."

Will sighed again, holding his face in his hands. He looked weary. I almost bought the performance.

"Adam, all this time I've been doing consults for you pro bono. I don't have any problems with that. But now, with this thing going to court, if you want my help... Well, I have expenses and overheads to cover."

"I understand."

"I'm glad you do. For a criminal case like this, I'll need a retainer of twenty-five thousand dollars. It's expensive, but you won't get better."

"Fine by me."

He raised his eyebrow. "How are you going to pay me?"

I smiled. "Do you accept cash or cryptocurrency?"

He chuckled. "It depends on the situation. Why?"

"I have a cryptocurrency portfolio, in addition to traditional savings in the bank."

"Call me old-fashioned, but I prefer cash."

I had just barely enough cash in the bank to cover his fee. At least I had other savings.

"Understood. The funds should be ready by the end of the day. But I'll need you to pass instructions to someone outside who can act on my behalf."

"Of course. We can do this after I leave. But you do understand that this is just my start-up costs. As the case progresses, there will be more expenses."

"I'm good for that."

He looked at me oddly. No doubt he was wondering how a cop like me could afford the city's finest lawyer. I simply met his gaze and said nothing.

"Well, then," he said. "We can get started. But there are two things you need to know."

"What's that?"

"The first is bail. You've been charged with murder in the second degree and deprivation of rights under color of law. Frankly, I don't know if you'll even be allowed bail. Even if you are, bail for a single count of murder could potentially be as high as one million dollars."

"What happens I can't make bail?"

"You'll either be detained here, or transferred to a supermax prison, with other rogues. For your sake, I hope it's the former."

Me too. There is no love for former cops, especially among rogues. Sending me to max security would be akin to sending me to a war zone.

"If you can't afford bail," he continued, "you can hire a bail bondsman. But you'll have to pay ten percent of the bail upfront, and you won't get it back."

"We'll cross that bridge when we come to it," I said. "Until we know how much bail to post, *if* the judge allows for bail, there's no point worrying about it."

"All right, but I just want you to keep that in mind."

"What's the second thing I need to know?"

He hesitated. Steepled his fingers. Looked down. Licked his lips. Looked back up.

"The DA unmasked you."

My breath caught in my lungs.

"How?" I asked.

"During the press conference today, he gave the media your name, alias, and photograph."

My muscles tightened. My pulse quickened. Heat gathered under my clothes. I breathed. Slow. Steady. *Calm.*

"What about the Prime Privacy Protection Act?" I asked.

"Privacy protection can be voided under specific circumstances," Will replied. "The HCPD summarily terminated you yesterday, immediately after your arrest. You're no longer a public employee. You're no longer eligible for P3A protections."

If I made bail, the gangs of Hollow City would come hunting for my head. If I didn't, if I were transferred to supermax, I'd be trapped in a prison full of bloodthirsty rogues.

I didn't know which was worse.

"I know it's a lot to take in," Will said. "But we'll handle this one step at a time."

"We're going to fight this," I said.

"All the way to the bitter end."

27

THE AMERICAN DREAM

T he court held the arraignment the following day.
It was a circus. District Attorney Stephen Carter showed up in a finely-tailored dark suit and red tie. Not to be outdone, Will Dawson dressed in a bespoke black wool suit with a purple silk tie, matching them with a fine gold watch and exquisitely polished leather shoes. Reporters crowded the gallery, representing news networks from around the nation, and the world. The families of the decedents, a motley collection of men and women and children, occupied most of the remaining seats, dressed in funeral blacks and whites and grays. Near the front row, right behind the defendants' table, my mother, father, and brother shrank in their seats.

And there was me, the main attraction.

As the deputies marched me into the chamber, the cameramen aimed their lenses, placing me front and center. Here he was now, Amp the fallen Prime, exposed as Adam Song, in his prison jumpsuit and heavy chains.

I stood ramrod straight, head held high, my gait measured and precise, the way Drill Instructor Pritchard had demanded so many years ago in Camp Pendleton. Even as I settled into my seat, I kept my back erect, my eyes trained on a spot above and behind the judge, my hands safely tucked in my lap.

Judge Robert Magnus, his face a professional mask, formally opened the proceedings. In dry legalese, he covered the preliminaries, before getting down to business.

"Adam Ko Yeung Song," Magnus said formally, hopelessly mangling my name, "you are charged with the following: six counts of murder in the second degree, all felonies; and two counts of deprivation of rights under color of law, all felonies. Do you understand the charges against you?"

"Yes, Your Honor," I said.

"How does the defendant plea?" Magnus asked.

"Not guilty, Your Honor," Will replied.

Will, the DA, and the judge went back and forth for a while, deciding on the date for the preliminary hearing. They settled on a date six months from now.

Now came the time for the bail hearing. The DA stood to make his case.

"Your Honor, Primes have been gifted with incredible powers, setting them above the level of ordinary humans. Primes in public service must be held to the highest standards. In this case, Mr. Song has consistently and repeatedly failed to meet those standards."

Carter described my recent OISs in painstaking detail, all for the benefit of the press.

"In the first shooting, Mr. Song confronted Mr. Ruiz and Ms. Vega in their bedroom. While Mr. Ruiz was armed, Mr. Song did not give Mr. Ruiz a reasonable chance to surrender. Mr. Song shot him multiple times in the torso and the head, killing him immediately. Ms. Vega moved to cradle the body of Mr. Ruiz, and Mr. Song again shot her repeatedly in the chest and face.

"During the second shooting, Mr. Song admitted that he saw two suspicious individuals—Mr. Christian Alvarez and Mr. Manuel Velazquez—loitering outside his apartment, but he chose to confront them. When they approached him, Mr. Song stepped aside and saw Mr. Alex Desoto and Mr. Roderick Cortez step out of their vehicle.

"Mr. Song tripped Mr. Alvarez, then killed Mr. Velazquez with his bare hands by slamming his head into the sidewalk. Mr. Song then ran for cover around the block. He drew his weapon and chose to wait in ambush behind a car. When Mr. Alvarez, Mr. Desoto and Mr. Cortez approached, Mr. Song chose to engage them.

"He shot Mr. Cortez in the chest and the head. Then he shot Mr. Alverez in the hand, effectively disarming him, before shooting him again in the head. When Mr. Desoto tried to drag Mr. Velazquez's body to safety, Mr. Song shot Mr. Desoto several times in the torso and the head. At that time, Mr. Desoto did not pose a lethal force threat, nor was he armed.

"Your Honor, Mr. Song brought military tactics to police work. He has coldly and ruthlessly gunned down six people in two separate shootings. It may be true that the victims were criminals or associated with criminals, but justice must serve *all* people.

"Furthermore, Mr. Song has engaged in six shootings in six years on the HCPD and has killed a total of fourteen individuals. Most police officers never fire their weapons even once in their entire careers. This presents a highly unusual and disturbing pattern of violence throughout Mr. Song's career in the HCPD. Mr. Song has acted not like a cop, but like a cowboy, and there is no room for cowboys in the police department.

"Your Honor, I hold the position that the men and women of the Halo City Police Department represent the city's finest. However, Mr. Song has not acted in accordance with the department's standards of professionalism and used his status as a police officer to unlawfully deprive six individuals of the right to life.

"We must uphold standards of discipline and professionalism within the police department. We must demonstrate that no one, not even Primes, are above the law. I submit that Mr. Song be remanded without bail."

The judge nodded sagely. "Very well. Does the defense have any comments to make?"

"Yes, Your Honor," Will replied.

"You may proceed."

Will stood and cleared his throat.

"The Song family came from across the ocean to make a new life in America. Adam Song, an immigrant and the son of an immigrant, has integrated splendidly in our society.

"After graduating from high school, Mr. Song volunteered to enlist in the United States Marine Corps. He volunteered again to join the Marine Raider Regiment, one of the finest Special Operations Forces in the world. After a decade of faithfully serving our nation abroad, he returned home to serve us again.

"Mr. Song joined the Halo City Police Department and studied for a criminal justice degree. In his spare time, he obtained an instructorship position in a martial arts school and provided self-defense training to ordinary citizens. After four years on the streets, Mr. Song was headhunted to join the Asian Gang Unit, where he specialized in the triads and Chinese street gangs.

"One and a half years ago, on Rebirth Day, Mr. Song gained his powers as a Prime. He dutifully reported his abilities to his superiors, then volunteered once more to serve the city in the Special Tactics and Rescue team.

"Mr. Song's DD214, his certificate of release from active duty, shows that he has served with distinction. He has participated in combat overseas in support of our freedoms, and has earned multiple awards for valor in combat. In his ten years of service, he has never been court-martialed, and he has earned an honorable discharge.

"Mr. Song served in the HCPD for six years. He has never had a substantiated complaint filed against him and has never been accused of any color of law violations. When he became a Prime, he discharged his duties without fear or favor, and has received numerous commendations for outstanding service in the line of duty.

"Your Honor, Mr. Song is a paragon of the community. He is the personification of honor, duty, and country. He has chosen, again and again, to serve our nation and our city in the military and the police. He has faithfully and unceasingly carried out his duty, and all he asks is the same as every immigrant has ever asked for: a fair chance.

"Mr. Song is more than a man and a Prime. He is the embodiment of the American Dream."

A lump gathered in my throat. My heart squeezed into myself. My eyes trembled. No one had ever said anything like that about me. Phrased like that, I could almost believe Will's words.

But the whole world was watching me. I swallowed the lump, breathed, and listened to Will's conclusion.

"Furthermore, the prosecution has neglected to mention the following details. In the first shooting, Ms. Vega moved to Mr. Ruiz's body in a manner suggestive that she was about to take his rifle. She had placed her hands on the weapon, making it a case of self-defense.

"In the second shooting, I must mention that Mr. Desoto was a Prime. During the assault, Mr. Desoto called down lightning at Mr. Song, who evaded the lightning only by virtue of his superhuman speed. Even unarmed, Mr. Desoto indeed posed a lethal force threat. My client was justifiably in fear for his life.

"In light of Mr. Song's character and in recognition of his stellar record of service to the city and the nation, coupled with the life-or-death circumstances Mr. Song was thrown into, I request that Mr. Song be allowed bail, to be set at the court's discretion."

Judge Magnus steepled his fingers, as though deep in thought. This was still a show, and all the world was watching.

"Under ordinary circumstances, given the severity of the charges, and Mr. Song's status as a Prime, bail would not be granted. However, this is an exceptional case, involving an exceptional individual.

"Given Mr. Song's service and his character, the court sets bail at ten million dollars."

Sighs, long and low and deep, filled the court. My heart pounded in my head, overriding all other sound.

"How could you?!" someone yelled. "You can't just let him—"

Magnus banged his gavel. "Order! I will have order in the court!"

"He's a killer! You can't grant him bail! You can't!"

"ORDER!" Magnus boomed. "Sir, if you do not sit down and remain silent, you will be found in contempt of court!"

The heckler grumbled and sat down.

Magnus cleared his throat. "Now, as I was about to say, the court will impose additional bail conditions on Mr. Song. Mr. Song, you will surrender your passport to your attorney, and you are restricted from traveling outside Halo City. This will be enforced with an ankle monitor. Do you understand?"

"Yes, Your Honor," I said.

"You will surrender your firearms and ammunition to the Halo City Police Department, and you may not purchase any additional weapons or bullets between now and the conclusion of your hearing."

"Yes, Your Honor."

"You will not have any contact, direct or indirect, with any witnesses. This includes telephone, email, even a letter. If you see any of them on the street, you will cross the street and walk away."

"Yes, Your Honor."

"Very well. Are there additional comments or questions?"

"No, Your Honor," the DA said.

"No, Your Honor," Will echoed. "Thank you."

28

MIDNIGHT MOON

One million dollars. It was the price the bail bondsman set. An astronomical sum, but not impossible. I steeled myself to relay instructions through Will, calling in every marker I held.

But barely an hour after the hearing, my father signed a check for a million dollars, and just like that, I was out.

"Don't worry about it," Aaron said. "We can afford it. Just worry about staying out of jail."

"But—" I began.

"It's okay. The most important thing is you're out now."

My parents remained silent.

We are Songs. We never say sorry, goodbye or thank you.

Still.

One. Million. Dollars.

"Thanks," I choked out.

Father waved his hand dismissively. "It's nothing. We can earn it back."

We were never rich. That money should have gone to college education for the children, vacations, retirement...

And yet...

They signed away their future for my present.

Shi Shifu would say that we all get what we've earned. It was universal law, the law of karma. I don't know what I'd done to deserve this. I don't know if I could ever repay it.

But a man never shirks from his responsibility, and a son never forgets his family.

And El Trece never forgets its feuds.

Out on the street, just past the boundaries of polite society, blood calls for blood. Now that everyone knew who I was, who my family was, all my enemies would come rushing for me and mine. It was only a matter of time.

You'll always pay for what you've done. Good *and* evil.

It wasn't over, of course. After a pair of deputies fitted me with an ankle monitor, after I was formally released, a pair of police officers, Sarah Kruger, and Michael Renner, escorted me to their car. It was time to hand over my guns to the state.

Kruger drew up a document on her police smartphone, listing every firearm and every cartridge I'd ever purchased and registered with the state government.

"We're going to need you to hand over everything on this list," Kruger said.

"I can't give you the ammo," I said. "Not all of it."

"Why not?"

"I expend thousands of rounds every year on training," I said.

"Just give us what you have," Renner said.

"All of it?"

"Yes," he said firmly. "The court order extends to ammunition too."

The cops drove me to my storage unit. As I waited, I called Angel on my Nullphone.

"Hey Amp," she said tiredly. "What's up?"

"Shane O'Neil," I said. "Did you treat her?"

"Yeah. We just completed her treatment, actually. How did you know?"

"Everybody knows that when an officer goes down in Halo City, Angel will come to save her."

Angela laughed. "You're such a sweet talker."

"Thanks for helping her. How is she doing?"

"She's resting now, but she'll be fine. She's completely healed. Physically, that is."

"Mentally? Emotionally?"

"There's nothing my powers can do about that."

Nor mine.

At the storage unit, under the watchful eye of the cops, I handed over a gym bag. The officers laid out the guns and boxes of ammo on the floor and methodically counted them off against their list. I got out of their way and watched.

They bagged up everything. Every ammo box, every handgun, every 'assault weapon' I'd ever owned. Tens of thousands of dollars' worth of ordnance, all purchased at my own expense. Kruger and Renner made resupply runs back to the car for more evidence bags and borrowed a trolley from the storage facility.

"Is that everything?" Kruger asked, gesturing at the pile of hardware.

"It's everything on your list, isn't it?" I replied.

"We're missing some ten thousand rounds in assorted calibers."

"Hey, I told you I train a lot. We're talking hundreds of rounds per session."

"I still have to account for them," she insisted.

Renner wiped the sweat off his brow. "Yeah, we mark them as expended."

"All of them?" Kruger asked. "C'mon, we should check the rest of the stuff in here."

"Wait a second," I said. "Your warrant authorized you to seize the registered weapons and ammo in my possession. I gave you everything I had. You do not have the authority to search my possessions."

"I need to confirm we have everything."

"You've already done that. There's no need to go through the rest of my stuff."

"We need to—"

"Do you want me to call my lawyer?" I asked. "He's Will Dawson. Maybe you've heard of him."

"Sarah, drop it," Renner said.

"What?" Kruger asked.

"We've got everything we came for," Renner said. "We've carried out the warrant, and he's been cooperative with us. We're done here."

Kruger eyeballed my bags and boxes, shot me a dirty look, and left. Renner winked at me and followed her out.

Back at their car, the cops issued me a receipt, then offered me a lift back to Loong Moon. I arrived in time for dinner. My father had prepared all our favorite foods, and this time he said nothing about the quality of his apprentice's work. In the space of an hour, we ate and drank and said little, none of it substantial.

No mention was made of the court case.

We're Songs. There are some things we never spoke about.

But at the end of the meal, when the last of the crumbs were swept away and the final glasses emptied, I faced my family and said, "Thanks again."

"Don't worry about it," Aaron said.

We're Songs. That's enough.

Aaron drove me back to the church. The priests were there, waiting. They had prayed for me since the arrest, and they offered profuse thanks to God that I was released on bail. I didn't disagree. I lit a candle and placed it on the altar.

Once I was back in my room, I sat on my bed and took inventory of what I had left.

Backpack. Chest rig and runner's rig. Nullphone and burner phones. Laptop, with Kali Linux and peripherals. Crypto hardware wallets and other electronics. All legal and accounted for, and I still had unfettered access to the HCPD's intelligence database. The cops hadn't taken my live blades either, and the hardwood sticks in my training bag could double as weapons.

And, tucked away in the storage unit, was the rest of my war chest.

Forty thousand dollars and change in illegal cash. Body armor.

And a duffel bag filled with unregistered guns. The rifles and shotguns I wasn't required to register with the state. Tucked away in the crevices of the bag were magazines and boxes of ammo.

And, of course, there was also the Mossberg I'd buried in the forest. But it would have to wait there until the ankle monitor came off.

You don't fight a war with what you want, only what you have at hand when it kicks off. But all things considered, all this was much better than having nothing at all.

I thought I could have resolved this matter with a few phone calls, an off-the-books stakeout, a couple of black ops. I guess I was sorely mistaken. I hadn't achieved much. Ruiz was still out there, and El Trece's cyber expertise was still mostly unknown. And there was no telling what the Triads would do.

The past two weeks were simply the opening skirmish of a longer war. A war that would come whether I liked it or not. This was not an armistice, merely a ceasefire for all sides to regroup and rearm. I had to be ready for what was coming.

Under the midnight moon, I laid out my gear and cleaned them one by one.

END

MORE HEROES UNLEASHED!

For more heroes unleashed action, check out *Heroes Fall* by Morgon Newquist - available now on Amazon in hardcover, paperback, and Kindle formats!

ACKNOWLEDGMENTS

Writing a story in a shared universe is certainly a novel experience, and I'm glad to have so many people willing to help me keep my facts and the story tight. I would like to thank the following:

Thomas Bridgeland, Carlos Carrasco, Kevin Menard, and others went through the first draft and offered a wealth of advice. Without their help, this book would surely be a lesser work.

Tushar Ismail helped me choreograph the action scenes, patiently working through the problems I'd presented him and showing me better ways to move, and helped me work out the finer points of improvised rappelling from a rooftop.

Drew Dill provided excellent legal advice, helping Adam Song and Will Dawson navigate treacherous legal waters.

Russell and Morgon Newquist, for inviting me to play in their world and doing a stellar job in preparing the manuscript for publication.

The PulpRev and Superversive movements, for continuing to inspire me and so many others through their conversations across the Net.

And of course, Jasmine, for language and naming support, and for her time, energy, and love.

HOLLOW CITY

SONG OF KARMA, BOOK ONE

By Kai Wai Cheah

Published by Silver Empire

https://silverempire.org/

Cover by Kasia Suplecka and Steve Beaulieu

❀ Created with Vellum

CPSIA information can be obtained
at www.ICGtesting.com
Printed in the USA
BVHW031413211221
624587BV00002B/192